FORWARD

As I conceived this story, one of my biggest challenges was to create a fictional, economic collapse that would seem realistic to the reader. When I actually began writing, I couldn't help but notice how disconcerting, economic news seemed to dominate the headlines with increasing frequency. Things got a little surreal as I would write fiction and then watch similar real-life events unfold on the nightly newscast. The riots in Greece and France, economic protest in London, and budget gridlock in Washington, D.C. all seemed to coincide with the pretend world being created inside my word processor. The Texas wildfires of 2011 were another example. It was a little uncanny at times how I would finish a section and then watch it being played out in real life. Honestly, I wasn't trying to write a script for cable news.

As we were finishing the final edits, economic protests led to fires and violence in Oakland. At one point my editor even suggested we consider accelerating the timeline in the book.

All the while, *Holding Your Ground* (my first book) was climbing in sales, eventually making the top 100 Best Sellers on Amazon. The emails, letters, and customer reviews all relayed the same basic message: *Thank you for writing the book. It helped.* People are concerned, some even frightened, and the book made them feel like they can have some control, regardless of future events.

I pray the remainder of my work remains purely fictional.

Holding Your Ground played a greater role in this book than one might think. More than anything else, I consider myself a problem solver and teacher. My experience as an instructor has proven that some people learn well using an instructional guide like *Holding*, while others do better with a scenario, or story based environment.

This led to my desire to write a novel (or story) that utilized the methods described in *Holding* while using "real life" situations. In reality, this book is intended as entertainment, not as a example of how someone should conduct themselves in a real life survival situation. I hope the readers have fun with it and perhaps pick up an idea here or there.

Prologue

AP Press Release - Washington, D.C. 08:00 April 20th, 2015

The U.S. Commerce Department today announced that the Gross Domestic Product declined by almost two percent for the first quarter of 2015, resulting in the third straight quarter of contraction. Most analysts were hoping for a slight increase in the GDP, as today's announcement indicates that the United States economy has officially entered a depression.

Mark Goldberg, senior economist at Baker, Dean and Morgan, stated, "Three straight quarters of decline is the textbook definition of a depression. Soaring energy costs, natural disasters and federal debt are all contributing to the retraction in the size of the U.S. economy."

In related news, The Department of Labor announced yesterday that first time claims for unemployment benefits rose to 1,241,000 last week, increasing for the 42nd straight week. The economy lost 210,000 net jobs in the private sector and an additional 121,000 public sector positions were eliminated.

When asked about the grim economic indicators, White House spokesman Jim Grease replied, "We see light at the end of the tunnel. The downward trend in manufacturing actually slowed last quarter, and we believe that is a positive sign."

The United States unemployment rate now stands at 19.4 percent, ranking as the 7th worst among the G-8 nations. Japan currently ranks first with 22.4% unemployment; the United Kingdom and Germany round out the top three.

On a positive note, oil fell $3.11 per barrel yesterday to $344.96. Declining demand from developing countries was the root cause of the selloff according to traders.

Houston, Texas – July 30, 2015

Private Training Facility – Fort Bend County, Texas

The whine of the miniature, remote control dune buggy gave away its position before his eyes even detected its movement. In a single motion, he pivoted his body left, dropped to one knee and aimed the rifle--but he was too late. Scooting over a low embankment, the target disappeared out of sight and out of range. Stinging sweat rolled into his eyes, and his legs were beginning to seriously protest the day's activities. He listened carefully, trying to detect his target's direction, but the thick air was absolutely silent. *What the hell am I doing here*, he thought, *it's so hot even the fire ants are hiding underground.* He decided to flank the vehicle's position, zigzagging to his right, moving as quickly as his legs could support the additional forty pounds of body armor, ammunition and supplies strapped to his chest. He pushed himself hard the last few feet to get an angle on the target, but he just couldn't gain enough momentum. Worse yet, the drone of the toy's engine indicated it had rolled into a strand of trees that was now blocking his shot.

The "toy" was a common remote control vehicle that could be purchased at any hobby store, typically to the delight of a 5-year-old boy who discovered it peeking through the boughs of a Christmas tree. While such a device could bring a smile to a young man's face during the holidays, it rarely produced anything but agony at this facility. This specific model had been modified with a coat hanger which carried a paper bullseye two feet above its frame. The inexpensive child's toy was an excellent training tool as it allowed students to test themselves against a moving target controlled by rather crafty instructors. This particular one was known by the trainers as the "Dune Buster," but all of the students at the facility called it the "Ass Buster," because it was wickedly fast.

Today, Bishop was the student, and the toy was the master. Not only was it faster than he was, it didn't seem to mind the heat. He had been hunting the little bastard for twenty minutes while cocooned in an oven of Kevlar, and it was taking its toll. His exhausted mind returned to questioning the wisdom of training in this weather. While the blistering Texas sun was bad enough, it was the blanket of humid air pressing down that was making the exercise insufferable. *This is like trying to swim*

3

fully clothed...upstream...in hot water...with sharks around, he mused. He gathered his strength and pushed off for one last effort.

In a safety bunker twenty-five yards away, two instructors were watching Bishop through a small slit as he tried to maneuver for a shot. A momentary smirk formed on the lips of the older man as he remarked to his comrade, "He's falling for it."

"They always sucker for that move. Are you ready?" replied the other gent as he lifted the paintball rifle to his shoulder.

"Let's nail this guy and get back into the air conditioning."

The senior instructor positioned the joystick commanding the toy to move away from the student, baiting him out into the open.

As the toy began rolling again, Bishop adjusted his direction, and in doing so, exposed himself to the bunker. He centered the red dot on his riflescope and began to squeeze the trigger when two paintballs struck him in the thigh, mixing their red coloring with the sweat that had soaked his pants. The sting of the impact caused Bishop to miss the shot and then roll to the ground panting for air and cursing under his breath.

He opened his eyes a few moments later and looked up at two smiling instructors. "That was too easy, Bishop. An old dog like you should know better," the older fellow said as he offered a helping hand.

"You guys suck."

"Oh now, don't be bitter, Bishop. Everybody falls for that trick. Besides, I could have hit you in the ear with those paintballs, and that really hurts, so don't start whining like a little girl. Now be a good lad. Clear that rifle, and join us for some cold iced tea."

Bishop looked at his watch, "Oh shit, I can't. I have to go downtown and file paperwork today. Thanks for the offer though."

Northwest Freeway

Bishop gave the pickup truck some gas and accelerated up the entrance ramp. He was behind schedule and trying to get out of the city before the roads filled with the afternoon rush. He had always thought that "rush hour" was an interesting term, as in this gridlock, no one could "rush" anywhere. When the freeway came into view, he realized it was too late. There were five lanes of bumper to bumper traffic stretching as far as he could see. *So the economy sucks?* Even with gas prices above $6.00 per gallon and unemployment over 20%, enough people managed to clog the roads every afternoon to cause a "non-rush hour."

After merging into what was more of a parking spot than a moving line of traffic, he glanced over to see a truck almost identical to his own in the next lane. It was simple male bravado for both drivers to size up the other truck. *So that's what it looks like going down the road,* they both thought. The other driver, wearing a 10-gallon hat and a western shirt, raised a bottle covered in a brown paper bag and toasted Bishop's truck. After giving his vehicle's twin a quick look, Bishop motioned to the cowboy with a nod and flashed a "thumbs up" approval. *At least he looks like he belongs here.*

While his parents claimed he was a natural born citizen of the Lone Star State, Bishop often mused that he was a victim of a "birther conspiracy" and really didn't fit in. He didn't like beer, preferred vintage Rock n' Roll to country music and didn't care much for horses. As a boy, he had used dirt bikes and ATVs on the ranch – horses were for parades and shows. But his most egregious sin was his dislike of traditional cowboy garb. He owned a single 10-gallon hat, and the last time it was on his head was four years ago at the rodeo. The matching pair of calfskin boots sat in the closet, a layer of fine dust obscuring their multi-colored hues. *Give me a good pair of jump boots any day* he often thought. "I still have my guns and drive a pickup, so I guess they won't revoke my Texas citizenship any time soon," he had once joked with a co-worker.

Bishop hadn't had any reason to go to downtown Houston for a long time. He avoided traffic whenever possible because the inactivity frustrated him. He had dreaded this trip since learning that all employees were required to file their annual insurance papers in person, at the downtown headquarters. The visit to the training facility had been scheduled in a vain attempt to salvage the day, but his performance had been a disappointment. *Hurry up and wait---just like the Army. I am 37 years old, and life is half over,* he thought. *The sand is running through the hourglass faster than ever, and I don't have the sand to waste on paperwork and traffic.*

He sighed and turned the radio to a local news station to determine if the traffic were the result of an accident or just normal congestion. The news consisted of the typical bad economic indicators, followed by optimistic spin from a government spokesman. He maneuvered the truck into a lane that was creeping forward a little faster than the others and settled in for a long ride home. The radio finally reported that the slowdown on the Northwest Freeway was only congestion, and traffic was moving well a few miles ahead of him. Perhaps he wouldn't have such a terrible drive home after all. *Five years ago, I would have been stuck out here for hours. Maybe the Second Great Depression was not an entirely bad thing?*

No, he decided, *it was not a good thing . . . no matter how you looked at it.*

Many of his friends, despite vaulted degrees and esteemed careers, were not doing so well. It seemed like each day someone he knew posted messages on Facebook about being laid off or looking for work.

He was lucky he supposed. A job with a company that did petroleum exploration all over the world had provided some security. He was essentially a highly paid watchman, but could boast that he had traveled widely and experienced great adventure. That thought caused him to snort out loud. *Adventure was such a bullshit word.* The truth was more like being in the wrong place at the wrong time and yet lucky enough to survive. His mind drifted back to when his current "adventure" began.

Bishop had been deep in the middle of a dream---something about a warm, clear night and soft grains of sand squishing between his toes. On the nightstand, his cell phone started its screeching assault. *Shit!* It was way-too-early AM, and he decided to ignore it. As his brain happily returned to its deep REM state, the phone began firing its second salvo almost immediately. He rolled over and through squinted eyes checked the caller ID. The number displayed was an odd format he didn't recognize. Angry and still half-asleep, he answered the phone, "This had better be good. You are interrupting my debut as a porn star, and I'm right in the middle of a scene with two Asian girls who aren't afraid of each other."

The voice on the other end had laughed and said, "Bishop, you old pervert. That gut hangs over your belt too much to be a porn star, and besides, your pecker belongs on a mouse."

Bishop yawned and protested in a gravelly voice, "My gut doesn't hang over my belt."

The caller was Spider, an old Army buddy who seemed to drift in and out of his life, but a friend nonetheless. "Bishop, I'm in Iraq working security for a U.S. company. The wife of one of my guys has decided to hatch their kid a few weeks early, and we just sent him home to the states. I need a guy who knows a little about pipelines and a little about rifles. Are you still looking for work? ....Bishop, are you there? ... Wake up dipshit! Oh, and by-the-way, the food over here ain't half bad," he rambled.

Even today, Bishop had to smile at the naivety of his response, "What the hell does a pipeline have to do with rifles?"

Bishop's recalling of that old phone conversation suddenly reminded him that he needed to let his bride know where he was. He picked up the cell and called Terri. "Hey babe, I'm going to be stuck in traffic for a bit, but it's not real bad," he said.

Her response was hurried. "No problem---Cindy was over and blabbed for 20 minutes. I'm trying to finish balancing the checkbook, get in the shower and make you something to eat. Some people have way too much time on their hands, you know? I have this new recipe I wanted to cook for you, but I don't think I'll be able…"

"I was just thinking about picking you up over my shoulder, carrying you back to the bedroom barbarian style and doing a little *cooking* myself."

"I have to do a deep-dive into these insurance forms for Mom, and that's no fun. Do you know how many pages these things…"

"I promise you my idea will result in a *very deep dive.*"

"… and the girls from the bank are having a meeting at the YMCA for the charity…"

"My idea involves a meeting *at the Y* as well."

"Oh, and I got the mail. You received your membership renewal for the…"

"I got your *male*, right here darling, and this *member* won't need any *renewal.*"

Terri feigned frustration at the innuendo. "Bishop, are you even listening to me?"

"Sorry babe, this traffic is such *a slow grind*, it distracts me."

She laughed and in a low, sexy voice said, "I'll *distract* you plenty big boy. Get your *slow grinding*, *deep diving male member* home, and I'll deliver a *renewal* that will make you sleep for hours."

"Sounds good babe . . . love you."

"Hold on a sec, I forgot. Can you stop and get some milk, oatmeal, dishwashing detergent and a dozen apples on the way? Love you, too."

Bishop laughed, hung up and turned up the radio to listen to the news.

"This just in to the news room - A spokesman for Houston General Hospital has informed KTRT that a bankruptcy judge has ordered the facility to cease operations in three days. Furthermore, the hospital is requesting anyone with a family member or dependent, currently admitted at their Medical Center complex, to make arrangements for immediate transfer of the patient to another facility. The General Hospital System has been ordered by the court to execute these bankruptcy procedures immediately. Any patient not transferred voluntarily will be automatically relocated to neighboring City Hospital in the next few days."

The station went on to give details of the financial troubles of the hospital system, the delay in Medicare and Medicaid payments from the government and other background information. Another announcer reported that City Hospital had no knowledge of any large transfer of incoming patients. A spokesman for City Hospital said that the facility was at capacity and would not be accepting any new patients.

Bishop's phone rang, and he didn't even have to check the caller ID to know it was Terri. "Hey Darling, are you listening to the radio?"

A now very serious voice replied, "No, but it is on the TV news. What are we going to do about Mother?" Terri's mom had cancer and had been admitted into Houston General two months ago. She was not expected to hold on much longer and spent most of her days sleeping from the heavy pain medication.

Bishop was at a loss. "No idea. I just heard the report myself."

The tone of Terri's voice became even more stressed, "Oh my God, Bishop! They are showing nurses and doctors walking out of the hospital. It looks like they're abandoning the patients. Bishop, what will happen to Mom?" Terri broke down and could no longer be understood between sobbing and blowing her nose. Bishop tried several times to calm her, but communication was impossible. She finally managed to blurt out that she needed to settle down, and she would call back in a bit.

Bishop worshiped the ground Terri walked on, and it put a knot in his gut anytime she was hurting. They had met five years ago and married eight months later. Terri worked part time as a bank teller and kept busy with their suburban home. She rounded out Bishop's life, and he considered her not only a great lover, but a partner as well. Terri was "with him" all the way. They were beginning to talk about having children when the economy improved and their savings allowed. While houses were cheap, loans were difficult to secure. It had drained all of their resources to obtain the American Dream. Terri's job at the bank had made the difference.

Terri lost her father years ago and had been raised by her mother. Consequently, she and her mom were very close. When the doctors had informed them of the cancer, it had been the worst week of their lives. In reality, Bishop hoped the kind old lady would pass on soon. Her quality of life was terrible, and the cancer was clearly taking its toll every day. He would support Terri through the grieving process, and then they could continue on with their lives. *No, I can't go there*, thought a guilty Bishop. *That is not fair to Terri or her Mom. If I were lying on my deathbed, would I want someone thinking that way about me?*

Bishop called Terri back, "I'm not far from the hospital and will head over there to see what's going on. You know the news media, always sensationalizing everything. At least I'll be able to check and make sure she's okay." He ended the call with a calmer wife and began to switch lanes to get off of the interstate. *I hope moving Rita does not involve a lot of forms and paperwork. I've already had enough chicken shit paperwork for one day.*

His dislike of paperwork sent his mind back again to Iraq and Spider. He had agreed to take the job with Spider, and after going over various details over the phone, had begun the "process." He had to snicker at the word "process," as the experience was more like a steady diet of pure, pasteurized *chicken shit.* For three days he was fed an unending meal of passport verification, State Department regulations, work permits, insurance documents, a Last Will and Testament, next of kin forms and all kinds of mind numbing paperwork. For dessert, he was given an intrusive physical topped off with several inoculations. Why hadn't he just told Spider, "Go to Hell," and gone back to sleep?

The flight to Baghdad included two stops, was totally boring, and thus exhausting. Bishop exited the plane onto a small stainless steel platform and immediately received a blast of hot air right in the face. While he had been raised in West Texas and was accustomed to heat, this experience was on a totally different scale. It was as if someone had turned on a hair dryer and pointed it at his head. He followed the other passengers into a line that was Customs, which amounted to a few cursory questions in broken English. The ancient Iraqi man at the counter asked him, "Country of birth please?"

"Texas – oh, I mean the United States of America."

The old gent smiled and waved him through. *They do that every time*, the Iraqi thought. *I wonder why only the Americans from Texas think their state is a different country.*

Spider was late picking him up at the airport because of traffic. Bishop loaded his gear in the back and mumbled under his breath, "Hurry up and wait." As they pulled out, Bishop was shocked at the volume of cars and the lack of rules. Spider worked the big, black SUV around everything from Mercedes Benz sedans with gold trim to mule-drawn carts loaded with rags and baskets. At one point, he quickly pulled over and stopped. "What's up?" asked Bishop.

"U.S. Military convoy is coming around," replied Spider, "If you don't pull over, they'll shoot you." Sure enough, traffic cleared, and several Humvees and troop carriers came speeding past. On the back of the last Humvee was a sign that read, "STAY BACK 300 METERS OR YOU WILL BE FIRED UPON." Bishop had a good laugh over the fact it was printed in English.

At that point of the war, there had only been a few short news stories about terrorist activities in Iraq, as the "Insurgency" was just getting started. The victory on land had been quick, but the celebration had been short. The Iraqi people expected the Americans to solve all of their problems immediately after toppling the old regime. The Americans were only there to kick the Iraqi Army's ass. Nobody said anything about rebuilding a country, and Bishop had to smile thinking about thousands of Army Officers who no doubt were complaining about the "*Chicken Shit*" involved in changing their original mission.

Bishop had joined the Army for one very specific reason – college money. He signed up for Reserve Officers Training Corps (ROTC) because he didn't have enough money, grades or athletic ability to go to college any other way. His degree was in Engineering, with a major in Fluid Dynamics. This was not due to any passion for things fluidized, but because his counselor had advised him that a wonderful job in the oil business awaited all who understood the science. What the counselor had not told him was that finishing in the bottom 50% of a small class, from an unknown West Texas college did not provide for a six-figure resume. He had, however, managed to acquire a love for certain aspects of fluid during his college years - mostly involving the panties of co-eds. After graduation and all of the associated parties, a hung-over Bishop reported for active duty. The Army gave him four years of college; they expected four years of service in return.

The Army had been a big, fat nothing for Bishop. His expectations of military life were completely different than the actual experience. Growing up on the ranch, he had been raised around firearms and loved shooting. He had believed his training would include exposure to some serious firepower. In the end, he estimated that he had fired more rounds each summer as a kid than he had shot the entire four years in the Army. Bishop thought the military would teach him how to fight, get him in peak physical condition, and turn him into a warrior. There was very little training on how to fight. The physical conditioning was easy for him, and there was almost no training whatsoever to turn him into a badass.

One of the few positive experiences was attending the Airborne School and ending up stationed at Fort Bragg. Nothing special or gung-ho here, as every Army officer had to go through Airborne School. He had never flown on a plane before, let alone jumped out of one. Skydiving was actually fun.

What Bishop did learn was a lot of new terminology, such as "Chicken Shit," and "Hurry up and wait." He spent three and a half years in Signals and G2, or Army Intelligence. Given his degree, the Army wanted him to operate base sewage and water systems. He thought that sounded like a *really shitty idea*, and eventually ended up as a messenger boy behind the

"Green Door." He, like every other peacetime Officer, requested every class, school and opportunity that he could find, only to be denied almost all of them. His degree was not from an "Army" school, and his family was not an "Army" family. The limited seats in the various schools typically went to those who were part of that inner circle.

To be fair, Bishop could not blame it all on some hidden political society. He was not exactly the model Officer and Gentleman. Bishop had developed issues with absolute authority, especially when lives were on the line. The Army expected men to execute a battle plan that was based on time-tested, empirical results. The plan was never discussed, questioned or enhanced for the current situation. It simply was THE plan and was to be executed without question. No idea or modification, no matter how creative or brilliant, would be considered. While the military did change its tactics based on new equipment or lessons learned, the process was very slow. If it had worked during WWII, it should work now. Unless the plan resulted in "unacceptable casualties," it was just fine.

Bishop didn't believe this was the right way to run any organization, and that put him at odds with command. One of his performance reports summed it up best, "This officer has a mindset and desire to be a warrior---a highly skilled individual fighter. This unit requires soldiers, or men who fight well in a team environment with defined and dedicated roles. There is no room in this Division for individuals, regardless of how motivated."

He had to smile as he thought back. In addition to his authority issues, he suffered from ADDDI, or Attention Deficit Disorder Due to Intercourse, as he had developed quite the reputation with the ladies off-base. While his service record would definitely not be studied by any war college, there were several pretty, young girls who missed him after he was reassigned to the Reserves and moved back to Texas.

The traffic pulled Bishop's mind back to present day as he maneuvered the truck through the side streets in the congested Medical Center. Driving in this area was an adventure in itself. One of the largest concentrations of medical facilities anywhere in the world, the Houston Medical Center consisted of over 30 hospitals, numerous teaching facilities, and hundreds of research and procedure labs. Almost every major medical university in the south maintained some presence in the Medical Center. For years, the petroleum and medical industries had been the economic backbone of the city. The cluster of large hospitals, office buildings and the supporting restaurants and shops was really a small city unto itself. It also had a very healthy "non-rush" hour of its own. *A healthy rush hour for the Medical Center*, Bishop thought - *Terri will love that one.*

As Bishop worked his way through the side streets and shortcuts, he could not believe his "luck" when he found an open parking spot less than four blocks from the hospital. He parked his truck and headed for the building.

A Hospital in Pain

Dr. Richard Hopkins was practically on the verge of tears for the first time in 30 years. He had built his department from scratch and invested all of his time, energy and emotion into the facility. This morning, when the emergency staff meeting was called, he assumed it was simply another update on the legal proceedings and financial troubles that the hospital system seemed to always be experiencing. He really didn't understand any of it, nor did he really care. As long as the nurses and technicians showed up for work, and he could order tests, the rest of it was mundane, useless information. He thought that management was wasting precious time that could be devoted to healing people. When the meeting began, the hospital President spoke quietly and went directly to the point. "We have been denied any more time to reorganize our debt. This morning, a judge rejected our final appeal and ordered the facility to shut down by Friday of this week. We cannot make payroll nor pay our suppliers." No one said anything at first - either from shock or lack of understanding. After a few awkward moments of silence, one of the department heads asked what this meant. Dr. Hopkins thought the President could not have been more clear – no paychecks, no medicine, no labs and no procedures. The hospital was closing.

Walking through the corridors of the facility after the meeting had broken up, he regretted not having paid more attention to the previous warning signs that the facility was in trouble. There had been dozens of briefings and financial presentations. As he reflected on the proclamation, he realized no one should have been surprised by today's announcement. He consoled himself in that he was not the only one who seemed shocked by the cold reality of business and money. Following the President's bombshell, everyone seemed to go through the Kubler-Ross stages of death and dying. At first, it was denial – they won't let the hospital close. Then they progressed through anger, depression, bargaining and finally, a kind of numb acceptance. Dr. Hopkins did not even call his wife or any of his friends - he simply walked out and headed toward his office to pack up his belongings.

A heated argument brought him out of his fog. The head of a nursing department was being confronted by three of her staff. "What do you mean NO PAYCHECKS?" yelled one. "You expect us to continue to work through Friday without pay? To hell with *your* moral code---the parking here costs me $20.00 a day, and if I'm not getting paid, I'm not coming to work."

Another nurse chimed in, "I haven't been paid for my overtime for two months. I pulled double shifts and had to pay for daycare. We are eating oatmeal. How can I do this?"

Dr. Hopkins started noticing other aides, nurses and even some interns leaving with boxes. One orderly was pushing a hospital bed loaded with personal items and a coffee maker down the hall. "My God," the physician thought, "I wonder if I can find any boxes to pack *my* belongings in?"

Brenda Mitchel had been an R.N. at Houston General for 14 years. Unlike so many who entered the field for job and financial security, she chose nursing for the gratification of helping people. She was a Christian woman . . . self-sacrificing, and believed strongly in her responsibility to the sick.

Brenda recognized the signs that the hospital was in trouble months ago. The cuts in benefits, lack of new equipment and weeks going by without overtime pay on her check stub could only mean one thing---the facility was struggling. After the news of the closure spread like wildfire throughout the facility, Brenda quickly decided to stay and help until the last patient was transferred. She began preparing a mental checklist of what each of her patients would need in order to be moved. As she sat at the nurse's station making entries into the charts, two other nurses approached.

"Brenda, we're leaving. We wanted to stop and say, 'Goodbye,'" said the older one.

"How can you leave?" she replied, "We have 34 people in this unit. They need us. We took an oath, and besides that, it's against the law for us to leave."

The two women looked at each other and then down at the floor. For a moment, Brenda thought she was getting through to them, but then the younger nurse responded in a quiet, almost inaudible voice. "Brenda, I just can't. I have enough gas to make it through Friday, and that's it. Management is responsible for this, so let management take care of the patients. I need to use what gas I have to look for another job."

Dr. Hopkins rounded a corner only to be confronted by a patient in a wheelchair. Her soft gray hair, line-etched expression, and forearms sprinkled with brown spots were clear indicators of her advancing age. She lifted her bony finger to get the passing physician's attention. "Doctor – do you know where my nurse went? I can't find anyone, and no one answers the buzzer. Where did everyone go?"

Only then did it dawn on Dr. Hopkins that the staff was leaving, and only a handful was left to take care of the patients. His mind was racing. The needs of the thousands of patients would quickly overwhelm any staff that did remain loyal to their oath. How many would stay? Nothing in medical school had prepared him for a situation like this.

He decided that he would stay and honor his oath, that there was really no other option as he would never be able to sleep at night knowing he had left the sick behind to fend for themselves.

When Dr. Hopkins reached his department's small section of the building, he was almost run over by an orderly pushing an ultrasound machine down the corridor. "Whoa," said Dr. Hopkins, "Where are you going with that?" The orderly was not even from his department. The interloper just stared - first at the physician, then at his ID badge - and then continued pushing the expensive machine, almost running. As the doctor caught his breath, he noticed that his department was in complete chaos. Papers littered the floor, drawers were pulled from desks, storage closets were open, and their contents scattered. *We are being looted* he thought, and reached for a phone to call security. The phone rang for more than a minute, but no one answered at the hospital's security desk. *If this is going on all over the hospital, they're probably very busy. I'll call the police.*

Lt. Michel Porter was an 18 year veteran of the Houston Police Department. He had survived numerous staff reductions because of his record and the fact that he had been injured in the line of duty. Porter was responsible for Sub-station #4, which included the Houston Medical Center area. He had watched the number of officers assigned to the department be reduced by almost half since he had left the academy.

Repeated budget shortfalls, a bad economy, and numerous mistakes by city politicians had resulted in deep cuts almost every year. When he had been promoted to station commander six months ago, he had inherited responsibility for 16 square blocks of business and residential territory. On paper, it looked as if it should be an easy beat. Mostly commercial, with a few blocks of affluent residential neighborhoods, any reasonable analysis would indicate a small police presence would be all that was required. Actual criminal activity and paper analysis were in disagreement. Lt. Porter, or Big Mike as everyone referred to him, understood that the Medical Center was one of the largest, sweetest targets left for criminals in the city.

A flailing economy delivered a double blow to law enforcement - reduced staff coupled with an increasingly desperate population. A desperate population committed more crimes. The Medical Center was one of the few places left in the city where you could drive for several blocks without empty storefronts and half-empty parking lots. Employees and hospital visitors came and went throughout the day and night. Restaurants and shops remained open and had customers at all hours as well. Customers meant money, and money was a magnet for the desperate. At first, the complaints had been about beggars pestering hospital staff as they reported for work. When the economy worsened, beggars became knife-toting muggers. Soon muggers became robbers brandishing pistols---that is until the organized gangs moved in, and the run-of-the-mill gangsters were forced out. Were it not for the fact that the hospitals had hired large numbers of private security, the situation would be much worse. Most of the private security officers were actually policemen who were let go by the city. The quality of security provided by these private police forces made a big difference in keeping things under control. Big Mike knew most of those ex-policemen drew as much or more pay as when they were in the department and wondered how much their cost had contributed to the financial issues facing Houston General.

Lt. Porter had listened to endless debates at both headquarters and the city council meetings. The Medical Center was one of the few "bright spots" in the city when it came to tax collection. The debate always centered on "social redistribution" versus "reward and reinvest in what is working." Shouldn't the area generating the revenue receive the lion's share of the funds? The council members argued that the city could not be seen as "protecting the rich" while poorer neighborhoods were left to become the Wild West. Lt. Porter was beyond contemplating that age-old debate any further. He simply wanted to get in his 25 years and retire. The constant battles with low morale, stretched-too-thin resources, and the other consequences of a shrinking force had taken their toll on him and his family. Only the love for his fellow officers kept him in the game. He sometimes felt a small hint of remorse over the fact that he tried to protect his officers more than the citizens of the city. It was only a small tinge and always passed quickly.

The duty sergeant interrupted Big Mike's thoughts with a louder than normal knock on the doorframe – a sure sign that something was wrong. "Lieutenant, there is a problem down at Houston General. We have received several calls of looting and hospital employees stealing equipment from the building. I guess they had a big announcement this morning that the place was shutting down on Friday, and now the rats are abandoning the ship and taking lots of equipment and even prescription drugs with them."

Big Mike digested that information for a second and then asked, "Who's running their security shift this morning?" The sergeant said, "It's George, and it took me quite a while to get him on his cell. There is a crowd gathered in front of the building, and he has all of his guys trying to keep things in order. He says he needs help and needs it right away."

Another officer appeared over the Sergeant's shoulder and said, "Boss, we have a problem down at Houston General. You better flip on the TV and check it out. It looks pretty serious."

As Bishop walked to the front entrance, he began to notice nurses and other staff leaving the facility carrying their personal effects and looking either bewildered or disgusted. When he turned the corner heading to the front doors, a large crowd blocked his way. Many of the people were simply curious what all the fuss was about. There were at least three television news teams, complete with vans pointing satellite dishes at the sky. The crews seemed excited, filming the growing crowd of spectators. Several hospital security guards were trying to keep anyone from entering the building, and this was causing tensions to rise quickly. Already there were a few heated arguments in process.

Working his way through the crowd, Bishop overheard a man shouting at one of the guards, "What do you mean I can't go in? I was told to get my wife out of this place, and now you won't let me go in? How am I supposed to get her out?" Several others were echoing similar protests. Bishop realized there was no way he was going to get in through the front door, so he reversed course and headed along the side of the hospital. As he walked along trying to figure out what to do, a side emergency exit door opened. Two men in scrubs looked outside, and then began to pass out boxes. Bishop waved as he walked toward them, but they paid no attention to him. He entered the door between them.

A little disoriented, he made his way to the main lobby and didn't even notice the absence of the volunteers who normally manned the information desk. He went to the third floor, exited the elevators, and proceeded to room 323. As he entered the room, the stench almost overwhelmed him. Mrs. Rita Peterson, his mother-in-law, shared a room with two other patients. Clearly one or more of them had soiled themselves and hadn't been cleaned up. He ignored the overwhelming odor and preceded to the last bed where Rita was lying.

Rita's eyes were open, and she was moaning. He had seen her awake only briefly in the last month and had not heard her make any noise at all. She was trying to move, and obviously something was wrong. He was relieved that the smell did not seem to be coming from her, but then realized she was in pain. Her thin brows were clenched, and she was grinding her teeth at the same time as trying to yell out. Her weakened body was shaking badly. Bishop moved to her side quickly and took her hand, repeatedly asking, "Rita, Rita, what's wrong? Are you okay? Tell me what's wrong."

Rita's eyes cleared for a moment and she whispered, "THE PAIN. Oh lord it hurts so bad." Bishop hurried to the foot of the bed and located Rita's chart. He had spent enough time at her bedside in the last few months to know a little about how the nurses charted. He flipped a few pages and realized no one had made any entries in the record all day. Rita was in pain because she had not been given her medications. He looked up to see that her IV drip was almost empty as well. She and all of the other patients in the room seemed to have been ignored by the hospital staff.

Bishop rushed out of the room and toward the nurse's station. He was outraged and was going to protest the treatment of his mother-in-law. As he approached the station, he noticed another patient trying to get out of his room and struggling. "Help me...someone please help me...I am not well," the older man was saying. Bishop heard crying and another voice calling, "Nurse...please come here," as he walked down the hall.

Bishop knew before he got there that the station was deserted. He could hear monitors beeping and small alarms going off before even turning the last corner. Sure enough, no one was around. He noticed a cart with locks on the drawers and a set of keys lying close by. Each drawer contained several small paper cups full of pills with a room number and patient name written on them. He knew this was the med cart, and Rita's pain control medications might be there. He searched for a while and found a syringe labeled with her name. He ran back to Rita's room, squirted the syringe toward the ceiling to remove any air, and then injected the medication into her port just as he had seen the nurses do several times before. The effect was almost immediate, and she relaxed.

There was no alternative but to get her out of the hospital, so he went to search for a wheelchair. He found one, but then realized there was no way to keep her in the chair even if he did move her from the bed. There had to be another solution. He checked several doors, but they were locked. He remembered the keys, and spent almost half an hour trying countless keys in different locks and eventually found a gurney. It was lighter than the bed, and he knew he could load it into the back of the truck.

As he pushed the gurney back toward her room, he practically ran over two guys coming around the corner. "Sorry," he said while reading the badges around their necks. Both of their IDs said "Cafeteria" on them, and Bishop wondered what they were doing up here. He almost started laughing at them because one of them reminded him of Bluto from the old Popeye cartoons, and the other one walked just like Daffy Duck. They looked at each other and then at Bishop, probably wondering why he had a smirk on his face.

Bluto grumbled, "We need that cart---official hospital business."

"No can do pardner – I'm using it. I think there are some more in that closet down the hall," Bishop replied, pointing over his shoulder with his thumb and trying not to laugh.

"I don't think you heard me," was the tense response. "This is official hospital business, and YOU can go get another cart." Daffy, clearly the brains of the operation, chimed in, "We also need to see your wallet...errr...your ID."

Bishop gave a frightened glance at both men and stuttered, "You... You...You want my ID?"

Bishop was not an intimidating physical specimen by any means. Barely six foot and less than 200 pounds, he had figured out a long time ago that bluffing his way through a confrontation was rarely a valid option. He was also a natural born smartass and had a lot of trouble controlling his mouth. This combination had caused him to learn the hard way--- surprise was the best advantage.

Bluto reached for the gurney and started to pull it away from Bishop who held on tightly, and that surprised the big man. Bluto, as Bishop had anticipated, shifted his left foot for balance and started to give the cart a hard pull. Bishop gave it to him, pushing as hard as he could. The guy completely lost his footing as Bishop thrust the gurney at the wall causing Bluto's back to slam hard against a mounted fire extinguisher. Spinning the cart sideways to block Daffy, Bishop took two steps and struck Bluto hard in the Adam's apple with the edge of his hand. He spun around to face Daffy before the big man had finished sliding down the wall, clenching his throat and trying to breathe.

Daffy was holding up his hands in the "don't shoot" position and backing away. He decided he had business elsewhere, and quickly spun around and ran off.

Bishop looked down at Bluto and could see all of the fight had left him. "You better get that looked at bud. It's hard to be a looter if you can't breathe. By the way, has anyone ever told you that you look just like Blu . . . . Oh, hell, never mind." He grabbed the gurney and started heading back to Rita's room.

He disconnected her IV and rolled Rita from the bed onto the gurney as gently as possible. His plan was to take her to another hospital, so he threw her chart onto the gurney as well. She seemed not to notice any of this. He glanced at his watch and realized almost two hours had passed since he had talked to Terri. He would call her once he had Rita in the truck.

Ali Benzilla Shenfeti hated America. Not because of religion, or holy wars or even the influence of his mosque. Ali hated America because of what it had done to his father. At great risk, his father had helped the Americans in the first Gulf War by providing information about the Iraqi forces in Kuwait City to the Americans. He had despised Saddam more than the infidels. After the war the American consulate had recognized Ali's father was at risk if he stayed in the region . . . so they granted him political asylum and eventually, U.S. citizenship.

Ali had been uprooted with his mother and siblings and flown to the United States. His father had researched various American cities and settled on Houston, Texas. For the first few years, everything had gone according to plan, and life was good. The State Department had assisted in a small business loan, and a new family enterprise was established. Shenfeti Medical Supply was born with a family celebration in the back of the firm's new warehouse. It was really nothing more than a gas station that had gone out of business, but Mr. Shenfeti acted like it was a new 100,000 square foot facility.

Mr. Shenfeti worked tirelessly and grew his business delivering bottled oxygen and other supplies to customers in the Medical Center area. It was not long before he had three trucks and enlisted his son as a driver. Despite his limited English, Mr. Shenfeti had worked hard, enrolled his children in school, and allowed his wife to become more "westernized."

Ali had struggled with the West in general, but especially America. He played soccer while all of the other boys were interested in basketball or American football. He was one of three Muslim children in his class and the only one who was openly in love with Allah. This didn't go unnoticed by his classmates. Regardless, he and his family survived, and even flourished in Texas until 9/11.

As Ali later told his Mullah, it was as if someone had flipped a light switch. The discrimination was not open at first, but more like an underlying current of hatred. Orders for his father's business slowed, and longtime customers suddenly chose competitors for no known reason. Family friends no longer called or stopped by. Eventually, his father lost the business, having to sell out to a rival. Ali was retained as a driver because he knew the routes and the customers. Mr. Shenfeti became depressed and then ill. He died less than two years later of a heart attack in Houston General Hospital, one of his company's very first customers. Ali's hatred of all things American increased every time he made his weekly delivery to Houston General.

Ali was unaware of the hospital's financial problems or the announcement that morning. He pulled his delivery truck into the loading dock only to find everything locked down and a sign on the office door saying that the hospital was closed. This angered him even more as the hospital had dozens of his empty oxygen tanks, and he was responsible for exchanging them for the full ones on his truck. The hospital also used acetylene and other volatile gases for its labs and processes, and his truck was full of those as well. Barely keeping his temper in check, he shifted the truck into reverse, deciding his boss could deal with the situation later. As he tried to turn the corner on the way to his next customer, he found his path blocked by the large crowd of people gathered in front of the building.

Big Mike ordered all available radio cars be sent to Houston General and called downtown to request help. He left the station and quickly proceeded to the hospital. By the time he and most of the officers from the area began to arrive, there were over 800 people gathered in front of the building, and the crowd had overflowed onto Fannin Street, a major traffic artery in the area. Big Mike had to pull his cruiser to the curb almost six blocks away because of stranded cars full of angry drivers. As he was walking to the building, he saw something fly through the air and strike one of the big two story windows on the front of the hospital. The glass shattered, throwing sharp shards into the crowd and raining down on top of the front line security officials guarding the building perimeter. Before the yelling and screaming was over, another projectile was launched from the crowd, and a second window exploded, causing even more bedlam. Big Mike radioed back to the station and told dispatch that they had better issue the riot gear and requested more officers be sent immediately. Big Mike gathered up three of his men and proceeded to push to the front of the crowd, never noticing the white truck with the O2 sign on the door.

Ali had just had enough. The events of the day overwhelmed common sense, and he started honking his delivery truck's horn while inching into the crowd. Most people simply moved aside or tried to get out of the way, but eventually his truck bumped into three men who had walked out of a local bar, drinking beer, and watching the show. One of them turned around and yelled back at Ali, "Look at this Mexican honking his fucking horn. Go back to Mexico, asshole! If all you fuckers went back home, maybe we would have jobs." If Ali had not been so angry, being mistaken for a Mexican would have been funny. When the three large men started moving around to the side of his truck, he reached under the seat for the sawed-off shotgun he kept there.

Bishop didn't even try for the front door while pushing the gurney. He had waited on four different elevators before he could finally fit in with Rita and found it a bit odd that no one riding on the elevator questioned him at all. When he made it to the main floor, he started pushing Rita toward the side door he had used to enter the building. He found the exit and opened it to look out on the side street. There were lots of people around, and he could hear honking coming from the direction of Fannin Street where the big crowd was gathered. He began pushing Rita out of the door.

Ali pulled the shotgun out from under the seat at the same time he opened the driver's door of the truck. He kept one foot on the sideboard as he intended to just show the rednecks the shotgun, not use it. He pulled it out of the cab and started to level it toward the closest of the men.

Something caught Big Mike's eye. As his head pivoted toward the truck, he saw the driver pull the shotgun out of the cab. Big Mike screamed, "GUN!" at the top of his lungs and tried to pull his 9mm service weapon from its holster, but the closeness of the crowd stopped the draw. One of his officers heard the shout, and managed to clear his weapon despite the press of people. His shot went high because he rushed it.

Ali heard the shot and actually felt the round go over the top of his head. He believed one of the rednecks was shooting at him and began to chamber a round in the pump shotgun. His finger never made it to the trigger.

Big Mike managed to get his weapon clear as the crowd instinctively moved away from the first shot. This gave him the space he needed. His training kicked in, and his thumb released the safety while his arm brought the weapon in line with the target. He pulled the trigger, and the hammer fell on the firing pin. A 110-grain full metal jacket bullet exited the barrel of the pistol at 1,125 feet per second. It missed Ali low and to the left, passed through the front and back windshield, and struck a full tank of oxygen right below the valve, shearing the stem and causing the slightest spark.

The escaping oxygen, ignited by the spark, burned its way inside of the tank where the pure gas fueled an even greater combustion. The steel tank could no longer hold the pressure and exploded, sending searing hot fragments flying into the bed of the delivery truck, piercing the skins of several other full tanks.

That first, single tank would not have caused a very large explosion, and the damage would have been limited. But when the high velocity steel fragments shredded the other tanks in the truck, the mixture of escaping gases immediately formed a small vapor cloud. The military refers to this type of cloud as a "fuel air mixture," and the resulting release of energy is the most powerful known to science short of a nuclear detonation. To the naked eye, it all looked like one big explosion.

Anyone within 100 feet was killed instantly by the shock wave, their internal organs turned to mush. Within 150 feet, the fireball killed many others as the oxygen already in their lungs was ignited at over 1200 degrees. Those individuals unlucky enough to be within 250 feet of the explosion suffered the effects of the flying debris.

Bishop had just started pushing Rita out the door when the shock wave caught her gurney and tore him the rest of the way through the exit, still hanging onto her. Rita was killed instantly as her gurney was hurled almost 20 feet through the air, pulling Bishop along with it. When his head finally cleared enough, Bishop knew he had cracked a rib, and it felt as though he had dislocated his shoulder. The angle of the building absorbed most of the blast and had saved his life. Lying disheveled and stunned over the legs of Rita's gurney, his fuzzy mind drifted back to a similar experience years before.

After his in-country Iraq orientation, Bishop had been issued a rifle and gear. Spider then took Bishop out to see the "junk" they were supposed to protect. Spider's company had been contracted to guard a pipeline which was considered to be a prime target for the insurgents. The problem was that it was impossible to guard the entire section they were responsible for as it was much more than just a straight line of big pipe.

There were valves, pumps, safety lines and spurs all up and down a five mile stretch that Spider's team was to protect. The whole situation was complicated by the fact that the equipment was a mixture of Russian, French, and American machinery. It had been purchased from whoever Saddam had been on speaking terms with at the time. As newer equipment had been installed, the old, broken pieces had been left right where they were.

The man Bishop had replaced was an oilfield engineer who had been trying to figure out how all of the rusted "scrap" functioned. Spider's team needed to know the role of every piece in order to prioritize how they would protect it. The important components would receive full- time protection while non-critical or non-working equipment would be subject to timesaving random patrols.

On the third day, Spider and Bishop were on their way back to the security company's compound, driving their usual route. They attempted a turn and ran right into the Baghdad police blocking the street. After several minutes of hand gestures and words neither side understood, they finally discerned that a street festival was in progress. The road was closed. Spider started trying to work his way back through the side streets, alleys and roads. Many were still blocked by debris, courtesy of the United States Air Force, and in short order they were lost. They drove through suburban Baghdad for 20 very tense minutes when they finally spotted a US Marine Corp Humvee ahead. As they got closer, they realized there were actually several Humvees, loaded with lots of Marines, and both men relaxed.

Spider parked the SUV and left to find the officer in charge of the convoy. A gunnery sergeant told him that the LT was in a shop trying to buy ice. Spider went off to talk to the man while Bishop decided to hang around a group of young marines and shoot the proverbial shit. One of the young men was telling stories and doing a pretty good imitation of President Bush. He was a bright-eyed young corporal from Spokane, Washington and Bishop took an immediate liking to the kid.

In a few minutes, someone yelled "Mount up ladies!" and the Marines all began to shuffle toward their vehicles. Spider reappeared, telling Bishop they were going to join the Marine convoy and were to take the third spot when they pulled out.

They fell into place behind a Humvee and had gone about half a kilometer when Bishop noticed that the streets were suddenly empty of people. "Hey Spider, where did all the people go?" Spider looked around and started to say, "Oh shit" when the Humvee in front of them rose straight into the air. Bishop could remember seeing the rear tires rise off of the ground and then the windshield of their SUV turned snow white with cracks from the blast wave. The next thing he remembered was the seat belt of the SUV strangling him as he was hanging by it.

Their SUV was lying on the driver's side, and Bishop was suspended above a groaning Spider. He managed to put a boot on the console and tried to undo his seat belt, but it was jammed. He pulled his fighting knife from his chest rig and sliced into the seat belt once, then again and finally cut through. He used his rifle barrel to punch out the glass from the passenger window and pulled himself out. Once he was on top of the passenger door, he looked back inside to check on his buddy. Spider was trying to clear his head and was bleeding out of his nose, but he gave Bishop the thumbs up and proceeded to unhook his seat belt. As soon as he was sure Spider was going to be okay, he looked up at the wrecked Humvee. It was lying on the driver's door as well, and the front half was missing. Bishop could see one of the Marines had been thrown free of the vehicle but could not see the other man. A small "puff" came from the underside of the Humvee, and he knew instantly that it was starting to burn.

Bishop hopped off the wreckage and ran toward the now burning Humvee. He found a foothold and climbed up so he could look inside and saw a Marine still strapped into the passenger seat. The fire was making the frame very hot under Bishop's arm. *I have to get that man out of here.* He pulled his knife again and sliced through the seat belt. Bishop reached in, grabbed the man's plate carrier and pulled with everything he had. He pulled so hard that the momentum carried him and the Marine off of the side of the Humvee and they landed in a heap beside the vehicle. He knew something was not right even before he hit the ground. He should not have been able to pull a fully loaded man out like that. He sat up to check it out and grasped that he had pulled out only half of a man. The lower half was still in the Humvee. A stunned Bishop sat there staring at the man's intestines unraveling on the ground.

Bishop hadn't realized it at the moment, but his ears no longer functioned. During all of the turmoil, it had never dawned on him that there was a complete absence of noise. He noticed movement and looked up to see the Gunny motioning him to get down and mouthing something. *What was he saying?* *…..in….in…in coming….INCOMING!* Bishop started to lay flat when a mortar exploded 20 feet away causing the ground to shake so hard that he actually bounced. Hot air blew off his hat, and the dead Marine's body was flung on top of him. He shook his head to clear the bright white lines that were crossing his vision. He started to get up, but his legs would not answer the commands being sent by his brain. It was the first time in Bishop's life that he was so frightened he could not move. *No,* he thought, *Oh God please not now, not in front of the Marines. Move, God Damnit! Move your ass,old man.* He willed his legs to start pumping in any direction. He managed to get up and had made two half-crawling steps when the Gunny waved violently for him to get down again.

The second mortar hit right as Bishop's cheek made it to the hot sand. His legs were picked up and flung sideways by the force of the blast. He ended up completely disoriented with grit in his mouth and eyes. His next memory was of being dragged away, face down, from the burning Humvee and seeing combat boots landing step by precious step on both sides of his head. Two Marines were dragging him away from the kill zone. They pulled him behind a low wall where a corpsman started looking him over.

Once the corpsman had verified that Bishop was both unharmed and one of the luckiest people he had ever met, Bishop drained three full bottles of water. With his senses recovering, he started slowly wandering around. The Marines were waiting on their CO to fly in on a bird so that a full report could be made. *So the Chicken Shit Syndrome is not unique to the Army*, he thought. The Lieutenant in charge of the convoy appeared at Bishop's side to check if he was okay. Bishop asked, "What the hell was that all about Lieutenant? What happened?"

"The terrorists have a new trick; Division calls them Improvised Explosive Devices or IEDs. They take old artillery shells and make bombs out them. Most times, they plant them next to the road and wait for us to go by. Every now and then, like today, they get real clever and lob a few mortar shells or have a sniper fire rounds at us right after the detonation. They have no chance against us in a stand-up gunfight, so they're doing this shit to break us down." He thanked Bishop for pulling his man out of the fire and proceeded elsewhere to take care of business.

It was then that Bishop realized he had not seen the young corporal who did the Bush imitations and went to find him. Bishop approached the Gunny and asked where the kid was. The Gunny gave him an odd look and said, "You pulled half of him out of that Humvee, sir. He rests in that bag over there."

Everything became clear in Bishop's mind. He remembered asking Spider where all of the people had gone, and then the explosion occurred. He looked back along their route where people had already returned to their shops and stalls along the street. He then thought about the obvious effort required to plant the roadside bomb and then walk off the distance for the mortar crew. *All of those people back there could not have missed seeing that bomb being buried or the terrorists counting steps as they walked away.* He glanced over at the half-full body bag, and his rage boiled over.

He grabbed his rifle and began walking toward the Iraqi people on the street. He began shouting at the top of his lungs, "You knew! You rotten fuckers, you knew! Why didn't you warn us? I'm going to kill every last one of you fuckers! A hundred of you bitches are not worth that kid!"

Bishop was pulling his rifle up to his shoulder when a very large hand grabbed the weapon and spun him around. It was the Gunny, and he calmly said, "Sir, you're not going to kill anyone with that weapon. You don't have a magazine in it." Bishop just blinked as it took a second to comprehend. He looked down at his M4 and broke out laughing. It was empty and as dangerous as a baby rattle. The nervous laughter was contagious, and a few nearby Marines got a good chuckle as well. He shrugged his shoulders and headed back to find Spider. He wanted to know when they were going to blow this pop-stand.

The Double Tap

In the parking garage across from the hospital a news crew had been setting up cameras to cover the riot. A wide pillar had deflected most of the blast wave, and a camera ended up pointed at Bishop and Rita lying in the street. The picture was beamed back to the station for several minutes as the crew was too disoriented to realize they were broadcasting live. The picture of an elderly woman lying disheveled in the street with a man half-draped over her gurney was one of those rare images that would change history. The live footage was broadcast throughout the world. A single frame would be published in all of the major newspapers over the next few days.

As Bishop's head began to clear the cobwebs, he checked his body for major injury. He had enough presence to slowly flex and move everything to see what worked. He discovered his left arm wasn't responding well, but it felt like shoulder pain and not a broken arm. *There goes half of my sex life* he thought. It hurt like hell to breathe. He managed to get up and check on Rita, but it was obvious she was gone. He sat down and covered her face with a sheet after giving her a kiss on the forehead. *That's from Terri.* The blast had killed her instantly; and in a way, Bishop was glad it had been quick. He immediately felt guilt at his sense of relief and then pushed it out of his mind. He decided he would just lie back down and wait on help to arrive.

When Ali's delivery truck had exploded, the blast shattered every window for three blocks. There was a crater in Fannin Street over 20 feet in diameter and 10 feet deep. Several cars and trucks on the street had been blown over or set on fire. Houston General Hospital lost the stone facade for its first three stories. The entire first floor was devastated. The office building across from the hospital suffered similar damage, and one corner looked close to collapse. Bodies littered the street in both directions. The blast set off car alarms as far away as NASA. Some thought Houston had been hit by a nuclear bomb because of the small mushroom cloud that rose over the scene.

Bishop, of course, knew none of this. He was gathering his wits to stand up when he smelled something rotten in the air. *What is that?* It took his mind a few seconds to register the odor. *GAS!* Adrenaline pumped through his body, and he managed to get to his feet and start moving away from the area as fast as he could. He could hear the whine of sirens close by and expected to see help arriving at any moment. Instinct directed him to put distance between himself and the blast zone. He suddenly remembered the truck was parked nearby and headed in that direction. Two police cars went roaring past, followed closely by an ambulance. Seeing that help was arriving actually gave him more strength. He could now hear an orchestra of sirens in the distance. It sounded like there were hundreds of emergency vehicles descending on the area. Bishop was almost to his truck. He reached in his pocket for the keys when his shadow became very intense, and suddenly the entire street was flooded white with light. While this blast wave didn't knock him down, he could feel the heat and heard the roar as the ground shook for a second time in less than five minutes. He turned to see a giant fireball rise over the top of the five-story hospital. The leaking natural gas had been sparked, and Bishop could only hope that the first responders were not close when it had exploded. He made it to his truck and reached for his cell phone. It was gone. *Well shit*, he thought, *Terri has to be going insane with worry. I have to get in touch with her somehow.*

Terri had been glued to the TV watching the coverage. The media had helicopters and ground coverage. The station she was watching had a reporter interviewing someone right in front of the hospital when the truck exploded. The screen went completely white, and she heard the voice of the anchor, apologizing for apparent loss of signal. An uneasy pause of about 10 seconds ensued, when the station switched to the helicopter view. The devastation from the aerial feed was clear. Terri was getting dressed for the trip to the hospital when the picture of Bishop and Rita lying in the street appeared on her television. While she could not be 100% sure with the smoke and the angle of the shot, she knew in her heart that she was looking at the lifeless bodies of her mother and husband. Her body began to jerk uncontrollably when the man stirred. She did not blink or breathe for several seconds until finally seeing him move again. He got up to check on the woman lying beside the gurney. She saw the man bend over, kiss the woman on the head, and then cover her face. When he reached for the blanket, his head rose up enough and Terri saw it was her husband. Bishop was alive ... but her mother was dead. She just sat stunned watching the television with hot tears of both relief and remorse rolling down her cheeks.

Bishop drove toward home. He didn't know what else to do. He was in extreme pain, and it was becoming harder and harder for him to catch his breath. Somehow, he kept on course, navigated the traffic, and ended up in his driveway. He managed to open the door and thought at least Terri wouldn't have to search for his body. He started to get out, but the step down out of the truck was his undoing, and he did a full-face plant into the grass. *The neighbors will think I stumbled home drunk and passed out in the yard.*

Terri heard Bishop's truck pull into the driveway and was on her way out the door when she saw him fall. She rushed to his side yelling, "Bishop, are you all right?"

"Well babe, there were these three big guys at the bar, and, well...you should see the other dudes."

"Bishop, this is no time for jokes." Terri's tone was unmistakable.

"Terri," Bishop said with serious eyes, "I am sorry baby, but your Mom is dead. I tried; I really tried, but she is gone. She didn't feel any pain."

Terri said, "Bishop, we can talk about that later. I am so relieved you made it home. Let's get you taken care of." She tried to help him up, but his weight was too much for her. She ran across the street and rang the neighbor's doorbell. With help from friends, they managed to get Bishop into bed, and a nurse friend came over to check him out. Terri decided to call for an ambulance and have Bishop taken to a local hospital, but was informed by the dispatcher that every available ambulance in the city was being diverted to the Medical Center. She decided to drive him there herself, but he would have none of it, half-heartedly vowing to kick anyone's ass who tried to move him from the bed.

Houston, Texas - July 31, 2015

Aftermath

Bishop had been lying in bed all day, watching the news and letting Terri take care of him. He was actually feeling a bit better, but needed to get both his shoulder and ribs checked out. The cable news channels were covering the Houston explosion from every possible angle. Over 1,200 people were dead, and another 650 were injured. The fires were still burning, and the Houston Fire Department was struggling with a combination of poor water pressure and a lack of manpower. The department suffered from cutbacks just like every other city agency in the last few years. The mayor had asked for help from Dallas and other nearby cities, but so far those departments had responded with only token assistance, as they were shorthanded too.

The initial reaction by several "experts" was that the whole affair had been a terrorist attack. The 24x7-news coverage concluded that the explosion was a truck bomb and that a sleeper cell of jihadists had taken advantage of the crowd gathered in front of the hospital and detonated the weapon. Bishop didn't buy it. The crowd at the hospital had been impromptu and compared to a football game or other event, had been quite small. If a terror cell were going to stage an attack, why go after such a small crowd?

Wall Street reacted poorly to the news. Already down by over 50% since the start of the depression, stocks plunged even further in anticipation of additional attacks and the reaction of the U.S. Government. The President had done what Presidents always do and expressed sorrow while pledging to bring justice to those responsible. America was already a war-weary country, and the vast majority of the population blamed 16 years of war for a large part of the current economic situation. While all but a skeleton force of U.S. Troops had been pulled from foreign battlefields, the money had been spent. Money that many believed would have been better utilized at home.

The prospect of more war, combined with an already unemployed and frustrated people, brought out protestors. Clashes with police were becoming common in every major city. It didn't help that Houston General was part of a nationwide system of hospitals with facilities in 12 major metropolitan areas. While no other medical center experienced a disaster like Houston General, the emotional and economic ripples were felt throughout the other eleven communities. This compounded an already tense situation in these areas that led to protests, mobs, and even minor looting.

In Atlanta, riot police had been deployed, and two young men had been killed in the resulting encounter. As the news of the shootings spread, it wasn't long before a full riot broke out. The nation witnessed violence on a scale not seen since the Rodney King verdict in Los Angeles years before.

Atlanta was burning.

Houston, Texas - August 1, 2015

It was late afternoon when a Houston news producer reviewed the video that his now deceased crew was transmitting back to the station before the explosion. The newsroom had been in complete turmoil since the hospital had been attacked. They had lost four co-workers in the blast, and that shock combined with an unending series of major news events had resulted in everyone's forgetting about the film from that day. The producer and a sound engineer were watching as the female reporter interviewed a spectator from the crowd. The questions and answers were almost indiscernible due to the noise of the mob, so the sound engineer was trying to block out the background noise. The producer stopped the footage playback and pointed to the edge of the picture where he could see the side of a truck holding several storage tanks. In addition to the containers, the producer was intrigued by the figures of three men who were facing away from the crowd and were preoccupied instead with the truck.

"Can you isolate from that direction?" he asked the engineer. The crew that day had been equipped with the station's latest digital video and audio equipment. The engineer pulled up a computer display with dozens of multi-colored lines and began typing and clicking with the mouse.

After about three minutes, he said, "How's this?" and an audio began to play.

Both men sat in shock as the slightly warbled voices began to play over the computer's speakers. "Go back to Mexico, asshole! If all you fuckers went back home, maybe we would have jobs. Let's kick his ass!" A few minutes later, they managed to enhance the video, and Ali's shotgun could be seen in the picture. "This is priority one," said the producer. "Get this on the air now! Someone get me New York on the phone, and oh, yeah, call the FBI too."

KFOR News Houston began reporting that the explosion at Houston General Hospital was not a terrorist related attack, but was the result of a racial incident. The network then showed the clip of the three white men, moving toward the cab of a delivery truck and what appeared to be a Mexican man in the truck's door pulling out a shotgun. The audio made it obvious what was going on. The cameraman had instinctively moved his camera toward the police officer who shouted, "Gun!" and a shot pierced the air. The picture then went blank, and the network anchor began to explain the source of the video.

Within a few hours, every news outlet in the world started playing the video clip over and over. Most people were relieved that it wasn't a terrorist attack. On television, it appeared to be a simple argument that had somehow gotten out of control. The following morning, the stock market recovered slightly, and many people exhaled in relief. They had no idea how premature that relief was.

North Houston Suburbs

Bishop was watching when yet another "Breaking News Alert" flashed on his TV. He almost ignored it because it seemed like every five minutes there had been some event that the cable news warranted as special, new, or important. Most of them were just a new spin on old news, complete redundancies at best. When he saw that this report concerned the Houston incident, he watched with more attentiveness. *I told you so*, he thought as the report ended.

He was tired of lying in bed and was about to get up when he heard Terri come home from work. As she headed toward their bedroom, he decided to play possum and avoid another scolding about "rest." He closed his eyes and pretended to be asleep.

He heard Terri move quietly around the room for a bit, and then there was no noise at all. He waited almost a full minute and was about to peek to see if she had gone. The sound of her voice made him jump, as she was standing right next to the bed.

"I knew you were awake. Faker!"

Bishop protested, "I was not awake. You just scared the shit out of me."

Terri was not to be distracted, "How do you expect to get better if you don't rest? How are you feeling?

He decided to be coy, "Well Nurse Terri, I have this inflammation problem, and was hoping you could help me with it."

Terri's face flashed concern for about one second until she caught on. She playfully replied, "You're swollen? Where baby?"

Bishop's hand reached beneath the covers and with an innocent voice, "It's really swollen right down here nurse, and it's *very* uncomfortable."

Terri reached down and pulled back the covers revealing Bishop in his boxers. She slowly pulled her skirt up to her waist saying, "I think I have the right medicine for that problem. You just lie still, and let Nurse Terri apply a special treatment."

She gently straddled him on the bed and began to rub against the area in question. Bishop responded immediately with a moan and said, "Oh Nurse…Oh, that seems to be making the problem worse."

Terri's expression changed from fake lust to pure mischief. While keeping her hips moving, she leaned forward and gave Bishop a kiss. As she started to lean back, she purposely put her hands on his chest and applied just a touch of pressure. Bishop inhaled sharply as his wounded ribs smarted, "Ouch."

Terri dismounted him immediately. She didn't even give him a chance to protest.

"That's not fair Bishop. You get a girl all excited and can't perform? I thought I had another 20 years of good service out of you before you started wearing out. Do you need blue pills already?"

Bishop protested, "You little shit. Why if I could catch you, I'd show you a performance."

Terri knew she had him, "Oh, there you go again. You're teasing me, and it's mean. You know I don't like mean men."

Bishop pointed to his underwear, which now looked like a small camping tent, and said, "A tease, huh?"

Terri looked down and grinned. "I think some ice would help with that swelling. Hold on a second, and let me get an ice pack out of the freezer," she said and turned to leave.

Bishop reached out to catch her, but pulled back quickly when the sharp pain in his ribs protested. "Ok, you win. But when I'm better, you're going to pay."

Terri sat down on the edge of the bed and played with his hair. She gave him a look of pure love, and they smiled at each other.

"You poor baby, I feel so guilty. Let me make it up to you," she said as her hand gently moved to the elastic band in his underwear. She slowly kissed him with little pecks all the way down his chest and onto his tummy. Right below his navel, she stopped, looked up at him, and whispered, "Lay back and relax."

Ten minutes later, Bishop was falling into a deep, satiated sleep.

Terri looked down at him and smiled. *What a wonderful man I have*, she thought.

She had "met" Bishop via an internet-dating website. After weeks of complaining to co-workers about how she hated clubs and bars, someone suggested she try the web. She had initially scoffed at the idea. Raised in a conservative mid-western home, Terri considered online dating as something for overweight losers who couldn't find true love any other way.

She was sitting alone in her apartment on a Saturday night. Her date for the evening had just called and cancelled. It was no big deal as her suitor was just the latest in a string of lukewarm relationships. *What the hell. What do I have to lose? I should try that internet thing.* She searched the web and picked a dating site that appeared to be more about relationships and less about casual sex. After filling out a profile and posting what she considered her best picture, she decided to enter the chat room and watch.

It was only a few minutes before the computer dinged, and she saw that she had a message in her in-box. Before she could figure out how to open the message, a second and then a third appeared. *Wow*, she thought, *that must have been a really good picture.*

She exchanged emails with Bishop for over two weeks. She really couldn't tell what was different about his messages or why she had focused on him out of the dozens of men who contacted her. After a few phone conversations, they agreed to meet in person.

Bishop insisted they meet somewhere that was very public, and she was glad. The news reports of women being murdered by men they had met online were not lost on her. She recalled being so relaxed just sitting and talking with Bishop. It was the best date she'd ever had. As she thought back, she smiled, realizing Bishop had played her like a violin.

They met at a popular coffee shop in a good part of town. He passed the first test by being on time. He passed the second test because he looked like his picture. He kept his eyes above her neck and was on the way to acing the initial exam. They ordered coffee and found a table. He didn't pull out her chair, nor did he pay for her drink, and that was a bit of a surprise. She decided to take charge of the situation and said, "I know the primary reason why you're here. You want in my pants, and I want to tell you right now it's not going to happen... tonight. I'm not that kind of girl."

"Good," he said without pausing. "I've had my fill of casual sex. I was hoping you weren't looking for a quick lay. I found out long ago that sex without chemistry is like 'woo-hoo,' but sex with chemistry is 'woooooooo-hooooooooooo.' I'm the kind of guy who takes a little time to develop chemistry, so if you think you can behave yourself, we should get along just fine."

They talked about so many topics that night that she couldn't remember them all. After finishing a third cup, Bishop had looked at his watch and said, "I have to get going. I'm leaving on a business trip for a few days. If you would like to go on a real date, I would very much like to see you again. Send me an email after you think it over."

He had walked Terri back to her car and never even hinted at wanting to "escort her home."

Sleep had not been an option that night as she continued to replay their entire conversation over and over in her mind. She finally settled on what had attracted her to Bishop the most - he spoke very little about himself. She realized that he had continually asked questions about her and then listened. It had been refreshing. Without thinking, she got up at 1:48 AM and sent Bishop an email saying she would love to go on a date. After she hit the "send" button, she cursed herself for doing so in the middle of the night. *That's not how you play hard-to-get,* she thought.

They went on a few dates and after leaving a lousy movie before it finished, decided to get a late night burger. There was a surprisingly long line of people for the late hour, probably due to the movie crowd. As they stood in line waiting, three young men came in wearing gang colors and spouting foul language. Bishop looked at the three and was amused because they reminded him of Larry, Curley, and Moe. He leaned over and whispered his observation to Terri, and she admitted the similarities made the three thugs appear less threatening. Moe was clearly the leader and was quite annoyed with his inept comrades. Curley was a big dude with a shaved head who kept looking around the room like he was lost. Larry was simply fascinated with the dollar menu and paid no attention to anything else. At one point, Bishop caused Terri to laugh out loud when he whispered, "Watch out for the two finger eye poke and the double slap – they're experts you know."

After their language drew a few dirty looks from other customers, Moe declared, "We ain't got time for this shit," and proceeded to cut in line. Terri watched as Bishop tensed and noticed his hands had balled into tight fists. She was just about to suggest they eat somewhere else, when he reached out and touched Curley on the shoulder. In a nerdy, super whiney voice Bishop complained, "Excuse me. You're cutting in line. You probably don't realize it, but it's extremely rude and makes the other customers uncomfortable."

Curley didn't say a word for a second. He half turned, sized Bishop up, and then undressed Terri with his eyes. Curley showed backbone, and threatened, "Mind your own business, Old School. Fuck off before me and my boys take your lady outside and have a l'il fun with her."

Bishop turned, looked at her, and smiled. He nodded toward the exit door and made a motion with his hand indicating she should "go over there." She hesitated at first, but he winked and repeated the signal. She thought they were going to leave and walked over to the door to wait on Bishop. Curley had turned his back to Bishop and was focusing his attention on the menu above the counter. As soon as Bishop saw Terri was clear, he took a deep breath and moved.

He grabbed Curley by the belt with one hand and the jacket collar with the other. Bishop lifted up and back on the belt, while pushing down and forward on Curley's collar. Curley reacted as expected, throwing out his arms to maintain his balance. The moment Bishop felt the man's weight shift, he pushed hard with both legs. The helpless Curley was propelled head first into the cash register, sending it flying from the counter. Bishop didn't even take the time to face Moe. Just as he released Curley, Bishop's foot shot out and struck Moe right on the side of the knee with a savage kick. Terri heard a loud "yelp" and saw Bishop spin and hit Moe squarely in the solar plexus with the heel of his hand. Moe went down, unable to hold his knee and gasp for breath at the same time. Larry took all this in but didn't move. Bishop took one step toward him and said, "The manager is probably calling the cops right now. Do you want to hang around and talk to them?"

Larry started helping his friends up and out of the restaurant while Bishop stood over them and watched, even offering to assist a few times.

After they had left, Bishop walked toward Terri and said, "I'm really not that hungry, are you?" They left quickly as well.

For the first 15 minutes of the drive home, neither of them spoke. She finally couldn't handle the silence anymore and said, "What was that all about?"

Bishop thought about his answer for a moment, "Terri, I think you're a wonderful girl and hope you have similar feelings for me. There's one thing you should know about me – I cannot handle personal injustice. It does something to me, and it always has. I think it started in elementary school with playground bullies, and it just has always been that way. It gets me into, um, well, uncomfortable situations now and then. I hope you can accept that about me."

She had to laugh at the phrase "uncomfortable situations," and that broke the ice. The rest of the trip home, she tried to deal with the mixture of emotions going through her. Was he a danger to her? Was he a danger to others? Was he overly confident? Could she handle being with someone who did not have a healthy aversion to confrontation?

In the end, she decided to continue to seeing him and as she looked back, believed that was one of her best decisions ever.

The Georgetown End Run

Timothy Bose had served as a United States Senator for sixteen years. He was an experienced, albeit frustrated, politician. The honorable gentleman envisioned being President of the United States, but his polling numbers and lack of name recognition indicated that he had little chance. He was an intense student of history, especially concerning politics, and could recite from memory details of how every major leader had come to power since the beginning of civilization. While this skill was not unique in Washington, he could have also written a thesis on how each of them had *fallen* from power. And that was what made him think differently about governing than anyone else.

He had been waiting for an event that would focus America. A strong conservative and a keen observer of the human animal, he reached the conclusion that the American people were like confused waves on the sea. The economic tide and changing winds had left his once proud nation listing without direction or purpose. Such an event would be even better if it focused the nation's attention on him and away from any opposing candidate.

As the disaster in Houston unfolded, he made the obligatory patriotic statement to support the people and the Commander in Chief. When new information about an "illegal Mexican" playing a key role in the explosion had surfaced, the Senator saw his opportunity. Washington's "Inner Beltway" went silent as experts, consultants and think tanks digested the news. Advocating certain positions, views and policy was going to be complex as everyone instinctively recognized the situation as a potential powder keg. After all, the Hispanic voting block was more powerful than ever, and there was the upcoming election to consider. Yet at the same time, white, middle class America was suffering badly from the depression. While the rest of Washington went into analysis mode, the Senator had his aide schedule a news conference. Being first out of the box had its advantages, and most of the major news networks clamored to hear what he had to say.

He worked until late in the night preparing his opening comments and refining his position. *This is it*, he thought, *how I handle this situation can make or break my dream for this country*. While he would never have admitted it publicly, Germany in the early 1930s served as his model. The German people, under the Treaty of Versailles, were suffering horrible economic conditions at that time. Adolf had been a brilliant, if not ruthless political mind and had seized the one tangent that would unite the German people – a common enemy. Hitler picked the Jewish people as the focus of frustration and anger. Senator Bose would pick illegal aliens, and the situation in Houston would be his springboard.

He had to tread carefully as he wasn't an orator like Hitler. If he didn't position this correctly, bright political minds would pick up on his strategy and counter him brutally. He had no desire to see concentration camps in North America, nor did he feel that his race were superior in any way. He believed America needed a bold movement to unite her people and change her course. Japan wasn't going to repeat an attack on Pearl Harbor, and a surprise strike from any other world power would be nuclear and out of the question. Even when the world had believed that the Houston incident were a terrorist attack, the country hadn't united like it after 9/11. *No*, he thought, *I have to play this just right, and if I do, I can change the course of this great nation.*

United States Senate Press Room #3 - August 4, 2015

The Senator's news conference started right on schedule with an eclectic assortment of attendees representing every publication from *The Houston Chronicle* to *The Associated Press*. Bose began with a prepared statement that conveyed the proper mix of outrage, remorse, and professionalism. He began by discussing the composition of America and how its greatness was directly related to the immigrating masses from the four corners of the globe. At first, everyone listening thought, "Great speech, he is going to tell everyone not to take out their frustrations on the Hispanic people for the sins of one man," but then his tone and pace changed. He started quoting historical references to non-military invasions of various empires throughout history. He gradually worked in rule of law, and then dropped his bombshell 30-second news byte:

"The Department of Labor indicates that 24 million Americans are out of work. The Department of Homeland Security estimates that there are 24 million illegal aliens in the United

States. Does everyone think these numbers are just a coincidence? We have always said we can't possibly round up 24 million illegal aliens and deport them. Well, I think we can. I'm going to introduce a bill this afternoon into the Senate that will authorize Immigration Control and Enforcement to hire an additional 2 million agents. This will employ our people and provide a kick-start to the economy. Furthermore, the bill will temporarily grant ICE special powers of enforcement, search, seizure, and arrest. This legislation will also create a special court system to process the deportation of every single illegal in the United States of America. Finally, funding will be available in the form of a cash reward for information leading to the deportation of any illegal. I will be happy to take questions now."

The group of reporters erupted, and cameras flashed all over the room. The Senator nodded at the first reporter:

"Sir, isn't what you are suggesting a breach of civil rights?"

"What I'm suggesting is more like limited Martial Law. Now, I understand that this is something which has never been proposed before. But Ladies and Gentlemen, these are unusual times, and we have to take a *new* course of action to meet these *new* challenges. Please consider that we currently have millions of Americans who are out of work. Our government is broke, and our cities barely provide basic services. We simply can't continue to do this anymore! Our citizenry is weary of supporting illegals. We have to ask ourselves . . . *Could the incident in Houston have been avoided if we had addressed this problem before it spiraled out of control?* Think about it. Would the hospital still be open if its bottom line had not been completely corroded by the excessive burden of free medical care? Would we have thousands of Houstonians dead or dying? We can structure this bill such that the rights of every single American Citizen are protected under our Constitution. Those who are here illegally deserve no protection under that document."

"Senator, what you are suggesting could expose immigrants who are here legally to tremendous discrimination and hardship. What do you say to them?"

"My bill will protect American citizens and those who are here lawfully. Those who are not should leave today because we are going to find you, and when we do, we will deport you. In addition, I have a message to those considering entering the country illegally – don't. If we have to put an armed man every ten feet along the border, we will. The border will be closed, ladies and gentlemen, and those that should not be here will be removed."

The questions and answers went on for another 15 minutes. When he was finished, the Senator went back to his office and began directing staff to write the new bill. He could not remember a time when his phones rang so much. He instructed the switchboard to take messages. He wanted all of his people focused on the language of his landmark legislation.

Cable news channels brought in their best analysts and talking heads to cover the Senator's announcement. At first, the consensus was that he had crossed the line and his political career was over. Within a couple of hours, however, the story started to change.

Both the House and Senate were overwhelmed with a 70% positive reaction to the Senator's announcement. The volume of telephone and email traffic regarding the interview was unprecedented. The website for The Department of Homeland Security crashed due to excessive traffic from those trying to apply for the new jobs. Many people simply offered to volunteer.

The powerful people in Washington are connected by the world's most advanced intelligence network, and it doesn't belong to the CIA or the NSA. Social media, internet, text, email, and cell phones all became hyper-active as information was instantly shared throughout the city. Press offices, think tanks, lobbyists, and elected government officials all received constant updates. It didn't take long before everyone knew Senator Bose had connected with the American people on a level not seen since 9/11.

The only people who were unhappy about the entire concept were the Hispanic political organizations and the Mexican government. Of course, the ACLU and other liberal organizations immediately protested the Senator's anticipated bill. The phones of the Hispanic groups were hot with activity trying to call in favors, making threats and organizing protests.

Bishop had been sitting up in bed watching the Senator's news conference. *Not good*, he thought.

After watching the commentary, he decided that Terri was just going to have to trade him in for a new model because he could not stay in bed one minute longer.

He got up and found that the more he moved around, the better he actually felt. He showered, dressed, and brushed his teeth. He had just polished off his third peanut butter and pickle sandwich when he realized he needed something to occupy his mind.

Initially, he tried to work out, but the pain in his ribs made him rethink that idea. Bishop headed to the garage and his beloved workbench. When he and Terri had been looking for their first home, there were just a few criteria that were really important to Bishop. The first was that he wanted a house that afforded a little privacy – something very difficult to accomplish on their limited budget. The second and most important feature was having a good area for a workshop.

When Bishop returned from the Army, he had decided to take his limited savings and relocate to Houston. After all, his degree had been chosen specifically for a career in the oil industry, and Houston seemed a logical choice to find a job. He quickly found that every person on earth with any sort of engineering degree was in Houston with the same idea. As one headhunter put it, "Every waiter and burger flipper in Houston is a petroleum engineer."

After a few months of searching, Bishop was still unemployed and running out of money. He had been going to the Veterans Administration and using their job placement service when he noticed a small note on the bulletin board:

HELP WANTED – Public rifle range has an opening for a safety/range officer. Must have firearms experience and be able to work weekends. Military training/experience a plus.

Bishop took the note down and called the number before reaching the parking lot.

Northside Gun and Range was not far from his apartment. He was connected with the owner, Richard, who asked if he could stop by that afternoon. Bishop had a job.

The pay was only a few bucks above minimum wage, but Bishop needed to work and did his absolute best. It wasn't long before Richard came out to the range and asked Bishop if he could come inside and work the gun store as his regular man had called in sick. Bishop really impressed the customers with his knowledge of firearms. When he got his next paycheck, he noticed it was higher than normal. When he mentioned the error, his boss said, "You sold three guns last week. That's your commission."

Eventually Bishop approached Richard and asked if he had a minute. "Sure, what's on your mind?"

"You know the economy keeps getting worse and the range business has slowed down. Why don't we take a few of the shooting lanes and make a pistol training area out of them? We can give private lessons as well as provide Concealed Handgun License classes if we get a certified instructor."

It wasn't long before Bishop was on his way to firearms school in Dallas, learning to become a state certified handgun instructor. The new offering by Northside brought in customers. Not only did the range do well, but sales in the gun store increased too. Richard paid Bishop a share of the profits.

Bishop was working on the range when a number of serious-looking gentlemen showed up to shoot their pistols. Bishop had never seen weapons like theirs and struck up a conversation. It turned out that they were competition shooters and were in town for a match. He heard them call their pistols "speed guns" and decided to watch the matches the next day.

He drove to a competing range where the matches were being held and was surprised when he had trouble finding a parking spot. He watched several different types of competitions and wanted very badly to join in. *This is so cool*, he thought.

He went to work the next day and told Richard about his experience, emphasizing how busy the competing range was. Richard was a big fan of NASCAR and decided that Northside needed its own competitor so the shop could plaster their man with advertising as if he were a race car. He purchased Bishop a very expensive "speed gun" and told him to "get real good" with it.

Bishop had always been a good shot as his father taught him the basics early on. As he got older, he could finish his chores on the ranch before it got too hot. Without much else to do, he spent countless afternoons exploring the washes and canyons on the property with his rifle. When school was in, he didn't have as many chores, so the late afternoons were spent stalking anything that moved in the west Texas mountains.

Bishop was bored to death at the range and did not often get a chance to sell rifles, so he put all of his energies into practicing with the pistol. He had been hard at it when Richard said, "We have to do something different. You are using up all my profits in ammunition. I want to do this, but we need to figure something out."

Bishop offered, "How about reloading?"

So Bishop learned how to reload ammunition and found that it not only saved money, it was therapeutic as well.

With his sore ribs and troubled state of mind, Bishop went to his garage and began reloading a batch of rifle rounds. He was so involved in his task he didn't hear Terri come home. When she realized he wasn't in bed, she knew exactly where he was. Terri never understood how someone as smart as Bishop could spend hours pulling a handle on a machine, doing the same thing over and over again. She started to open the garage door and paused when she heard him whistling. She stopped and listened to him for a bit and decided to leave him alone. *Oh well*, she thought, *if it makes him happy*.

Bishop finished reloading and was hurting a bit more than what he would ever admit. He still couldn't bring himself to go back to the bedroom, so he planted himself on the couch and started watching a documentary on the first Gulf War. Terri fixed a nice meal and brought it into the TV room on a tray. As Bishop reached for the food, Terri snatched the remote control and playfully said, "You fall for that every time."

"Damn," was all he could think to say.

Terri was hooked on a show called Celebrity Dance Hall. The program featured a myriad of celebrities partnering with professional dancers in a contest. Bishop didn't like the show and would have normally occupied himself elsewhere while Terri watched. He considered the bedroom, but decided watching the show while eating was the lesser of two evils.

As the first team finished their routine, Bishop couldn't help himself and heckled the contestants. A little later, he made additional condescending remarks while finishing his meal.

Terri gave him an aggravated look and said, "Bishop, just be quiet. I don't sit and make fun of your baseball players constantly grabbing their crotches and spitting all over the court, so either leave or hush up."

He managed to keep quiet for the next few segments, but additional criticisms soon followed before he caught himself and looked over to see Terri staring at him harshly.

Bishop decided if he were ever going to sleep again with both eyes closed he had better shut-up. It took all of the discipline he could muster, but he managed to make it through the rest of the program without additional comment. He even recovered a bit when he made Terri a bowl of microwave popcorn. When the winners were announced, Bishop didn't say a word. He watched Terri out of the corner of his eye, and when she wasn't looking, snatched at the TV remote. He was too slow. He then decided to try another approach, and using the tone of "a man and his castle," told her, "My turn to pick a program." This was a tactical error on his part as her response was a barrage of high velocity couch cushions. He retreated quickly to the bedroom to lick his wounds and regroup, smiling all the way.

He decided to clean one of his rifles until he was sleepy and went to pick one out. As he was looking through the gun safe, he saw the original "speed gun" Richard had purchased for him years ago and bad memories came flooding back.

Bishop entered his first match three months after he and Richard had hatched their plan. It was a local affair, and only about 40 shooters signed up. He entered three different competitions that all involved running through a "course" and shooting at several targets.

He finished in the top ten in all three events, and managed a close third in one. He later joked with Richard that the giant "Northside Gun and Range" patch on the back of his shirt had caused him discomfort and impacted his times.

The following week was the best ever for Northside, and Richard put Bishop full time on training. He purchased competition guns for rifle and shotgun based events, commonly called 3-gun matches.

For the next ten months, life had been grand. Bishop worked hard and spent countless hours on refining his technique and scores. He won his first local event a month later and placed in the top 50 in his first national event. Richard paid for him to go to Fort Benning for the Nationals, where he placed in the top 20 in two different competitions.

Business at Northside continued to grow every month.

Bishop landed after flying home from a national event in Phoenix where he had won for the first time. He hadn't called Richard because he wanted to surprise him with the big trophy, but as he arrived, he noticed several police cars in the lot. He parked quickly and ran toward the main building, only to have his way blocked by a big cop.

"Sorry buddy, you can't go in there - Crime scene."

Bishop knew, but had to ask, "Officer, I work here. What is going on?"

The cop knotted his brow, "You work here? Hold on."

The officer stuck his head inside the door and yelled at someone to come out. A man in a suit appeared and introduced himself as Lt. Davis, HPD Homicide.

Bishop really didn't remember much after that except that Richard was dead. He'd been killed during an attempted robbery.

The police never did make any arrests in the case, and the entire matter made Bishop's blood boil to this day. Richard's son took over Northside and sold the business within two months of his father's death. The new owners had no interest is competition shooting and judged Bishop to be an unnecessary expense.

He was back to looking for a job when Spider called and asked him to come to Iraq.

Cleveland, Ohio - August 4, 2015

An Unwelcome Gift

On the morning after Senator Bose's press conference the police headquarters in Cleveland, Ohio was presented with a group of 21 Hispanic men. They were herded up the station's front steps by men with rifles who claimed their prisoners were illegals. The riflemen were unemployed union construction workers who took a school bus to a building site in Westlake, forcing the drywall crew onto the bus at gunpoint. The Cleveland police arrested the union men for kidnapping and let the Hispanics go. It wasn't long before a large crowd gathered in Public Square.

The crowd formed when the families of the arrested union members tried to bail them out. The police station overflowed, and tensions began to rise. The families of the union men were forced to wait "outside" for hours before they could get their loved ones out of the jail. Someone made a sign, and a local news crew showed up in case the situation escalated. The presence of the news crew naturally drew rubberneckers, increasing the size of the crowd even more. A local conservative radio talk show host got word of the gathering and fanned the flames with live updates of the situation peppered with inflammatory rhetoric. Within hours, unions sent unemployed workers, complete with bullhorns and more signs. The composition of the onlookers was unusual in that the crowd contained both union members and hard line conservatives who were normally at odds. Both sides were outraged that American citizens were arrested on serious charges while the "illegals" had been let go.

By rush hour, the crowd had overflowed Public Square and filled Euclid Avenue past the theater district to the south and down the hill on Superior Avenue to the north. It merged with the regular crowd flocking to the Warehouse District where dozens of restaurants, bars and clubs were located. By six o'clock, thousands more angry commuters were stranded on roads made impassable by the angry mob. They had few options but to join in. Alcohol from the District combined with exasperated people caused tensions to rise even higher.

An impatient driver was managing a path through the crowd when he finally cursed at the wrong group of men. His car was turned on its side and caught fire. The people in the area were already compressed tightly against each other, and the burning car caused a surge in the masses. A large department store window gave way as dozens of people were pressed against it. The frame couldn't handle the pressure and collapsed inward. Someone reached through the empty window, grabbed an Apple Computer, and ran. Bedlam broke out.

The burning of cars was kind of a tradition in Cleveland. After the assignation of Dr. Martin Luther King, roving mobs torched dozens of vehicles, incinerating entire city blocks and shutting down parts of the city for days. In a desperate attempt to regain control of the area, the National Guard had had to be called in to keep order. For more than a week, Cleveland's citizens were confined to their homes under a mandatory curfew. Like the rest of the world, they watched in horror at the almost non-stop broadcast of the burning of their beloved town. But while others could just flip the channel and forget about the devastation brewing outside, for the residents of Cleveland it was not so easy. The unmistakable odor of ash permeated their homes. Children who ventured to peek thru the window blinds could see burning vehicles in the street, just yards from their own lawns. In the minds of many citizens, the legacy image of that incident was of burning cars.

As she watched today's news bulletin, the current Mayor of Cleveland was unsettled by an overwhelming sense of déjà vu. As an eight-year-old girl, she had been terrified when the 1968 riots were in progress. She watched the events of the afternoon unfold, and one consistent thought kept running through her mind – "NEVER AGAIN." When the pictures of a burning car reached the City Hall conference room, she turned to the Chief of Police and said, "Stop this thing. Stop it right now!"

Cleveland was one of the few metropolitan areas that still maintained a mounted police force. Primarily used for parades and crowd control at sporting events, there were 48 officers trained and equipped to use horses in the line of duty. At the football stadium parking lot, the entire force was marshaling in preparation to enter the fray. The plan was simple; the mounted police would form two lines and enter Public Square from different directions. Behind the 24 horse-wide-wedge would be another 75 officers on foot, many equipped with riot shields. They would push the crowd back causing them to disperse. Behind the horseflesh battering rams would be officers equipped with tear gas and masks. They would gas the cleared area to keep the crowd from reforming behind the wedge. All over the city officers were pulled from numerous stations to supplement the small army gathering at the stadium.

A few miles east of downtown Cleveland, Bob Spence sat in his run-down one bedroom apartment watching the news unfold. Spence, as everyone called him, had been a Cuyahoga County Deputy Sheriff, but had been let go almost a year before due to budget cuts. After an honorable discharge from the Marine Corps, he had joined the ranks of local law enforcement, thinking this was a good direction for him. When informed that he and dozens of others were being "reduced," it was a complete shock to both him and his family. He began drinking a lot and started hanging around with the wrong crowd. It had been in a neighborhood bar where he had met a small group of men who referred to themselves as "The Force." If they had been aware of them, the FBI would have classified The Force as a neo-Nazi Class Three Organization – meaning they talked a big game and sported a lot of ink, but were essentially innocuous. The Force was neither radical enough nor large enough to be on the FBI's radar and was practically unknown to law enforcement.

Spence's wife had divorced him some months before. His unemployment benefits had run out, and between strings of part-time jobs, he had started selling drugs in order to eat. His latest swastika tattoo had caused what family he had left to disassociate from him. He was a bitter, angry man who had little hope for the future – with the exception of a single plan. Spence had a scheme to relieve some of the local banks of their excess holdings. He and The Force had been working on it for several weeks, but they could never figure out how to implement it without considerable risk of being caught.

The Force was the only "family" he had left. Since he had considerable inside knowledge of police procedures, he quickly rose to power as the group executed numerous petty crimes for pocket cash. He observed the riot unfold, and realized this was the opportunity they had been waiting for to execute their plan. He knew that the size of the crowd would dictate a concentration of officers in the area. He had participated in numerous emergency drills involving everything from terrorist attacks to the Browns winning the Super Bowl and the subsequent celebration getting out of hand. It was understood that the outlying police stations would be sending reinforcements to help downtown. This would mean a shortage of manpower in the suburbs, providing the necessary reduction of risk in their plan.

This was just the situation they needed to make their plan work. After a few quick phone calls, The Force was assembled in Spence's apartment. A quick discussion and all agreed – it was now or never.

Each man went over his specific role in the plan. Spence's military training had taught him that simple was always best in any operation. Stress, unforeseen events, and the fog of war would derail a complex plan. Everyone should know their job forwards and backwards. After an hour of reviewing times, locations and responsibilities, the group allocated the necessary equipment to execute the plan, and headed to their jump-off points.

The first step was to acquire a bulldozer. One member knew where several were parked on semi-trailers at a construction company. Construction was slow because of the depression, so the lot always had several units idle. Having been laid off from the construction business, he knew how to operate both the truck and the dozer. It was also known that the keys to the truck and the bulldozer were carelessly kept above the visor. Within 20 minutes, Spence's cell phone rang, and the voice on the other end said, "I have a D8 CAT on the way."

The Shaker Heights suburb of Cleveland remained an upscale address, and many of the streets were still lined with the residences of Cleveland's "old money." These families had worked together over the years to everyone's mutual benefit and profit. After his "reduction" Spence had been able to land a job here as a part time security guard. He had discovered that a local synagogue had an investment club. These Jewish businessmen determined some time ago that gold was the place to be and had converted a significant sum of money into bullion. Spence's security company had been hired to escort a rather large shipment of lockboxes to a neighborhood bank. He estimated that there were almost 400 pounds of .999 pure gold sitting in those boxes, all stored in the vault of the Shaker Square Branch, 2nd National Bank. *Typical Jews*, he thought, *too damn cheap and too damn paranoid to keep their money in a more secure downtown bank.*

Even with a reduction in the number of local police, Spence knew that their chances of being caught robbing a bank were high. The local station would still have at least ten radio cars in the area. State Police and county reserves would be on the way to fill the void left by diverting resources downtown. To increase The Force's chance of success, he had purchased an eight-pound container of Winchester 748 smokeless gunpowder at a local sporting goods store. Typically used to reload rifle and pistol ammunition, the substance was legal, readily available, and would not draw attention. He then purchased a length of steel pipe at Home Depot and proceeded to construct four rather large pipe bombs. He added in a little gasoline, Vaseline and cannon fuse to create a highly effective bomb. Over a period of a few weeks before the riot, his crew had stolen four common trashcans, the same type as typically used outside of any bank branch.

Each fuse had been carefully measured and timed. The trashcans were numbered and painted with the name of the bank to which they were to be stationed. One member of The Force owned an old panel van that the group had used for a few previous crimes. It came equipped with a large magnetic sign that referred to the fictitious "North Cleveland Facility and Landscape Maintenance Company." Members of the team had a uniform shirt, complete with a patch showing the word "Service" printed under their fabricated logo. Fake name badges and pairs of worn work gloves rounded out the disguises. The four bombs, complete with trashcan facades, were loaded into the van.

Two blocks away from the 2nd National Bank branch, code named "Fort Knox," the truck carrying the bulldozer parked in an empty lot. Wearing hard hats, reflective vests and carrying "Caution" flags, the bulldozer crew started the enormous machine and backed it down from its trailer. Spence's cell phone rang again, and the voice delivered its coded signal, "Ready 5 at Fort Knox."

The van made its way to one bank branch after another, spread over almost a square mile of suburban Cleveland. As the crew parked in the lot of each closed branch, they would light the long cannon fuse and place the new can near the front door of the bank. Each man wore a baseball hat low over his eyes and was careful not to look up at surveillance cameras. Spence knew the cameras at the bank branches were not monitored, but were simply recording video tape. He knew the picture quality was low and that if his men were careful, they would not be identifiable, even under close scrutiny. They had also picked four bank branches that all used the same alarm monitoring company as Fort Knox. Their logic was that while one alarm would cause stress in the control room, five alarms would cause complete anarchy.

As each can was delivered, his cell phone rang, and a report would be made indicating, "Easter Egg in place." The cannon fuse was a very reliable, slow burning method of setting off a bomb. Each trash can bomb was timed to explode in sequence a few minutes after its predecessor. Easter Egg One would explode in one hour, with the rest following in ten-minute intervals. When the last bomb had been planted, Spence looked at his watch and smiled. *Right on time*, he thought. He dialed the bulldozer crew and simply instructed, "Go," and hung up.

As the dozer left the nearby parking lot, the first bomb exploded. The trashcan had been placed to the side of the main entrance of the bank, and the blast shattered both sets of doors at the entrance. A fireball ensued that could be seen rising over 100 feet into the air. The alarm was immediately engaged.

At the ABT Security Center five miles away, a yawning operator was half watching one of several computer screens in front of him. He was monitoring the commercial alarm cluster which was typically boring as compared to the residential center down the hall. *At least down there*, he thought, *a cat sets off a house alarm now and then.* His computer began making an annoying beeping racket, and he clicked the mouse to see which alarm had been tripped. He saw that it was a bank branch and looked at the time on the display. It was clearly after closing time, so he clicked on "Notify Police of Alarm." The computer connected to the closest known police station in proximity to the alarm and the downtown police headquarters. An automated message was sent to both stations. As per procedure, he picked up the phone to call the station just in case the computer system failed. After talking to the special police operator, he called his supervisor.

The dispatcher keyed her microphone and announced a bank alarm and possible robbery in progress. She identified four specific cars in the area and requested they respond. Three of the cars acknowledged almost immediately and began heading toward the address with sirens wailing. Spence was standing outside his car about four blocks away from Fort Knox. He had barely heard the explosion almost a mile away, but saw smoke coming from that direction. What he had no problem hearing was the radio car a few blocks away when it turned on its siren and sped off toward the bank The Force had just attacked.

The police were pulling up in front of the now burning bank branch when the second bomb detonated. It was one mile away from the first bomb, and the responding officers didn't hear or notice it. They were busy establishing a perimeter around the first branch and calling for the fire department.

The ABT operator heard two new alarms and then saw confusing alerts on his screen. He first noticed the smoke detection alarm had triggered at the first bank branch. Was the bank on fire? A moment later, the computer flashed a second door alarm at a completely different bank.

"What the hell? Sir, could you please look at this," he asked his supervisor. It was quickly determined that there were now two banks involved, and again the police were notified.

The dispatcher had just requested a response from several units on the second alarm when the third bomb exploded. Unfortunately, two of the bank's ATM customers had been walking up to the bank machine when the third blast occurred. Both were lying dead on the ground before the ABT Operator noticed the new alarm. *Something's wrong* he thought as he looked over his shoulder at his supervisor. The supervisor was a retired police captain and was now very suspicious. He instructed the operator to follow procedure, but pulled his cell phone out of his pocket to call an old partner who happened to be in charge of the dispatch that night. When his ex-partner and fishing buddy finally answered his third call, he said "Hey ....it's kind of crazy right now, can I call you back?" The supervisor replied back with "No, don't hang up. I'm watching all of these bank alarms. I think we have a diversion on our hands."

"I was just thinking the same thing. Hold on a second, I have a report coming in from the third bank."

A few seconds later, the report came in concerning the two bodies found in front of the third bank. Both the ABT supervisor and the dispatch officer concluded that the bank robbers had messed up on the third bank and blown themselves up.

The delay on the fourth bomb was just a little longer than the first three. The CAT dozer was rolling down the alley behind

Fort Knox at full speed, when the fourth bomb detonated some 10 blocks away. The driver pointed the 80,000-pound machine directly at the back of Fort Knox and applied full throttle.

The resulting collision was impressive. The back wall of the bank gave way like cardboard. Two feet inside the outer wall was the back of the vault. Built in the 1940's, the safe was a room with walls of 2-inch steel plate surrounded by another 12 inches of re-enforced concrete. For all of its imposing structure, the vault's walls were no match for the kinetic energy released by the 5 foot high hardened steel blade of the CAT. The back corner of the vault shredded like paper, hardly even slowing the big machine down.

The dozer stopped once it was clear, and Spence's men poured into the gap. With crowbars they began popping the lockboxes open one by one. They emptied many into large canvas laundry bags while carrying out others intact. In less than four minutes, they were out of the branch with untold valuables and 300 pounds of gold. ABT didn't even report the fifth alarm at Fort Knox until the robber's van was leaving. By then, there wasn't an available police car for over two miles. The Force drove slowly through traffic having to stop twice for speeding fire trucks on their way to bank fires.

The driver looked over and asked, "Spence, which way are we heading?

"I always wanted to check out Acapulco." Spence replied with a wry smile on his lips.

In addition to the four fires started by the bank bandits, two of which had spread to multiple structures, the Cleveland Fire Department was fighting no less than four large blazes started by the disturbance downtown. Two of the downtown fires were burning out of control because the riot prohibited moving in equipment to fight them.

Cleveland was burning.

A New Job

Bishop watched the news reports on the Cleveland riots and it troubled him. *Why do politicians always stir the pot?*

He went to their pantry and checked the boxes of stored food and dry goods. Living along the gulf coast meant hurricanes, so having several days of food stored in the house made sense. As he looked through the big plastic bins, he noticed a few items that were missing or low. He made some notes to go over with Terri on the next trip to the store.

Bishop was feeling much better physically and made up his mind that he was going to work out. He had decided a long time ago that he was not going to be a big muscle guy. As he had played an assortment of sports in high school, it became clear that he was never "the best" at anything, but was "close to the best" at almost everything. As a teenager, this circumstance had been difficult to deal with mentally. He had moved from sport to sport, working to be the school's star at *something*, hell, *anything*. While he always made the team, someone else was always "the best."

He found this to be true with lifting weights and exercise as well. He was never going to be a power lifter due to his frame, and yet got bored easily doing countless reps to build endurance. He had settled years ago on a routine that did a little of both. He didn't lift for personal image or appearance; he did so because it burned stress. He always felt so much better after using his muscles.

Bishop went to his personal gym, which was actually a spare bedroom that Terri "let him use." He set up one of the machines and started to warm up when the pain in his chest made him weak at the knees. After recovering, he decided he would at least do some pushups, but never made it past kneeling before his body told him in no uncertain terms – not yet.

He wasn't in the mood to reload, and everything in the gun safe was spic and span.

Now thoroughly disgusted, he decided he would head to the company range and at least get a little trigger time. After all, how could shooting a gun possibly hurt his ribs?

As Bishop drove to the offices of his employer, Hamilton, Burns and Root, or HBR, his mind drifted back to the way he landed this crazy job in the first place.

After all of the reports and debriefing following the ambush, Bishop and Spider went back to their original routine in Iraq. They were out by the pipeline one morning when a company truck pulled up. The driver got out and walked toward Spider, who was clearly on edge about the visitor.

It was Spider's boss, who was known as "The Colonel." Bishop continued to inspect a pumping house when Spider and The Colonel approached him.

"Bishop, this is The Colonel. He is the Global Security Director for HBR," said Spider.

Bishop held out his hand, acknowledging the gentleman with a nod and a single word, "Sir."

The Colonel, as expected, shook Bishop's hand with an iron grip. After the stern handshake, he began in a rapid fire, staccato voice: "Son, I had an unusual call from the Marine Corps yesterday. Normally, when I get a call from the Marines or the Big Army, it's to bitch about my guys getting drunk or trying to have sex with FEMALE enlisted personal who have zero fucking business in a combat zone."

The Colonel stopped and spit to emphasize his disdain for females in combat, and then continued.

"This phone conversation, however, was different. It seems that the Marine Corps wanted to thank me for hiring someone with a full set of balls who gives a rat's ass about more than himself. Now personally, I think this is BULLSHIT. Personally, I think there was a reason why you pulled that man out of that burning wreck. I don't know if you and he were gay lovers, if he owed you money from a poker game, or if you were trying to fuck his sister back home. Personally, I don't care. What I do care about is having one, as in a *single*, 24-hour period where I don't have some punk Bird Colonel pulling on my nuts with a pair of pliers. Today was the first day that has occurred in as long as I have been the bouncer in this whorehouse. Do you follow me so far son?"

"Yes, sir."

"Now, does this mean I want in your pants, boy? That is a complete negative. I have all kinds of people wanting to blow hot air up my ass every-single-fucking-day. Most of them are a hell of a lot smarter and damn sure prettier than you are. What I DO want is for you and Spider to get THIS security operation 100% UN-FUCKED pronto. Do I make myself understood, son?"

"Yes, sir."

"GOOD! When you get back to CONUS, call my office, and talk to me about a full-time job. I know that Spider here sucks a goat's ass every morning for breakfast, but he's all we can afford on this job. Don't hold *him* against *us*."

The Colonel spun around and headed back for his truck as Spider struggled to keep up with him. On the way, he looked at Spider and said, "That boy don't say much – does he?"

Three weeks later, the first-time father who returned showing off pictures of his brand-spanking new baby boy relieved Bishop. Bishop was pleased to hear that Mom, new baby and Dad had all made it through the ordeal. After arriving back in Houston, he had done nothing but eat and sleep for three days. Spider had lied; the food had sucked.

After catching up on the mail, bills and calling a few old lady friends, Bishop decided he really didn't have that many options, so he put a call into HBR early the next morning. He was informed that the Global Security Director wasn't available and a message would be left for him. Ten minutes later, his phone rang, and it was The Colonel. Even long distance, the voice boomed, "Son, I want you to execute a shit, shower, shave and breakfast – in that order. You will then don class A civilian dress. Immediately proceed to 1417 Willard Street, downtown Houston. Go to the third floor, Suite 317. Enter the suite, and ask for Mrs. Porter. Son, Mrs. Porter is a dear, *personal* friend of mine. I want your back straight, your gut in and you will address her as Mrs. Porter or Ma'am. Is all of this clear so far son?

"Yes, sir."

"I'll be perfectly frank here, young man. Should you piss off, disgust, or offend Mrs. Porter in any way, I will personally tie your body into knots, dip it in salt, and eat it like a pretzel while enjoying a beer. Is that clear?"

"Yes, sir."

"Mrs. Porter will have all of the required paperwork and your job offer in writing. If you don't like the offer, then you can shove-the-fuck-off. If you like the offer, then execute Mrs. Porter's instructions *exactly* as she requires in an efficient, high-speed, low-drag manner, and then be on your way."

The phone went dead.

Bishop was hired by HBR to be a "Project Engineering and Security Specialist," which he found a very fancy title. He believed the job should be called "Night Watchman for Middle-of-No-Where Oil Projects." When HBR was looking to drill, pump, explore, survey or produce energy in some remote land, the company would send along security experts to talk to the local law enforcement, study the surroundings, and then evaluate potential risks or problems. When HBR rolled in millions of dollars' worth of equipment and personnel, they wanted their folks working, not worrying about local rebels, or having to bribe the local warlord.

While all of this sounded simple on paper, Bishop found reality was far more complex. First of all, HBR wasn't going to avoid any project that could make the company money over mere security risks. Even if a drilling site were right in the middle of a Chinese Army base, HBR was going to bore it, and The Colonel's department had to keep it secure.

Fair enough, thought Bishop, given enough money and enough weapons, almost any location can be made secure. The problem was that in many of the places HBR worked, a foreigner walking around with big, military grade weapons was frowned upon at best, and normally outright illegal. In addition, there were often no local law enforcement or friendly military around. Bishop had joked once that they could be doing a project in the middle of a tropical forest and not see anyone for weeks, but as soon as one of his guys displayed a rifle, an entire brigade would appear out of the jungle to arrest them.

The Colonel's department also included Executive Security. This was considered the best job in the entire operation. When HBR executives traveled to various remote projects, the Executive Security group served as their personal bodyguards. Ever since an HBR Vice President had been kidnapped and held for four million in ransom, the company had decided it was cost- effective to have bodyguards. Referred to as "the tier one operators," or T1s, these were the hardcore, ex-Special Forces guys. Bishop had to deal with the T1 operators on a regular basis, and really didn't mind. At first, he had been concerned that they would act as if they were "gods of war," but that rarely ever happened. When a VIP was visiting one of his locations, he would normally brief the T1 guys, answer a few questions, and everything went fine.

As Bishop pulled into the HBR Security Offices, he realized that he was indeed a lucky man. One of the benefits of the job was a healthy "continuous education" budget. This meant that the company had its own shooting range, training facilities and employees could attend classes on everything from the latest security systems to seminars sponsored by weapons manufacturers. Just a few days before, he had been at the South facility chasing around a toy robot through the pine woods. *Toys*, thought Bishop, *we are all a bunch of boys with very cool toys.*

He carried in his weapons, checked them in at the front desk, and enjoyed four hours of drills, timed courses and just destroying paper targets. *There's nothing like blowing the hell out of something to cheer a guy up.*

The Cleveland Dominoes

In Phoenix, a bar owner was running radio advertisements all afternoon protesting the Senator's legislation and offering free beer to anyone who could prove he or she were in the country illegally. It was a sting operation, and hundreds of people were arrested and detained by the county sheriff.

The leaders of HISPOLA, the leading lobbyist fighting for immigration reform, started to organize protests and work stoppages. They had a very good turnout in El Paso, San Diageo, Los Angeles, and San Francisco. In Denver and St. Louis, the few hundred marchers were met by several thousand Senator Bose supporters, who quickly shouted down the protestors.

Bishop watched all of this with great interest while mending. He had gone to the doctor that morning and had been told to take it easy on the ribs and shoulder for a few more weeks. He and Terri had finally received possession of Rita's body. After a brief but sincere ceremony, her last wish was granted. She was cremated and her ashes scattered over the Gulf of Mexico. Bishop was proud of how well Terri handled Rita's death. While she grieved openly, she also kept busy, and they seemed to grow even closer than before.

A sealed package arrived in the Houston FBI office five days after the explosion. It was addressed "Urgent – Agent in Charge Meyers," and contained the forensics information that had been analyzed to date. Agent Meyers really wanted to know more about the truck and how the explosion had occurred. A local hospital supply company had reported a delivery truck and driver missing and had even supplied an inventory listing along with the bill of lading for the truck. He was sure that the truck shown in the news video belonged to the supply company, and it was technically possible that the materials on board could have caused a blast of that size. The problem was that the missing driver was listed as a U.S. Citizen, of Iraqi descent, not a Mexican. Meyers could understand the misidentification, but needed to be 100% sure before he filed his report with Washington. The entire affair had become such a political hot potato, and he didn't want to make any mistakes. He opened the package and began reading the report. A half hour later, he asked his assistant to call Washington and get him the Director.

The Houston Fire Department (HFD) had a problem. The inferno ignited by the hospital explosion and subsequent gas leak were still burning. The department barely kept up with the volume of calls before the disaster and was completely unprepared for the size and scope of the current firestorm. Equipment and men were beginning to fail after combatting flames, smoke, ash and heat for five consecutive days. The primary hotspot in the Medical Center was contained, albeit barely. The fire had consumed 14 square blocks, but had not breached the perimeter established by the department. While HFD had performed at heroic levels to maintain control of the Medical Center area, other areas of the city were suffering due to the diversion of the local units. There were now three multi-unit fires burning, and their containment was optimistic at best. The Mayor called the Chief to inform him that he and the City Council were receiving complaints that the "poorer neighborhoods" were being neglected.

"Have you received any word of units coming from other cities?" asked the Chief.

"No. The civil unrest is widespread, and after the arrest of those union men in Cleveland, no one wants to send us any assets. Most departments are already shorthanded. We're on our own."

"We have a weather issue as well. There is a front moving through tonight, and the winds could be a problem. If we don't get a lot of rain with that front, I don't know if we can hold the Fifth Ward."

"Would it help if we called for civilian volunteers?"

"No, this is not a forest fire in the mountains. Our problem is lack of equipment. I've had seven engines fail in the last 24 hours. We have three more of our biggest pumps acting up. A lot of our stuff is well past its mean failure hours and should have been replaced three years ago. Most of my men have been on the fire line for over 48 hours straight and are going to need a break soon."

"I know you're doing your best Chief. I'll keep working the phones, and the Governor is pledging to help. Let me know if there is anything else I can do."

"Dust off any plans you have to evacuate the Fifth Ward, and pray for rain without wind. There's a storm brewing in more ways than one."

The Fifth Ward was one of the poorest areas in Houston. Primarily a minority community, it consisted mostly of run-down residential neighborhoods and abandoned warehouses. The HFD had been fighting a four square block fire started by an unattended barbeque grill being knocked over by a dog. When the storm front passed through in the early hours of the morning, it brought winds of 30 mph and little rain. The fire jumped two main avenues that had been "the line" established by HFD. In their day, the two large mills would have been the economic hub of the area. Now vacant and deteriorating, they were evidence of urban sprawl and manufacturing's abandonment of the inner city. Within 20 minutes, both buildings outside of the perimeter were totally engulfed in flames. Unfortunately, the entire area consisted of commercial structures that had been constructed before fire suppression systems were even thought of. This, coupled with an abundance of older homes built very close together, provided perfect tinder for the blaze. The emergency alert went out, and the police hurriedly evacuated sleepy citizens. It was all the fire fighters could do to keep a corridor open for the people trying to get out of the way.

Before dawn, the Morris Street Transfer Station of Houston Power and Light was consumed. The damage done to the city's electrical grid by the Medical Center explosion had been bad enough. When Morris Street went down, the entire grid failed. All over the area transformers popped and sparked leaving the nation's fourth largest city completely dark. The waking city rushed to offset the inefficient interruption in its morning routine.

The first service to be majorly impacted by the power outage was the city's traffic system. The outage showed no mercy on the effectiveness of the unending string of traffic signals crisscrossing Houston. As a result all across the city, every intersection was a traffic jam - resulting in thousands of angry citizens caught in total gridlock. Emergency medical services, police, and the few unallocated HFD units were slow or completely unable to respond. With literally no movement in traffic, frustrated commuters rolled down their windows and cut their engines. Some sat in their cars, cell phones in hand, letting someone know they were delayed. Others just sat, overwhelmed by the persistent sound of thousands of car horns blaring from all directions. As the day heated up, no doubt tempers would as well.

Even the areas not threatened directly by fire were severely impacted by the power outage. Grocery stores, banks, office buildings and small businesses across the city could not function. The food and medicine stored in over 1,000,000 refrigerators would spoil and rot. Gas pumps didn't work, and stores could not process credit cards. ATM machines refused to give any cash.

Most citizens initially dealt with the situation the same as they would a power outage from a thunderstorm. However, the local news stations soon reported that Houston Power and Light expected it to be at least 10 days before service was restored to the entire city – that is, *if* the fires did not destroy further equipment.

Without electric power, the city's water pumps stopped working. With over 160 trucks simultaneously pumping water out of fire hydrants, the pressure dropped within five minutes. The city's backup generators tried to do their job, but were designed to handle residential water requirements after a hurricane, not the entire HFD watering fires all over the city. The resulting line pressure was insufficient for the big firefighting equipment, and the volume of water being used to fight fires slowed to a trickle.

Within a few hours, both fires were so large they created their own weather. Not since Dresden, Germany in WWII had the world witnessed a metropolitan firestorm of such magnitude. Without the millions of gallons of water being delivered by HFD, the fires became super-heated and began to consume the oxygen out of the air. Giant funnel clouds of flame, ash and cinder reached skyward for thousands of feet. One firefighter reported that "the Devil has unleashed hell's own tornados."

On the surface, each blaze caused hurricane force winds of over 100 miles per hour as the greedy flames devoured more and more oxygen. The air around the surface of the fire was pulled in and then shot skyward like a giant geyser of super-heated gas. More than one unfortunate firefighter was sucked into the inferno as he tried to hold his position.

If the Mayor had not had the foresight to order city busses staged in critical areas, the death toll would have been much worse. All over the city, busses carried despondent citizens with nothing but the clothes on their back away from the fires.

The Chief made the call at 5:58 AM. "Everybody pulls back," was all he said.

Houston was dark and burning.

Tehran, Iran - August 6, 2015

The Plan

The building looked just like the hundreds of structures that lined the streets of Tehran. But upon close observation, every window contained modern steel frames, not the weathered wood typical in the area, and this building had no available parking in front. A closer examination would also reveal several oddly shaped structures along the roofline, which were observation and defensive posts manned by soldiers of the Revolutionary Guard Special Operation Services.

The Ministry of Intelligence and National Security of the Islamic Republic of Iran, or MISIRA, was well known by western intelligence services. The organization was responsible for espionage, counter-espionage and the Iranian Secret Police. MISIRA was considered to be well-funded and capable, but limited in reach. The internal structure of the Iranian government was such that no one branch entirely trusted any of the others, which limited the range and scope of its operations. MISIRA had another basic restriction that kept it from being more effective. Iranian law required it to be controlled by a Doctor of Islam - an Ayatollah.

General Melli found himself staring at the large bank of high definition monitors mounted on the wall of the "INROOM-USA." It had been difficult to look elsewhere in recent days. This single facility provided more useful information at less cost than the entire agency's other resources combined. Start-up cost was minimal, and there was very little investment associated with its operation. The IROOMUS, as everyone referred to it, was a big Western media-viewing lounge. Satellite signals from every cable and network news organization were pirated and sent to this room. On the next floor, a select group of translators created closed caption scrolling text at the bottom of each screen. There was a time delay controlled by the computers so that the translation text matched the video. The advertisements were censored as they often contained offensive images and even the most holy could be harmed by viewing their corruptive content. Any organization that covered events in the United States on a regular basis, such as Al Jazeera, was also monitored. There were other "rooms" that covered Japan, Europe, Russia and other major regions of the globe.

Israel had its own special room, because as far as the politicians were concerned, it didn't exist. The General sighed out loud at that thought. He was a soldier, and a damn good one by any standard, but he failed to grasp the subtleties of the Islamic state. His sigh caused the older man sitting next to him to focus his attention on the General. "My son, something troubles you?" asked the Ayatollah.

The general nodded toward one of the big screens, "The great infidel beast is ripping itself to shreds, Teacher - just as you predicted."

"An easy prophecy," he said with a wave of his robed arm. He slowly stroked his beard and said, "Is it time to awaken the revolution on their shores?"

"Yes Teacher, I believe it is. If I understand this Senator Bose and his new law correctly, our agents would be at risk of discovery if it is enacted. We have invested so much, and the beast is now so weak. Their people are fighting amongst themselves, and their economy is on the edge of complete failure. I think the time is now – with your blessing."

The Ayatollah was watching an American news broadcast. A picture of the young man and older woman lying in the streets of one of their cities was being shown again. He found it interesting that of all of the images that could have been chosen by the broadcasters, this was the one they had selected as the icon of the story. It was an image of weakness and decay, rather than strength and recovery. He did not know who the two people were, but he would have selected something more positive and reassuring if the decision were up to him.

"The council approves," was his simple reply.

General Melli's mind visualized the faces of his 23 agents that now lived in America. There were originally supposed to have been thirty, but seven of the operatives had failed to embed themselves. One was captured by the Border Patrol while trying to enter the country. Two others had been killed in a traffic accident while being transported. Three more had embraced the wicked western lifestyle too whole-heartedly and were "eliminated" as security risks. The seventh died of natural causes.

The General thought the plan was his greatest work. He knew Iran had no chance against the United States in open warfare. Even with their small arsenal of nuclear weapons, Iran would be crushed in a matter of days. The General also understood that an invasion of North America was impossible. As Admiral Yamamoto of Japan had said before WWII, "There is a rifle behind every blade of grass." The General had done his best to educate the Supreme Council in that toppling of the great Satan must come from internal rot, not external force. It was actually the American media that had given him the initial concept for the plan. With illegals crossing the porous southern Mexican Border at will, there were several news reports over concerns that Al-Qaeda could send terrorists into the U.S. The General had supposed that was a great idea and began forming the plan.

Initially, he thought that finding 30 Spanish-speaking operatives would be difficult, but this concern was unwarranted. The MISIRA operation in Morocco provided over 50 dossiers for individuals that met the requirements. The second concern was the protection of Iran should the operation be discovered. General Melli had a healthy respect for the United States, and unlike most of his peers, he did not want to anger or unite the great power against his country. As he refined the plan, he arrived at what he thought was a most creative solution. The agents would believe they were working for Al-Qaeda, not Iran. The concept of Al-Qaeda sparked great passions in the hearts of many believers, much more so than any "cause" associated with Iran. Al-Qaeda was respected, shadowy and could provide all of the logistics necessary without raising any suspicions of state sponsored terrorism. After all, the plan involved actions and deeds that were clearly overt acts of war.

What the General was most proud of was the sheer simplicity of the plan. For years, a number of ideas had been suggested regarding destroying America. All of them had been rejected due to complexity, expense or a low probability of any success . . . but he understood two critical concepts about America that seemed to have escaped previous planners.

The first involved the American media. The sheer breadth of coverage enabled almost instantaneous communication among Americans. If something happened in New York, everyone in Los Angeles knew about it almost instantly. The capacity to spread information was a great asset to the government - if the information were accurate. If the information were inaccurate, it could be a debilitating factor. This effect was compounded because initial "reports" were almost always inaccurate. If this could be manipulated, it could act as an "effect multiplier."

Additionally, the geography of America and its supporting infrastructure had two primary weak spots. The first was that a large percentage of oil refinement was concentrated in a very small area. This strategic fact would have been kept secret in virtually every other country in the world but the United States. Every year when hurricane season started, this weakness was covered widely and openly in the American media. The second vulnerability was the transportation system, which linked the enormous land mass together. This much-envied system provided more than just economic arteries for the country.

A highly capable rail system, combined with an almost infinite capacity of land-based transport, provided insurmountable issues to any plan designed to cripple or seriously harm the country. The Americans could move people, supplies, and assets around very quickly and in great quantities.

At first, the General thought any plan would require attacking all of the oil refineries along the Gulf Coast. That task was impossible due to the sheer number of facilities that would have to be disabled. He almost dismissed the entire operation a second time, when he researched the number of kilometers of surface roads. Again, the sheer scale of the targets made any realistic operation impossible. It was the study of the American reaction to 9/11, created by a junior officer, which made him realize that he did not have to disable all of these capabilities – the Americans could do that for him.

The young officer's work had pointed out the obvious to the oblivious – if aircraft are being used as a weapon against them, they ground *all* aircraft. One officer had commented that if trains had been used as the weapon, then the Americans would have closed all of the tracks. Even though the attacks had stopped, the cautious government had kept thousands of aircraft grounded for several days, causing great economic stress and compounding the results of the attack. The General could now see a weakness in the American armor.

There was another event that occurred by the grace of Allah.

During the first gulf war, Saddam sent many of his aircraft to Iran to keep them from being destroyed by the Americans. He also sent a few warehouses worth of his best chemical weapons. Iraq never asked for them back, so the Revolutionary Guard decided to reverse engineer some of the more potent weapons. A particular nerve gas of the VX variety had the greatest promise, and resources were focused on it. The result was an aerosol based nerve gas that was easy to handle, had a good shelf life, and could be concentrated or diluted to reasonable volumes.

Within four hours of the council's approval, 23 very carefully worded emails were sent from sources in Europe, Asia and Mexico. In the United States, those same 23 people received their emails, which to the casual viewer, looked like common spam advertisements. Embedded in each message was the order to execute their objectives at a specific date and time.

Terrorist Bug Spray

Raheb was known as Roberto to his co-workers. He attributed his odd Spanish accent to being an exchange student when he was younger. Raheb's job was simple enough; he sprayed for mosquitoes. A burgeoning industry, "mosquito trucks" trek along interstates and subdivisions alike, spraying a cloudy mist of insecticide in the air. The technique is often referred to as "fogging," and occurs while most folks are settling in for a bit of shut eye When Raheb's email arrived, he paused for a few moments. America had been good to him, and he had come to think of the people as fair and generous. His doubt was short lived. He reminded himself that his family would be very well taken care of in Jordan after he accomplished his mission, even if he didn't survive.

Survival was not a big concern for Rehab. He had been trained by his Al-Qaeda leader for over a month on how to handle the "soup." After he crossed the border with Mexican papers in the middle of a hot New Mexico night, it was simple enough to secure the bus ticket to Chicago. Arriving in the Windy City, he mingled with the illegal Hispanic community and worked assorted odd jobs doing everything from landscaping to low skill construction work. It wasn't long before funds were transferred into his modest bank account, an "inheritance" from a wealthy Mexican uncle who had passed away.

He purchased the used Nissan pickup truck easily enough for cash. The fogging sprayer, holding tanks and other equipment required for his mission were acquired through the internet and local supply stores. He assembled everything in the garage of his apartment, purchased a magnetic sign for his truck and became "West Side Pest Control" practically overnight. On three different occasions, he filled the truck with the normal insecticide and patrolled suburban neighborhoods in the early morning hours to verify everything worked correctly. He was never hired or paid, he was just testing the equipment and passing police cars ignored him.

Raheb took pictures of his equipment and emailed them to his "family" back home in Mexico. While anyone looking at the emails may have questioned why he took so many pictures of the steel storage tanks in the back of the truck, overall the correspondence implied he was a proud new business owner showing off.

After accomplishing the first stage of his mission, he settled into a quiet, isolated routine of reading the Koran, praying, and making sure his truck and equipment were well maintained. He drove the truck once or twice a week to verify his route and become familiar with the territory. He took walks to the local grocery store, paid his rent right on time, and occasionally went to the bank. His only problem in life was a combination of boredom and the anticipation of when, or even if, the email would arrive.

The UPS driver delivered a new shipment of insecticide two days after Raheb received his email. The three steel tanks contained the exact same labels, warnings, and fixtures as the ones he had previously tested. Raheb knew that was where the similarities ended and took extra precaution storing the tanks in his garage.

The morning of D-Day, Raheb awoke early and prepared his truck. As per his training, he checked the local weather report and verified that it would be a typical sunny day with calm winds out of the Southwest. The direction and strength of the wind was critical to his mission. *Perfect*, he thought, *Allah smiles upon me*. He dressed as instructed; and before leaving the apartment, disconnected the gas line that fueled his hot water heater. He could smell the gas leaking as he locked the door for the final time. He went down the steps to the garage and double-checked his equipment. He started the truck and proceeded on his route to the Dan Ryan Expressway.

His arrival was timed perfectly as the local traffic report indicated that the seven lanes of inbound cars had clogged the massive roadway. The average speed was less than 5 miles per hour and already two fender benders were causing "gawkers" to bottleneck the flow.

Raheb worked his way onto the entrance ramp and slowly merged with traffic. Although he was heading north, and the wind was from the southwest, it wasn't strong enough to affect his work. He made his way cautiously to the inner most lane. He could see a long, flat stretch and made sure the shoulder was clear of any emergency vehicles or accidents. He reached in the seat beside him and pulled on the hazmat mask, equipped with a high quality micro air filter and put it on. He wore a homemade suit that was mostly latex and duct tape. It was important that the "soup" not touch his skin or be inhaled.

He flipped on his emergency blinkers and pulled onto the shoulder that separated the north and southbound lanes and accelerated to 20 miles per hour. He reached for the pump switch on the dash and turned it on. *God is great*, he thought.

In the back of Raheb's truck, a high compression pump engaged and began pulling the "soup" out of the two five-gallon steel tanks. The pump mixed the substance with the amount of air required, and the nozzles shot a cloud almost 70 feet into the air out both sides of the truck bed.

The "soup" was VX1 Nerve Gas, one of the most deadly chemical weapons ever developed. A single drop on exposed skin would kill a person in less than two seconds, and when inhaled, it was even more deadly. VX1 was only slightly heavier than air, and its molecules were so tiny that they would pass right through the average filter. It was odorless, had no taste, and thus offered no warning.

As Raheb's truck passed hundreds and hundreds of slow-moving commuters, the cloud of death created by his fogger fell slowly onto the roadway. Death was practically instantaneous. A few of the dying pressed downward on their gas pedals, but bumped harmlessly into the car in front of them. The speed of the northbound traffic was already so slow that traffic helicopters didn't notice anything at first.

The southbound traffic was a completely different story. Going against the rush hour masses headed from downtown Chicago, the counter flow was moving at 30-40 mph. At least it was until Raheb's poison was inhaled by an 18-wheel truck driver who died instantly and rolled his rig, causing a spectacular crash blocking several lanes. The southbound side backed up instantly, and now Raheb's cloud had double the number of targets. The Chicago EL, or Elevated train, ran on tracks laid between the north and south lanes of the expressway. Every half mile there was a platform built in the middle of the super-highway. Hundreds of morning commuters were waiting for trains in these open-air stations. They died where they had stood, toppling over on top of one another.

Raheb's tanks held enough gas to spray continuously for 30 minutes. As he slowly moved along the shoulder, he kept his speed at a constant 20 mph. At one point, an annoyed cab driver saw Raheb approaching in his rearview mirror. The cabbie decided that Raheb was just "one of those jerks" who could not wait their turn like everyone else. He swerved his cab over to block the shoulder. Raheb had been ready for this and slowed down to follow the cabbie for a few seconds. As his cloud killed the drivers behind him, it created an opening when their vehicles stopped. He changed lanes, passed the cab, and proceeded on his tour of destruction. After going almost five miles, Rehab exited the Dan Ryan and proceeded going south on the Skyway.

The Skyway was an elevated roadway passing above the rooftops of several neighborhoods. He drove through an automated toll lane, but did not have the mandatory electronic transmitter in his truck causing a red light to flash over the lane. A Chicago Transit Authority traffic cop saw the violation and pulled out to give the violator a ticket. The policeman's hand never made it to the switch to turn on his lights as he inhaled the gas and died instantly. As the Skyway elevated to its 128-foot height, the victims of the gas changed. The surface streets and sidewalks below the drive-over were littered with the bodies of those who had fallen.

Raheb heard the pump change its tone indicating he was running out of the poisonous gas. He drove for another few minutes and exited the Skyway in Indiana. He moved along the surface streets of suburban Gary until he found a run-down carwash well away from any main street. He pulled the truck into the bay and looked around. That early in the morning, not many people were washing their cars. Seeing he was alone, he dropped coins in the machine to quickly spray down the truck and himself. He took a box cutter knife and removed his latex suit, discarded it in the trashcan, and removed the magnetic signs from the truck.

He drove another few blocks to a city park that would be incredibly busy later in the day. He found a remote spot and parked the truck. He used a tarp to cover the spray pump and exchanged his license plates for ones that he stole weeks ago. He slowly walked for almost a half an hour and entered a small diner that served breakfast. He ordered coffee and watched the television over the counter to see the results of his work. A few hours later, he hailed a cab, rented a car, and secured lodging at a Detroit inn. His plans included a short layover, entry into Canada, and eventually a flight to Germany.

The time of 8:30 a.m., Chicago time, had been carefully selected by the General's staff. It was 9:30 in Boston and 5:30

in Los Angeles. The fogger in Boston was actually a city maintenance truck that had its nozzle and pumps hidden amongst road cones and other equipment stored in the back. The yellow warning lights on top of the truck ensured it passed the morning traffic flow unnoticed until it was too late. In Los Angeles, the I-5 was already packed with commuters trying to beat rush hour traffic. It was precisely 6:00 a.m. when a converted ambulance, flashing red lights, began its trip of terror.

Within 30 minutes, the United States of America suffered over 30,000 deaths at the hands of three terrorists. The carnage had only just begun.

A line of stalled traffic would normally attract the attention of the Chicago Transit Authority immediately. A line in both directions would double the chances of someone seeing the odd pattern on the city's wide network of "traffic-cams." What caught their attention this time was the *lack* of traffic beyond the point where Raheb had exited to the Skyway. The Dan Ryan was practically empty after that. A call went out to the authority's own police department and within minutes Officer Patrick Merrill was bypassing the hundreds of cars trying to enter the expressway via ramp #114. He drove his cruiser along the shoulder of the ramp and eventually reached the expressway. He started driving at a high rate of speed along the shoulder to get around the honking, angry masses of people who could not move an inch. He looked in his rearview mirror to see another set of red lights a short distance behind him and recognized the car of an Illinois State Trooper who was quickly catching up with him. He welcomed the backup while wondering which of the troopers was bringing up the rear.

Officer Merrill had driven just over a half mile when he finally entered the kill zone caused by the attack. He never noticed that all of the honking had stopped. A few hundred feet ahead, a car was blocking the shoulder and appeared to have run off of the road and struck a guardrail. He stopped just short of the accident and thought it strange that there was little damage to the vehicle, and that no one was standing around like he had seen a hundred times before when driving up to an accident. It was almost as if the driver had just parked there. As he rushed to the side of the car, he could see the driver was slumped over the steering wheel. He tapped on the window of the car and said loudly "Transit Police." The driver didn't move. He rapped a little louder and still received no response. He looked down and noticed the door was locked. The State Trooper had parked his cruiser and was walking up behind Officer Merrill, who turned and looked back at the trooper and moved his arms in the "I have no idea" motion and then laid his hand on the roof of the car. There was an invisible film of VX1 on the surface and it killed him. He just fell over, dead before he even hit the ground.

The State Trooper froze mid-step and quickly knelt down and drew his weapon. A veteran of both Iraqi wars, the only time he had ever seen a man fall like that was when he had been shot by a sniper. The Trooper keyed his shoulder radio and reported, "Officer down! Officer Down! Possible sniper at mile marker 115 Dan Ryan Northbound." He quickly moved to a nearby car for cover. He was moving as fast as he could and grabbed the fender of the car to keep his balance. He was dead in seconds.

The Chicago Police Department and associated law enforcement agencies lost seven more officers before a paramedic wearing latex gloves was checking Officer Merrill's body discovered no one had been shot by any sniper. At that time, only one thing was certain - anyone entering the area seemed to die immediately. Almost two full hours passed after Raheb had first turned on his pump before authorities realized they had been the victims of a chemical attack.

Cameron, Louisiana – August 10, 2015

Cameron, Louisiana had been practically devastated by Hurricane Ike. After the storm, 90% of the buildings were damaged or destroyed, and many people never rebuilt or returned. Once an oil town with the majority of its employment centered on the offshore drilling and gas production industry, it now looked more like a ghost town from a "B" horror flick.

When someone bought the old Mobil gas station on Marshall Street and started doing repairs, the few remaining residents were happy. Within a few weeks, a hand-painted sign announcing "Ramirez Welding and Repair" hung out front, and an old mobile home was being hooked up outside the building. The few folks who stopped in to welcome the new business all heard the same story about Mr. Ramirez losing his business in New Orleans from Katrina. He had been saving money to reopen his welding business as soon as possible.

There was very little oilfield work in the area, but the residents overlooked that fact in favor of blind optimism that maybe the good old days would return. A local farmer broke the axle on his grain wagon and needed a welder. His regular man was on vacation, so he decided to give the "quiet Mexican guy" a chance. Mr. Ramirez did an excellent job repairing the equipment and charged less than half of what the farmer had expected. After telling a few of the locals the story at the café, Mr. Ramirez started doing a legit business at his shop for shrimpers, truckers, and farmers.

Of course, Mr. Ramirez wasn't from Mexico, but he was a welder by trade. He had grown up welding in Iranian oil fields and knew the equipment and industry like the back of his hand. He had two sons who had left Iran to fight the Americans in Iraq. Both had been killed in that conflict. The Iranian government did not tell Mr. Ramirez the entire truth about the situation, but they channeled his hatred of America into a very motivated and loyal man.

While he did not know the intended target or use of the devices he was creating, he would make certain they were built *exactly* as the drawings specified. Not long after his shop had opened, four shipping containers were delivered that "required repairs." Mr. Ramirez began creating a very unusual pressure vessel with concave sides inside each container. He was turning the 20-foot long steel containers into what explosives experts called a "shape charge." Developed right before WWII, both German and British scientists worked on methods to direct an explosion's energy in a single direction. Sometimes referred to as "focused explosives," the method used a bowl-shaped "backstop" that directed the energy in one direction. Shape charges were now commonly used in practically every type of anti-armor munitions.

Mr. Ramirez finished his work several months before the email came. He had thought that the message might never arrive, but had no alternative other than continuing with his business and keeping his story straight. When the email finally came, he happily filled the pressure vessels with the contents of several "welding tanks" stored around his shop. A very specific mixture was transferred to each shipping container. Over the next two days, four flatbed trucks arrived, and the big steel containers were winched onto each one. On the back of the flatbeds were bags of common industrial chemicals that had been slowly gathered over the previous months so as not to attract attention. The bags were emptied into shipping containers. A cell phone was wired into a specific place on the side of each pressure vessel, and the container doors were closed and padlocked. The trucks left Cameron without attracting any attention.

Timed to coordinate with the gassing of Chicago, each of the trucks leaving Cameron had traveled to its destination bridge. Truck #1 had traveled the shortest distance, slightly over 100 miles to Baton Rouge. The truck began its climb up the causeway to the Horace Wilkinson Bridge, which carried I-10 across the Mississippi River at a height of over 170 feet. As the driver approached the second of four trussed peaks, he started downshifting, hitting the brake, and attempting to switch lanes. He had studied numerous photographs of the bridge and had practiced crossing it with his rig over a dozen times. At precisely the right location, he hit the emergency flashers and stopped the truck, partially blocking both of the inner lanes. He checked his position, and lurched the truck forward about four feet for exact placement before setting the emergency brake.

A few of the angry drivers behind him honked, but this was the Deep South where most people thought it rude to sound their horns in protest. The stranded drivers saw the trucker climb out of the cab and open the hood. He then walked to the side of the bridge and pulled out a cell phone. Believing the truck was disabled, motorists began to focus their attention on getting into the one remaining open lane and ignored the driver.

Acting as if he were talking on his cell phone, he continued to walk further from his truck. When he was about 100 meters away, he looked at the cell phone again, pressed the "Send" button, and started running.

It took about 3 seconds for the call to be put through to the cell phone in the shipping container. The phone had been modified to transmit an electronic signal rather than ring, igniting the bomb. The blast did not cause that much damage to the surface level of the bridge, but that wasn't the target. This truck sized shape charge directed its energy straight down. Over 350 pounds of molten copper shot through the bottom of the shipping container at hypersonic speed acting like a 20 foot long saw blade. It cut through the blacktop and plate steel surface of the bridge without losing energy. The structural tower, supporting the west fulcrum of the bridge, was directly below the container bomb. It was embedded over 100 feet into the bottom of the river and was sheered completely in half in two different spots.

The bags of aluminum powder, phosphorous and nitrates stacked in the top half of the container ignited less than a half second later. This was technically a separate bomb, and created an enormous pressure wave downward onto the already crippled bridge.

The reinforced concrete tower split in half and collapsed upon itself leaving over half of the deck unsupported. The deck swayed back and forth for almost 15 seconds before collapsing with over 600 feet of the span falling into the Mississippi below. Thousands of tons of concrete and steel landed directly in the navigation channel blocking the mighty river to all marine traffic. One of the busiest waterways in the world was now closed.

In the few seconds required for the deck to fall, a motorist had picked up a cell phone and filmed the collapse. The video would be aired repeatedly all over the world to the horror of most viewers. They would learn that 113 people were lost as their cars and trucks fell into the river. While the death toll may have been minimal when compared to the nerve gas attacks, the graphic images of cars, mini-vans and trucks sliding down the steeply angled deck before falling into the river became the iconic image of the attacks that day.

At St. Louis, Memphis and Cairo, IIllnois similar explosions occurred within 13 minutes of each other. Although the bridges at Baton Rouge and Memphis were the only two that fell into the water below, the others sustained enough damage to close them for months.

There were over 200 bridges crossing the Mississippi river. The destruction of four of them was hardly enough to split the United States geographically. The General's plan, however, had worked perfectly. He didn't have to divide the country - the Department of Homeland Security would do it for him.

The two most important orders ever issued by a United States President were within one hour of each other.

The first order was "Close the bridges."

The second, "Close the roads," made the first obsolete.

Houston, Texas –　August 10, 2015

Bishop and Terri were both feeling disheartened. The night before they had been enjoying a wonderful sunset from their front porch, but the mood turned melancholy as the splendor grimly reminded them of the world's troubles. After the sun had set, the sky to the south continued to glow. The couple lived 23 miles north of Houston and despite the postcard colors, they knew it was evidence of the raging fires devastating Houston proper. The radiance was an orange haze of flame and ash permeating the air. Fortunately for them, the wind was driving the flames south. At least they didn't have to abandon their property like countless thousands of others. The football stadium was littered with homemade tents and sleeping bags where many of Houston's newly homeless were sleeping. Exceedingly long lines formed outside of local churches where displaced folks hoped for a cup of cold coffee or a peanut butter sandwich.

The Governor of Texas called up the National Guard to help the Houston police cope with the massive number of homeless and to assist with other tasks. He had also ordered the cities of Austin, Dallas, and San Antonio to send firefighting equipment and workers to assist. It was unclear just how much help was coming, but the HFD would welcome anything they could get.

Since Terri had the day off, Bishop and she had planned a quiet day at home with a little grocery shopping scheduled for the afternoon. While Bishop polished off his BLT on wheat, Terri snuggled next to him on the couch to see the local news at noon. The teaser before the show indicated that a local cardiologist would be interviewed later in the broadcast, giving valuable advice about triglyceride control. *A healthy dose of indigestion to go with my lunch* thought Bishop. He was about to flip the button on the remote when yet another Breaking News Alert stopped him.

For the first 20 minutes, they sat watching in complete, stunned silence.

The news was showing footage of Chicago and the Dan Ryan. Mile after mile of cars were sitting on the expressway, looking like they had been parked or abandoned. The news reporter commented that hundreds of them still had their engines running. As a helicopter camera started zooming in, they could see unmoving people sitting in several of the cars. When the camera panned to a school bus full of children slumped in their seats, both Terri and Bishop had to dry their eyes.

The story sounded almost the same in Boston and Los Angeles.

The next scene was the cell phone film of the bridge. While the casualties were not nearly as horrific, the footage of major sections of the bridge falling into the Mississippi River was more graphic, leaving no doubt of the nature of the devastation.

The picture then switched to the President, broadcasting from Air Force One. Bishop had to give the man credit for putting on a good show and trying to calm the American people. The President reminded everyone, "We have been attacked several times in our history, and each time the United States of America has overcome the challenge." He went on to recall how America had reacted to the 9/11 attacks. "We pulled together like no other time in our history and responded as one nation. We, as a people, must now do the same thing. The number of our citizens murdered in cold blood is greater than 9/11, and our resolve will not waiver. We will overcome just as we did during those terrible days."

Bishop's response was one, single, eloquent word. "Bullshit."

Terri gave him a puzzled look as he muted the sound on the television.

"Terri, when the terrorists attacked us on 9/11, unemployment was at 4% and the economy was healthy and growing. Most people don't realize how close we came to financial disaster then. If you read the 9/11 Commission Report, it spells it out in black and white – we were very lucky."

She nodded, and he went on.

"Look at us now. Unemployment is 20%, almost every major city and state is on the verge of bankruptcy, and our infrastructure has been largely ignored for twenty years. We have fewer cops, fewer firefighters, and citizens have fewer financial resources to fall back on. Do you think the Medical Center fire would have been burning for more than a week if the fire had been started five years ago?"

Bishop stopped talking when the TV picture changed to a man neither of them recognized. He was speaking to a large crowd with intense passion on his face. Terri turned the sound up and heard the guy ranting, "The Rapture has occurred! Jesus has taken his worshipers to Heaven! The end times are upon us!"

Bishop muted the sound again and just looked at Terri shaking his head. Gathering his thoughts, Bishop continued, "See what I mean? As a people, we are so weak financially, and everyone's morale is low. The President can say what he wants about recovery, but I have to wonder if the country has enough strength left to pull through this."

Terri said, "I don't know Bishop. Church doesn't sound like a bad idea right now."

When the news broadcast started repeating everything, Bishop muted the television again and looked at a very frightened Terri. He didn't blame her for being alarmed. He was scared.

"Bishop, are we safe here?" she asked, a vague, unsettled feeling growing inside her.

"We are as safe as anywhere from terrorists, if that is what you mean?"

"Yes...ummm.... NO....ummm.... I really don't know what I mean."

Bishop understood what they were both feeling and fought the urge to simply glue himself to the TV set, devouring any little bit of new information that became available. Thinking that it would be best if they did something productive, they got dressed and began to take inventory of their supplies "because it was close to Hurricane season," or at least that's what they told each other.

Bishop started off by going to the garage to check the gas cans. Following the last storm, their neighborhood had been without electricity for six days. Like many Houston homes, they had a small gasoline generator that could keep the refrigerator and freezer running and provide for a fan or two. At that time, they had a single 5-gallon can of gas in the garage, and that lasted less than two days. They had lost hundreds of dollars' worth of food, spoiled in the refrigerator, when there was no more gasoline to supply the generator. When things had gotten back to normal, Bishop purchased nine more cans and kept them full. Or at least he tried to keep them full. Gasoline has a limited shelf life and will turn into an unusable lacquer. This meant that he had to cycle the gas constantly, pouring it in their cars and then refilling the cans. After a few years, he had gotten into the bad habit of not keeping the cans full until the storm season was close.

As he picked up each can from its shelf, he found that all but two were empty. He carried the empty cans to the truck and put them in the bed.

He had already checked on their food and bottled water supply and updated the grocery list.

Terri was in the bathroom going through their supply of shampoo, medicine and the most critical item of all – toilet paper, another lesson learned from the last hurricane.

Bishop walked in, "Hun, are you about ready? I think we need to get going. A lot of people are going to have the same idea."

"Ready."

They jumped into the truck and headed for the corner gas station, eight blocks away. They had driven a few blocks, when Bishop looked up at the Centennial Bank and nudged Terri. "Look at that," he said. The bank's parking lot was full, and two police cars were parked on the sidewalk in front of the doors. A line of people came out of the building and around the corner. "Maybe they're selling tickets to the next Celebrity Dance Hall Show," commented Bishop, which earned him a punch on the arm.

Terri said, "For once, I am glad I'm not working today. I hope all the girls at the bank are handling it okay without me."

As they neared the gas station, Bishop realized they were too late. Everything with an engine was in line, stretched down one lane of the street they were on, waiting to fill up. As they worked their way cautiously to the corner, they could see that both streets had cars going in every direction waiting to pull into the station. "Shit," said Bishop, "I didn't realize the lottery pay-out had gotten so big. Look at all these people trying to buy tickets at the last minute." Terri shot him a dirty look.

They bypassed the gas station and headed for Food World. As they approached the strip mall that housed the giant grocery store, they again ran into snarled gridlock. Bishop looked ahead and noticed that the traffic lights were completely dark. He noted the business signs on both sides of the street were unlit as well.

"I hope the power isn't out at Food World," Bishop mused.

"Well, having the power out would slow us down for sure."

"That's only part of it," Bishop continued. "How can they check people out without power to the registers? How can people pay with debit cards?"

They didn't bother to attempt a turn at Food World. The parking lot was overflowing, and the police were trying to control the crowd. "Damn it Terri, I didn't know it was double coupon day. Look at all of those thrifty shoppers."

"Bishop, there is no need for the bad jokes. I'm fine," Terri said in her most reassuring voice.

"You told me humor was sexy."

"HUMOR *would* be sexy," was all she said.

They drove in silence for a bit, trying to come up with another viable plan. Every single store they passed that sold any type of food, medicine or fuel was overflowing with people. At one point they passed a home improvement super store, and Bishop could see two men fighting in the parking lot. He didn't mention the skirmish to Terri, but she had already noticed the rather large crowd of spectators that had gathered.

They finally pulled over in an empty lot to think a bit. Terri rolled down her window to get some fresh air, and they both heard music playing. Across the street was a church, and there were dozens of cars parked around the building. It was Thursday. They gave each other a puzzled look.

Bishop said, "Come on Terri, let's go check it out. I need to stretch my legs anyway."

As they entered the Church, they could hear singing. A smiling man approached them and said "Welcome." Bishop shook his hand and asked, "Is there a special service today?"

"No my friend, there is no special service today. A lot of us watched the news this morning and decided we needed to come and say a prayer. The organ player came and decided to add some music, and everyone just started singing. I'm sorry that we can't offer any message or communion to you, but you are welcome to have a seat and join us."

Bishop smiled at the man and said, "That is message enough, sir. Thank you, we will."

They stayed at the Church for about 30 minutes and then left, feeling renewed.

As they were driving home, Bishop turned to Terri and said, "I have an idea. I'm not so worried about food, but gasoline is critical. I know where there is a big tank of gas, and we might be able to get some if we're lucky."

Bishop drove to the HBR offices and found it odd that only a few cars were there. He pulled around to the back gate and hit the intercom button. A voice said, "Good morning sir. Would you please scan your badge for verification?"

Bishop swiped his badge, and the voice said, "Thank you sir." The gate opened, and they drove into the back lot and parked. The guard met them at the door, "Bishop, is everything okay?"

Bishop explained to him what they had seen. He continued, "Paul, I want to fill up my truck and gas cans from the storage tank. I know that is unusual, but I'll sign the paperwork and use my account."

The guard smiled and said, "Fine by me. Let me get the forms and turn the pump on for you. I may do the same myself if the boss says it's okay."

HBR kept a 500-gallon above ground tank in the back lot. The company had a few security patrol cars that were used to keep an eye on its many facilities around the city. Bishop filled out the paperwork required by HBR's bean counters and pulled around to the tank. He topped off the gas in his truck and filled all the gas cans. On the way out, he stopped to let Paul know they were leaving.

"Bishop, be careful going home. The President has ordered all of the roads closed. Everyone is supposed to stay at home and off of the streets," he said.

"Are you going home?"

"No, I don't have anyone at home. I am going to stay here and keep an eye on the place for The Colonel."

Bishop and Terri kept some energy bars and bottled water in the truck. They gave them all to Paul.

Bishop waved a final good-bye to his co-worker as he drove away. "I will try to get back and check on you later, Paul."

Feeling better about the gas, Bishop and Terri started for home, but had to take a different route because the police had shut down the main road. "Probably an accident," he told Terri.

They were driving through a neighborhood when Bishop noticed a patrol car come up behind them quickly. The lights flashed on, and Bishop pulled over. A man with a hat and shirt that said "Police" on them exited the car and walked up to Bishop's truck. He paid special attention to the gas cans in the back as he walked by while Bishop paid special attention to the man's sidearm, which was not standard police issue.

"License and proof of insurance, please."

"What's the problem, officer?"

"I noticed the gas cans in the truck. We have had reports of looting in the area. May I see your license and proof of insurance please?"

Bishop made sure that his hands remained in plain sight on the steering wheel. He said, "I have proof that I obtained this gas legally sir. If you would like, I can reach into the console and show you the receipt.

"I would like to see that, but first I need your license and proof of insurance."

Bishop smelled a rat. The guy was nervous and wasn't wearing a badge. Considering the day's events with law enforcement resources stretched thin while having to protect every gas station and bank, what cop would have bothered with them? Besides that, most would have accepted the proof and been on their way to more important tasks.

Bishop said, "I'll be happy to provide you those, and no offense, but I'd like to see your ID first please."

A strange look registered on his face before he replied, "Look buddy, I am a reserve deputy. I got called up this morning early, and I don't have time for this. Are you going to cause me trouble?" The man reached to his side and unsnapped the holster of his pistol.

"No sir, not at all. Here, let me give you my papers."

As Bishop slowly reached for his wallet, Terri opened the glove box and found the insurance card. Bishop handed both over, and the cop merely glanced at them and handed them back. Now Bishop was almost certain the guy was not a real cop. A real cop would have taken the documents back to his car and either used the on-board computer or called in the numbers. He thought about just putting the truck in gear and taking off but figured the damn fool might pull his weapon and start shooting at them.

The "cop" said, "I will need to confiscate this fuel. If you want, you can go to the station tomorrow and show your receipts, and it will be returned to you. We have orders to confiscate any goods that may have been looted."

Bishop watched as the guy gave his little speech and noticed his right hand drifted down to his side, in easy reach of his weapon. He was absolutely sure now that he was not a real officer.

"Please step out of the vehicle, sir."

"I would prefer not. I have a busted leg, and it hurts like hell."

"Sir, please step out of the car - *now*."

"Ok, ok...no need to shout," and Bishop got out of the truck, faking a bad limp and pain.

The officer asked Bishop to stand by the hood of his patrol car. He then reached in his window and popped the trunk. As Bishop limped back to the patrol car, he noticed the emblem on the door was for a private security company and had the word "Neighborhood Patrol" written underneath it.

The man opened the gate of Bishop's truck bed and grabbed two cans of gas. He proceeded to walk by Bishop with a can in each hand. As he passed, Bishop took one quick step, and pulled the guy's sidearm out of his holster. "What the fuck..." the guy said, and dropped the cans.

Bishop threw the pistol as far as he could into the weeds. The guy paused and then took off running after the pistol. Bishop reached into the patrol car and took out the keys. He threw them as far as he could on the other side of the road. He then picked up his two gas cans, loaded them back in his bed, hopped in the truck, and took off as fast as he could.

When he was sure they were clear, he looked over at his pale wife and said, "Thanks babe. You got me out of a ticket."

"What the hell are you talking about?" she asked with a clearly puzzled look on her face.

"He told me he was going to let me go with a warning because he felt sorry for you being stuck with an ugly fuck like me."

"Bullshit. Why did he go running over to those weeds?"

Bishop said, "I told him you had lost a pair of your panties over there the other day," and braced for the impact of her punch.

"Bishop, that doesn't make any sense," she smiled. "He already has lots of my panties at his house."

Not falling yet

They drove straight home and unloaded the gas cans. Then, Bishop got busy. The incident with the "reserve deputy," combined with the crowds of people at every bank, gas station, and grocery store, had shaken him down to his core. He wondered how long it would be before the real police officers themselves had to do something – anything – to feed their families. Even if the cops held to their oaths, would they show up on the job or begin to scavenge food for their hungry kids? How long would the police have gasoline for the squad cars? Without any threat of arrest by the police, how long would it take before anarchy took hold?

Terri's house, as he often called it, had a quality alarm system installed when it was built. Bishop upgraded the system with alarm screens and better glass break sensors a few months after they moved in. For years, he had been comfortable with their security despite an overall increase in crime.

Then two separate events occurred that caused him to rethink how secure their home really was.

The media attributed the first event to the worsening economy and had been termed "Flash Mobs" by the press. A Flash Mob consisted of a group of twenty or more people who would enter a store individually. At a pre-arranged signal, normally sent over cell phones, everyone would pick up something of value and rush out of the store with it. The store's security, designed for individual shoplifters, couldn't cope with the "mobs," and they easily escaped with the loot. The mobs used social networks, cell phones, and other technology to coordinate their targets, rendezvous times, and greedy schemes. Initially, only retail stores had been besieged. It didn't take long before smaller, more ruthless groups of armed home invaders formed and began using the same methods. Media reports of upscale homes being "mobbed" by small gangs of five to eight burglars became common. Some entire neighborhoods had been plundered.

The second event was a training class that Bishop and several other HBR personnel attended. That class completely changed his outlook on home security. The subject had been "breaching," a term best explained as the forcible method commonly used by law enforcement and military to enter a home or building. Like most people, Bishop had seen films of the DEA or other police units busting down the front door and pouring into drug dens and terrorist hideouts.

The tactics and procedures taught that day had been far more encompassing than a simple "stick" of men using a ram to knock down the door and follow each other in - shooting the surprised bad guys. Bishop learned that the "real" methods used were far more complex than what was shown on TV. An example given at the class was called an "enveloping breach," meaning more than a single entry point into the structure is used. The instructor discussed a tactic where the police would make noise and have men at the front door, but the actual breach would be via the back door - what Bishop had called a "head fake" in basketball.

The sheer speed and force demonstrated by the professionals during the class made Bishop think hard about his home. When he learned that drug cartels, gangs and other organized criminals used very similar methods, he decided to devote some time and money so that he could sleep well at night.

Bishop wasn't a drug dealer or terrorist, so there had never been any concern about the police raiding his home. While their neighborhood was not affluent enough to be a target of flash mobs just yet, there was an undeniable trend of attacking more modest areas. The wealthier communities had the funds to increase security and take other precautions to counter the new crime wave. This invited the criminals to lower their expectations and target areas of modest housing. A neighborhood of slightly more expensive homes than Terri's had been recently raided less than a mile away.

After hearing of that incident, Bishop decided that they needed a better plan for the security of their home. While he didn't anticipate a complete collapse of society, he understood that if things got worse, they might have to take extreme measures to protect themselves and their property.

He had analyzed several solutions ranging from high-tech and high-dollar electronic devices to cheap plywood covering all of the doors and windows. The problem for Bishop, as an occupant, was having enough warning or time to react to the breach. The more warning the occupant has, the more likely the breach will turn into a bloodbath for the entry team, or invaders. Bishop's alarm system, if not bypassed, would give him less than three seconds to react. If he were in bed, watching television, or practically anywhere in the house, that just was not enough time to make a difference. He shuddered at the thought of Terri being there by herself.

Boarding up windows and doors would buy time, but it also eliminated some important benefits. You can't open a window to let in the breeze if it is covered in plywood. Covered windows are just not practical or enjoyable to live with. The same logic applied to doors. He didn't think Terri would accept all of the doors and windows being covered with plywood and the resulting dark home. Her new curtains would most likely be an issue as well, and Bishop was not brave enough to even think of going there.

A few weeks after the class, Bishop settled on a solution that cost him less than $50.00 and wouldn't cause Terri to refuse him sex for the rest of his life. He purchased a few bags of steel picture hooks that screw into the wall. They were not heavy duty, or individually strong, just common little hooks - $2.00 for a bag of twenty. He then found cargo nets used to secure items in the back of a pickup truck. The thin mesh nets were made of nylon and stretched slightly.

Bishop could screw 20 or so of the picture hooks around a door or window frame and then hang the net. The contraption let in sunlight and could be removed in a few minutes to open a window to let in plenty of air. In each net he threaded 5 to 10 small "jingle bells," used as Christmas decorations, to serve as noisemakers.

For anyone trying to "breach" the door or window, the nets would be a nightmare. They could not be cut or removed without the bells ringing. The nets would hold a door in place even if an explosive charge defeated its hinges and locks. While the individual hooks were not that strong, 20 of them would withstand a tremendous amount of force. The entire system could be removed once the threat had passed leaving only a few, small, easily repaired holes.

After their experiences of the day, Bishop didn't even hesitate. He spent the rest of the afternoon screwing in the small hooks. Terri didn't protest at all.

Washington, D.C. – August 11, 2015

As the situation unfolded and the fog began to clear, the President and his staff realized that the United States had been attacked on a scale that made 9/11 look like a minor skirmish.

The primary task immediately concerning the staff at numerous federal, state, and local agencies was to determine the residual life of the nerve gas. Boston was expecting rain in a few hours, and there was anxiety over the deadly gas affecting the water supply.

The Army's CBRNE team, a military acronym for Chemical, Biological, Radiological, Nuclear, and High Yield Explosive; was on-site in Chicago. The Center for Disease Control (CDC) sent their team to Boston. Los Angeles was basically frozen and waiting on the results from the other two cities. The Marines from Camp Pendleton, being the only force of any size in the area equipped with complete hazmat operational capability, were on their way.

It was seven hours before the CDC identified the agent as a VX Nerve gas derivative. The White House was advised that the active agent, in a completely exposed state, would become ineffective after 14 hours. Furthermore, water would actually weaken the agent and was an effective neutralizer. Suddenly, everyone was praying for rain.

After it was made public that it was a nerve gas attack, the President's order to close the roads was, as a practical matter, unnecessary. Most people would not have left their homes or businesses regardless. In that way, the confirmation eased the situation. The run that morning on gas stations, grocery stores, and pharmacies stopped as suddenly as it had begun when everyone rushed back to their homes in case of another attack.

From a pragmatic perspective, it was impossible to fully implement the executive order. The police blocked off all of the bridges crossing major rivers with relative ease, but closing roads exceeded their resources. After several calls with quite a few prominent elected officials in the President's circle of influence, the decision was made to declare martial law and to establish a curfew. This action gave would give workers and travelers the time to get back to their homes and families and then stay put. Of course there would be exceptions. Employees at hospitals, nursing homes, prisons, and power plants, as well as, law enforcement officers and first responders had to be allowed to go back and forth. Processes to enable this movement were established.

It quickly became clear that these exceptions were not going to work. The police on the ground realized that their roadblocks, searches, and questioning of drivers created long lines of potential targets. In more than one location, nervous police officers anticipating another attack shot at an impatient driver who tried to bypass the line of cars. Tensions were running high.

Exhale

It also became clear that people had to eat. As one expert stated, the average American has less than three days' supply of food at his residence. The men manning the roadblocks began to encounter people who were hungry or needed prescription medications refilled. The sick were trying to get to doctors. Business owners were trying to get to their shops.

After three days without further attacks, the restrictions of martial law were eased. Most officials believed that this attack was similar to 9/11... that the terrorists were a "one trick pony" and there would be no further attacks. Everyone began to relax and focus on recovery. While inspection lanes for trucks remained at bridges and tunnels, regular traffic was allowed to flow unimpeded.

The General and his staff had anticipated this "period of relaxation." Four of the email recipients were to execute what military planners called "Secondary" or "Follow On" attacks. The General's plan had been somewhat flawed, however. He believed it would take four days, not three, before the lifting of martial law.

Covington, Kentucky – August 16, 2015

Bridge Anyone?

Five days after the gas attack, Alberto left his apartment in Covington, Kentucky and walked to the lobby of The Towers High Rise Apartments. The Towers was one of the few tall buildings on the south side of the Ohio River and offered a grand view of the Cincinnati skyline. Alberto was actually a former Major in the Lebanese army who had been given a crash course in basic Spanish. He had crossed the border at Brownsville, Texas two months ago.

Alberto rang the buzzer at the front door labeled "Management Office" and heard the surprised voice of a woman answer. "Oh, how good!" he said. "I am so pleased you are open with all going on. I am Alberto, and I would like to look at your apartments if is okay."

Susan, the apartment manager, was happily surprised to have a possible tenant. She had just been going over the complex's financials, and the numbers didn't look good. Expensive apartments were not leasing well in this economy, and she was more than a little worried. She lived in the building and had come down to the office more to escape her cabin fever than any anticipation of renting a unit.

Sue hit a button on the intercom system and saw a well-dressed, handsome, middle-aged Hispanic man on the monitor. She said, "Hold on, I will buzz you in."

She left the office and proceeded to the lobby where she introduced herself and reached out to shake hands with Alberto. He smiled widely, took her hand and kissed it. This caused her to giggle, and then be embarrassed at her reaction. She was 31 years old and could not remember anyone ever kissing her hand. *What a clod I am*, she thought, *he probably thinks I'm some country bumpkin.*

Alberto rescued her with, "I am recently transferred to this city. I love the water and the tall buildings and want a flat that will show me both."

"Please have a seat, and I will check on the units we have available. Would you like something to drink?" she replied. Sue knew damn well which units were open. What she could not remember at that exact moment was how well she had brushed her hair that morning. *This guy was really good looking, and what a charmer!*

Alberto watched the young woman walk away and noticed that she swung her hips more than before. He cursed his sinful mind and refocused on his mission. She was tiny, even by Middle Eastern standards. He estimated her at less than 5 feet tall, weighed no more than 100 pounds, and would not pose any physical threat to him. That concern out of the way, his mind drifted back to her walk, and he realized he had not had a woman in several months. The training, transportation, insertion and other necessary tasks to arrive at his destination had kept him completely occupied. As he watched her return, he felt a familiar stirring in his loins and dismissed it immediately. *Besides*, he thought, *those breasts are probably not real. They are far too large for such a small woman.*

Sue checked herself in the mirror of the office restroom, pressed her dress down, quickly brushed her hair, and applied just a bit of powder. She had thrown on a summer dress that morning. She examined her dress in the glass, thinking it didn't look professional at all. *Oh well*, she thought, *too late now.*

She returned to the lobby with a piece of paper and a ring of keys. She informed Alberto that the building had three different units on higher floors that would offer a wonderful view of the river and skyline. As they proceeded up the elevator, she learned that he came from a wealthy family in Mexico City, but had been educated in Brazil as a small boy. His family had recently purchased a small business in the area, and he was going to be here to help with the transfer. She looked for a wedding ring – there was none.

As they entered the first apartment, she moved to the wide bank of sliding glass doors that opened onto the balcony. She pulled back the blinds to show the view. This unit was on the 12th floor and sported a single bedroom plan. She was a little disappointed when Alberto didn't seem to be impressed. He merely walked over to the window, looked out for a few seconds, and then asked to see the other units. *He has a wife and family,* she thought. *He needs more bedrooms.*

They rode the elevator up to the 17th floor, and as before, he quickly went to the window, looked at the view and asked to see the next unit.

The final riverside unit was on the 18th floor, but it too was a one bedroom. Her heart grew heavy as she put the key in the door because she was sure she was not going to close a sale that day. She, even more than the leasing company, really needed the money, and he was such an interesting and good-looking man.

Susan could tell within a minute, apartment 18C was exactly what her prospect was looking for. After checking the view, he asked the right questions, such as "who lives below this flat?" She reassured him that 17C belonged to a gentleman who traveled extensively.

He asked about the next-door neighbors in A and B, and she told him that one was a banker and the other was a retired lady who was away on a cruise with her daughters. She turned to show him the size of the kitchen cabinets and never saw him coming toward her back. He buried the six-inch fighting knife in just the right spot and pierced her heart. Susan died before she could even inhale from the shock. He dragged her body to the bathtub and laid it down.

Alberto grabbed the building keys and left hurriedly. He returned to his shabby apartment a few blocks away, retrieved two common-looking suitcases, and returned to the high rise. The entire trip took less than 15 minutes. He rode the elevator to the 18th floor and entered the apartment, sat the cases down and opened them. He quickly assembled an enormous rifle.

The Barrett .50 BMG rifle was a very heavy piece of equipment. The barrel alone weighed over 25 pounds. The entire rifle tipped the scales at close to 40 pounds fully equipped and loaded. Designed for military snipers, the .50 BMG was the largest, most powerful rifle caliber legally available to the general public. Alberto had not believed his trainers when they had told him he could simply enter any U.S. gun store, and purchase one. He had purchased this specific rifle at a gun shop in Texas right after his arrival in country. Not only did he buy the rifle, he also purchased a Schmidt and Bender 24 power scope and a Barrett computer controlled ranging device.

Even more impressive than the rifle were the rounds it fired. Originally developed for Browning Machine guns in 1910, the bullet delivers 15,000-foot pounds of energy on target. Even the most powerful hunting rifles deliver an average of 2,000-foot pounds. Until 2010, the world's record for the longest verified sniper kill was with a .50 BMG rifle. While there were other calibers that could match the big .50's capabilities on distance and accuracy, none could deliver such a punch at long distances.

As Alberto loaded the weapon with match grade ammunition, he thought back to his sniper training in the mountains of Lebanon. He would be shooting in a downward trajectory over a great distance. Normally, he would compensate for the angle, but the Barrett computer would perform the math and adjust his scope automatically for him. He tested the rifle and matching components several times at a public shooting range and had developed complete "DOPE," or Data On Previous Engagements for the weapon after several visits.

There was one special piece of equipment that had been manufactured and mailed to him. Often called a "silencer" by the general public, the correct term was a "Cancellation Device," or CAN. Alberto had seen a few American movies where the CAN all but silenced the weapon, and he laughed at the concept. In reality, a CAN would eliminate a lot of the sound, but on any large weapon, especially the .50, it would be clear to anyone within hearing range that a weapon had been fired. The purchase of a CAN in the United States required a special background check and paperwork. The General had been concerned that Alberto's cover would not pass the more detailed inspection, so he had one shipped as a machine part. It was the only "illegal" piece of equipment with him that day.

Most snipers practice a method called "shoot and scoot" in order to avoid capture. Alberto was uncomfortable with the fact that he did not have a mountain pass or forest to "melt into and disappear" after his mission was accomplished. He did have his shabby apartment, and that would have to do.

When his email arrived, Alberto disassembled the rifle and used a grinder to remove all of the weapon's serial numbers. This step was necessary to delay having the weapon traced back to him quickly. The delay would give him more time and options for escape should there be a change in plan or a postponement.

He took the powerful binoculars and scanned the I-65 Bridge crossing the Ohio River below him. He could see a single line of cars backed up for several miles on both sides of the river waiting to cross. A different lane held all of the larger trucks, and police were inspecting each before being allowed to cross the river. As he went down the line of trucks, he was looking for specific features on each one. He finally found what he was looking for on the seventh truck in line. The diamond shaped signs on the white tanker indicated both hazardous and explosive contents on board. He started timing how long each inspection took. After watching three more trucks proceed thru the checkpoint, he was able to calculate with reasonable accuracy the average time spent scrutinizing each vehicle. The next task was to study the trucks on the Ohio side of the river. He estimated they were approximately 2,500 meters away, at which distance it would be next to impossible to hit a man, but an easy mark for a target the size of a tanker.

It took almost two hours before the lines of trucks provided him with exactly the pattern and timing he needed. He slammed the magazine into the rifle and adjusted its bi-pod. He looked through the scope and touched the keypad of the computer. A small motor turned the scope turrets, and he centered the crosshairs on the first truck and squeezed the trigger. The rifle bucked hard against his shoulder, but he recovered quickly. Before the round even struck the first target, he sighted the weapon to a second target and pulled the trigger. A third target was entering the bridge when he centered on it and fired yet again. He had ten shots in the magazine and did not intend to waste any of them. He then examined the traffic waiting on the Ohio side and identified three additional targets. He followed up with four shots on the Kentucky side. Only one of the tankers on the bridge showed any signs of being damaged. It merely caught fire.

Alberto had been told to expect this, and quickly shoved another magazine into the weapon. He repeated the exact same shot pattern, and this time the results were spectacular. It had taken only 60 seconds for him to fire 20 shots. In that one minute, two explosions had occurred on the bridge, while a third tanker was spewing poison gas. On the ground three more vehicles burst into flames, and poisonous chemical vapors streamed from the remaining trucks.

Alberto surveyed the success of his work. He left the dead girl and rifle right where they lay and quickly vacated the apartment. He rode the elevator down to the third floor and used the stairs the remainder of his descent. After eyeing the quiet lobby, he escaped via the back emergency exit and walked calmly to his apartment. Two hours passed before sirens screamed on their way to The Towers High Rise Apartments. By then, Alberto was almost 100 miles away.

In Pittsburg, an analogous plot was executed, except that in "The Steel City" the shooter targeted two bridges and managed to damage an additional five trucks.

The response from the Commander in Chief was swift and unforgiving. The bridges were closed again.

Ships and very smart rats

Bishop and Terri had stayed at home since filling the gas tanks at HBR. Bishop was finally able to work out, although certainly not vigorously, and kept himself busy with reloading and running.

He was jogging through the neighborhood when he noticed some neighbors packing up for what appeared to be a long vacation.

Bishop ran in place and called out from the street, "Heading to Disney World, Bill?"

"Hey, Bishop, good to see you out, Bud. How are you feeling these days?" the man responded, while simultaneously shifting baggage in the rear of the SUV.

"I'm just about back to normal, thanks for asking. You guys heading out?"

"Yeah - brother-in-law has a ranch, and we thought we would ride this one out up there. Terri has a key to our place here, Bishop. We probably won't be back for a while, so if you guys need anything, you're welcome to what's left inside."

Bishop went up the driveway, shook Bill's hand, and said, "Good luck buddy. Do you have a weapon with you?"

"I have that pistol you taught me to shoot. I grabbed my Daddy's shotgun too. I don't have very many shells for it though."

Bishop teased, "How much do you think I can pawn that big screen of yours for while you are away?"

Bill smiled and waved him off.

Bishop got home and went to his closet. The results of his reloading were stored there, and he had thousands of rounds of ammunition organized in clear containers by caliber size. He grabbed some shotgun shells and threw them in a bag.

When he saw Bill and his family driving down the street, he waived them over to the curb and handed Bill the bag. "Terri and I made up some snacks for you guys. Hope you don't need them. They're very spicy."

Bill looked in the bag and then back up at Bishop and grinned. "Thanks, man. Hope to see you guys soon," he said and pulled off.

Bishop would never see them again.

Washington, D.C. – August 18, 2015

The President was meeting with his cabinet. He had spent more time in the situation room during the last 20 days than most Presidents had in their entire terms. As usual, the news was not good and getting worse. The Chief of Staff was discussing his third PowerPoint slide, and it looked like he had many more to go.

"Mr. President, we have two major issues right now, food and energy. Swarms of people surround almost every food outlet in the country and have since the attacks. The shelves are bare, and we can't get trucks into the major metropolitan areas fast enough to replenish the supply."

The Secretary of the Commerce Department interrupted him, "It doesn't do any good to deliver food. People are so scared right now they are hoarding. Even when we have the Army escort trucks in, the shelves are empty in less than ten minutes. We had riots at distribution centers in San Diego and Denver yesterday. Five more people are dead. On the black market, a can of soup is going for $20 in some places."

This statement caused the Secretary of Homeland Security to inject his view. "We can't move the trucks any faster. Do you want another Chicago on our hands? The public blames the terrorist right now. If it happens again, they will blame us. We are barely holding on. Another attack and I can't guarantee what will happen. Mr. President, we have over 200,000 people protesting on the Mall this morning, not 500 yards from this room. So far, they remain peaceful. The Marines from the Washington Navy Yard have been deployed in front of the White House and the Capital Building, along with the D.C. Police, but there are only 400 of them. If that crowd decides it wants us out of office, the Marines and the Secret Service will not be able to hold them. My analysts tell me the public is on the edge, and another event will push them over it."

Several in the room shuddered at the concept of a complete revolt and what might become of them if a mob stormed the White House. One of his advisors interjected, "Mr. President, perhaps we should move the administration to Camp David?"

The President looked at the man with fire in eyes and said, "ABSOLUTELY NOT! This country has endured greater threats than this, and I am not going to be the first President to turn tail and run, especially not from the American people!"

After the President's outburst, the room remained silent for a few moments.

The head of the Secret Service looked down at the floor. He had intended to recommend that the President visit Camp David shortly after this meeting was finished. In reality, he thought Fort Hood, home of the 1st Calvary Division and their 1,200 battle tanks might be a better idea.

Finally, the Chief of Staff cleared his throat. The President, slightly calmer now, addressed the advisor. "Please continue."

"As I was saying Mr. President, we have *two* problems. Energy is the second. Electrical grids are failing all over the country. Almost every part of the U.S. has experienced issues ranging from complete disruption to rolling brown outs. The combination of fuel shortages, naturally failing equipment, and inability of maintenance staff to travel freely to perform repairs precipitated this dilemma. These same issues are also impacting the delivery of gasoline. Failing infrastructure, lack of personnel, and extended delays in spare parts delivery are all taking their tolls on refinement, production, and distribution. The public is hoarding fuel as well. Gasoline is now in very short supply in the Northeastern states as well as along the West Coast. Availability of diesel is practically non-existent. Sir, I received a call from the Governor of Iowa yesterday. He told me that there was only enough diesel fuel in the entire state to harvest 5% of the crop this fall. While I haven't verified his claim, he also told me that the Governor of Nebraska had called him that very morning to ask if he could spare any diesel fuel for their harvest."

The President paused. "Gentlemen, I would like to take a short break. Let's reconvene in 30 minutes." As he pushed his chair back from the table and stood up, his personal secretary handed him a stack of telegrams and messages. He accepted the stack, and as he walked out of the room, began to flip through them:

The Chairman of the New York Stock exchange wants to know when they can reopen.

The head of the Dairy Producers Association wants to know what he should do with 10.5 million gallons of spoiled milk and 30 tons of rotting cheese.

Governor of Florida....

Governor of Maine....

The Director of the FBI requests an urgent, private call immediately.

He almost flipped past that last one. *Odd,* he thought, *why would the Director make such a request without coming through the normal chain of command and Homeland Security?*

After he left the situation room and was alone with his secretary, the President instructed, "Get me the Director of the FBI on the phone please."

The Director made it clear to the President that he needed to see him, immediately and in private. This was not a matter that could be discussed over the phone. The President started to schedule the appointment for later in the day, but the Director would have none of it. "Sir," he said in a stern voice, "You need to know this information *right now.*"

"How soon can you be over here?" the President asked.

"Sir, I'm already in the White House and waiting outside your office," was the reply. He was shown in immediately.

Fifteen minutes later, the President sat the three-page briefing on his desk, closed his eyes, and began to rub his temples. He had gazed outside for a few minutes at the well-manicured grounds surrounding the White House, then turned to the Director and said, "How sure are you of this information?"

"I'm positive, sir. There is no doubt. The National Security Administration (NSA) confirmed my inquiries, and while they haven't put two and two together, facts are facts."

The President stood and walked out from behind his desk. The Director, as a show of respect, stood as well. The President went to the pair of facing sofas in the Oval Office and sat down, and said, "Take a seat Director. Explain this to me. I need to know the details. What you're telling me is that a foreign power has attacked the United States of America. Not terrorists, not some vague zealot organization, but a foreign country has committed an overt act of war. I need to know the details."

The Director sat and began.

"Sir, a Chicago traffic camera captured the license plate number of the truck spraying the VX. The address of the owner was traced to an apartment complex that had been destroyed by a gas explosion and burned to the ground that very morning. We initially thought he was an illegal from Mexico, but one of our agents interviewed a local storeowner and found out that the suspect had an aversion to pork. It seems a mistake by a sacker had caused the man to return the offensive meat and had threatened the storeowner's life if it ever happened again.

We then traced every delivery made to the address. He had received tanks of insecticide two days before the attack. We attempted to trace the source of the shipment, but it dead-ended. This was clearly a very professional job. We had almost given up when an analyst on loan from the CIA said he had seen this before. It took a few days, but he found the case file from Iraq in 2009. The exact same method used to originate the shipment of VX had been used before. It was a front for an Iranian weapon's shipment.

We asked the NSA to focus on all cell, email, and phone traffic originating outside of the country and going to the Chicago man's accounts. It took the supercomputers at Fort Mead a while, but we have matched up identical emails, originated out of MISIRA in Iran and received in Chicago. They were lost in the net for a while, but then at least 23 people in the United States received emails of identical content. We now have hard evidence that 11 of those 23 people were involved in the attacks against us.

Last night, Border Patrol intercepted a man trying to cross from the U.S. into Mexico. This man finally started talking two hours ago. While he claims that he was working for Al-Qaeda, he identified a picture of a known MISIRA agent in Morocco. Sir, he said the agent was his instructor. He welded the bombs used to drop the bridges and was trying to get back home to Iran."

In addition sir, the man in Houston, the alleged "Illegal Mexican" was actually from the Middle East. This information has been verified. I believe the man's truck was to have been used as a weapon by design."

The President held up his hand and stopped the Director. "How many people know of this?" he asked.

"I typed the report personally sir. Just you and I have the entire picture."

"Can we backwash it?" asked the President.

"Yes sir, I will have other case files assigned to the inquiries made to verify these facts. No one will be able to trace the questions back to the reason they were being asked after I backwash it."

"Good. See that it's done, and thank you. I will be in touch soon."

"Those rotten sons of bitches," was all the Chairman of the Joint Chiefs could say after finishing the FBI brief. He quickly looked up to apologize to the President and the Chief of Staff, but both men waived him off.

"Mr. President, as one of the world's most knowledgeable experts on warfare, I do not know how to advise you on this situation sir. My initial reaction as a United States Army Officer and a patriot is to roll right over there and kick their sorry asses, but I don't know how our nation or the world would react to that. Given the events of the last few days, I'm not sure if we can even afford the postage to deliver the threat."

The Chief of Staff chimed in, "General, the political situation here at home requires that this matter, and our response, be handled in a different way. No one will debate that. The President and I have to ask, can we execute Blind Drop without any leaks?"

The General pondered the question, but only for a moment. "Sir, if you were to share this report with the five Air Force Officers required to execute the mission, I would stake my life that not a single one of them would ever say a word."

The President was staring out the windows again, seemingly lost in thought. He slowly turned, "General, let Iran know we are *unhappy* with their actions. Deliver the message *hard*. Let them *never* forget what happens when the United States of America is attacked. Proceed with Blind Drop as soon as possible."

Missouri – August 20, 2015

Two days later a single B2 Stealth Bomber lifted off from its home at Whiteman Air Force Base, 80 miles southeast of Kansas City. After 15 years of war, such flights were so commonplace that any locals awake at that hour wouldn't have paid it the slightest attention. The two-man crew welcomed the mission. They had personally performed many of the pre-flight tasks, normally the duty of the ground crew, in order to keep prying eyes away from its secret purpose. The loading of the special cruise missiles had been especially stressful, however. While both men had flown with nuclear weapons as part of their training, this was their first "real" mission, and both officers were proud that they had been selected to execute it.

The aircraft's captain often wondered how he would feel if ever ordered to deploy nuclear warheads against an enemy of the United States. While he had never doubted he would execute those orders to the best of his ability, he had questioned how he would feel afterward. This mission was different in many ways. Being personally briefed by the Chairman of the Joint Chiefs and the Secretary of the Air Force was motivating enough, but after he read the justification for the strike, he was eager to execute his orders.

The jet reached a cruising altitude of 50,000 feet and both crewmembers ran their checklists twice. There really wasn't much for them to do. A technological marvel, the B2's computer- controlled systems could almost fly unassisted. The two humans onboard were merely a backup in case the computer systems failed.

Above the Atlantic Ocean and moving over 12,000 miles per hour, a low Earth Orbit Satellite deployed its solar panels into a 100-foot wide set of "wings." Its enormous bank of Ultra Capacitors began to store the sun's energy being collected by the panels. Like a battery, the capacitors could "store" electrical energy, but unlike chemical devices, they could discharge their power at virtually any rate required. The Satellite's purpose required millions of volts of energy.

The Satellite was the best-kept secret in American Military history. It had become operational in 2007, when it was tested for the first time in conjunction with the Israeli Air Force. Israel had bombed the Syrian Nuclear Reactor being built at Deir ez-Zor. While the world was not particularly shocked that the Israelis had destroyed the facility, what did surprise most military experts was that they got away with it. Syria was equipped with the latest Russian-built anti-air defenses and radars, and their system was considered by many to be one of the best in the world. Israel attacked the reactor using common F-15I aircraft which should have been detected and shot out of the air before even getting close to the doomed Syrian reactor. As inquiries were made, several different stories were leaked, including such lucidities as "Israeli secret agents had covertly installed a 'kill switch' on the radar when it was being installed in Syria."

Of course none of this was true, and most experts knew that tale, as well as many of the other explanations, was ridiculous. The saying that "truth is stranger than fiction" was actually accurate in the case of the Israeli attack. IRISS, an acronym for Inter-wave Radar Integration Suppression Satellite, was a weapon that generated a beam one kilometer wide – from orbit. The beam energized an aircraft's surface, blocking any radar waves from bouncing back. Harmless to pilots and crew, the beam could be directed to follow a flight of attacking aircraft making even non-stealth units invisible. While the Israeli Air Force didn't know how the Americans had pulled it off, their aircraft flew to the target without so much as a warning light flashing on Syrian radar screens.

The United States had used IRISS on very few actual missions. Like any secret weapon, the more it was exposed, the greater chance of its discovery. And of course, once uncovered, counter-measures could be developed. The mission to kill Osama Bin Laden had been an exception. IRISS had been used to "plow a road" through Pakistani air defenses opening a corridor for the American helicopters delivering their teams.

The problem for Blind Drop was not the B2 bomber itself, but the refueling planes required for its long flight toward Iran. Several friendly and unfriendly militaries knew that American refueling tankers flew an identifiable pattern in a predictable number of areas. Additionally, mid-air refueling required the massive airborne gas stations to fly in a very straight line at a very precise speed while they were transferring fuel. It was not difficult to track the big planes when they went into their refueling flight pattern. If no other aircraft was detected on radar, it was a safe bet that a stealth aircraft was being serviced. One could simply trace the line between the tankers and have a surprisingly close vector on the "invisible" planes.

During the two wars in the last 15 years, the United States could care less if China, Russia, Great Britain or Japan knew where their bombers were headed. What were they going to do – call the Taliban and let them know a B2 was on the way? This operation, however, was different. No country was to have any evidence or warning of the flight, so IRISS was used to "hide" the refueling tankers as they met the B2 somewhere over the Indian Ocean.

After several hours of flight, the B2 started its approach run. The flight and ballistics computers were functioning perfectly as the plane lowered its altitude to less than 100 feet over the Indian Ocean. The doors opened underneath its main fuselage. One by one, two Tomahawk Mark 8 Special Purpose Cruise Missiles were launched.

Initially, the pilots thought that there had been a malfunction when they did not see the normal exhaust flare associated with the Tomahawk's jet engine. Their instrumentation reassured them that all was well, and the captain remembered that these were very special missiles.

The Mark 8 was essentially identical to any other Tomahawk except that it was a stealth weapon. The body was coated in a substance that absorbed radar waves rather than bounce them back. Odd shapes and angles further assisted to reduce its radar signature. Even the relatively small jet engine used to power the missile had its exhaust vented to defeat heat-seeking technology. During the tests at Area 51 in Nevada, one radar operator claimed the Mark 8 bounced back less radar signal than a common house fly.

As the B2 banked away and headed home, the first missile accelerated to 600 mph. The second missile obeyed its programming and continued at 500 mph until a gap of 150 miles had been established between the two. It then increased its speed to keep pace with its sibling.

As Tomahawk One crossed into Iranian airspace, a single monitor in the White House situation room indicated the progression of both missiles on a regional map. The President,

Chief of Staff, and Chairman of the Joint Chiefs all stood looking over the shoulder of a very attentive Air Force Major.

The missile traveled over the low-lying swamps of the Iranian coast along the Gulf of Oman. Within a few minutes, it began to transverse the valleys of the Zargos Mountains. Its twin continued to follow, precisely 150 miles behind.

Double Tap Squared

The President asked, "Can this Officer still send a self-destruct message?"

"Yes sir," replied The Chairman as he leaned over the monitor. Pointing to a small series of numbers in the corner of the screen, he indicated, "Sir, this is the altitude of the weapon. In a few minutes we should see this number begin to increase rapidly. If we don't, that means the missile is malfunctioning, and we should self-destruct the weapon."

He then looked at the Major and asked, "How long before phase two?"

"Three minutes sir - W94A warhead now armed sir."

The four men watched the screen without comment for the next three minutes. Right on time, the numbers started increasing so rapidly that reading the values became almost impossible. The Major's hand had been hovering over the keyboard, but he noticeably relaxed when the indicator started climbing.

The Chairman looked up at the President. "Last chance, sir."

The President continued to stare at the screen and simply said, "It's a go."

Ten seconds later the altitude indicator read 88,000 and paused. On the screen, the small dot that had represented the first Tomahawk changed to a bright white circle.

"Detonation, sir."

"Initial indicators are within one meter of designated target."

"Full yield."

"Clean burn," continued the Major in a monotone voice.

In the desert of Western Iran, almost 200 kilometers southeast of Tehran, a bright white light appeared in the noon sky. Unless one was looking directly at it, the detonation was hardly noticeable. There was no blast wave, mushroom cloud, or fireball - just a quick, hardly noticeable white light in the sky for less than two seconds.

It took less than a thousandth of a second for the electromagnetic pulse, or EMP, to reach the surface of the earth. Trillions of charged electrons crashed into the terrain at the speed of light, creating what could be described as a giant blanket of static electricity.

For a distance of 400 miles in any direction, anything using or connected to electricity suddenly stopped functioning. Electrical conduits attracted the energized particles of the EMP wave, and surges of millions of volts gathered in electrical wires, contacts, semi-conductors, and circuits. The EMP generated over-voltage charges in virtually all unshielded electronic devices, and this caused them to immediately burn out. Battery-powered watches, automobile engines, elevators, and air conditioners failed. Even if a device were shielded in some way, the electrical power grid failed completely. In Tehran alone, over 80,000 transformers exploded along with every voltage regulator on the city's power grid.

The Iranian military and some critical government agencies had fail-over capabilities at many of their locations. Hundreds of circuits switched from primary to backup generators and power systems.

The second Tomahawk was 12 minutes behind the first. It traveled an additional 50 kilometers north and west of the first missile and began its climb.

Its detonation ensured that all of the backup capabilities were fried as well.

In the White House situation room, the Chairman of the Joint Chiefs was heard to quietly utter, "Now that's what you call a double tap."

World Reaction

In London, Moscow, Beijing, and numerous other capitals throughout the world, important phones began insistently ringing and were immediately answered. Sensors all over the planet had captured the fact that there had been not one, but two nuclear detonations over Iran.

Satellites were repositioned, and embassies in Tehran were called, mostly without anyone answering. When the initial reports began to drift in, everyone expected the Iranian capital to be a smoldering heap of carbon and glass. As usual, it took a number of hours before the facts became clear.

Speculation ran rampant. Had the Israelis finally had enough? Had the Iranians been testing a new weapon and simply screwed it up? Had the Iranians pissed off the Russians somehow? The Americans?

In less than a second, the entire Nation of Iran had been transformed into a Stone Age society and really, no one cared. What did concern many world leaders was that the same might happen to them.

The Non-United Nations

Two days later, in an emergency session of the United Nations the Iranian ambassador was given the floor. He started to speak:

Members of this great body, two days ago, the peaceful Nation of Iran became the second country in history to be attacked with nuclear weapons. Our country has been deeply and gravely injured and for no reason. We are at war with no one. Our armies are only for our defense. We do not occupy any other nation's territory, nor do we threaten their citizens in any way, yet we have been attacked. The only country to ever be attacked in such a way was Japan. The only other country desperate enough to use these weapons of mass destruction is the United States of America. I stand before you more than a representative of my humble people. I address you, as a fellow human being and citizen of this planet. In recent weeks, the sins of the United States have invoked the wrath of God upon them. The wounded beast has struck out and attacked without reason or logic. This beast could turn on any of you at any moment. Something must be done to contain this great evil or you could all suffer the same fate.

The entire chamber erupted in a confused mixture of applause and heated conversation. After several minutes, the attendees settled down and the Ambassador of the United States was given the floor.

Fellow diplomats and representatives, the United States of America did not attack Iran. The Iranian Military was conducting tests of illegal nuclear weapons and was too incompetent to control the exercise. Not one piece of evidence has been presented to this body that indicates the United States had any role in this event. The United States believes the results of the accident are being exaggerated. Where are the pictures of the damaged buildings? Has anyone witnessed a single victim? Where is the evidence? No, ladies and gentleman, this was not an attack but a prime example of gross incompetence. Immature children should not play with dangerous toys.

Again, the chamber erupted with mixed reaction.

As expected, sanctions and reparations were proposed, and a vote taken. The sanctions included a ban on exports or imports from the United States, which, even before a vote, threw the world's commodity markets into turmoil. Without the U.S. importing oil and exporting grain, the entire world trade system was at risk.

In addition, the United States was to pay Iran Ten Trillion dollars in reparations.

The United States lost the vote by a considerable margin. Many countries cast their votes because they sensed weakness in America rather than feeling any concern for Iran. Many others had different reasons, such as a compromised America furthering their strategic plans. After the vote was read into the record, the American Ambassador requested and was granted the floor.

Members of this body, with the full authority of my Government, I hereby declare the withdrawal of the United States of America from this organization. My nation will no longer be a member of the United Nations. Furthermore, please consider this official notice that all non-American citizens have ten days to leave our country. This very building will be occupied by the New York City police department after that time, and anyone remaining will be arrested and deported.

My country has had enough of the parasitic governments represented by this organization. In addition, I would like to take this opportunity to announce our withdrawal from NATO. All American military units will be recalled immediately. Our naval carrier battle groups and all associated support operations are being recalled as well. All air wings of the United States Air Force are being recalled from foreign lands. God help all of you – you are on your own.

Within 24 hours, China was looking at Taiwan with a gleam in its national eye. Without the American Navy at their back, Taiwan was very nervous.

In Columbia, the heads of several drug cartels recognized this move as an opportunity to further their agendas. Without the American DEA and Special Forces supporting the government, the Columbian leaders were very nervous.

North Korea was already assembling massive tank formations and pointing them at South Korea. The government of South Korea was very nervous.

All across the globe, ancient adversaries, rebel groups, and more recent political foes were re-thinking their strategic plans. In India, Pakistan, Vietnam and Thailand plans were being modified that no longer could include any response from the Americans as either friend, or foe.

It was less than 48 hours before the first shots were fired. China sent a flight of 48 aircraft toward Taiwan to "test the reaction." Taiwan scrambled all of its interceptors and played cat and mouse with the Chinese until both sides had to land and refuel. As soon as the last fighter was on the ground in Taiwan, a radar officer saw 400 Chinese planes pointed straight at them. This time, they didn't turn back and were not there to play any games.

Within three days, nine regional conflicts and four full-fledged wars had begun.

Houston, Texas – August 25, 2015

No more microwaves

Bishop woke up at 5:00 a.m. as usual. He rubbed his eyes, threw on a pair of shorts, and headed for the kitchen. He poured water in a cup and stuck it in the microwave. Terri was always on him to drink less coffee so he got in the habit of making his morning brew in the microwave. *After all,* he thought, *there is no way she can count the cups this way.*

He hit a button on the microwave, and it didn't beep. He looked up and noticed the clock was off. It took his sleepy mind a whole minute to figure out the electricity was out for the entire house.

They had been without power several times in the past few weeks. Normally, it was out for two to three hours before being restored. He had started to hook up the generator twice, only to have the power come back on as soon as he was close to finishing. *Just like washing your car will cause it to rain*, he thought.

Bishop stuck his hand in the refrigerator and checked the temperature. It felt like the power had not been out long, so he didn't have to worry about the milk spoiling just yet.

He wanted his coffee and was not going to wait on the power to come back on, nor was he going to hook up the generator - not until he had some caffeine. He poured some water in Terri's teapot, plodded to the back porch, and fired up the gas grill to heat his water there.

He finished his coffee, exercised, and then grilled some bacon and eggs. He made a little extra and took it into Terri who was still in bed. "Wakie Wakie...eggs and bakie," he said.

Terri rolled over and moaned, "Daddy, I don't wanna go to school. I'm sick."

"Terri, the power is out again. I had to slave over a hot grill to cook this, so wake up young lady."

She rolled over, sat up, and yawned. Bishop sat the tray on her lap. She poked at her breakfast at first, but when Bishop came back in, the tray was empty, and Terri was back asleep.

It was mid-August in Texas, and the average temperature on any given day was close to 100 degrees. Without electricity, there was no air conditioning, and modern houses were not designed to maximize airflow. By noon, Bishop decided it was time to hook up the generator and keep the fridge and garage freezer good and cool.

He was walking through the kitchen and heard Terri rattling around in the pantry. "What's up, babe?" he asked.

"I'm just looking for something you can cook on the grill for lunch. This primitive camping is kind of nice for a girl as far as not having to cook." A slight grin crossed her lips before she continued. "You are going to do the dishes using the garden hose, aren't you?"

"Darling, I think we had better start thinking like it was a Hurricane and eat the stuff out of the freezer and fridge first."

She nodded and smiled, but he could see the concern in her eyes. He wondered if she could see the fear in his.

Bishop hooked up the generator and ran the cords to the freezer and fridge. He had a very small, one room window air conditioner that he could mount in the bedroom if necessary. It was a very difficult job, and he had only done it after the most severe storms. The power it consumed was about all their small generator could handle.

When the power had not come back on by late afternoon, Bishop found their emergency radio in the hurricane box and cranked the handle several times. He flipped it on and found that most of the radio stations were not broadcasting. He finally dialed in the station that was the "Emergency Broadcasting Network" frequency for the Houston area.

"Again, Houston Power and Light is advising all of its customers that it may be some time before service is restored. A spokesman informed KTHN that the fire has consumed another sub-station and has also severed a high voltage transmission line. Our sister station in Dallas reported power outages were widespread in the metro area before contact was lost with them earlier this afternoon. We will bring you more information as it becomes available. Now on to other news, China announced today that it was beginning a series of criminal trials concerning its recent reacquisition of the province of Taiwan…"

Bishop turned the radio off and went to the garage. It was time to install the small air conditioner.

It was dusk when he finished the installation job and noticed some neighbors out in the street talking. He decided to join them. The tone of the conversation was predictable. Everyone was concerned about what was going on. Most of the folks were experienced storm survivors, and almost everyone had a reasonable amount of food and their own generators as well. The general tone of the conversation was optimistic and positive.

"Hey Bishop, what have you been up to?" asked one neighbor.

"I was just installing the little window AC for the bedroom. I don't know about wasting the gas on that, but we sure do sleep better in the cooler air."

"Oh, I wouldn't worry about it much. They will have the power on in a week or so. We have a little extra gas if you run low."

And so the conversations went. There was no way to tell if everyone really believed things would be back to normal soon or not. Bishop really had his doubts and after a short time said goodbye to the neighbors.

He went back in the house and found Terri planning meals. "Bishop, I think we have about 30 days of food. I'm sorry babe, but I got a little lazy and used some of our Hurricane supplies rather than run to the store. Will the generator hold the freezer for 8 days?"

"It should if we only run the bedroom AC at night," he replied.

"I've filled both of the bath tubs with water, and we still have hot water. How long do you think that will last?"

Bishop looked puzzled, "Our hot water heater uses natural gas. I don't know how long that will hold out. The city water should by okay at least a few more days, depending on how full the tower was when the power failed and how much fuel they have for the backup generator. People will start hoarding water, so that will make a difference.

Terri smiled, "Well, at least I can have a hot shower tonight. "

"Terri, we will have to make a decision soon. It takes us 70 gallons of gas to get to West Texas. We won't have enough if we run the generator more than 10 days or so. I don't think we can count on getting more gas."

Terri frowned, "I don't like the thought of going out there either. Once we go, we probably will never come back, at least not for a long time. We have worked so hard for our home here."

Bishop looked down, "Terri, I don't want to be a downer, but I have a bad feeling about all of this. It just seems like the world is in a downward spiral, and nothing can stop it. While heading to West Texas would be a difficult trip and a very primitive life, it sure beats dying."

Bishop's father returned from Vietnam with issues. He struggled with adapting to normal life and finally convinced his young wife that he would do better if he were away from "all these people." One of the men he had served with was from western Texas and claimed his family owned a large ranch there. He had always told Bishop's father that there was a job waiting on him anytime.

Bishop's parents relocated to the ranch after a few phone calls and letters. His father worked as a ranch hand, and his mother helped in the kitchen and with household chores. A few years later, Bishop was born.

Terri had once asked Bishop who he was named after.

"Dad had been a pretty good chess player before the military got a hold of him. He told me once he couldn't think of anything else, so he named me after the chess piece. I've always been happy he didn't decide on 'Queen'."

The lifestyle of even the most sprawling ranches in West Texas can be harsh. Bishop's mother never quite adjusted to life on the ranch and finally had enough. After the divorce, she returned to her family in Tennessee. Bishop went with her at first, but he had always been a daddy's boy and loved the ranch, so his parents reached an agreement that Bishop would spend summers with his mother. That arrangement became irrelevant when his mom died in an automobile accident when he was 12. Just five years later, his father died of cancer when he was 17.

Before his death, Bishop's father had been a foreman at the ranch and was highly regarded. Years later, the owners decided there was no way to keep the ranch going, so they divided up the thousands of acres and sold most of it off. A small track was reserved for Bishop in honor of his father.

Bishop loved the land, but could not find the words to explain why it warmed his heart to spend time there. Located at the southern end of the Davis Mountains, it was an arid landscape with little value. The environment was harsh - no trees and little vegetation. His 250-acre track had one very important attribute however – a spring. Used for years to water cattle with a windmill-driven pump, it had never run dry. Bishop had unhooked the windmill some years ago, but the structure was still there and could be functional once again. The property contained a very tight box canyon with high, steep walls. Years ago, Bishop purchased a used camper and kept it at the back of the ravine. They were not luxury accommodations by any sense of the word, but beat sleeping on the ground.

Houston, Texas – August 28, 2015

Is that fireworks?

Bishop sat straight up on the couch, covered with sweat and not sure of where he was. His mind cleared after a few seconds, and he recognized his surroundings. He had been dreaming about gunshots. He checked on Terri, and she was in the bedroom, safe and sleeping soundly in the cooler air. He scouted the house, peering out the windows at the completely dark neighborhood. Everything seemed fine.

He started for the fridge to get a drink when he heard a distant popping noise. *That was what woke me up*, he thought, *I wasn't dreaming after all.* He quickly went to the back porch, shut off the generator, and listened. It was difficult to be sure with a couple of neighbors' generators still running close by, but he thought he heard a car engine and voices.

He waited several minutes . . . just listening, but didn't hear anything more. As he was eyeing the generator, he realized something was wrong. "Oh shit!" he said out loud. He had fallen asleep and not changed the plugs to power the freezer. He ran back through the house into the garage and pulled open the freezer lid. Bishop was relieved at the sight of frost lining the side of the unit and the still-frozen food stash. He went back outside, changed the plugs, and re-started the generator. *That was close*, he thought, *I have got to pay more attention.* He stayed up listening and walking around the house for another hour before returning to bed. *I almost lost four days of food* was his final thought before sleep took over.

Tehran, Iran – September 1, 2015

The smell was what had initiated the search. No one had seen the General or the Teacher at the MISIRA headquarters for several days. This was not unusual. After everything electric had stopped working, chaos had occurred, and the staff had been distracted. The organization could not easily contact its many operatives, and over 90% of the equipment had been completely fried. A few computers, housed in the basement, still functioned, but were worthless since the outside connections had been destroyed.

The underground cells were off limits to all but a very select few, and the elevator used to access those lower levels required a special key card to operate. After five days, everyone started to notice the smell of decaying flesh coming through the air conditioner vents even though no air was circulating.

A search for the source of the odor ensued, and both the General and the Teacher were eventually found suspended mid-shaft in the elevator car. Both men had died of dehydration.

The Grave Diggers

Bishop went through his normal morning routine of making coffee on the grill. He hit the start button and put the teapot in its normal position. He returned a bit later only to find that the water was still cold. *Damn*, he thought, *there goes the gas.*

He started to switch the grill from the natural gas to propane, glad he had two full tanks, when he heard what sounded like a gunshot, and it was close. Before he could react, there was a second and then a third shot. He ran into the house and woke up Terri to tell her what was going on. He grabbed a rifle and headed out the front door. By the time he had walked a short distance, there were several neighbors standing on their own front lawns. "Where did it come from?" he asked. Everyone pointed toward Roger's house.

Bishop could see Roger sitting on the ground staring at a body lying next to him. Roger's wife was standing nearby with her face in her hands. Naturally concerned, Bishop rushed over. "Roger, are you okay man?"

"Oh God," he said, looking up at Bishop with a face full of pure horror.

Bishop bent down to check on the body. It had blood pooling underneath and two holes in the center of the chest. It was a young man that Bishop had never seen before.

"What happened?" Bishop asked.

"Oh God, I don't know what happened. I just, I just...I just don't know."

Several neighbors began walking up to get a better view of the situation. A couple of the women took Roger's wife inside.

"Roger, tell us what happened. Come on buddy. It's okay. Cindy is fine. Everything is all right. What happened?"

"I heard a noise outside and saw someone in my driveway. I grabbed the gun and went out there, and this guy was under my car. I could see his legs. I asked him what hell he thought he was doing, and he rolled out from under the car, pointing a gun at my face. He took a shot at me and missed. I don't know... I shot back, and he went down."

Two of Roger's friends consoled him as he began sobbing uncontrollably. Bishop asked someone to get a blanket and motioned for the guys to get Roger away from the body. With Roger away from the car, Bishop was able to size up the situation. He found a pistol under the dead guy's arm, as well as a screwdriver and an empty milk jug under Roger's car. A neighbor covered the body with the blanket.

Seeing the commotion, Terri ran up to find out what was going on. Bishop, trying to recreate the scene in his own mind replied, "Roger heard this guy under his car and challenged him. The dude took a shot at Roger and missed. Roger fired back and killed him."

Terri asked, "What was he doing under the car?"

"He was stealing gas. He died trying to get a gallon of gas. What a fucking waste."

"How do you steal gas from under a car? I thought you needed to suck on a hose or something?"

"That is the slow way. See the screwdriver? You punch a hole in the bottom of the gas tank with that and then let the gas drain into the jug."

"Bishop, shouldn't we call the police?"

"How are we going to call the police? There are no phones."

Bishop turned the body over and checked it. He found a wallet that was empty except for a motorcycle driver's license listing an address of an apartment complex about a mile away.

"What a dipshit. This poor guy was just plain dumb," Bishop said, shaking his head in disbelief. "This whole thing *really* bothers me."

Terri replied, "He was probably just desperate, Bishop. Don't you think you are being a little harsh?"

"It bothers me because he died for a gallon of gas. How long before he would have killed someone for their sandwich?"

Bishop realized how cold his statement sounded and wondered for a second what he was saying. He mumbled to Terri, "Sorry babe. I'm having trouble wrapping my head around all of this. This street is full of good people living decent lives and to see this sort of thing here is, like, some sort of nightmare."

Bishop joined a few of the neighborhood men. They talked about what to do for a few minutes, and the men agreed that they would load the body into a pickup and take it to the closest police station.

Bishop didn't agree, "I don't think that is a good idea. First of all, it's a waste of gas. Second, I don't think you will find any police at the station. Even if you do, you might be in trouble for messing with evidence at a crime scene. Besides, what are *they* going to do with the body?"

The debate continued for a few more minutes, and they determined that some of the men should walk to the police station to see what the police wanted them to do. Bishop didn't like that idea either, but thought it was better than the original.

He and two other guys were going to make the trip, so he went home to get ready. He grabbed his rifle, load gear and a side arm. When he went back out to meet the other men, they looked up at him with an expression that seemed to ask, *What the hell is that?*

Bishop had put on his body armor, which was a thick-looking vest. On top of that, he had put on a "chest rig," a harness that contained many small pouches, each full of different types of equipment, including a medical kit and other items. Three of the pouches contained extra rifle magazines.

One of the men joked, "Are we going to war?"

"I'm uncomfortable with this trip. I think if one guy is desperate enough to walk a mile for a gallon of gas, there is a good chance there will be other very desperate people. I have heard bangs and pops for the last two nights, and I don't think it was firecrackers. Besides that, carrying all this shit around gives me a good workout."

His two traveling companions digested his reasoning for a bit and felt they should at least bring along their rifles. They had to make a second trip home when Bishop asked them if they had brought any water.

"Water?" they asked.

Bishop responded using a patient tone, "It's over a mile to the police station. It will be over a hundred degrees on the way back. When was the last time you walked two miles in that kind of heat carrying a rifle? What if we have to detour and it's more than two miles?"

When the "team" was finally ready, including rifles and water, the three men began trekking down the street. Bishop's housing development had been started in 2008, right before the housing bubble had burst in the market. Originally, the large tract of land was to have included several streets and entrances off of the main road in the area, Cypress Boulevard. The developer had managed to construct a single street and build less than 50 homes on it before the housing market had evaporated. The remainder of the land was vacant and covered with a tangle of wild vegetation.

When Bishop and Terri were shopping for a home, he liked the fact that there was only one way in and one way out. Traffic would never be an issue since the single street dead-ended. No cross streets existed, and a nature preserve bordered one entire side of the neighborhood. They couldn't afford a larger piece of property within commuting distance and really liked the home, so they had taken the plunge.

As the men left their street, they walked single file down Cypress. Something kept nagging at Bishop. They had made it four blocks when it finally dawned on him that there was no sound. The fact that there were no automobiles was not a surprise, but what did bother him was the lack of sound from home generators, children playing, or other normal human noise pollution. He had grown used to the sound of generators on his street and now that they were out of earshot, he couldn't hear any motors running at all.

"This is kind of spooky," he said. "I don't think we are in Kansas anymore."

They noticed the smell as they were approaching the first residential area between them and the police station. Bishop thought he knew what the smell was, but didn't want to freak the other guys. As they went around a small bend in in street, they saw a SUV at the side of the road. The hood and back hatch were both sticking up in the air and as they got closer, several buzzards flew off.

"Guys, I think we should go back," Bishop recommended.

"They may need our help."

"I think they are beyond our help, but if you want to check, I suggest we spread out a little and get on both sides of the road," Bishop replied with warning in his voice.

The two men with Bishop just shook their heads and went running up to the SUV. They didn't get very close before one of them turned around and went down on his knees and started to vomit. The other man stopped 40 feet away and just stared at the scene.

Bishop didn't walk directly to the SUV. He made a very slow circle around it looking both at the nearby homes and at the ground. After he had finished his circle, he slowly walked up and took it all in.

There were open suitcases and paper bags surrounding the vehicle. Clothes, shoes, and other personal items were strewn all over the street and sidewalk. Bishop used his rifle barrel to lift the lid of one of the suitcases, and underneath was a spent cartridge. *So*, he thought, *they had pulled all of this out of the back after shooting.*

He walked around the back and noticed that there were a few bullet holes in the brake light and a few more through the back hatch door. He looked in the backseat and then quickly spun away. Lying there, in pools of dried and blackened blood, were two small children, one still strapped in a car seat.

Bishop pulled himself together and walked around to the driver's side. What he saw there almost took him to his knees. A man's body was lying on its side with his hands bound behind him using his own belt. There was a single bullet hole through his head. He had been executed.

Bishop walked away quickly fighting a mixture of boiling anger, disgust, and fear. He went over to the other men and all three of them stood silent, looking in every direction but at the SUV.

"We should head back," stated one of the guys, "there are no police. If there were, this would not be left sitting here like this."

"Shouldn't we do something with their bodies?" one of the other men asked.

"What do you suggest?"

"Fuck, I don't know. I'm a goddamned real estate agent. How the fuck would I know? Jesus Christ, I just want to go home."

Bishop thought that was a good idea, but something was still bothering him about the SUV. He tilted his head to one side and said, "Hang on a minute, I want to take one last look around, and then we will head back."

Bishop walked up the street in the direction that the SUV had come from. He had gone about a block when he saw a woman's purse next to the road. It appeared to have been thrown out the window of a moving car. It was scuffed up, and the contents had been flung around. He continued another 50 yards or so and found two more spent cartridges on the ground.

He played it out in his mind. The family had packed up and left in the middle of the night. A car had come up behind them and perhaps tried to get them to pull over. The man probably refused, and a chase ensued. The followers had started shooting at the SUV, and the woman in the passenger seat thought they were after her purse. She threw it out the window in desperation.

Woman? Passenger seat?

He spun around quickly and began running back to the SUV. When he got close enough, he yelled out, "Guys, let's spread out – the woman is missing. She might still be around here."

Bishop's companions gave him a puzzled look and mouthed, "Woman, what woman?"

He ran up to the scattered luggage and looked around for just a second. He held up a woman's dress with his rifle barrel and asked, "Who does this belong to?" Then he pointed to the open passenger door and said, "Who opened that door?"

Both men gave Bishop a look of "Oh shit!" and began to look around.

Bishop scanned the area for a minute and focused on a privacy fence about 50 yards away. It was the closest structure to the SUV, and he started walking toward it. As he rounded the corner of the fence, he saw her.

She was curled up in a fetal position next to the barrier, naked except for a pair of white socks. Her back was turned to Bishop. He approached her slowly and said in a gentle voice, "Hey there. I won't hurt you. It's okay. I promise I won't hurt you."

She didn't move.

Bishop could see she was breathing. He kept a good distance while he moved until he could see her face. Her eyes were open but did not focus. Her nose had been bleeding, and her face was bruised and swollen. Tears streaked the dirt on her face. She just lay there, not moving.

Bishop turned to the other men and said, "Find me something to cover her up with - hurry."

He kept talking to her in a calm, steady tone and unhooked the canteen from his belt. He poured water on his hand and slowly rubbed some on her lips. She showed no reaction.

One of the men ran up with a sleeping bag that he had scavenged from the van's belongings, and Bishop covered her up. This seemed to affect her, and she stirred for a second.

Bishop considered the men and said, "This lady is in shock. We have to get her out of here. Grab some of her clothes, and go get her purse up the street. We will carry her back with us. Stay where we can see each other all the time. Whoever did this might be back."

Bishop ran to the back of the SUV and found two suitcases with wheels, the kind people pull through airports. He had a length of Para-cord, an extremely strong rope, in his kit and used it to tie the two suitcases together. Then, using his knife to cut rods from the two fishing poles still in the back of the

SUV, tied them on for support. His creation reminded him of Rita's gurney and that, of course, was its purpose.

He carefully lifted the woman and carried her to the makeshift gurney. The group proceeded back to the neighborhood, pulling the victim and keeping an eye out for trouble.

As they returned, a few of the neighbors who were outside dropped what they were doing and came running to help. Bishop turned to one of the men and said, "I think we need to block the entrance to the neighborhood. I'm going to pull Terri's car up on one side, but we need another car to completely block the street."

"I got it," he replied and hurried toward his house to bring a second car.

Bishop explained how they had found the woman and a little bit about what she had most likely endured. A neighbor lady just shook her head. She walked over to the small crowd that had gathered, issuing orders for the victim to be moved inside. Bishop handed the neighbor the woman's purse, and she quickly located the woman's ID. "Her name is Brenda Mitchell. She is a R.N. Supervisor at Houston General," she said.

Terri came running up and gave Bishop a big hug. She had been waiting by the window for him to return.

"Are you okay, Bishop?"

"I'm fine."

"Liar. You are not," she stated flatly. Something in his eyes made the hairs on her neck stand on end.

"Why did you ask if you already knew?" he said way too sharply.

"Bishop?"

"Terri, I want you to start keeping your pistol on you all of the time - understand? And I mean *all* of the time. Don't take a piss, don't cook, and don't even sleep without that pistol within reach. Please Terri, I mean it."

"Okay, Bishop. Was it that bad baby?"

"It was *that* fucking bad. I want you to go get your pistol. Then I want you to go up and down the street and knock on everyone's door. We need to have a neighborhood meeting in the cul-de-sac at 7:00. It will have cooled off a little by then."

Bishop checked on the victim and saw that she was being well taken care of. The ladies got her to drink something, and her eyes appeared more focused.

Bishop then headed to the house for Terri's car keys. He had siphoned all of the gas out of her sedan for the generator but figured there was enough to get it the short distance to the entrance of the subdivision. He was right.

He then went to his garage to retrieve the wheelbarrow. Of course the tire was flat because he never used it. But after working the hand air pump, he threw in a shovel and started toward Roger's house. He picked up the lifeless body of the gas thief, dumped him in the wheelbarrow, and covered him back up. He turned around and started down the street toward an empty lot in the back of the neighborhood.

As he pushed the wheelbarrow down the road, he started thinking, *what a morbid sight I must be, something never before seen in this neighborhood, not even at Halloween.* He thought about shouting, "Bring out yer dead! Bring out yer dead!" like an old movie he had once seen. That thought, combined with the stress of the entire situation, made him laugh. The realization that he was pushing a body down the street and preparing to dig his first grave made him stop and wonder if he were losing it mentally.

Someone yelled, "Hey Bishop, hold up!" and he instinctively turned around to see who it was. A couple of the men were walking along behind him carrying shovels and some other items. "We'll help," one of them said grimly.

It took them almost three hours to dig the hole. There had not been a serious rain in Houston for weeks, and the lot had been hard packed in preparation for building a house. They were all soaking with sweat and had sent for water twice. When the grave was about four feet deep, they had had enough and dropped the body inside. As they started to fill the hole, one of the men began to hammer and made a small cross out of scrap lumber. "What was his name?" he asked. Bishop had put the man's wallet in the blanket before throwing the body in. "Just write 'Looter,'" was all he said.

They had just finished when Bishop looked at his watch. Entombing the body in the parched Texas earth had taken longer than he thought, and it was almost 7:00. As the burial detail meandered back, they could see a crowd had already gathered. *Damn*, thought Bishop, *no time to take a shower.*

Neighborhood meetings had become commonplace after hurricanes. When the power was out for extended periods, everyone had seemed to naturally gather in the big, open cul-de-sac. Cookouts, social meetings and even the serving of a cold beer had occurred.

In the rare circumstance that the group had to solve a problem or make a decision, the tradition was for each household to speak for five minutes, in order by address number. Everyone knew this gathering was one of those meetings. At a little after seven, the first homeowner stood and cleared his throat.

I call this meeting to order

Bishop and Terri lived at number 27, almost in the middle of the pack. As Bishop stood and listened to each speaker, he realized this meeting had been a bad idea. The speakers seemed to fall into two main groups, those who were convinced that everything would be back to normal soon, and those who had zero idea of what to do. Most people had enough food for the time being, and the water was still flowing. Almost everyone was worried about having enough gasoline for the generators, and two people were running low on critical medication.

Later, looking back, he realized he must have been quite a sight to see when it came his turn. He was still wearing his load gear and carrying his rifle. He was soaking wet with sweat and had blood from the shooting victim on his shirt and vest. His ensemble was complete with a healthy coating of dirt from the afternoon's grave digging session.

When it was their turn, Terri smiled as Bishop stood to address the group. His neighbors were gathered in a circle of lawn chairs, surrounded by tables covered with bottled water and an assortment of snack crackers. He passed her his rifle, cleared his throat and began to speak.

"I want to begin by apologizing to you all for my appearance. It has been an *interesting* day. I want everyone to know what I believe we should do and why I think it's the right course to take. To begin with, I believe that local government has ceased to exist. On Cypress, a very main street, we found dead bodies this morning that had been there at least 10 hours. We haven't received any mail for days. Has anyone seen a police car cruise the neighborhood recently? Has anyone heard a siren? A fire truck? An ambulance? "

Bishop looked around to see that everyone was either shaking the heads "no" or looking down at the ground. He continued:

"I believe we are on our own, at least for a while. None of us know what is really going on out there. I have been listening to the radio on and off for days trying to get news of the outside world. There is nothing on the air but marching band music. Here is what I suggest we do. First of all, we should take an inventory of anyone in the neighborhood that has medical training. We should set up our own little clinic right here on this street."

Bishop heard some whispers and saw some heads nodding in agreement.

"We are in danger from looters and other predators. I recommend we establish our own 'Neighborhood Watch' so that we have some security. Finally, I think we need some sort of organization, like a council. There will probably be a lot of very difficult decisions facing us in the coming weeks, and I don't think it's practical to vote on every issue. There are 49 homes on this street; I suggest each block of ten addresses elect a representative. That would give us a council of five. Everyone should agree to abide by the decisions of the council. Lastly, I believe it would be a good idea for us to have a regular meeting here every night. Thank you."

As soon as Bishop sat down, everyone else started talking all at once. He sat next to Terri, and they held hands as he wondered how long she would be able to tolerate how badly he smelled. As if she could read his mind, she reached over and gave him a kiss on the cheek. Most of the remaining speakers agreed with Bishop's ideas, and a few had other thoughts to offer as well.

It was not long before it was completely dark, and the residents of the neighborhood were in their homes, revisiting the events of the day. Bishop told Terri he wanted to take a walk and check the neighborhood's roadblock.

As he approached the two cars blocking the entrance, he noticed something was not right. As he got closer, he smelled gasoline. *Fuck*, he thought, and pulled his night vision off of his vest.

Bishop had been a strong believer in Night Vision Devices, or NVD's, since he had first used them in the Army years ago. The security personnel at HBR were all issued their own monocles or goggles. Bishop had selected a monocle that he could either hold to his eye like a spyglass or mount on his rifle to be used with the regular optics.

He turned on the NVD and held it up to his eye. The darkness suddenly turned into a green, alien landscape. He could see everything very clearly, and while Terri's car appeared exactly as he had left it, the other vehicle had a growing dark spot under its gas tank. Someone had recently spiked the tank and taken the gas.

Bishop mounted the little night vision scope on his rifle and raised it up to a ready position. He slowly moved around the cars, prepared for trouble. Being alone, his progress was very deliberate and methodical, as he scanned in circles so that no one could sneak up behind him. He worked his way around the cars and out onto the street. As he looked down Cypress both ways, movement caught his eye. He saw three men, all with rifles slung over their shoulders. They were carrying jugs and cans.

The optic on the rifle gave him a pretty clear indication of their distance. They were just over 600 meters, or about seven football fields away. While he knew he could scare the hell out of them, the chances of hitting them at this distance were very low. He considered chasing after them for a second, but decided that was unwise. He wasn't so worried about the three to one odds. He was more concerned about what else he might run into on the way there or the way back. Bishop decided he would send them a message and brought the rifle up to his shoulder. He elevated the crosshairs to about 60 inches above their heads to compensate for the bullet drop and was slowly squeezing the trigger when he heard a car engine behind him. He lowered the rifle and scrambled to some bushes at the side of the road.

He saw a light coming down Cypress, but it didn't appear to be headlights. The light would come on for a few seconds and then go off for a bit. Whatever it was, it was moving very slowly. Bishop brought the rifle up so he could look through the NVD. It did not take long before he could make out a pickup truck, and in the bed of the truck were several men. He could also see rifle barrels. The driver was not using his headlights for some reason. The men in the back had flashlights, and it looked like they were searching the sides of the road at the same time as trying to provide the driver enough light to steer the truck.

As it got closer, Bishop could see why they did not use the truck's headlights – they had been shot out. Through the night vision, he could see that the windshield and hood were full of bullet holes as well. *These boys have been busy* he thought. He backed further into the underbrush next to the road and went prone. He did *not* like this situation at all. There were at least six of them, and he had hardly any cover that would stop bullets. Besides the bad odds, Bishop did not want an encounter with these guys as they had already been in a fight or two and were not likely to run. He had decided to let them pass and hope they did not see him, when he heard one of them shout, "Hey! Look at that! Look at the pretty thing over there."

Terri had gone looking for Bishop when he didn't come back right away. She smelled the gasoline and heard a car engine and decided to see what was going on. She had just gone around the cars when a flashlight beam hit her directly in the eyes and caused her to look away.

The truck sped up and came right at Terri. She started to take a step back and run, but realized she wasn't going to make it and froze. The pickup braked and stopped about 20 feet from her, and she could see the outline of several men hopping over the sides of the bed. She reached toward her back pocket and remembered she did not have her pistol. *Oh hell*, she thought, *Bishop is going to be so pissed*.

Bishop had a clear mental picture of what was happening before the truck ever stopped. He got up and moved out of the bushes as fast as he could. He was moving toward the truck as the men came pouring out of the bed. Bishop's stomach knotted when he heard one of the men say, "I like this street. This one is prettier than the one last night. Let's have some fun again!"

He knew if they got close to Terri, he was going to have an even bigger problem. He raised the rifle to his shoulder and yelled, "Terri! GET DOWN! NOW!" Before his lips had finished his warning to her, his finger started pulling the trigger.

She heard a shout and was startled for half a second as shots were being fired. She half-knelt, half-dived to the pavement and covered her ears.

Bishop had the advantage of both night vision and surprise. His first and second shots hit two men directly in the chest, and both went down instantly. He did not have an angle on the others as the truck blocked his view. He dropped to a knee and started laying fire under the truck, hoping to skip the bullets into the men on the other side. He sensed, more than saw, another one fall. One guy managed to rise up over the bed and loosed two shots in Bishop's general direction, but they were not close. Bishop saw the driver's door open and a leg stick out. He put three shots into the door, and the driver slid to the ground. He was moving toward Terri, wanting to get between her and the truck. As he quickly walked toward her, he punched rounds into and around the truck. He was about four steps away from Terri when he heard his bolt lock open. He was empty. He hit the magazine drop button on the M4 and felt it fall out. He reached to his chest and pulled out a full magazine, but dropped it on the ground in haste. He reached for another and managed to slam it into his weapon, when one of the attackers rose up and let sprayed several shots. One of them hit Bishop in the chest. He remembered falling right on top of Terri, and then a small, black circle appeared in his vision. He couldn't get his breath and his brain would not control his body.

The men were not sure if they had hit anyone, and it took them seconds to regroup and muster the courage to stick their heads up. Terri was jolted when Bishop fell on her. She didn't know who it was at first, but then recognized his rifle. Her hand was right next to the pistol on his belt, and she unsnapped the holster and pulled it out. She kept whispering, "Bishop? Are you okay?" while trying to watch for the men shooting at them. She rolled him off of her and felt him breathing. Her hands ran up and down his body in the dark, feeling for blood. Out of the corner of her eye, she saw movement and the outline of one of the attackers approaching. She flicked the safety off the pistol and pulled the trigger, but only heard a soft click. *What in the hell did he teach me to do*, she thought. She finally remembered and worked the slide on the big pistol. She pulled the trigger again, and it roared. She pulled the trigger three more times quickly.

The remaining attackers decided they had had enough. They slowly backed away, then turned and ran.

When several men from the neighborhood finally came to the rescue, Terri was still on the ground holding the pistol. She almost shot one of them by mistake. They helped Terri off the ground, and two of them picked up Bishop, who moaned and cursed when they grabbed him under the arms.

Bishop's head started to clear, and he found himself lying in the grass. There were all kinds of people standing around with flashlights shining on him. He felt his chest where the bullet had struck but didn't feel any wound. Terri was beside him and held up his body armor with a bullet stuck in it. She said, "This saved you, but it hit you right in your bad ribs. I think you are going to be sore."

"Are those bastards gone?" he said weakly.

"Yes. The men are down at the entrance checking around. It's going to be okay. You saved me."

"Where the hell was your pistol, Terri?" he said, before closing his eyes.

He was having dreams of being under a waterfall, the cold water felt great. He woke up in his bed and tried to sit up. His ribs protested, and he decided that could wait.

Terri came into the bedroom with a cup of coffee. She sat it down beside him and just smiled. He looked at her belt and noticed she had her pistol tucked inside it. That made him smile. He then felt down his body and confirmed he was naked. He smelled his armpits and realized he was squeaky clean. "How did I..." he started. Terri interrupted him, "Cindy and a couple of the women helped me clean you up. We wanted to check that you were not hurt anywhere. You smelled awful Bishop. All the girls thought so."

"Great. The first time I get naked with more than one woman, I can't remember it; and I stunk to high heaven. That's just great."

"Don't worry, hun. We had plenty of fun without you."

Bishop just moaned and rolled his eyes.

The Alamo Houston Style

It was almost noon when Bishop woke up, but he didn't realize how late it was. *I sure am spending a lot of time in this bed these days*, he thought. He managed to get up without too much effort and made himself a cup of coffee using the grill and teapot. He was sipping the hot brew when he looked at his watch. *Oh shit*, he thought, *we have to get started*.

Terri was out by the street talking with some neighbors when he found her. She looked up as he approached and asked "How is my hero feeling?"

"Just peachy keen. Terri, I need to talk to the guys. It's important."

Terri replied in her best official tone, "Talk to me, sir. I am your official block councilwoman. How may I help you?" she said with her eyebrows going up and down.

"Seriously Terri, those guys from last night are going to be back. For a while they will fume over the ass-kicking they took, and then will be back mad as hell. We need to be ready."

"Bishop, don't worry about it. Our guys are taking turns down by the entrance. We organized shifts to keep watch. They even have a signal whistle."

"They won't come to the entrance. They will come through the woods."

"What? What are you talking about?"

"Terri, that's what I would do if I were them. They know there are people here with guns and ammunition. They know they haven't looted this street yet. We hurt them badly last night, so they'll try a different way. Can you get all the guys together? We have a lot of work to do before it gets dark."

"Sure. Where do you want them?"

"Ask them to meet by our garage."

Bishop opened his garage door. He searched in a cabinet for a bit and found what he was looking for. He went to his bedroom closet, filled a bag with shotgun shells, and then went back to the garage.

The neighborhood men started arriving one by one. As soon as most of them were there, Bishop said, "Hey guys, thanks for coming over. I think the gentlemen who attacked us last night will be back, probably tonight. I know we have guards at the front now, but I don't believe we will be attacked from that direction. I wouldn't if I were them."

"How do you think they will come at us, Bishop?" someone asked.

"If I were them, I would come in from the woods over there," he said pointing. "I would scout the neighborhood and see the guys at the entrance. I would bypass the guards, work my way through the woods, and attack from a new direction."

"Bishop, there is no way we can guard all of that ground all night. How the hell are we supposed to cover the entire area?"

"I have an idea that I think will work. We need an early warning system, and I'm pretty sure we can make one. Does anyone have fishing line at home?"

A couple of the men did, and ran off the get it. Bishop pulled out a big piece of cardboard and a marker and started drawing a map of their street. He had just finished when the men returned with spools of fishing line.

Bishop motioned them all close and pointed at the map. "Here is what I think we should do" and outlined his plan.

There were some questions and a few suggestions. Within an hour, everyone agreed on the strategy; and they proceeded installing the early warning system throughout the neighborhood.

The first step had been to use a two-story house, one on each side of the street and as close to the middle of the neighborhood as possible. With agreement from the owners, they went to the second story of each house and noted on the map where the blind spots where.

Then they hung the fishing line as tripwires outside. They used hammer and nails, small hooks and anything available to hang the lines and cover the blind spots. While one crew was rigging the wires, Bishop was showing others how to build the noisemakers. He had a bag of mousetraps that he had picked up a long time ago to use in the attic. He showed everyone where to drill a hole in the traps, glue a small nail and a shotgun shell to create a noisemaker. If the trap were sprung, the nail would hit the shotgun shell and go boom.

"Where the hell did you learn this shit, Bishop?"

"I took a class once in the Army."

After they made the "booby traps" as one man called them, they went around the neighborhood carefully hooking them up to the fishing line tripwires. Bishop checked each one and thought it was the best they could do in such a short time. Everyone met back at his garage.

"I only have two night vision scopes. After I mount them on the rifles, we will use one in each house on the second floor. They will only fit on my rifles, so I need the guys manning the watch towers to learn how they work."

Everyone wanted to learn, so Bishop spent the next hour teaching the basics of an M4 carbine. Some of the men had been in the military, and it came back to them quickly. "The M4 is just a newer version of the old M16," he told them. "All of the controls are the same."

It was starting to get dark, but Bishop had a few more things to go over.

"We won't be able to tell exactly which tripwire they hit. All shotgun shells sound the same, and the noise will echo around the houses. The guys in the watchtowers will have the best chance of seeing or hearing which one was tripped. I have numbered them on the map. You guys should all do the same. If they go off, everyone should meet at this house, right here. This is our rally point."

Bishop reached in his bag and pulled out a bunch of glow sticks. He handed each man one and said, "If you hear a shot, break this stick, and hang it around your neck on the way to the rally point. It will keep a friend from shooting you. Once we have gathered at the rally point, we will take them off and go after the looters. "

"One more thing – It's possible that they will try an enveloping attack, or diversion. They may send two guys in here first and then a bigger group comes afterwards, from another direction. Don't fall for it. Unless you are supposed to meet at the rally point, stay at your post and keep a sharp eye out. If the rally point gets in trouble, we will shoot a flare and that will mean come and help."

Everyone thought they were ready and knew their job. Bishop was exhausted, so he readied all of his gear by the door and went to bed.

Breach

Bishop had given each watchtower a Walkie Talkie and kept one as well. He sat it next to the bed and throughout the night, every hour, he heard, "One OK," and then, "Two OK."

He set his watch alarm for 3:00 a.m., and it started beeping. He thought it would be after three if they were coming at all. After his alarm sounded, he heard guards check in again over the radio. He had made some coffee before going to bed and warned it up on the grill. He put on his load gear, slung up his rifle, and strolled out into the cool, early morning air. He keyed the radio and said, "This is Bishop – I am walking to the rally point, so don't shoot me."

He walked slowly down the street, stopping to drink coffee, and listen at every block. He made it to the rally point and sat down on the curb to finish his coffee.

"One - movement - I have four men with rifles walking through the woods. They're using flashlights. I could shoot them right now."

Bishop keyed his radio, "One, don't shoot anybody. Until they come over our fence line, they're hunting deer for all we know."

Bishop made sure his weapons were ready and just waited. After a bit, he keyed his radio and said, "Two, how does it look over there?"

"Two. All clear here Bishop. Do you need help?"

"Two. Thanks, but I got it. Keep watching."

"Okay."

"One. Bishop, they're heading for our fence, right behind #44. I don't think there is a booby trap there."

Bishop wished he had made a map to bring with him. He was pretty sure that #44 was not covered, but was having trouble remembering exactly where each tripwire was. He also had a much bigger problem than his memory. He had planned on one of the booby traps being tripped and the other guys rushing to the rally point. It now looked like the bad guys were going to cross the fence where there weren't any alarms, and he had no way of calling the others for help. He was on his own.

Bishop keyed his radio as he headed for #46, right next door to where the strangers were headed. "One. I am heading to #46. I'm going by myself. Do you have a clean shot at where they are going to come through the fence?"

"No, there's a roofline blocking my view. They're almost to the fence. One guy just pulled out a crowbar, and they lifted another guy over the top of the fence. I saw his head pop up and look around."

Bishop moved as fast as he could without making a lot of noise. He decided to try and catch them coming through the fence where the opening would create what the T1 guys called a "fatal funnel" – essentially a narrow gap that channels people into a known opening where they can be dealt with. Bishop made it to #46, ran along the side of the house, and entered through a gate into the back yard.

A six-foot high privacy fence with a gate at the end separated the yards of #44 and #46. He made it to the gate and gently pushed it open. He heard the crowbar prying wood off of the fence and in the moonlight saw a board popping off and falling into the grass. It wasn't long before a second board went flying off. He saw a head peak through the opening and look around. A foot came through next, followed by a leg. Bishop raised his M4 and waited until the man's hip was through the opening, then aimed for the fence where he knew the man's upper torso would be. He fired three shots in rapid succession. He moved his aim slightly left, fired, and then sprayed three more rounds to the right. The 5.56 NATO rounds he was using were 69 grains each. At 2850 feet per second, they went through the thin pine fence as if it were paper. He then charged the fence, but couldn't see anything moving.

"One - where are they?"

"Bishop, you hit three of them. Two are not moving and the third is on the ground. The last guy is running."

"One, please hurry down here with my night vision. I don't want to worry about these guys anymore. I'm going after him."

"Ok. I'm on my way."

It took less than a minute for the lookout to get to Bishop and hand him the monocular. Bishop mounted it on his rifle, and then used it to look through the fence where he could see three men lying on the ground. The third was rolling around holding his shoulder. Bishop went through the opening and kicked the man's weapon away. He figured the runner would try to get back to the road, so Bishop headed to cut him off. He looked through the NVD, ran 20 steps, avoiding trees and brush. He had repeated the process for about five times when he paused. He could hear someone fighting through the undergrowth to his right. He took a knee and scanned the area. He saw the man, who in the darkness had bumbled into a large patch of thorn bushes. Bishop could see the guy was about 150 meters away and struggling to get through the painful stickers. He centered the small red dot of his riflescope on the man's chest and thought about the looters. *What would they have done to Terri and the other families in the neighborhood?* He then remembered what they had done to that family in the SUV. When his mind flashed an image of the small children, dead in the backseat, he pulled the trigger.

Houston, Texas – September 8, 2015

Established Order

Bob's job was to monitor the Emergency Broadcasting Network twice per day. He didn't mind listening to John Philip Sousa and the other marching band music being played around the clock. Every hour, a pre-recorded voice would come on the air:

You are listening to the Emergency Broadcasting Network. Stand by for emergency instructions and information.

There would be a pause, and then the National Anthem would play, followed by another hour of marching music. This cycle repeated every day, over and over. There was never any news and he noticed that the music was exactly the same every day.

He was 79 years old and had to use a cane to get around. He often thought about his son and grandsons who lived scattered around the country. He knew they were good men who had married good women, but he still worried about them. His heart was heavy, wishing the lot of them were closer to Houston.

Before all of the turmoil had started, he would talk to one or two of them almost every week. While he sometimes had trouble keeping their names straight, no one seemed to mind. A few times a year, they would either visit him or take him to a wedding, funeral or family other event.

Their mother passed away four years ago, God rest her soul. She had been not only Bob's wife, but his lover and friend. Nothing could ever replace her.

He made it to the kitchen and found a candle left by one of the nice neighborhood girls. He fumbled with the lighter and got it to burn. The kitchen was filled with a warm glow. He turned off the flashlight to save the batteries. The candle was very short, and he thought he was going to have to ask that neighbor of his for another one. *Damn it! What was her name again?*

Bob went to the sink with a cup to fill with some water. He lifted the faucet and only a little spurt came out. He tried again and still nothing. *Odd*, he thought, *is there something special I'm supposed to do? These new times are so confusing, but at least my neighbors stop by often, and I have a job. Job? Oh, yes, I need to listen to the band music.*

He tried the refrigerator water. *Damn, I keep forgetting, there are no more refrigerators.* He finally remembered the water had stopped working two days ago. He found that fancy bottled water someone had left him on the counter and made a cup of cold coffee. He made sure it was the steel cup, and then held it over the candle for a while. *At least it makes it warm*, he told himself.

He picked up the small radio and turned the crank to give it power. It reminded him of the Army, so many years ago, where he would see crank radios like this. He turned it on and smiled when the music came on. He sat back and his mind drifted away to a trip he and mother had taken with their new baby son years ago.

His trip back in time was interrupted by a new sound he had not heard on the radio before. Every few seconds, he heard static over the top of the music. He moved the dial on the radio, thinking he had bumped it off of its station. That didn't seem to have any effect. He turned it some more, but the annoying noise still persisted.

He would have to get his neighbor to look at it when he asked her about another candle. He settled back into thinking about his son.

Bishop had fallen asleep on the couch again. He woke up hot and sweaty, but that was nothing new these days. They had stopped using precious gasoline to cool air days ago. He heard a distant rumbling and initially thought it was an explosion. A little concerned, Bishop became very still to see if the noise repeated. Seconds later, there was a flash of light, the windows rattled, and the whole house shook to its foundation. He smiled for the first time in days. A thunderstorm! They had not had significant rain in weeks, and it would cool off the air!

He went to the garage without even making coffee and gathered up his buckets and plastic bags. He went outside to set up rain traps.

Bob was sitting at his kitchen table drinking his cold coffee. The radio played the same announcement it always did, but then he heard a new voice.

Your attention please. Your attention please. This is Major Robert Danforth of the 112th Transportation Regiment,

Federalized Texas National Guard. I have an announcement. To all civilians of Houston, Texas and surrounding areas, the United States Army, by order of the President of the United States, has established Martial law for the City of Houston. In addition, all city and state agencies have been federalized. All employees of the city of Houston or the state of Texas should report to the Federal Building at 1200 South Main Street as soon as possible. You should bring identification and will be assigned specific duties.

All civilians within the Interstate 610 loop are ordered to remain in their homes until contacted by local authorities. For the safety of all citizens, this order will be strictly enforced and violators will be shot on sight.

All civilians residing outside of the 610 loop are hereby ordered to report, as soon as possible, to checkpoints established at every major intersection of the 610 loop and interstates 45, 59, 10, 288 and 290. Additional checkpoints are being established at all major surface roads as well.

You are required to bring identification and will be assigned temporary housing and duties. The United States Army will provide basic shelter, security, food, water, and medical care.

Family units may be temporarily separated in order to provide shelter.

No weapons of any kind are permitted inside of the 610 loop.

Personal property is subject to confiscation.

Able-bodied adults, between the ages of 16 and 65, will be expected to perform assigned tasks and labor.

These orders are issued by General T. Wilson Adams, Major General, United States Army.

End of message.

This message will repeat in 30 minutes.

Bob had a piece of paper and pencil next to the radio. He was trusted to write down anything he heard out of the ordinary, and this was surely not ordinary. The voice had rattled off the information so quickly he couldn't write fast enough to get it all down and was embarrassed he had not done his job. The static had not helped, but he now understood it was lightning causing the interference.

He looked outside and saw that it was almost dawn. He could see the flashes of lightning and hear thunder close by. This was important information and he had to let someone know quickly. Maybe Rosie would know what to do. She was always up before the sun.

Rosie lived alone too. She had lost her husband to a heart attack years ago, and Bob and she had become friends. He had found that they had many things in common, and he enjoyed spending afternoons with her just sitting and talking about "life back in the day." He hated to admit it, but her mind was sharper than his, and she helped him with his mail, bills and other business.

They had been sitting together complaining about doctors and healthcare, when she mentioned her heart medication. After comparing the labels on their prescription bottles, they learned they took the same drug. After the electricity had stopped working, he went to visit Rosie, and she did not look well at all. She had not filled her prescription and had run out a few days before. He went back to her house later that afternoon and took her his pills, along with a "little white lie" that he had several months' worth of tablets and was glad to share.

He would take the radio and his paper to Rosie's house. She would help him write it all down so he could do his job. If he hurried, he could make it there before it started raining.

Bishop was running around the house setting up rain traps. The city water had finally run out a few days ago, and they had been using the water stored in the bath tubs to flush the toilets. He shuddered to think about the sewers failing. There were a few in-ground swimming pools in the neighborhood, and he knew they would be used for flushing and laundry next. *How long will those last,* he worried.

As he came around the corner, he saw Old Bob walking down the street carrying something. He seemed like he was in such a hurry. Bishop thought it was odd that he was going to visit Rosie this early. As he watched him moving down the street, Bob suddenly stopped walking. He seemed to take a minute to catch his breath and started again. After about ten steps, he stopped again, and this time Bishop could see him hold his chest. Bishop ran to the door, and yelled for a sleeping Terri to come quickly, and ran to Bob assistance.

This is not good, thought Bob. His chest was tight and he was having trouble taking in air. He thought he would be all right if he could just get to Rosie's and sit down for a bit. She would get him some water and show him pictures of those grandkids of hers. He forced himself to keep walking a few more steps when a sharp, stabbing pain went through his chest.

He sat down hoping this pain would pass. He looked up to see someone running toward him and was happy to see it was his son! *What was he doing here? What a wonderful surprise!*

By the time Bishop reached him, Bob had already sat down right in the middle of the road. Bob was smiling at Bishop as he made it to his side and said, "My son! What a wonderful surprise! I have to tell Rosie about the news on the radio, and then I want you to tell me everything! Can you help me get to...."

Bishop caught him as he fell over. He gently laid him down on the pavement and felt for his pulse. No pulse. He listened to the old man's chest, no heartbeat. He was going to do CPR and ripped open his shirt. He looked up at Bob's face and saw he was still smiling and wondered for a second what had made him so happy. Bishop put his hands on Bob's chest in the proper place and started to push down. For some reason, he hesitated, mesmerized by the serene look on the face of a man he respected so much. *Even if I revive him, we can't help him recover,* he thought. *I wonder if he would ever be this happy again.*

Bishop pushed down once on the old gentleman's chest and felt his ribs give a little. Bishop's ribs were not fully mended themselves, and the thought of breaking bones stopped him cold. Bishop could not bring himself to do it. *Go with your dignity and that big smile, Bob. I hope someone does the same for me one day.*

It started pouring rain. Bishop just sat in the street next to Bob's body and really didn't notice the downpour. Terri came running to them and could see what had happened. She sat down next to Bishop and held him in the rain. For the first time since it all began, Bishop wept.

Funeral for a friend

The storm lasted almost all day, and despite everyone staying inside, news of the radio broadcast spread quickly along with word of Bob's death. The following morning everyone gathered at the makeshift cemetery. At Bishop's request, the lot being used to bury the dead had been divided into two sections. One, often referred to as the "Happy Hunting Grounds" was for friends. The other, referred to as "Hell's Gate" was for looters and other predators. *I wonder which side will fill up first*, Bishop had thought when they first labeled them.

After someone said a few kind words, the crowd slowly moved to the cul-de-sac, and a neighborhood meeting started. Each council representative was responsible for certain critical items, like food or medical care. As they ran through their reports, it became clear that the group was running out of food and medicine. Rosie told everyone that Bob had given her his heart pills, and a somber mood came over the little assembly.

Bishop was not surprised when his neighbors started tearing each other apart at the meeting. Minor bickering, pointed questions, and even a few insults contributed to the already low morale of the group. Eventually, one of the neighbors suggested making a plan to head downtown to the Army encampment. "After all, we are all going to go, aren't we?"

A couple of others commented the radio broadcast seemed to describe a Nazi labor camp, and they would die before going to a "concentration camp."

This sparked a huge debate that lasted over an hour. One of the council members finally got things back under control by standing on his chair and yelling at the top of his lungs.

The conversation settled down a bit, and another council member took the floor, saying, "We have two options. Either we stay here together, or we all head to downtown, and let the government take care of us. If we split up, there will not be enough people left to guard the neighborhood and do the work. I suggest we take a vote."

Bishop stood up quickly and said, "If I may, those are not our only two options. Some of us may decide to try and make it to family or other locations. That is a third option."

Bishop's statement caused another round of arguments to surge through the meeting. Before long, people grew tired of the fighting and began to drift off. A shoving match broke out between two of the men, and someone fired a pistol in the air to break it up.

The irony of the whole situation was not lost on Terri. Bishop's words at the first meeting had helped pull everyone together. Now his words had pushed everyone apart.

Time to leave

Bishop and Terri made a light lunch and were eating on the back porch. It seemed like every meal these days was "light." Bishop guessed he had lost at least ten pounds. *Not such a bad thing,* he mused. They sat and ate in silence, each knowing that a difficult conversation was ahead, and both wanting to avoid it. It was Terri who finally "manned up" and began to speak.

"Do you think we should head for west Texas?"

"I don't see where we have any option. I have listened to that broadcast several times, and maybe I'm over analyzing it, but I don't like it at all."

"What's bothering you about it?"

"The Army would have received orders to 'Establish order and protect as many citizens as possible.' It doesn't take a brain surgeon to realize that means taking over the cities. The denser the population, the more 'Established Order' bang they get for their buck. I just don't see how they can do it nationwide without a very heavy boot heel on the population's throat."

"I don't get it?"

"There are about 2.5 million soldiers in the military if you count the Reserves and National Guard. Sixty percent of those are Air Force and Navy. That leaves about one million 'ground troops' if everyone shows up. I don't know how many of our guys stationed overseas got back home before it all fell apart, but normally about 200,000 of those ground troops are in Korea, Japan, Germany and other locations."

"So, I still don't get where you are going with all this."

"Let's assume that they were brought back home, and there are one million men available to the Pentagon. The top ten metropolitan areas have over 60 million people. That is a ratio of 60 to 1 even if they don't use any men to control their own bases and forts. They don't have enough people to 'Establish Order,' and it's clear in that broadcast."

"How is it clear? I didn't hear that," she stated, clearly now intrigued.

"Did you notice they established their checkpoints at the inner loop, not the outer loop where many more people live? The broadcast also said that city and state employees were now part of the Federal Government and under the command of the military. That means cops, firemen, teachers, and meter maids. There is no way the Army wants to be involved with a bunch of undisciplined, untrained city workers. They would only do that if they were desperate for manpower."

"So you don't think there will be any 'Established Order?'"

"Oh, they will establish order all right. They will make people toe the line or kill them. A dead person is an orderly person, after all. Remember the part about looters being shot, and citizens being ordered to remain inside of their homes? The military will use the same tactics they use on new recruits. Idle minds are dangerous minds, so they will make everyone work like dogs, doing whatever menial task they can think of. Exhausted people don't cause as much trouble as energetic ones."

"You make them sound horrible – almost like invaders."

"Well, in a way, that is not far from the truth. I actually feel sorry for the Army. Can you imagine the problems associated with executing their orders? The officers will be judged on how many people they feed and keep alive, not how many people are happy. They are being handed millions of unwashed, hungry and sick people who have little hope in the future. They don't have the training or resources to accomplish this mission. Their bigger problem will be the demoralizing of their own troops. Can you imagine worrying about your family back in Bumfuck, Iowa while you are being ordered to shoot fellow Americans caught stealing food?"

"Wow Bishop, you have a dark mind. So we should pack up and 'Head West Young Man?'"

Bishop thought about this for a minute before he responded.

"Terri, when we go, we will technically be criminals and open game for any military or law enforcement that still exists. Given bandits and a desperate population, we would have to worry about every other human being between here and there. That is over 600 miles of very dangerous travel."

"Wouldn't we have the same problem here?"

"Yes, and it could be much, much worse. It has been just over 30 days since the stores were emptied. Many people are probably still hiding and using up what food they have, but it has got to be running out. Hell, we were better prepared than most, and we are running low. There are four million people in greater Houston. If even half go to the Army that leaves two million desperate souls looking for food."

Terri digested Bishop's reasoning for a little bit and asked, "How would we eat in west Texas?"

"There are deer and jack rabbit in the area. We have some food in that self-storage bin we rented. I know enough about the local plants that we can probably make it. We will never get fat, but we won't starve," Bishop said half-smiling. "Don't worry babe. My Dad had a great recipe for Cactus Bread."

She thought some more about what he had said. Going out to the "ranch" had been fun the first few times. It had been something different to do and a new place to explore. After a while it had gotten old, and they hadn't gone last fall. She finally decided that Bishop was probably right and really, it didn't matter to her as long as they were together.

She went over and sat next to him. They hugged each other for several minutes. She finally smiled and said, "Bonnie and Clyde it is! Let's be on the dodge together, Clyde."

Bishop surprised her and just looked down. He got up and paced around a little bit. She knew enough to just let him stew. He finally stopped and looked at her with very serious eyes and said, "Terri, we have big problems with this trip. We don't have enough gas to make it. We will need to scavenge on the way, and if we can't find any, we could end up stranded and walking through the middle of nowhere. We really *are* going to be Bonnie and Clyde."

Terri just smiled and said, "I have seen pictures of Clyde. Your ass is much nicer than his. Let's get going."

The Packing of Memories

Bishop liked to joke about his "old beat-up Texas Pickup truck," but in reality it was a very nice vehicle. A late model 4x4, it had four doors, leather seats and most of the conveniences found in a luxury car. It even had a sunroof. The backseat had more room than most sedans, but that meant the bed was not that large.

He and Terri pulled the camper top out of the garage and installed it over the bed. It provided extra waterproof storage and also served to block the contents of the bed from view.

They started loading the truck, which proved a difficult task. Because of the hurricanes, they had made a list years ago about what to take if they had to "bug out." That list had been compiled with the belief that they would eventually return to, at worst, a wind-damaged home.

Now they were bugging out, and may never return. After a few terse confrontations over what was being stacked by the back door, they decided they would gather everything up and then go through it together.

Many items were easy to include, such as the few boxes of food that remained and a bag of outdoor clothing. As they were gathering their belongings, they couldn't help but think about years of desert living without being able to replace anything. During a break, Terri's mind drifted back to sitting in Sunday school, wearing an itchy starched pinafore and tight black patent shoes. She couldn't help but draw a parallel between their situation and Exodus's account of Moses and Israelites. *Are we going to depend on Manna from the sky?*

One of the harshest disagreements started over shoes. Bishop packed two pairs of athletic sneakers, a pair of good hiking boots and a pair of combat boots. Terri started it all by teasing him, "You are worse than any woman I know. Look at all of those shoes. We aren't going on vacation; we are going into the middle-of-nowhere to survive."

Bishop took her teasing way too serious and reached into her bag and pulled out three boxes of maxi-pads. He held them up and said, "I like a fresh girl as much as anyone, but do you really need five years' worth of hygiene products?"

"Yes I do. Given your attitude, I plan on being on the rag 24x7 for a very long time," she retorted.

"I'm glad you warned me, although lately, I probably wouldn't have noticed any difference."

And so it went most of the morning.

Bishop tried to take special care in the order that he loaded the truck, but it was hopeless. Every time he thought he had it worked out, his mind would create some potential situation where he needed quick access to something now buried in the back. In the end, he decided to just get as much in there as he could and deal with it all later.

He went in the back door and found Terri sitting on the floor crying. In her lap were several family photographs she had taken off the walls. She looked up, sniffed and said, "I don't suppose these should go, should they? They would take up a lot of room and probably get broken anyway."

Bishop bent and tool Terri's hand, "I left room for them Terri. They are important, and I want to take them. You should grab our wedding album and all of the paperwork in the lockbox as well."

Terri sniffed and looked up at him, "Oh Bishop, you are just being nice to me. They're not practical and won't help us survive one single bit."

"Baby, I disagree. We are going to need hope, now more than ever. We have to believe that things will get better and that one day life will return to normal. We need a connection to our past, no matter how bad things get. If you don't pack them, I will."

Terri smiled, stood and they hugged for a few minutes. After that, the packing went smoothly.

The Trash

One of the most serious problems facing the council was trash. It was the smell of all of the garbage that caused the issue. After a few days sitting out in the hot Texas sun, the odor became unpleasant to say the least. Normally, trucks would remove the offending waste twice a week. When the trucks stopped coming, the smelly bags had piled up and the stench was overwhelming. Someone had joked about the odor affecting home values in the neighborhood, but not many laughed.

At first, the council's solution was to burn the garbage. The smell of the fires from downtown Houston drifted their way on occasion, and everyone thought the addition of burning the neighborhood's rubbish would go unnoticed by any nearby predators. It was also common to see house fires in the distance. The combination of candles, abandoned homes, and the absence of any fire departments made plumes of smoke on the horizon a common sight. The smoke from a smaller blaze wouldn't draw any attention.

This seemed like a reasonable method until one evening the trash pit fire almost got out of control. The lack of rain had created an almost perfect environment for brush fires in the surrounding dry vegetation. A strong breeze quickly spread the flames, and the fire soon had the potential to burn down the entire neighborhood. Only a heroic effort by several people forming a bucket line and the water from a nearby pool saved the day.

So the council decreed that burying the smelly bags of trash was a better solution. Bishop's wheelbarrow was one of the few in the neighborhood, so it had become common to "barrow it" for trash removal.

Taking out the garbage quickly became one of Bishop's least glamorous jobs. He had to find which neighbor had borrowed the wheelbarrow, retrieve it, fill it with his own bags, and push it down the street to the dump site. Of course the accompanying shovel was bound and determined to fall out several times during the trip, normally banging into his leg as it fell. Everyone was responsible for digging his own hole, and in the dry, hard soil, that was backbreaking work. The elderly residents had no chance of excavating any holes, so it became a courteously to dig out a little more in order to create a place for their trash. With heat over 100 degrees and a rifle in hand, taking out the trash was a multi-hour pain-in-the-ass chore that had to be done every few days.

As Bishop was removing the last of the garbage from the house, he told himself this was one part of their current situation he wouldn't miss. He looked down at his hands and realized how callused they had become. *It's no wonder*, he thought, *it seems like we are always digging a grave or holes for trash. Mom always said if I didn't pay attention in school, I would end up working as a ditch digger – little did she know.*

Terri decided to join Bishop as he pushed the wheelbarrow up the street one last time. She knew he was dreading digging the hole, and decided she would go along to lend moral support. More importantly, she wanted to see their street one last time.

As they walked together, Terri thought about how some aspects of this new life were not all bad. Clothes, strung across makeshift lines, billowed in the breeze, and she loved the smell and feel of sun-dried laundry. Children played outside and they seemed to form closer relationships than before. She had to smile as two bicycles went flying past pulling wagons in what the kids called "chariot races." Were it not for the fact that the nearby "babysitter" was carrying a rifle, it would have been a scene right out of 1930's small town America. The babysitters had weapons because the parents were concerned about kidnappers taking the children and holding them for ransoms of food - or worse. It had been agreed that the armed supervisors would stay vigilant, but as concealed as possible.

The smell of cooking fires and outdoor grills often filled the air with wonderful aromas. Since there were no longer any working refrigerators, left overs and extra portions were often shared with neighbors. *One thing's for sure – now I know who can cook on this street and who can't.*

Friends waved as she and Bishop passed. Many of them were doing chores, which prior to a few weeks ago, would have seemed strange or out-of-place. One woman was carrying a bucket of water from the swimming pool into the house. *No doubt to flush the commode.* Another man was carrying a bundle of fire wood back to his home from the nearby woods. The fact that he was armed made the scene only slightly surreal.

Terri watched Bishop start to dig the hole for the trash and realized how much weight he had lost. She had not weighed herself for weeks, but knew that her clothes fit looser. The combination of physical labor, the constant perspiration from lack air conditioning, and an absence of junk food did have its benefits. She had to admit her body felt better and had more energy than before.

As they walked back home, she thought about leaving the friends they had made the past few years. She was worried about the old folks as well as the families with young children. This new lifestyle had to be more difficult for them and probably required more adjustment than she and Bishop had to make. Word had spread that most of the elderly couples were heading together to the army checkpoints, and everyone planned to gather, see them off, and wish them well.

Families with teenagers seemed to be having the most difficulty adjusting. Already, there had been one attempted suicide and the parents of the young adults were struggling to help them adapt. Video games, social networks, and school gatherings had been abruptly removed from their daily lives. Most of the teenagers had friends they couldn't contact and were just as worried as anyone missing a family member. Being stuck with Mom and Dad in the equivalent of a social deserted island was difficult for them. The few kids of similar ages scattered up and down the street began to band together, but the loss of their network of friends weighed heavily on teens. One young man had commented to Terri that he had dreamed of getting his driver's license for the last year, only to reach the milestone a week before the shit hit the fan. He wondered if he'd ever learn to drive now.

Terri listened as Bishop and she walked past two young boys openly arguing over which one was going to be the "looter" and which one was going to be the "guard" in their game. She contemplated if it were a bad thing that "Looters and Good guys" had replaced "Cowboys and Indians."

Part of her wanted to stay and try holding their ground, but she knew deep down that they were making the right choice. The decision would have been easier if there weren't so many families determined to stay and make a go of it right here. Or was it they had nowhere else to go? She and Bishop had done everything they could to make it work here. No one had contributed more, or tried harder – but it was simply unsustainable. There were already households on the street that were out of food. Some men had attempted to hunt small game for a few days, but had found nothing. There was no place to fish or trap and while some gardens had been planted, even a bumper crop would not feed everyone for long. People had taken to gathering various eatable plants and roots, but each day they had to venture further from the neighborhood to find a meal. Already there had been two tense encounters with other scavengers in a wooded area nearby. The land could not support the density of the population.

Terri and Bishop's instincts for self-preservation had overridden any loyalty to the neighbors. She felt like they were leaving them all to die, but in reality they were leaving for a chance to live. *Were they being selfish? Where they placing themselves before the greater good of the community?* She shuddered as she thought about millions of people reaching that same conclusion but having nowhere to go. How long would it take listening to their children cry from hunger or watching loved ones die of starvation, before everyone would turn on each other? How long could any group of people hold together in those circumstances? How many peaceful, good people out there were on the verge of throwing away moral values to secure food? *Bishop was right – people would be the problem.*

The fact that she and Bishop didn't have any close family was a blessing in these times. She knew several people were deeply concerned about loved ones that they could no longer contact. One couple had two children away at college and had not heard a word from either since the collapse. Those parents went through the motions of living, but anyone could see it was eating them alive inside. The father had even approached Bishop and offered him everything they owned if he would drive to the university and bring back his children. Terri remembered that as one of the worst nights for Bishop. He had tried to gently explain to the man that there was simply no way they could do it. It would take several men away from the neighborhood, leaving all of the families exposed, and it required more gasoline than existed on the entire street. Even if they had the gasoline, what if they lost men? What about *their* families?

The man had pulled out a file of his extensive investments and bank accounts and offered it all to Bishop - if he would just bring home his son and daughter. When Bishop had refused, the man had left quietly, and had never looked Bishop in the eye again.

"What are you thinking about babe?" Bishop's voice brought her back. They continued walking toward their house, each looking at their surroundings like they would never see them again. Terri finally broke the silence.

"I'm worried about these people, and I'm trying to find a silver lining inside of this nightmare we are living in. It's difficult Bishop. Do you realize these kids will never feel the joy of driving a car?"

"Some people would say those freedoms we enjoyed is what caused all of this. Think about all the gasoline we wasted and the air pollution we created. After all of this eventually burns down, think about how clear the air will be."

"Oh Bishop, that's silly. You aren't going green on me, are you?"

Bishop wiped the sweat dripping from his forehead and said, "We are all going green now – whether we like it or not. I sure hope that global warning thing reverses soon."

The Route

That afternoon, they spread maps and guide books all over the table and planned their route. Bishop wanted an itinerary that avoided large population centers, like Austin and San Antonio, but still allowed for scavenging. They determined they would travel in the dark, using night vision instead of headlights. Bishop had freaked Terri out once by doing this on a vacation. They were driving along at night, and Bishop had brought the monocle up to his eye, turning off the headlights while on a remote stretch of road. Terri could only see a solid black windshield and yet the car was moving at highway speed. She demanded that he stop it, or she would puke. He later showed her that the monocle provided a better view for the driver than the headlights.

Any route was risky, and it was almost impossible to bypass civilization. There were just too many people on this side of The Hill Country, a 100-mile wide stretch of land that ran through the center of the state. The Texas Hill Country separated the coastal plains of eastern Texas from the arid west and had become a popular area for retiring baby boomers. The once small towns in the region had grown significantly because of retirement homes and the influx of people they attracted. It would be difficult avoiding those areas on their trip.

One advantage they did have was an old book Terri had found at a garage sale. It was a Texas Atlas that claimed to have "every road, both paved and unpaved" in Texas. It was the size of a phone book, but it became critical to their planning.

After spending hours poring over maps and guides, Bishop needed a break. He remembered one more important task to finish and left the house. When he didn't return for a bit, Terri went outside and found Bishop's head sticking out of the sunroof of the truck.

"Let me guess," she said, "You are going to make a sign that says 'Spring Break 2015' and flash it to everyone as we drive down the beach."

"Actually, I was thinking the sign would say, 'Show me your tits.'"

Bishop explained to Terri that she was going to be driving most of the time while he reclined in the backseat. "I'm an important man and deserve to be chauffeured around," he teased.

Bishop was a little insulted because Terri found that remark very funny - way too funny. He explained that he was going to ride with his head outside of the sunroof so he could have a clear 360-degree view and be able to shoot quickly if needed.

All day long while they were loading the truck, he saw neighbors packing up and leaving. Most stopped to say good-bye on the way out of the neighborhood. While many of their friends had decided to head downtown and take the Army up on their offer, others had decided to take their chances and try to make it to family or friends in rural locations.

There was also a good-sized group that had decided to stay, and they were gathered in a nearby front yard, watching everyone leave and talking things over. Bishop walked over to them and joined in their conversation, which focused on the decision to stay put.

He offered to give them the weapons he didn't have room to pack, and a couple of the men walked back to the house with him to retrieve the guns.

Terri gave one of the wives a set of house and car keys and everyone shook hands, hugged, and extended well wishes. It was dusk when Bishop and Terri started the truck and left. Both of them were very quiet as they thought about leaving their first home together – both of them believing they would never see it again, but afraid to say so out loud.

Houston, Texas - September 9, 2015

Terri was driving with a night vision scope while Bishop sat in the backseat. He had a rifle with the other night vision mounted on it, and had arranged the contents of the cab so that he could pop up through the sunroof to scout, or shoot if necessary. They drove without lights for safety and without air conditioning to save fuel.

Their route was going to turn what would normally be a 12-hour drive into almost three days on the road. Taking the back roads and avoiding towns was going to cause a lot of zigzagging, and that ate up time. Bishop had plugged the route into the GPS navigation system, happy to see the device still worked. *At least no one has knocked down the satellites - yet.*

They had a full tank of gas in the truck, 28 gallons. Bishop had another ten gallons in cans. The cache of fuel was his biggest concern, because at best, it was half of what they would need to reach to the ranch.

He had told Terri to drive slowly to conserve gas, but he really wanted her to go slow so that he could scout the road ahead and potentially avoid trouble. He discovered right away that sticking his head up through the sunroof was not the perfect idea. If the truck were moving more than 35 mph, the wind made it difficult to focus and keep the night vision steady. He dug his goggles out of his kit to help with the wind drying his eyes. *I hope bugs won't be as bad since we aren't using headlights.*

As they drove down Cypress, Terri seemed to struggle with steering using the NVD. As he watched her, he noticed her eyes darting from one side of the landscape to the other. He realized that the problem was not with the functionality of the tool; but with her natural curiosity about the world outside of their little neighborhood. Bishop had started to snap at her to pay attention, but then remembered she had not been off their street for over a month. Other than overgrown yards and weeds already sprouting in parking lots, things really didn't seem that different when looking through night vision. *Rose colored glasses* he thought.

As he stood with his head and upper body sticking out of the sunroof, he scanned right and left looking for trouble. He noticed that practically every store and shop had been emptied. One corner gas station had burned completely down. They continued tracking north and west, not seeing another soul.

"Bishop, someone is behind us," Terri said with a nervous tone.

He spun around and didn't need the night vision to see the headlights some distance behind them. He watched for about ten seconds and calculated the car would catch them soon. "Terri, turn off this road up here."

"Won't they see our brake lights?" Her breathing had changed, and her voice was a little shaky.

"No, I removed the fuse."

"Isn't that illegal? You know I don't want a ticket on my record, Bishop. It would cause our insurance coverage to go up."

They both nervously laughed as Terri turned off of the road.

"Go up about two blocks and stop."

They entered a residential neighborhood not unlike their own. Terri pulled over, and Bishop got out of the backseat and stood beside the truck. He asked Terri to keep a lookout for anyone approaching from the other direction.

He stayed beside the truck and watched as the car that was following them passed by where they had turned and kept going. He couldn't tell what kind of car it was and didn't care. He opened the door to the truck and found Terri looking around at the houses through the NVD. "These houses have all been looted, Bishop. There are clothes and trash all over the yards. I think there is a dead body up the street."

"Back up slowly Terri, and stop before you get back to the main road. I want to get out again."

"You really should cut back on the coffee. If you have to pee every ten minutes, we will never get anywhere."

Terri slowly backed the truck up and stopped. Bishop stood on the sidewalk, scanning the street up and down for a few minutes to verify that the car had indeed left the area. He got back in the truck, and they continued on their original route.

Terri swerved again and apologized. She just couldn't help looking around.

"How about I describe what I'm seeing? Will that help? If we lose a tire from *your* hitting a curb, *you* are going to have to change it right out here in the middle of no-man's land."

"I guess that might help. It's killing me not to be able to look around."

They drove for another few blocks, and Bishop said, "Hey babe, that store is having a two for one deal on bread today. We should stop in and stock up." Terri tapped the brakes.

Bishop carried on, "Hey darling, gas is ten cents cheaper over there. Remind me to fill up at that station next time."

Terri purposely swerved the truck, banging Bishop and his sore ribs into the side of the sunroof.

"Ok, I get the message. I'll shut up."

They drove on in silence.

It was impossible to leave suburban Houston without crossing a major freeway. Bishop believed this was one of the most dangerous parts of the route. Not only were there countless places to hide, the underpasses and overpasses provided a perfect place to ambush or ram another car. Bishop had no intention of traveling one single inch on any freeway, but they would have to cross some of the big roads.

As they approached the Tomball Expressway, Bishop had Terri pull over and park a few blocks away. He got out of the truck and said, "Lock the doors and don't let anyone in but me."

"Very funny."

"Seriously, I'll be back in a few minutes. If you hear shooting, wait ten minutes and then leave. If I'm not back in 20 minutes, then leave. Go back to our neighborhood, and stay with friends."

"What do I do if someone comes near the truck?"

"Run over them."

"What do I do if they have a gun?"

"Run over them faster."

Terri loved to play Devil's advocate. "What do I do if they are cute?"

"Ask them their sign, and then run over them."

"Gotcha."

Bishop made his way quickly toward the overpass. Without street lights, the area was completely dark. He cut behind a fast food place at the corner and used abandoned cars as cover. He wanted to have a look under the bridge.

He made it to the overpass, stopped, and looked around. He didn't see or hear anything and was about to leave when a small light flashed in one of the cars under the bridge. *Someone wanted a cigarette.* He moved a little closer so he could look inside the car. It was a late model, large Mercedes Benz, and inside sat four young men. They had the windows down, and he was close enough to make out the tattoos on one guy's arm. He was just about to move closer, when another guy stuck his head out of a large truck across the road and yelled, "Hey you stupid shit, put that out. You can see the cherry for twenty miles."

"Oh fuck off bro'. There ain't nobody coming tonight. We ain't caught nobody for two nights. Let's get out of here," came the response.

Bishop was unsure of what to do. Taking out either vehicle was simple. Taking out both would be dangerous. While he couldn't see any guns, he was sure these thugs were armed. The truck was dented along the passenger side, and he suspected they used it to block the narrow roadway. The Mercedes crew would then hop out and do the dirty work. It was a simple, but effective trap. As he scanned around the numerous cars littering the area, he noticed several were "shot up," confirming his fears.

He checked the time and decided that he and Terri should cross elsewhere.

After Bishop returned to the truck, he told Terri what he found, indicating they were going to have to try to cross under at the next exit. They made their way to the next underpass, and Bishop scouted their path. He returned, happily announcing it was all clear. They made it to the other side without problem.

Only 600 miles to go

They drove until the sun began rising behind them in the east. The false dawn created a memorable image of red and orange ribbons penetrating the dark blue of the night sky. The bright colors failed at first, seeming to give up as the night kept control. As the sun made its way over the horizon, Terri felt an inner peace that always seemed to warm her soul with a new dawn. She hadn't had this feeling since the collapse.

"Bishop, do you feel a warm spot inside of you when the sun rises?"

"Every single time - It's like a relief that you made it through the night, and everything is going to be okay."

"I wonder if everyone feels it. It's so calming."

"I think most people do. It makes it even better having you here to share it. Given all we have been through, we need to relish all of these moments. Maybe they will help make up for some of the bad stuff. By the way, you are really doing well. I'm glad you are with me."

According to the GPS, they had traveled 85 miles from home and used almost a quarter tank of gas. They were driving through open farm country down a badly paved road when Bishop noticed a creek running parallel to them. He looked at the atlas and told Terri to watch for a gravel lane to her right. They found what they were looking for. It was more like two worn paths with weeds growing down the middle. She turned off the road and stopped at the livestock gate blocking access to the path.

Bishop climbed out and noticed it was light enough that they didn't need the night vision anymore. He approached the gate carefully and looked it over. There were spider webs between the gate and the fence. He looked down the lane and could see more cobwebs crossing the lane in the morning dew. No one had been down this path for a while.

He opened the gate and motioned Terri to drive in. He closed it behind the truck and asked her to follow him as he scouted the path on foot.

He walked down the lane looking for any sign that someone had been there, but found none. The lane passed through a small wooded area and ended at a tiny metal shed about the size of a phone booth. There was a large pipeline crossing the creek, and he verified that the place could not be seen from the road. He recognized the building as a flood monitoring station that would warn the pipeline company if the stream's water got too high, potentially damaging the line.

He motioned for Terri to bring the truck and park it. She got out of the vehicle and walking stiffly, immediately headed toward the woods, finding a bush to get behind. *Damn*, thought Bishop, *she has been in that truck for over 7 hours and never said a word.*

Terri began unpacking some things out of the back of the truck while Bishop nosed around. He walked about 400 meters in each direction and found nothing. They were in an isolated area which was just fine with him. As he walked back to their camp, he noticed there were some good size fish swimming in the creek.

Terri had hung a hammock in the trees and was already lying in it, sound asleep.

He quietly dug through some boxes and found what he was looking for, a small casting net. He went to the creek and with a few throws, caught six, small perch. He used a spare bootlace, strung the fish in the stream, and then gathered the driest wood he could find. He didn't like starting a fire because the smoke and smell were like a big, neon sign saying, "Here we are; come get us," but thought on their first day out it might be worth the risk.

He took some fishing line and a shotgun shell noise maker and set a tripwire across the lane, deciding to wait on the fire. He had been wearing the heavy load vest and body armor the entire trip, and it was beginning to get hot already. He stripped down, plopped down in the creek, and washed himself off. He finished a few things while letting the sun dry him off and then got dressed again. He moved his gear beside the hammock and sat down with his rifle across his lap. Terri had been asleep for about three hours. He would wake her soon, so he could get some shuteye himself.

As Bishop sat staring at the sky, he considered their progress. They had traveled half the distance he had expected and had used twice the gas. He was trying to reassure himself that they were doing the right thing when Terri's watch beeped. He looked over at her as she rubbed her eyes and looked around. It took her a second to compose herself, and she rolled out of the hammock. She came over and kissed Bishop and asked if everything were all right.

Bishop told her what he had done and highly recommended she get naked and skinny dip in the creek - after he was awake of course, and could *watch out for her safety*. She snorted at the "for your safety" part and gave him another kiss.

"Wake me up in an hour," he said, rubbing his eyes.

"Okay."

Bishop woke up four hours later to the smell of smoke and cooking fish. Terri was sitting on top of the camper shell, completely naked, with one of the rifles. It was loaded. "Everything okay?" he asked, knowing full well she was drying off her clothes in the sun and maybe working on her tan.

"I was attacked by wild animals, and you just slept through it."

"Wild animals? Huh?"

She pointed to the other side of the creek where three, sleepy-looking cows were calmly grazing.

"They do look pretty dangerous to me. I told you to wait until I could guard you before you went skinny dipping."

"You never warned me about pervert cows."

Bishop laughed, "Terri that was *utterly* ridiculous."

Fish for Breakfast

They ate the fish with a can of corn and toasted the meal with bottled water. They each slept another few hours before starting to pack up the campsite. An hour before sunset they reviewed their route for the night.

Bishop led the truck out of the lane, then unhooked and pocketed the tripwire. He watched and listened to the road before signaling Terri to pull out.

He closed the gate behind them, and they were on their way right as the sun set.

The rural area allowed better progress, and Bishop even relaxed a few times and ducked back inside the sunroof. In less than an hour, they were approaching the Brazos River, and Bishop felt the increasing tension in his muscles. River passages were very dangerous due to the limited number of bridges. All of the local roads naturally funneled traffic to those few crossings. The further they moved away from Houston, the better Bishop felt about running into looters and desperate, starving people. That distance did not mean they could relax. however, as he was sure that locals would be sick and tired of the fleeing masses escaping Houston and invading their space.

They started slowly going down into the Brazos River valley, and Bishop asked Terri to reduce her speed to around 10 miles per hour. It was critical that they find the right spot. Between 290 and I-10, there were only three river crossings. Two were at small towns, and the other was very remote. Bishop wanted to try the isolated crossing. After a few turns, he pointed to a small lane similar to the one they had left by the creek. Bishop could not check it for recent activity as well in the dark and had to gamble that it was safe.

Bishop wanted to scout the bridge before they approached. He strung a couple of quick tripwires and pulled a different rifle out of the back. He removed the starter motor circuit breaker out of the main fuse box in the engine compartment and put it in his pocket. It would be next to impossible to start the truck without it. With everything locked, he and Terri began their hike. He taught her how to use the night vision to plot a path and then move 20 steps. It was not long before they were moving through the surrounding woods at a quick pace, but it still took them almost 30 minutes to reach the river. They walked along the bank until they crested a small rise, and both of them stopped and stared.

Bishop initially thought he was looking down on a small town that had electricity. There were hundreds of flickering lights scattered on both sides of the river. The Brazos was about 200 yards wide at this point, but was low due to lack of rain. Spanning the river was an older two-lane bridge that carried Texas 591.

Bridge over troubled waters

They were about a half mile away from the bridge and slightly higher in elevation. As they looked down, Terri was the first to realize the lights were actually campfires. Bishop had traded his M4 for an AR10. The two rifles looked similar, with the AR10 being slightly oversized. It fired a .308 Winchester cartridge that was much more powerful than the smaller .223 used in the M4. The .308 had been a favorite of military snipers for years because of its range and was considered a standard by most hunters. Bishop had not brought the big gun to hunt, but rather to use the scope that was mounted on it. But looking at the scene before him he thought, *the extra firepower might come in handy as well.*

He raised the big rifle and braced it against a tree, adjusting the focus and magnification of the scope, which was almost as long as the rifle barrel.

Terri quietly whispered, "What is going on down there?"

"Both sides of the bridge are blocked by military Hummers and an armored vehicle. Cars are parked on both sides of the road for as far as I can see. It looks like people are just camping at the bridge. I can see sleeping bags and makeshift tents. And there are kids running around playing."

He pulled the rifle down and let Terri have a look. She scanned the bridge for a few minutes and then let Bishop take the rifle. "That doesn't make any sense. If the bridge is closed, why do all of those people stay? If not, why don't they cross? I don't understand it."

Bishop responded, "I can't figure it out either. If we can't cross here, then we have to go through a town, or go to I-10 or 290 and try there. If this crossing is that congested, those will be worse."

"What do you want to do?"

"I don't have enough information to make a decision. I guess I'll ninja down, snatch a prisoner, and make him talk."

"I have a better idea."

Terri told Bishop her idea, and he didn't like it one bit. It took her a few minutes of whispered conversation, but she finally convinced him that her idea was safer.

He handed Terri two energy bars from his vest. Terri handed Bishop her rifle and proceeded to walk toward the bridge with Bishop following her.

She came out of the woods, zipping up her pants like she had been using the bushes. She walked along the road where people were sleeping, sitting around fires, and talking. Nobody paid any attention to her. She walked a few hundred feet until she saw two children playing with a tennis ball. She sat down along the side of the road, pulled out her energy bar, and started eating it. It took the kids about 10 seconds before they noticed the pretty lady eating something. They stopped and just stared at her.

Terri held the energy bar up and made a motion of "come on over and have a bite." Both kids ran over.

When they got closer, Terri could see they were filthy. A boy of about 10 and a girl a little younger stood in front of her and nibbled on little bits of the energy bar.

"What are your names?"

"I'm Troy," replied the boy, holding out his dirty hand for another nibble.

"And my name is Chrissie," chimed in his sister, "and I'm eight years old."

"How long have you been here at the bridge?"

Troy replied between bites. "Three days, maybe more - I kinda lost count."

"Where are your parents?"

Chrissie pointed down the road and said, "They're back there. Mom is sick, and Dad told us to go play somewhere. He's been kind of mad since we got here."

Terri passed out the last of the energy bar and then reached for the second one. Both kids' eyes got big when they saw it. She opened it and tore off a little bite for each.

"I just got here. How come the people aren't crossing the bridge?"

Troy spoke first, "The soldiers, or at least that's what they say they are, won't let anyone cross."

Chrissie quickly chimed in, "Dad says they aren't soldiers. He says that's bullshit."

"Chrissie, shhhhh, that's a bad word," chided Troy. He continued, "Two days ago, a bunch of men with guns tried to get across. The soldiers killed them all. The soldiers have big guns, and they shoot really fast. Babababababababa."

Chrissie held her hands up to her ears when he started the machine gun noise.

Terri looked up to see a man pause and look their way. She could sense, more than see, Bishop's rifle rise up behind her in the woods. The man started walking over to them.

"What's going on? You kids okay? What are you doing lady?"

"I found a couple of energy bars in the glove box. These kids looked like they could use a bite."

"They didn't take your food?" He asked looking nervously in the direction of the bridge. He lowered his voice and said, "Lady, that's up to you, but I wouldn't be doing that out in the open. There are people here who would take those from you in a New York minute." He looked over one more time and continued walking down the road.

Terri continued, "Do the soldiers take people's food?"

"When we came to the bridge, a bunch of soldiers made us pull over. They took Daddy's pistol and put a hose in our gas door. They made us get out of the car, and Mommy started crying."

Terri handed out the last bit of the energy bar, and then the kids ran off without another word.

She turned around and after checking to see that no one was watching her, ducked back into the woods.

Ben and Maggie

Terri stumbled through the woods in the half-light of the campfires. She was beginning to think Bishop had lost her, but she kept walking. She was in almost complete darkness when he appeared out of nowhere and held his finger to his lips.

He handed her an NVD, and they headed for the truck. When they were almost in sight of the vehicle, he whispered to her, "They have snipers up in the trees. I saw two of them. We were damn lucky they didn't notice you feeding the kids."

"Bishop, what the hell is going on back there? Did you hear what those kids told me?"

When they got back to the truck, Bishop doubled checked the area. He wanted to make sure no one had found the truck and was waiting for them to get back. He and Terri got something to eat out of the boxes and sat on the tailgate eating and talking.

"Terri, I saw at least 20 men on that bridge. They have a Bradley Fighting Vehicle, which to us, is essentially a tank. They have at least two Ma Duce machine guns mounted on Humvees. They have snipers in the woods. We might as well try to rob Fort Knox as cross that bridge."

"What is a 'ma duce'?"

"A big machine gun – an M2 or Ma Duce."

"Oh, okay. So, who are those guys on the bridge, the army?"

"I don't know. We weren't close enough to make out any insignias or markings. They could be an army unit gone rogue, but I doubt it. They could be a bunch of guys that looted an Armory – who knows. One thing for sure is that they're acting like criminals."

After they finished eating, they continued to sit and rest. Bishop noticed Terri was swinging her legs like a kid who couldn't reach the ground from her chair, and it made him smile. In a normal world, they would have been sitting and listening to the crickets chirp and the distant sound of the river. Instead of enjoying the cool air of the night and looking up at the stars, they had to keep watch for bad men with guns.

"I'm at a loss," Bishop said, feeling defeated, "I have no idea what to do. I'm sure the bridges in the towns are worse, even if we could get through to them. The interstate bridges are out of the question. This sucks."

Terri looked at her watch and commented that it would be dawn soon. They should find someplace safe to spend the day. Bishop got out the atlas, and they started the truck to check their position on the GPS. He wanted to put some distance between them and the bridge before he could relax. They picked a small country road a few miles away. After a few minutes of travel, Bishop asked Terri to stop.

He was using the night vision and scanning the road when he saw an old barn. He got out of the truck and went on foot to check it out. He could see where years ago there had been a house, but nothing other than the edge of the foundation remained. There was no equipment or feed in the barn. It was empty. One wall had several planks missing and another had partially collapsed. He found the gate a little further down the road and had Terri pull through. They parked the truck in the barn, hoping a big storm would not come along and knock the dilapidated building down on top of them.

When the sun rose the next morning, Bishop walked the road to see if the truck were visible. It was. He found some fallen lumber from the other side of the barn and randomly stacked the planks to block the view of the truck. He sat up some trip lines and was happy with their spot for the day.

They snacked again and took turns sleeping. There was nowhere to bathe, so they used a little of their bottled water and a towel to clean up.

Terri had to 'use the facilities,' and took Bishop's cute little camping shovel to dig a cat hole. She walked away from the barn to the woods. After she had finished, she was stepping out of the woods and looked up to see an older man and a young boy staring at her. Both had rifles.

The old man said, "Howdy," and nodded.

Terri said "Hello there. You startled me."

"Is that your truck in my barn?"

"Yes it is. I needed some place to stay the night. I meant no harm."

"Oh, you couldn't do anything to that old barn if you tried. My name is Ben. This is my grandson, Ben."

"My name is Terri, pleased to meet you."

"Where ya from?"

"Houston."

"Seems unusual for a pretty lady from Houston to be out here all by herself."

"Houston is not a very good place these days. I had to get out."

"I've heard some stories from passers-by. Are you hungry?"

"No, thank you, but no."

"Well, my house is over those two hills. Ben and I were trying to bring down a deer to butcher. My wife Maggie, she's at home cooking green beans and wild onions. You're welcome to some hot food if you like."

"Thank you, really. I'll be on my way soon if you don't mind my staying in the barn a little longer."

"Ma'am, I think it's best for both of us if you don't stay too long in that barn. Those men at the bridge wander up this way now and then. If you've got gasoline or food in your truck, they'll take it. A pretty gal like you might even have more trouble than that. They tried to bully me into giving them what we had, but I convinced them we didn't have anything."

Terri saw Bishop moving quietly behind the old man and the boy. She tried desperately not to look at him and give it away. He was now within 20 feet of them and creeping closer.

"Thank you for the advice. To be honest with you, I'm not exactly alone."

Ben looked at her for a second with wide eyes. He glanced down at little Ben and then back at Terri. In a real low voice, he said, "He's got the drop on me, don't he?"

Terri smiled and nodded.

There was a moment of silence and without turning around, Ben said, "Mister, we meant no harm to this young lady. Please let my grandson go."

Bishop replied, "Ben, I'm not going to hurt anyone. I only wanted to thank you for your hospitality. You and your grandson have nothing to worry about from me."

Ben slowly turned around and looked at Bishop standing behind him. Bishop smiled, winked at little Ben and then slowly walked up and extended his hand to the older gent.

"Lordie. I must be gettin' old. No man could have snuck up on me like that five years ago. Damn."

"Terri's beauty has distracted many men. You shouldn't feel bad at all. Now what were you saying about green beans, onions and deer meat?"

Ben convinced Bishop and Terri that moving the truck from the old barn to the new one by his house was safer, and besides, he and Maggie would enjoy some company. Bishop agreed and they packed up and left. The house was only a mile away and Bishop liked the layout. The house and barn could not been seen from the road.

They met Maggie and she, as Bishop said later, was a "Grand ole Texas Gal," complete with big hair, apron and unending charm. Maggie was busy working in the kitchen and apologized about their lack of meat. The smell of the food being prepared made Bishop's stomach growl, and everyone laughed. Terri thought they could help with the meal, and she returned with a can of smoked ham they had in stored the truck.

After their bellies were full, everyone sat on the front porch and talked. The women and little Ben decided to retire early while Grandpa Ben and Bishop finished a game of checkers. When they were alone, Bishop's tone turned serious, "Ben, I have to get across that river. I thought this bridge was our best bet, but now I'm stuck."

Ben packed his pipe and struck a match on the side of his chair. He puffed a few times, filling the air with a sweet smell and thought about it for a little bit. "I wish the Dayton Ferry were still open. Old man Dayton would have given anyone a ride for five dollars. The ferry is still there, but there hasn't been a cable for years."

"You mean the boat part is still there?"

"Last time I looked it was. We all went hog hunting over that way about two years ago. I worked on the Ferry in the winter when I was a kid. While we were hunting, I walked over on the hill, and the ole barge was still tied up right where it had finished its last trip."

"Which side of the river is it on?"

"This side, but I know what you are thinking. There's no cable. It was sold for scrap a long time ago."

"Would you need a cable for just one trip? Would a heavy rope do?"

"It's hard to tell. That ferry is over 30 tons of steel. That's why it's still sitting there. It's not worth the cost of the equipment it would take to move it out. The river is low, but still moving pretty well."

"What do you think would happen if the ropes mooring the ferry broke?"

"The cable did break back in '64," he said as he stoked the pipe. "The barge took out the bridge. Slammed into the west side support and down she went. When they built the new bridge, they redesigned the original structure, making it stronger. The barge would probably just get stuck against the bridge support nowadays."

Ben and Bishop were soon joined by a long eared bloodhound that Ben introduced as Cooter. Cooter smelled Bishop's hand and then rubbed his leg with his nose. Bishop scratched behind the dog's ears for a few minutes and told Ben he wanted to set the truck's alarm.

"No need for that Bishop, Cooter will let us know if anyone comes around. He's no attack dog, but we'll know if anyone gets close to the place."

The Ferry

The next morning, Ben agreed to show Bishop the ferry road. They drove Bishop's truck, and it didn't take long to find the overgrown track about two miles north of the bridge. Bishop got out and hacked through some saplings. After about an hour, they were looking down at the ferry. It was just where Ben had said, tied to the east bank looking like it was ready to cross the river. Bishop walked down the ramp and onto the rusty barge. He stomped around on the deck to see if it were rusted through. It seemed solid enough. He checked the ties and found they were simple chains that could be lifted off the bollards.

As they drove back to Ben's house, Bishop kept thinking about all of those people trapped at the river. He kept seeing the faces of the little kids Terri had talked with. He had an idea, but if it didn't work, he and Terri would be trapped on this side of the river for a long time.

I can't fix every problem he thought. *My responsibility is to Terri.*

When they got back to the farm, Bishop pulled Terri aside and explained to her what he was thinking. She listened without question as he told her that if he plan didn't work, they were trapped. When he had finished, she chose her words carefully. "Bishop, I didn't sleep last night thinking about those poor people."

"I know how you feel. I had trouble too."

"Do it, Bishop."

Bishop went to Ben and laid out their plan. "I can cause a distraction. I can confuse the men on the bridge for a short

186

time. What I can't do is organize the people stuck at the bridge. I don't know how to communicate with them. For this to work, we will need their help."

Ben thought for a moment and then replied, "I think I know someone who can help with that." After telling Bishop a short story, he headed into the kitchen. A little later, Maggie came into the room.

Maggie folded her apron and sat down with Bishop and Terri.

"Ben said you needed to speak to me?"

"Maggie, Ben told me you and some ladies from the church delivered fresh water two days ago to the bridge people. Can you do it again? Will you do it again?"

She thought about that for a minute and replied, "I don't see why not. We used a horse and hay wagon from over at Shirley's place. The men at the bridge have no use for an old plow horse, so they let us pass. I don't think they're desperate enough yet to eat the horse."

"Maggie, I need you and the ladies to do something dangerous. I need you to deliver a message to some of the men trapped at the river. If you get caught, I don't know what they will do to you. Do you think you can do that?"

"Oh my!" she exclaimed putting her hands to her cheeks, "This sounds exciting. Will it help those poor people?"

"I hope so."

"What's the message?"

"Be ready to rush the bridge one hour after dark."

She moved her hands to her lap and smiled. "This is going to be such an adventure!"

Rum Runners

Bishop and Terri drove to the ferry, where he began chopping down small saplings with an ax Ben had loaned him. He stacked all of the wood he could cut and gather in the center of the barge. He then rolled six empty steel drums, once used to hold diesel fuel for the barge's motor, onto the ferry and set them around the edges. When he had finished, he had a stack of wood that would create one heck of a bonfire.

They returned to Ben's house.

Bishop pulled supplies out of the truck and disappeared into the barn. He took an old feedbag and cut it into a square. He cut three strips of four-inch wide paper. He took the smokeless gunpowder, a staple of his reloading bench, and poured a small line down each strip. He rolled the papers tightly the same way a cowboy rolls a cigarette. After he had made his gunpowder cigarettes, he took a knife and cut them into small sections. He put a small piece of tape on each end and soon had a nice size bag of very big firecrackers – minus any fuses.

Ben came into the barn as Bishop was cleaning up, and told Bishop he had something to contribute. He crawled into the loft, and came down with a five-gallon can of kerosene. Bishop smiled. "Perfect."

Everyone met on the porch and had a bite to eat. Maggie had just returned, and everyone rushed over to see how the first phase of their plan had worked. She hugged Ben and then broke into a wide, beaming grin, "Message delivered with a smile and a cool drink."

Bishop had six magazines for the big .308. Each held 20 rounds, but he only loaded them with 19 because they jammed less often that way. He took his .45 sidearm and four extra clips for it. Ben and Terri took him to the lane where they had first parked to spy on the bridge and dropped him off. His kissed Terri and disappeared into the woods without another word.

Ben and Terri drove to the ferry and arrived right at dark. Terri spread around Bishop's firecrackers exactly according to Bishop's instructions. When she was done, Ben took the kerosene and poured it on the large stack of wood. He unhooked the mooring chains and watched as the big hulk of steel slowly started drifting down the river toward the bridge.

Bishop made it to the observation point he and Terri had used the first night. He found a good position that offered him cover and yet had a clear view of the bridge. He deployed the bi-pod on the rifle and settled down to where he was in a comfortable shooting position. He adjusted the scope and checked the range. The bridge was right at 725 meters, or about eight football fields. The .308 had numerous documented kills at over 900 meters, so the range was well within the capabilities of the cartridge. The rest was up to him. He pulled out his notebook, making sure his flashlight was not visible outside of his hiding spot. He was loaded with 169-grain match hollow points, so he flipped his notebook to the page where he had recorded the history of that cartridge with this specific rifle. He thought the angle downhill was less than 15 degrees, and the humidity was about 75%. This all translated into a holdover of 59 inches, meaning he would have to hold the crosshairs 59 inches above any target.

Bishop knew he was going to have many targets, so he adjusted the elevation knob, counting the number of clicks very carefully. When things started happening quickly, he would only have to concentrate on the crosshairs, not the holdover.

The river had a bend right before the bridge and Bishop could see it perfectly. He went through the order of targets three different times until he got used to the pattern and the feel of the rifle. He could see the Bradley with its machine gun on top. Next to it was one of the Humvees with a big .50 on top of it. The second .50 machinegun was at the west end of the bridge.

He waited about 30 minutes and was beginning to think the barge was not going to make it . . . or something had gone wrong for Ben and Terri. He was watching the river beyond the bridge when he saw the edge of the barge come around the bend in the river.

He sat down the NVD and picked up the rifle. He found the barge more from the reflection of all of the campfires than from actually being able to see its shape. He waited until it had cleared the bend, raised his aim to an additional 38 inches high, and ever so slowly squeezed the trigger.

The rifle roared and pushed against his shoulder, but he didn't wait to see the effect. He centered the crosshairs, raised the muzzle, and let a second shot go at the barge in less than a second. The bullet flew over the bridge at supersonic speeds, and everyone there heard a "crack" from its sonic boom as it passed overhead. The first bullet hit the deck right in front of the stack of kerosene-soaked wood. The heat of the bullet would have ignited the fluid, but when it hit the barge's steel plate, a spark flew, and the woodpile ignited.

The men on the bridge were confused. Everyone thought they heard a shot from the south, but the mass in the river was to the north and floating toward them. The fire spread quickly, and the outline of the steel barrels became clearly visible. The man in charge on the bridge saw the barrels and the fire, and thought his team was about to be hit with a large bomb. He started screaming for everyone to shoot the barge.

Bishop saw the Bradley turret start to turn toward the barge. This move exposed the back of the man operating the big machine gun. Bishop sent the shot and watched the man flop and fall over. His next shot was at one of the Humvees. Just like the Bradley, the man on top was spinning the Ma Duce toward the burning barge. Bishop centered and sent another one. He missed, but centered, breathed and sent another round. This one hit his target. The third .50 caliber was dispatched with a single shot. Bishop's firecrackers started popping off, and to the men on the bridge, it sounded like someone was shooting from the barge.

Bishop intended on going after the snipers in the trees next, but as he scanned the bridge, he saw a perfectly silhouetted line of men side-by-side, firing at the barge. He lined up and started firing at each one in rapid succession.

After he had either hit or scattered the men on the bridge, he started looking in the trees for the snipers, but couldn't locate them. He figured they were always present, but perhaps they switched positions nightly.

While he was searching, he saw movement and was very happy to see about 30 men charging the bridge from the east. He moved to view the other end and saw about 15 men charging from west. He went back to the east, and saw a target shooting at the charging crowd. Bishop centered on him and sent one his way. The man fell over instantly as did the next guy, who tried to climb up on the Bradley, reaching for the machine gun.

Bishop felt, more than heard, the bullet go past his head. He rolled to his right immediately and knew his sniper friends were indeed on the job tonight. Bishop rolled twice and then stopped. He prayed they didn't have NVD. He then belly crawled forward 10 feet. Another round hit right at his original position, so he didn't think they could see anything but his rifle's muzzle flashes and were shooting at where they had seen them last.

He decided to check on the bridge again and saw the rushing groups of men were meeting in the middle. The bridge now belonged to the people.

As he was watching the celebration on the bridge, he noticed two men moving quickly toward him through the woods, leap frogging from tree to tree. He fired two shots, but missed both moving targets. He dropped straight back along the river about 40 feet and took cover in a shallow ditch. He was scanning with the NVD when he saw one of the men rise up and pop off two rounds in his direction. Every few seconds, the man would rise up and fire. *His buddy is trying to get behind me and cut me off.*

Over the next 15 minutes, Bishop and the two pursuing snipers fought a ferocious running gun battle through the woods. Almost every tactical move known was attempted by one side or the other. Bishop tried every trick he knew and a couple he thought of in the heat of the moment. The two snipers were clearly experienced in small arms combat and kept pressing their advantage in numbers.

The only things that kept Bishop alive for those few minutes were the NVD and his focus. Despite all his efforts, he was slowly, but surely being cornered against the river. He knew if they managed to pin him, he was dead. Several times bullets would rip into the tree he was behind missing him by inches. His return fire had at least nicked one of the men because he heard a yelp and cursing after that exchange of gunfire.

At one point during the gunfight, Bishop was on a knee, peeking around a large pine tree, when his vision filled with white flecks and it felt like his face was on fire. His initial reaction was "I'm hit," but he felt okay except for the blood running down his cheek. As he checked his face for injury, he pulled several splinters out of his cheek and forehead. Some were over two inches long and if he had not had on his "shooting glasses," he was sure he would have been blinded by the near miss.

He was out of options and beginning to think it was over. They had his back to the riverbank with one sniper on his left and the other to his right. If he retreated any more, he would be completely exposed on the open sandbar. He figured he had one option left. He reached in his rig and found the pouch with the smoke grenade, pulled the pin and threw the device a few feet in front of him, waiting until it started billowing white smoke. The smoke trailed south along the river, and Bishop crawled along underneath it. As soon as the white smoke had shielded him a reasonable distance, he turned and moved quickly away into the woods.

He didn't know if the snipers were going to continue their hunt after losing him in the smoke. Their side had lost at the bridge, and he hoped self-preservation would override any desire to continue after him. He slowly retreated back into the woods and headed for the old barn.

Terri picked him up on the road as planned. He was covered in sweat and still breathing hard. He drank a full bottle of water without pausing and wouldn't look at Terri.

"You okay?"

"Yeah, I'm fine. We need to get out of here."

"You were late. What happened?"

"I'll tell you about it later babe. Let's just go."

They returned to the farmhouse. Bishop washed himself off and cleaned his rifle in silence. Ben and Terri both tried to strike up a conversation, but it was clear Bishop just wanted to be alone with his thoughts.

It took him several hours to settle down, and when the rush had worn off he suddenly felt exhausted. Despite feeling weary and knowing Cooter was on guard, his sleep was troubled that night – his mind flashing images of men's bodies jerking and falling in the crosshairs of his scope. He didn't know it at the time, but those images would never leave him, always seeming to return in the dark of the night.

Head for the Border

After their successful bank robbery, The Force left Cleveland, always traveling south and west toward Mexico. They waited until reaching southern Indiana to take inventory of their haul and found they had done very well. They used pawn shops, gold buyers and other "below the radar" exchanges to slowly dump their gold and other loot for traveling money along the route. For the most part, they had kept to themselves and as far away from the law as they could.

When the terrorist attacks occurred, they had been trapped on the east side of the Mississippi in Memphis for almost two weeks. They had slowly converted part of their booty to cash at the city's pawn shops, allowing them to stay in upscale hotels where they ate very well. When the bridges opened, they worried about trying to cross with the van and being inspected by cops, so they sold it to a junkyard and purchased the nicest 4x4 pickup truck they could find for cash. The five big guys of The Force could not all fit comfortably in a single truck, so a cheap, but reliable sedan was added to their convoy. The heavy loot was put in the back of the pickup, and they purchased a hard cover to secure it.

As they made their way across the heartland, they ran into trouble several times. They almost lost their treasure twice, with one episode resulting in two dead men in Arkansas. Spence was not stupid, and he knew that civilized society was crashing around them. They were in a small town when they decided they needed more equipment and much heavier firepower than they were currently carrying. Spence, being an ex-Marine and former policeman, knew his weapons. In addition, three of the four crew had seen combat in Iraq or Afghanistan. They used a technique, similar to the one they used at Fort Knox in Cleveland, to crack the gun safe of a large sporting goods store in Oklahoma.

The Force wanted to get to Mexico and retire with their riches on some sunny beach where women and booze were cheap and plentiful. They had been tracking across northeast Texas when they saw an old man driving alone down an isolated road in a farm truck.

"Turn around – I just saw gasoline go by!" Spence yelled.

The driver of their truck braked and turned around quickly leaving their comrades following in the sedan wondering what the hell was going on. The truck accelerated and began to close the gap. The old farm truck was a heavier vehicle than The Force's pickup, so running it off the road was not an option. Spence had his driver pull up beside the old man so he could stick his pistol out the window and wave for him to pull over. It eventually took a shot across the farm truck's windshield before the frightened man pulled over and stopped.

Spence got out of his pickup and waved his pistol, motioning for the old man to get out. As he opened the door and slowly climbed out, Spence noticed that the license plate on the truck was from Mexico and decided to find out what he could from the old guy.

"Good afternoon. We were wondering if you had any Tequila to trade."

"No hablo ingles," he replied, raising his arms.

"Oh, come on now, we don't want to hurt you, we just want to trade. Are you hungry? Need anything?"

One of The Force walked up, and said, "Queremos comercio?"

The old man smiled and relaxed just a bit. Spence told him to lower his arms and that helped even more. He motioned to the back of the truck, and with Spence's nodded approval, he proceeded to dig around and pull out a bottle of Tequila.

Spence laughed and told one of The Force to go get some of their food. He looked at the old man and rubbed his stomach in a circular motion as if to inquire, "Are you hungry?"

The old man smiled again and nodded his head rapidly up and down.

Between their limited Spanish and their new friend's broken English, they found out that civil war had broken out in Mexico. The old man described drug cartels, remnants of the Mexican Army and a few police forces fighting for control. He described situations that made the U.S. look like Disney World.

After they had extracted as much information as Spence thought they could, he gave the man a bag of food and motioned that he could be on his way. Happy to be released, the old man smiled and started walking back to his truck. Spence raised his pistol and shot him twice through the chest.

One of The Force commented under his breath, "Spence, man, that was some cold shit right there dude."

"Fuck it – we need the gas. Somebody get the siphon hose, and let's see how much is in that piece of shit - get the food back too."

Spence was mad. They had gotten this far, and now he was thinking their plans would have to change. Maybe the man was exaggerating? Maybe he was just telling them all of that stuff about Mexico to keep them out of his country? *No*, he thought, *I believe him*.

As they drained the gas out of the farm truck, Spence moved to the side of the road and stared across the landscape. *We need someplace to hole up and find out what is going on.*

West of the Brazos

Bishop and Terri stayed at Ben and Maggie's the next day and started west just before the sun went down. They crossed the river with just enough daylight left for Bishop to examine the blood stains on the bridge. The evidence of the previous night's battle only added to his melancholy state of mind.

Something seemed wrong with Terri this morning, and he was worried about her as well. She had been vomiting, and he was concerned about some type of stomach bug given all of the different sources of water and food they had consumed. She thought it was just nerves, but agreed to let him know if she experienced any other problems.

As soon as they could, they got off of the two-lane highway and started making good time on country roads. They were headed almost due west, a course that pointed them straight at the high population areas of Austin and San Antonio. Bishop wanted to avoid these regions at all cost, and after the events of the last 30 days, Terri understood why.

When they were approximately 80 miles east of Austin, they 'hung a lewie' and headed straight south. They hadn't seen any other cars, and as they traveled up the rare hill in that part of the state, Bishop was always looking for lights in the distance.

Houston had been without electricity for several days before they left, but there was no way of knowing about other cities. If other towns still had electrical power, it could mean less desperate people, and probably some level of government law enforcement or security. Maybe even gasoline. Bishop kept hoping to see lights in the distance.

Ahead, he noticed a mail box and power lines branching off the main line running above to the road. They had been passing the occasional rural home without incident, and Bishop didn't think anything of it. More out of curiosity than concern, he always scanned the properties as they passed. When he looked over this time, he noticed a flashlight beam moving sporadically in the front yard. Terri saw it as well, and slowed the truck as a precaution.

Bishop, peering through night vision, could see what appeared to be a middle-aged woman in a nightgown with her back to a tree. She held the flashlight in one hand and had a large butcher knife in the other. In front of her were two good size dogs and while Bishop was watching, one of animals jumped at her as she slashed back with the knife.

Purely out of instinct, Bishop raised his rifle and shot one of the dogs. Terri, unprepared for the noise from the gun, jumped and exclaimed "Shit!" Bishop saw the other dog run off. The lady looked toward the truck, shone her flashlight in Bishop's direction, and he waved. She waved back, and then took her knife and moved toward the dead animal at her feet. Bishop's jaw dropped at what he saw next. The lady dropped to one knee and began to skin the dog. Bishop shook his head and then watched as she expertly began to remove the hide.

"Terri, let's go."

"Is she all right, Bishop?"

"Yes, she is fine. I think she might want us to join her for dinner, but I'm not hungry. Let's get moving."

As they traveled through the night, they didn't see another light or vehicle. Bishop considered moving over to a larger, faster highway that was paralleling them south, but decided against it. They had developed a routine that they used at every intersection and rise. Terri would stop the truck, Bishop would 'dismount' and scout over the rise or around the intersection. It was becoming more and more difficult to maintain their discipline since they never yet encountered anyone else.

It was almost 4:00 AM, and the GPS indicated they were approaching another intersection with a county road. Terri started to slow down and Bishop said, "Blow through it. Don't stop." She gave the truck a little gas, and they went right through. Bishop turned and watched the road behind them, immediately dreading his decision. Nothing happened.

"You are so reckless!" Terri teased him.

"Hey, sometimes you have to live on the edge and take risks."

"Well, I for one am glad to see you come out of that conservative shell of yours. Let your hair down, and party a little."

"We do live such a boring, mundane life, don't we, hun?"

They drove another 20 miles when Bishop started getting that serious look on his face and asked Terri to slow down. In a short time, he saw a farm lane leading off of the road and asked her to stop. He got out and scouted the lane before waving her in.

There was no gate, but he didn't mind as he was not planning on staying long. The next big obstacle on their route was only a few miles ahead of them, and he wanted to regroup and make sure they were ready. Stretching, eating, and visiting the "facilities" were all taken care of.

Interstate I-10 was a coast-to-coast freeway. It ran from Florida to California along southern portions of the U.S. In this part of Texas, it was a major traffic artery and the fastest way to head west from Houston.

Because of the sheer volume of traffic, almost every exit had sprouted truck stops, fast food joints, and hotels. Bishop wanted to cross under I-10 using one of the few roads that was not an exit, but that was impossible given their route and direction. What concerned him most were the gas stations. During the evacuation of Houston for Hurricane Rita, I-10 had become a 120-mile long parking lot – primarily because gasoline had run out, and fuel trucks could not get to the stations to deliver more.

During those crazy three days, people had basically lived at gas station parking lots or on the freeway itself. Police had to be called in to manage the lines at the restrooms even after the fuel was long gone. Bishop remembered seeing pictures of convenience stores with their shelves completely bare.

It was only natural that as Houston fell apart, evacuees would head west via I-10 and now would have been stuck at the exits, perhaps for weeks. One of the things that surprised Bishop the most about the Rita situation was the lack of planning by so many evacuees. They had *always* been able to put a debit card in a gas pump and fill up and there was *always* fuel and food at the next exit. After Rita was over, many of them appeared on local news stations telling their horror stories: "We left Houston and were heading to my cousin's house using I-10. We had half a tank and a couple of cold sodas in the car, so we thought we would be able to make it out of town and fill the car up once we were away from the crowd."

Bishop believed there would be hundreds of thousands of such people on I-10. By now, they were going to be very hungry and very desperate. It would not surprise him at all if societies had formed, complete with rules and leadership. The real victims would be the small towns within a few miles of the interstate.

During Rita, when the roads had completely closed, the small towns near I-10 had become saturated with thousands of hurricane refugees looking for food, water, and shelter. One small town resident said it best. "The locusts of Houston descended upon us in biblical proportions and consumed everything."

Bishop knew that the Rita locusts were still in a mental state that retained some measure of "hope" for a return to a normal life. They were running from a storm and at worse, would return to a flooded or damaged home and have to deal with FEMA. Now, people would have little hope left in them and that would make them even more of a threat.

The biggest problem facing Bishop right now was how close to approach the freeway before scouting on foot. Were the people like those they had seen at the Brazos River Bridge and packed together tightly? Had they spread out? How far?

Another dilemma was how much gear to take with him. A rifle might attract attention he didn't want. It could also be common. One thing was for sure, a moving vehicle meant gasoline, and he would bet dollars to doughnuts that gasoline was more valuable than gold. If he let Terri get the truck too close, all hell could break loose.

He looked at his watch – it was 4:30 AM. He had two and a half hours before daylight. He could quickly walk with a light load about six miles per hour, so he decided they would travel to within five miles of I-10. He looked at the atlas and could not find any roads close to the five-mile mark, so he decided they would proceed slowly and chance it.

They were almost to the five-mile mark when they saw the first fires on the horizon. For as far as Bishop could see east or west, there were flames twinkling in the distance. It immediately reminded him of the people trapped at the Brazos river bridge. They stopped the truck and just stared for almost a minute. If their situation had been different, the scene in front of them would have been beautiful. Terri commented that it looked like a field of fireflies. Bishop took out the big rifle and used its scope again. They were still so far away he couldn't make out much, and he needed to get a closer look.

They drove another hundred meters or so and Bishop could make out a fence line with trees lining both sides. The fence looked like it was separating two fields of some crop that had not yet sprouted. The field next to the fence line was smooth and flat. He jumped out of the truck and quickly climbed the fence to check the soil. It was firm and hard. He ran back to the truck, pulled out his wire cutters, and snipped the wire very carefully. He motioned Terri in, and after the truck had cleared, he quickly used duct tape to connect the wire ends back together. It would not hold long, but anyone driving by would never notice the cut wire.

He walked ahead of the truck as he had done before, travelling away from the road for several hundred meters. The field began to slope gradually downwards into a small drainage gully. The gully was cultivated, even at the bottom, so he had Terri drive the truck down into it.

In reality, they were parked in a ditch, but from the road, it would appear like an empty, flat farm field. Bishop stood on the bumper of the truck and put his head at the same height as the top of the cab. He looked back at the fence and could not see it. He had to climb almost on top of the camper shell before it came into view. Anyone driving down the road could look in their direction and see nothing but empty field.

Bishop dug around in the camper for a few minutes and pulled out a rifle Terri had not seen before. It was a space age-looking gun, mostly plastic with odd angles. She realized why he had chosen it when he folded the stock and slung it over his shoulder.

She was curious as she watched him pull out an old shirt, tear the sleeve, and then roll it around in the dirt. He put it on and then took a handful of soil and rubbed it all over his face and hands. He put on the torn shirt and then rolled his mask into what looked like a sailors cap and pulled it over his head. He took a black plastic trash bag, put some gear and a few magazines in it, and draped it over the same shoulder as the rifle. It looked like a makeshift backpack. She couldn't see the folded rifle under the cover of his arm, shirt, and dark bag.

He tucked one pants leg into a boot and slumped over, walking around trying to imitate an older person.

"Would you believe me homeless?" he asked.

She giggled, "Will you work for food? I could use a pool boy with soft hands."

"Seriously, do you see anything out of place?"

"No, you look like those poor people we see under the bridges at home. The only thing missing is a shopping cart full of plastic bags and three days' worth of beard."

He asked her to wait for him there until it became dark again. If he were not back, she should return to Ben and Maggie's. They hugged, kissed each other, and then he was gone.

Bishop walked to the edge of the field and then the road. He looked back with his NVD and still could not see the truck. He started walking down the edge of the road, glancing right and left with the night vision, wondering when he would run into the proud citizens of I-10.

He had walked about half a mile when he started seeing the distant fires again. The folding rifle, called an ACR, or Adaptive Combat Rifle, did not have any magnification on it. He was stuck with the NVD and his own eyes. He kept moving and started up a small rise. He had a bad feeling in his gut. Something was just not right, like someone was watching him. *Bullshit*, he thought, *that is just nonsense. You are getting paranoid.*

He was looking right and left and almost missed the overturned school bus sitting in the middle of the road. He stopped and listened for a bit, but could hear nothing but crickets and other sounds of the night. He was 50 meters from the school bus when he stopped to listen again. His boot lace was untied, so he knelt to tighten it and saw a thin line running across the road a few inches in front of his leg. *A TRIPWIRE!*

Thoughts stormed through his head like lightning bolts. He wanted desperately to raise his rifle, run, or hit the deck, but he didn't dare move. Bishop could make out the wire now that he was looking for it. He tried to trace the wire in both directions with his eyes, but couldn't tell in the dark what it was connected to.

He couldn't stand there all night, so he took a deep breath and slowly, ever so cautiously, took two full steps backwards and went to one knee. His head pivoted right and left, up and down for over a minute. He raised the NVD and did a very detailed search of the area, seeing nothing but the wrecked school bus, and the tripwire. *What the hell?*

He stepped back up to the tripwire and started following it to the right. This was a time-consuming process as he checked for other wires in front of him. He would very slowly move his hand from the ground up to the height of his head feeling for a wire and then take another step. He finally reached the side of the road and followed the wire to the fence. There was a small pine tree and the wire wrapped around it and extended up to an orange plastic pistol – a flare gun. Bishop had seen these before on boats. The Coast Guard had regulations that required most boats to have emergency signaling devices, often flare guns, on board at all times. *Someone*, he thought, *was pulling their boat and decided later that they needed an early warning device. Why here?*

He looked at his watch and was not happy. It had taken him over an hour to move less than one mile from the truck. He was still trying to piece all of this together when he noticed a second wire running off the flare gun. He traced it with his eyes as it went up the tree until it ended at a shotgun shell pointing right at his face. *Nice*, he thought.

Whoever had rigged the flare gun had decided they needed a safety, or a booby trap on the booby trap. This safety was designed to hurt or kill anyone messing with the flare gun. He also noticed the flare gun had a condom over the barrel, and what looked like grease around the breach. *Wow*, thought Bishop, *someone knew what they were doing*. The flare gun had been waterproofed.

He was still four miles away from the interstate and already had run into the most sophisticated, well-thought out device he had seen in years. It was going to be light soon, so he made up his mind to go back to the truck and regroup.

Terri had settled on sleeping in the truck's backseat. She had toyed with the idea of making a sun shade of some sort and resting outside, but was just too tired. She took her pistol and laid it on the floor beside her. Then she draped a shirt and towel over the windows. She was thinking about how long it would be before it got hot enough to turn the inside of the cab into an oven when she fell asleep.

The light of the false dawn was arriving as Bishop made it back to the field. He crossed over an uncut portion of the fence and walked back to the truck staying close to the tree line and stepping carefully on clumps of weeds as he went. He could clearly see his tracks from when he had left earlier, and wanted anyone in the area to see only the sign of a person leaving the field, not coming back.

He was getting ready to cut over to the truck and stopped to look around one last time. As he stood looking back the way he came, a large clump of bushes growing in the fence row suddenly stood up, and Bishop was looking right into the muzzle of a rifle.

The man pointing the weapon at Bishop was wearing a Ghillie Suit, and a damn good one, Bishop had to admit. He had walked right past the man and never seen him. The Ghillie was a shirt and pants made of mesh. Local vegetation was woven through the mesh to allow the person wearing it to blend into the surroundings. The camouflage was very effective, having been used by both military snipers and hunters for hundreds of years.

"I guess I have just met the man who set that tripwire up by the bus," Bishop said.

"You got really lucky there bud. I thought for sure you were going to walk right into that, and I was going to have to reset it."

The man looked Bishop up and down, "A PVS14 Night Vision, a Springfield TRP .45 and a Bushmaster ACR, Enhanced. Nice setup. That's some pretty good kit. You Army?"

"No sir, private security."

"Blackwater?"

"No sir, HBR."

"You don't have to call me sir. Master Sergeant will do. How did you get out here Mr. Private Security?"

"We drove."

The man actually laughed at Bishop's smartass remark and then continued the interrogation:

"Now you wouldn't be thinking of trying to get the drop on me with that .45, would ya?"

"The thought had crossed my mind Master Sergeant, but no, I know a pro when I see one."

The man looked over Bishop's shoulder and nodded. Bishop heard a rustling, and a second man rose out of the fence line bushes wearing a Ghillie. The Master Sergeant said, "This is my son, Kevin. He makes way to much fucking noise when he walks, but he is a crack shot and during the last month, he has proven he *will* pull the trigger."

"Seems like they grow up faster than ever these days."

The Sergeant nodded toward the truck and said, "That your wife?"

Bishop tensed and his weight moved forward to the balls of his feet. *What have they done to Terri?*

"Relax. She is sleeping in the backseat. She is fine as far as I know. We haven't turned into complete animals just yet, so chill."

Bishop relaxed a bit and said, "Yes Master Sergeant, she is my wife."

The Sergeant reached to his belt and pulled out a small radio. He raised it and said, "Clear." A second later he tilted his head listening through the ear bud connected to the radio. He looked at Kevin and said, "Grandpa is clear." He looked around one more time and said, "There is no one around, so why don't you ask your wife to join us. She has a 9mm sitting on the floor beside her, and I really don't want her firing off any rounds this morning."

Bishop started to turn toward the truck, but the move made Kevin nervous, and he had an AR15 pointed right at Bishop's head. Bishop decided he was very comfortable right where he was, so he called out, "Terri, Terri, you awake? Terri, wake up please."

Bishop saw the truck move ever so slightly, and then the back door opened and her head appeared. She said, "Bishop?"

"Honey, we have company. Could you please come over here without your pistol?"

"Bishop? Okay, let me put some pants on."

Terri started walking from the truck, and Kevin shifted his aim from Bishop to Terri. She had a puzzled look on her face because Bishop still had his rifle on his shoulder yet the two man-bushes clearly had the upper hand.

The Sergeant looked at Terri and shook his head. He said, "I know you have that pistol tucked in your pants young lady. Please don't reach for it."

Terri looked surprised and then sheepishly asked, "How did you know?"

"Because you were sleeping with your pants on, and I would have done the same thing in your shoes. Now, Mr. Bishop, I want to hear your story, and I need it quick. The Rovers will be out soon and all of us standing around here having a tea party is risky, to say the least."

It took Bishop about three minutes to give the Sergeant the condensed version. When he had finished, the Sergeant thought for a bit and then said, "You have two choices. You can come with us or stay here. If you stay here, you have a 50-50 chance the rovers will find the truck. If you come with us, I can guarantee better odds, and I have three beers I have been saving for a special occasion. Your call."

Bishop thought about that for a second, "What if we just go back the way we came?"

"Well now," replied the Sergeant, "that isn't going to get you to the other side of I-10, is it?"

Bishop looked at Terri who just shrugged her shoulders. Bishop nodded. "We'll join you."

The Sergeant looked at Kevin and ordered, "Point," and the boy left immediately. He then keyed his radio. "Break out the good china, we have guests."

He told Bishop and Terri to follow him in the truck and started walking toward the road.

As they hurried to the truck, Terri said, "Do you trust him? I mean, they could be cannibals for all we know."

"They already had the chance to disarm us, shoot us, kidnap you, and do all sorts of evil crazy shit if they wanted to. I don't see any other option right now. Besides, I could use a beer."

Bishop and Terri followed the Sergeant down the road in the direction of the school bus. Right before they got to the tripwire, Bishop watched as Kevin opened a gate that had been well hidden by its own Ghillie suit. Bishop had walked right past it just an hour ago. The opened gate revealed a driveway heading back into a wooded area.

As they turned in the lane, Bishop could see a single story ranch style home. The front yard was littered with clothing, overturned chairs, and dresser drawers. The home had also been on fire as Bishop could see smoke stains above two of the broken windows, and some of the siding was warped away from the wall. An older man wearing a radio and ear bud walked around the corner carrying a shotgun, but did not raise the weapon. He motioned for them to pull the truck around to the back yard. Bishop had just noticed something very odd about the back yard, when the man reached up and pulled back a big tarp so they could pass. The tarp had been painted with a picture of a yard, but when it was pulled back, Bishop could see a large pickup truck and a boat on a trailer was behind it. *Pay no attention to that man behind the curtain*, he thought.

Hiding in plain sight

They parked the truck where directed and got out. Bishop immediately started looking around and the Sergeant walked up beside him. He reached out his hand and said, "Master Sergeant Nick Williams, 6th Special Forces Group, United States Army, well, if there still is an Army or a United States. Please call me Nick."

Bishop shook his hand and said, "Please call me impressed. Nice camo job on the driveway."

"Thanks, but I thought the house was our best work. Did it look like it had been on fire?"

"It didn't burn?"

"No," he said as they examined the structure a little closer, "I painted those smoke stains with spray paint, and the siding damage is an old Styrofoam cooler I cut up and painted to match. It really fooled you?"

"It sure as shit did."

"I had been at Fort Hood for a few months on a training assignment. Kevin was staying with my Dad in Houston, and we had decided to go on a fishing trip up at the lake. You know, three generations and all that shit. Anyway, Dad had been saving up for it for months. We left Houston before all of the shit started, but the trailer broke down on the way. We were waiting on a part to be brought over from Austin when all hell broke loose."

"Who owns the house?"

"When we pulled off to wait, it became clear that the Shell station up the road was going to have trouble. We went looking for some place to stay, but with the brakes smoking on the trailer, we couldn't go far. I saw a "For Sale – Foreclosure" sign in front of this place and thought it might be empty. There was still some junk inside, but no one had lived here for quite a while."

Bishop and Nick walked around to the front yard. Bishop was staring at the school bus, curious, but not wanting to ask a stupid question. Nick noticed he was looking at it and waited a little bit before explaining, "The Rovers, or at least that is what we call them. They use busses or trucks or anything that can carry a lot of people. They drive around the countryside and stop every so often. They'll send out scouts looking for some place to loot or scavenge. If the scouts find anything interesting, the soldiers come in force. They swarm the place like ants."

"It looks like you had some ants show up at your picnic."

Nick laughed, but then his face turned sour, and his voice became bitter.

"They had driven right past here several times, and the camo had worked. We saw a flatbed 18-wheeler, a tractor pulling a hay wagon, and a couple of other "troop carriers," but they would just slow down, point and talk and then go on past. It was the school bus that got us in trouble. We had our dog with us, Chief, and he never did like school busses for some reason. Chief started barking, and they heard him and stopped. Before I could stop him, he went running after the bus. He was a good dog."

"Was?"

Nick's voice went low and cold. "They shot him right in front of Kevin. Kevin is 15 and should be chasing girls and playing basketball, not carrying a rifle and shooting people. Anyway, I had taken the powder out of some of my ammo and made a couple of small IED's with some pipe I found in the garage. I threw one at the bus, but I missed. The driver panicked though and flipped it on its side before they all got out."

As they walked closer to the bus, Bishop could see the roof was riddled with bullet holes.

Nick's voice returned to normal, "It took us a week to bury all of them. I wanted to just leave them for the vultures, but the smell got really bad. We were lucky, none of them got away. Dad got three, and I don't know how many Kevin killed. Ever since then, we've been trying to avoid the scouts. With the bus blocking the way, they don't bring anything heavy down this road anymore, but we still run into the scouts now and then. That's why I have the tripwires set up."

"Who are they? How did they organize so quickly?"

"The reason we left the Shell station was because four car loads of gang bangers showed up. I saw one of their tattoos, and I think they were that M13 or whatever it's called. Like sharks, they could smell fear in the water. They had guns, were not afraid to use them, and took over. After we left, I walked back there a few times to see if there were any news or if any food had showed up. The M13 guys were taking whatever they wanted from the stranded cars and all of the businesses. I got the feeling it was a 'join us or die' type of deal. I also got the impression they had no trouble recruiting from the hundreds of teenagers who were stranded with Mom and Dad. The last time I went, there were 11 bodies hanging from the overpass - so much for any resistance."

Bishop took it all in and thought about it for a while. They continued to walk around the yard with Nick pointing out all of the tripwires so Bishop didn't set one off by mistake. As they went under the tarp and into the back yard, Bishop could see Terri and Kevin petting a cat and talking. He looked around a little bit for Grandpa, but couldn't see him anywhere.

Movement caught his eye, and he saw the man up on the roof of the house with a pair of binoculars.

Bishop said, "Well, it looks like you are about as secure here as you can be in this situation."

"We are not going to be able to hold out much longer. Food and water are okay right now, but we are almost out of ammunition. I didn't have that much to start with, and my pipe bombs didn't help the situation. Kevin has four rounds left for the AR, and I only have a handful for bolt action. We are down to less than 10 shells for Dad's shotgun."

Bishop looked at Nick and smiled. "Well sir, let me show you something that might cheer you up a little."

They walked around to the back of the truck and Nick watched as Bishop moved some boxes around and pulled out a heavy plastic storage bin. Bishop pulled the top off, and the inside was completely full of shiny brass ammunition. Nick didn't say a word, but just stared for a full minute. He started to reach for one and then pulled his hand back and looked at Bishop to see if it were okay. Bishop nodded and said, "It's all homemade, but I never have any issue with it. Those are above military spec. They have proven to have plenty of stopping power."

The military's standard issue 5.56 mm ammunition had been criticized for years as being underpowered. Starting with the Vietnam War, where first used, reports of the enemy continuing to fight after being shot were common. In every conflict since, a movement has circulated in the Pentagon to provide the troops with a more potent cartridge. From his own experience, Bishop knew the problem was not with the cartridge, but with the bullet being used with the cartridge. The United States subscribed to the Geneva Convention, which prohibited any type of bullet "specially modified to damage flesh." This limitation resulted in U.S. forces being given simple "ball" ammunition to fight with. Hollow points and various other types of bullets had proven far superior, but were against the Convention's rules.

Field commanders also wanted shorter and shorter barrels on their weapons. This was not only to lighten the load of the individual solider, but because Iraq had been primarily urban house-to-house fighting. A shorter barrel on a rifle has numerous benefits in going around corners, fighting up stairwells and other common building features. The shorter the barrel, the slower the bullet exits, and thus less stopping power is delivered to the target. The 5.56, already questionable, became even less effective.

What really pissed Bishop off was all of the money the U.S. spent trying to replace the M16 and M4 rifles. They could have simply changed the bullet, at no additional cost, and solved the entire issue. Bishop did not know exactly how much had been wasted, both in dead American boys and research, but it was complete chicken shit any way you looked at it.

Bishop didn't subscribe to the Geneva Convention and never intended to. He made his ammo just as mean and nasty as he possibly could.

"Could you possibly part with a bit? I don't have much to trade, but I took one of the last deer around here a few days ago. I could trade some fresh hot venison stew," Nick offered.

"Would 500 rounds hold you over?"

"Oh my god! Really? You can part with 500? Kevin! Come over here, son. Look at what the nice man you almost shot this morning has for us!"

Bishop smiled and then asked, "What caliber is your bolt action?"

"It's a .308 Winchester."

Bishop grinned and reached for another box.

Campfire Stew

As they sat around the fire eating some very tasty stew that was heavy on meat and short on vegetables, the conversation was on everything but today's world. Jokes, army stories, family history, and tales of fantastic fishing filled the air. For a while, Bishop almost forgot he was living through a situation that resembled a Hollywood post-apocalyptic movie and not the great state of Texas in the year 2015.

As soon as everyone had finished eating, Nick stood up and looked at Terri. He bent slightly at the waist and swept his arm toward the house, "I'll show you to your master suite. Right this way madam." He led them into the house and then a back bedroom. There was no furniture in the place, so Terri was surprised to see a mattress lying on the floor. She couldn't remember how many days it had been since she had slept on anything soft. Nick pointed to the windows and the stacks of plastic bags. "Those are the bullet stops I made. We had a bunch of trash bags in the boat and we filled them up with dirt. They should provide protection in case Kevin is cleaning his gun and has an accident, or the Rovers decide to shoot at us."

Next was another pleasant surprise – the toilets worked. "There is an old well out back. Take that bucket and use it to fill the tank. It flushes just fine. It even comes fully equipped with a five year old Sports Illustrated for your reading pleasure." Bishop walked over, rattled the knob on the throne, and looked at Terri. "Now honey, you push this little thing down, and the bad stuff goes away. You don't have to dig a cat hole or use poison oak leaves to wipe with."

Terri walked over and lifted the seat up and down, "Now honey, this is the seat, and you leave it down after…oh, hell, never mind. You couldn't manage that even when you used one of these every day."

Everyone laughed, and Nick said, "I have saved the best for last." He led them out the sliding glass door onto a small patio. Hanging from the roof was a shower curtain on two pieces of pipe. "Lady and Gentleman, may I present to you one of the finest facilities known to the human race this side of the Pecos – A HOT WATER SHOWER! We brought a Solar Shower with us to use on the boat. It's really a big plastic bag that you fill with water and let the sun heat. It gets very hot, so be careful."

Bishop and Terri both looked at each other and simultaneously said, "Me first!"

Nick said, "It's big enough for two," winked, and walked off.

I-10 – September 13, 2015

Getting Involved

Bishop woke up early and went outside without waking Terri. Kevin was on the roof doing his shift of guard duty. Bishop nodded at him and went over to the coals of the campfire. Nick said they ran a fire anytime at night because the smoke wasn't visible, but not during the day. Bishop stirred the coals and determined there was enough heat to make some coffee. He heated water and stared at the fading stars losing way to the rising sun.

Nick walked up, happy to help Bishop dispose of the hot water for his coffee. "I have been thinking about how to get you safely on the other side of the interstate, and I just don't see how it can be done. The overpass is blocked by two large trailers that you would have to zigzag through slowly. There are two rings of sentries, and they have a very effective over watch guards on the building roofs. I've seen their weapons and from the looks of the scopes, they're probably some poor fellow's deer rifles. I'm sure they paid him a fair price for them."

Bishop was familiar with the term "over watch" from his days in Afghanistan. He knew it described sentries or guards who occupied an elevated position so they could watch "over" the area for which they had responsibility. He continued to quiz Nick. "Where do you think they got all of their weapons?"

"Well, as people ran out of gas, or became stuck, the gangbangers drove down the grass median and took what they wanted at gun point. I watched them do it once. They had a couple of 4x4 trucks and would load several gunmen in the back. I imagine they would just repeat this same strategy a couple times a day to see what they could find. This *is* Texas, and people were leaving Houston because they were frightened, so they probably packed up all the guns and ammo they could carry."

Both men took a few sips of coffee, and Nick continued.

"The first week or so, we would hear shots several times a day. I remember one afternoon, some old boy must have put up one hell of a fight. It sounded like Baghdad on a Saturday night. I could make out at least four different calibers of weapons being fired. That firefight must have lasted a full hour and used up hundreds and hundreds of rounds."

Bishop smiled at the thought, "Being a highwayman in Texas is not a safe way to make a living."

"I don't know how many of the original gang members are still alive. The last few scouts we took out were younger men, 16 to 20 years old, and they carried a mix of weapons. We would have run out of ammo a week ago, but we ambushed a scout, and he had a Mini-14 with two full magazines."

Grandpa joined them for a cup of Joe, but didn't say much. He was going to relieve Kevin in a bit and was trying to wake up. Nick continued.

"The leader of the gang was a big dude they all called 'The Hefei' which is Spanish for 'The Boss.' This guy is not stupid. When they first arrived, he enforced some very tight discipline. He even beat the living shit out of one of his guys when he tried to steal candy from the station. Three days later, they took whatever they wanted, but early on, The Hefei was gathering his Intel."

"It sure seems like they organized quickly," Bishop replied. "He must be a pretty good leader to have scoped out the lay of the land and acted that fast. I wonder if some of these kids could make a difference if they had gotten started right. What could a guy like that do in the Army or running a business?"

Bishop sucked down the last few drops of his coffee, and then stood to go wash his cup. He turned to Nick and asked, "What if The Hefei lost his crown? What if he weren't available to lead? What would happen?"

Nick thought for a second, "I don't follow. You want to snipe him?"

"No, I'm thinking about kidnapping him, and the ransom is our free passage."

"Bishop, he has some serious lieutenants, and they may be glad to be rid of him. They might be thinking it's their turn to be The Hefei."

"Maybe, but most 'leaders' like that have some sort of insurance. They know where the money is hidden, or have the contact for the drugs or whatever. If he has ambitious lieutenants, I'm sure he keeps something back for a safety net - something important to them."

"How would we snatch him? We don't even know his habits or movements."

"I don't know. I don't think either of us have enough information. Let me show you something."

Bishop went to the truck and came back with the big .308 rifle. When he saw it, Nick's eyes were like a kid on Christmas morning. Watching Nick fondle the rifle, Bishop joked, "I am afraid my rifle is going to file a sexual harassment lawsuit against you. I'm glad you don't like Terri as much."

Both of them laughed and Nick said, "I only have a 10x scope on my rifle. With this big monster you have here, we can see twice as far. I think I know what's on your mind, and I bet I know just the place to do it."

Terri joined them at the fire, but didn't drink any coffee. She sat, rubbed her eyes, and looked around. She could tell from Bishop's face that he was deep in thought, so she decided to let him be, opening a package of the oatmeal. After her offers to share were politely declined, she proceeded to heat more water and make breakfast.

Bishop finally came out of his trance and looked up at her, "I have some bad news baby."

"What?"

"I'm not going to bathe for a while."

"Well, at least I got you nice and clean last night."

The Billboard

Nick and Bishop were moving quietly and quickly through the underbrush. Bishop had loaned Nick one of the night vision devices, allowing them to avoid entanglements and people. They were approaching the outer rings of the 'campers,' the people who had gotten stuck on I-10 and had nowhere else to go.

Nick had warned Bishop how heartbreaking it was to see fellow Americans living in conditions worse than most third world slums, but he was still shocked at what he saw. People had constructed shelter out of just about anything they could find. Cardboard, car hoods, and even suit cases had all been used. It was well past midnight, yet there were still a few dirty children moving around. Bishop watched as the kids stalked a grasshopper. One of them pounced and came up with the prize, holding up a large kicking insect for all her playmates to see. The little girl immediately ran back to a woman with frazzled hair and presented her with the bug. The woman rubbed the girl's head, took the insect, and threw it in a small pot that was sitting on the campfire. After stirring the pot with a stick, the woman moved back to her couch that looked like the front seat of a sedan.

Bishop and Nick moved easily around this group and headed closer to I-10. They tried to stay in the shadows, but there was little cover in the area. Bishop was looking at several trees that were completely stripped bare of all limbs and bark. They looked like raw, white telephone poles. When Nick noticed him staring at them, he mouthed the word "Firewood," and Bishop nodded.

They skirted several more groups of people and finally made it to the interstate. After listening for several minutes and scanning with the NVD, they scrambled up an embankment and took cover behind what used to be a guardrail. The wooden posts had been cut below the steel rail and above the ground for firewood. The rail, too heavy to use, was lying on the asphalt surface.

Bishop almost lost control of his stomach from the smell. The combination of burnt plastic, decomposing bodies, and other odors he couldn't identify was overwhelming. After ensuring he wasn't going to 'blow," his refocused, looking east and then west. The scene before them was unbelievably apocalyptic. Despite Nick's earlier warnings, Bishop couldn't stop staring. He was having trouble comprehending the devastation on the roadway.

Both sides of the great highway were packed with cars, trucks and vehicles of every kind. A few were on their sides, some flipped over completely with their wheels pointing skywards. Several had burned and practically all of them had the hood, truck and doors open, a sure sign they had been scavenged. The few gaps that didn't contain a vehicle were covered with broken glass and other debris. Directly in front of them was a semi-trailer from a furniture store with the delivery doors wide open. Piles of cloth, cushions and lampshades were strewn all around the trailer bed. Bishop imagined the wood from the furniture was now being used to cook grasshoppers. Any truck that even hinted of edible cargo had probably been looted first.

Nick tapped him on his shoulder and mouthed, "You okay?" Bishop nodded, mentally snapping out of it. Nick looked again in both directions and then moved out with the grace of a big cat. Bishop put his hand on the ground to shove off and felt something odd. He looked down to see a partially decomposed human arm under his gloved hand. He wasted no time in following Nick.

They were about one mile east of the exit and had to stay in the traffic lanes for cover. They moved from wreck, to rusted hulk, to overturned van for several minutes. Bishop was on one knee behind a car waiting on Nick to scout their next move. He heard glass crunch and spun his head toward the noise. He didn't need the night vision to see a rather large skinny dog with huge teeth. The animal seemed to think Bishop looked like a good meal. Bishop couldn't shoot the dog as the noise would give away their position and attract unwanted attention. He had his knife, but doubted he could reach it in time. The dog didn't growl or snarl, it just stared at Bishop with stone cold eyes. As Bishop started to stand upright, the animal sprang.

Bishop knew the animal would go for his throat. The average person has a survival reaction of throwing up an arm to block the leaping set of teeth coming at his windpipe. Bishop had the same reaction, but managed to use his rifle barrel instead. The dog's powerful jaws gripped the barrel instead of Bishop, and they both fell to the ground. Bishop landed on his back with the dog trying to tear the barrel out of his grip. The animal viciously jerked its head left and then right trying to remove this hard obstacle out of its way and get to the softer meat it could sense behind it. After failing to pull the rifle out of Bishop's hands, the dog let loose of the barrel and reared its head for a downward strike. Bishop's hand struck out and landed a strong blow at the dog's throat right below the jaw line. The animal paused, completely surprised, and Bishop struck again in the same place, only harder.

The animal twisted off Bishop and staggered back. It lowered its head and made a sound halfway between a cough and a gag. It looked over at Bishop and repeated the same sound. It staggered in a circle once and then fell to its side. Its last vision was of Bishop's arm striking downward holding his knife.

Bishop just lay on the ground trying to catch his breath. He started to sit up once, but only made it to an elbow. He heard a sound behind him, and somehow managed to spin around holding his knife out. Nick was standing about ten feet away, leaning against a truck cab. He knelt down by Bishop and whispered, "You alright?" Bishop nodded and kept drinking in air. Nick handed him a bottle of water, and Bishop managed a couple of mouthfuls between gasps. Nick helped him to his feet and waited a few minutes until Bishop gave him the thumbs up sign. Nick leaned close to Bishop's ear and whispered, "I have seen a lot of shit in my day, but that one takes the cake. Now is not the time, but later I'm going to have to know who the fuck you are." Before Bishop could respond, Nick was gone.

They played leapfrog using the wrecks as cover for almost a half mile before Nick stopped and pointed toward the sky. Bishop tilted his head and could barely make out a pole that seemed to disappear into the stars. Switching to night vision, he could make out the sign at the top, complete with a voluptuous woman advertising a steak house at this exit. Bishop leaned over to Nick and whispered, "We should go there sometime; they have an endless salad bar and prime rib on Tuesdays."

They made their way to the base of the big pole and were relieved no one had camped there. Bishop tapped Nick on the shoulder and whispered, "See you tomorrow," as he climbed up the ladder.

Bishop was not a big fan of heights. To be accurate, he had no problem with heights, or falling from them for that matter. It was the concept of *the landing* that bothered him. As he mounted the pole, he couldn't help but take in the view. He could see small fires blinking in the distance in all directions. When he reached the top, he encountered his first problem – the pole-ladder ended at a trap door that the climber would push up, proceeding to the narrow railing that surrounded the sign. The trap door was padlocked with a high quality, heavy-duty lock. Bishop did not have any tools with him and was not a burglar anyway. He looked around for a few minutes trying to decide what to do. He could always retreat back to the house and try to come up with another idea. The thought of having to do that made him mad. It was taking them forever to get out west, and he was sick and tired of the driving, killing, and living in constant fear.

Thinking about wasting yet another 24 hours affected his common sense. He looked from the ladder to the edge of the rail several times and kept thinking *I can make that*. He took off his pack and strapped it onto his chest. With one hand digging around inside, he fished out a roll of duct tape. He started to pull the tape, but the noise made him jump, and he almost dropped the roll. *Plan B*, he thought.

In the next few minutes, Bishop secured himself to the pole-ladder using his belt and made a makeshift rope from his pack straps. He managed to swing the pseudo-rope over the edge of the rail and pull himself up. He did a "chin up," threw a leg over the rail, and pulled himself over onto the steel mesh walkway surrounding the billboard. He was covered in sweat and just lay there for a bit. After a pause, he pulled his pack and rifle up and sat with his back to the billboard, partially covering the huge letter "E" in "Endless Salad Bar."

The sign had been designed for men to climb up the pole and change the advertising. The steel mesh "floor" that surrounded the big billboard was only 30 inches wide. Bishop was sure that the maintenance men had some sort of safety line that attached to the rail in order to work with less risk. He had no such line, so he walked slowly around to the other side and looked down at the buildings below.

As he surveyed the exit he thought, *this place was probably not one of the more popular stops, even during good times.* There were two gas stations on opposite corners, a fast food joint, a small hotel, and of course, the Steak House. A few other buildings were scattered up and down the road, but Bishop had no idea what they had been. The parking lot of every business in sight was packed with vehicles, except the hotel. On all sides of the hotel, it looked like the cars had been pushed by a bulldozer into a neighboring field.

He was about 80 feet in the air and less than three football fields from the closest building. The vantage point was perfect.

Bishop moved around to the other side of the billboard, pulling a box cutter knife from his pack. He carefully sliced the bottom 40 inches of the vinyl sign for about 10 feet in length. He slowly peeled it off, getting all of the "Endless Salad Bar" lettering. The irony of thousands of starving people looking up at an advertisement for a Steak House was not lost on him.

He rolled up "Endless Salad Bar" before going to the other side. He pulled out a bag of very sticky brown goo, pinesap gathered from a tree at Nick's. He used his finger to dab his 'glue' along the top of his Endless banner and stuck it in place over the top of the same lettering. He let the bottom of his attachment hang loose. After cutting a small hole at the bottom of each end of his banner, he threaded in a short piece of line with a fishing hook at each end. A quick test proved he could secure the bottom of the banner to the mesh floor to keep it from flapping in the wind. He took his pack and rifle and pushed them against the base of the sign under his "tent." Lifting the bottom up, he rolled underneath it with his back to the board. He had made a small "lean-to" and from almost any angle the sign would look normal even with Bishop hiding underneath it. If someone were to study it, they would assume the bottom had started to peel off or was just fraying out. He positioned his notebook, pencil, and scope right where he could reach them and cut a small slit in the vinyl to spy through. He then took his beef jerky and water and tucked them behind his back. He adjusted his pack to be a pillow and thought taking a short nap now would be wise.

He didn't think he had been asleep long when a distant popping noise woke him up. The noise repeated several more times, and it took his sleepy mind a few seconds to realize it was gunfire. He could make out three slightly different tones of the sound, which he assumed were different types of weapons. The noise continued on and off for almost 15 minutes, and then stopped. *Somebody is having a bad night*, he thought as he drifted back to sleep.

When he woke up, he had to urinate very badly and laughed at himself for not having a plan for that. He could pee through the wire mesh floor under him, but didn't know how far the urine would fly given the height and breeze that was blowing. The sun was just starting to rise, so it was light enough for anyone looking up to see. He figured he didn't have any choice, and undid his zipper. He slowly worked himself a little more sideways so that he could put the tip through an opening in the mesh floor. He relaxed and let it go, sighing with relief. He looked down to see his stream flowing with the wind at least 30 feet. *What an arch! This gives a whole new meaning to the term "pissing contest."*

There would be no hot coffee this morning, but he had a drink of water and chewed on beef jerky. He had taken the big scope off its rifle, and it was sitting next to his head. He looked at his watch, 6:40 a.m. He observed his surroundings in the daylight to get his bearings and make sure he had not missed anything significant during the night. He quickly noted that there were three over watch sentries. All three of The Hefei's men were on different rooftops, and within sight of each other. *Smart*.

For the rest of the morning, Bishop watched people wander around, noting nothing of interest. *This probably looks identical to what thousands of refugee camps have looked like throughout history.* He began sketching all of the buildings and their features. He also did his best to sketch the guards, noting the weapons and other equipment they carried. As he documented the scene below him, the gloom and suffering of the place seemed to fill his mind. He was watching two children roll a tire around in the dirt when both of them stopped their play and looked up. He moved the scope in the direction of their gaze, and what he saw was completely out of place.

Two young ladies were walking out of the hotel together and smoking cigarettes. They were clean, with well-coiffed hair and impeccable dress. They were both tall, attractive girls who looked like they just stepped out of the local shopping mall. They chatted while casually making their way to the fence surrounding the hotel swimming pool. Walking a step or two behind them were two men who were clearly bodyguards. Bishop could easily determine their function by how their heads were constantly looking around instead of eyeing the pretty girls beside them. The gals addressed another group of young men, pointing and issuing orders. Bishop was fascinated as he watched the men set up folding tables and chairs complete with red-checkered tablecloths. *We are going to have a picnic* he thought. Before long, a large barbeque grill was rolled out, and smoke was meandering skyward. *No, it's a good old fashion Sunday BBQ. I wonder if the coleslaw is any good.*

The aroma of the smoking meat drew quite a crowd from the neighboring campers, and they headed for the BBQ in droves. When Bishop looked back at the tables, he could see several men had formed a perimeter around the area to keep the gathering refugees away. Within an hour, the crowd surrounding the BBQ was several people deep. He didn't notice any pushing or shoving; it was as if everyone were standing and watching a parade. It wasn't long before the attention of the crowd turned toward the hotel again, and Bishop was rewarded with his first view of The Hefei.

The Hefei was a large Hispanic who Bishop estimated was 6'5" tall. He was wearing a pair of blue jeans and a sleeveless leather jacket. He was heavily muscled with a clean-shaven face and head. He walked out of a room and waved to the girls as Bishop recorded his room number in his notebook. The Hefei made his way down the stairs, and with a security contingent in tow, proceeded to the grill. *That's how he maintains control*, thought Bishop. *The man can smoke up a batch of ribs that just can't be beat.* Bishop noted the bodyguards, their numbers and their patterns.

After The Hefei made sure all was well at the grill, he walked over for what appeared to be a somewhat private conversation with his bodyguards. About that time, Bishop heard several engines start on the other side of the interstate. From his angle he couldn't see exactly where they came from, but all of a sudden eight motorcycles were heading for the underpass. They stopped right before going under the bridge that carried I-10 over the road. He couldn't see what was happening under the bridge, but after a few minutes, the bikers put their machines in gear and started heading toward the BBQ. Bishop watched as they came out from underneath I-10 on his side and proceeded to the hotel parking lot. The put their kickstands down and all but one of the bikers stood beside their machines, pulling their rifles around, but keeping them pointed down. The lead biker walked up to The Hefei and they sized each other up, exchanged a handshake then gave each other a less than enthusiastic shoulder to shoulder hug. They talked for a bit, and Bishop would have given anything to hear the conversation. He could tell from the body language of the guards on both sides that this was no picnic.

A door at the Steak House opened, and men started unloading boxes of food and what looked like freshly butchered racks of beef. The meat was thrown on the grill, and the side dishes were distributed to the tables. The Hefei continued to talk to the leader of the pack, and Bishop noticed several hand gestures by both men. This tête-à-tête continued for some time until The Hefei turned and waved in the direction of his hotel headquarters. A door to a room opened, and two men were shoved outside. Their hands were bound behind their backs, and Bishop could see they wore similar jackets to the bikers. The guards escorted them down the hotel stairs where they were brought before the two leaders.

The biker king turned and waved at the bridge. Someone yelled, and Bishop heard another engine start. A pickup truck began to follow the same route taken earlier by the bikers. In the back of the pickup truck were three men on their knees with hands tied behind their backs. *I am watching a prisoner exchange.*

The exchange was completed without incident, with the ex-prisoners hustled away from the party. *It's never good to have undesirables at such a nice social gathering.* The conversations continued until the meat was sufficiently charred, and then The Hefei and his guests ate voraciously while hundreds of starving people watched in silence. Bishop couldn't understand why everyone just stood there and watched. *I would at least walk away rather than be tortured like that.* The guards took turns eating and keeping the crowd back. As soon as everyone had their fill, it became clear why the crowd was standing around. The men who had set up the tables began gathering the paper plates full of scraps in their arms, and then throwing them into the crowd of refugees.

People scrambled, pushed, and shoved for the remnants of the meal. Bishop saw one older lady fall. Everyone just ignored her. The Hefei sat up in his chair and enjoyed the show. With the girls at his side, he would point and laugh at the fighting masses. It took ten minutes before the feeding frenzy was over and the crowd began to disperse.

Someone put on music, and the two girls moved to the table closest to The Hefei. They started dancing with each other and tried to get The Hefei to join them, but he waved them off. The girls then went around and danced for the bikers, who were hooting and hollering and reaching out to grab them. Someone brought out bottles of booze, and the biker king offered up a box of cigars.

Both groups drank, smoked, and watched the girls dance for almost an hour. Suddenly, The Hefei commanded the music be turned off and the mood became somber. The girls left and all but the most important people went and did other things. *It's time for a serious discussion by the big wigs.* Bishop watched the dialogue back and forth go on for almost 30 minutes. He couldn't hear what they were saying, but the body language and motions made it pretty clear. He was watching a peace conference, and you only had peace conferences if there were war.

An agreement seemed to be reached because suddenly handshakes were exchanged and hugs were more genuine. The underlings were waved back to the table area. More food and drink was brought out and the music started again. Bishop saw one of the hotel doors open, and the two girls came out, this time in bikinis. He could hear the hoots and whistles from the big, happy family all the way to his perch.

The girls didn't waste any time. After throwing back a few, they proceeded to work their way around the various clusters of bikers and bangers, dancing up a storm. It wasn't long before their tops were off, increasing the party's tempo. *Honestly Terri, I didn't know they were going to have strippers at the party.* The Hefei stood next to the biker king and waved the girls over. Both of them bounced over and got on their knees in front of the smiling lead biker. *Probably want to double check that he didn't drip any BBQ sauce on his jeans.* They proceeded to unzip the man's pants, and Bishop could see that they were each doing their best to impress him. After a few minutes, the biker looked up at The Hefei, pointed at the blond and nodded. The Hefei made a sweeping gesture with his hand that said, "Be my guest," and after a quick zipper adjustment, the happy biker and the blonde proceeded to a room. *Sometimes it's good to be King.*

The brunette sidled next to The Hefei, but he pushed her away and waved in the rival gang members who had been watching the show with great interest. The boys were hesitant at first, but then all seven of them strutted over, and The Hefei shoved the dark-haired girl at them. Bishop could see she was not happy about this, but at this point really didn't have any choice. The riders started groping her and passing her around, trying to kiss her, and touching anywhere they wanted. She started to fight, trying to walk off twice, but it was too late. Two of them picked her up, carrying her up the stairs, kicking all the way. All seven went into a room with the girl and closed the door. *It pays to be a winner.*

The Hefei rose up and began walking around, talking to the remaining men. Bishop studied the man closely and figured he was a natural leader. In the distance a horn started honking, and everyone tensed up. The guards moved in close around The Hefei, and the over watch shooters went on high alert. A pickup came into view on the road and was moving fast. The guards stopped it before it could even get close to The Hefei. A man was lying in the bed of the truck. Bishop could see that his leg was bleeding, and someone had applied a tourniquet. After some arm waving and heated conversation, the injured man was granted an audience with The Hefei.

Whoever he was, he must have had important information, because Bishop could see The Hefei listening intently. The leader waved over one of his guards, and a chair was pulled up for the injured fellow. Another guard rushed back with a map that was unfolded on the ground in front of them both. There was a lot of pointing at the map and various arm motions, while The Hefei seemed to pay particularly close attention. At one point The Hefei's head tilted slightly, almost quizzically. Immediately, the injured guest took The Hefei by the arm, steering him toward the corner of the hotel. When the newcomer reached out to touch The Hefei, Bishop thought the poor guy was a goner because all of the bodyguards raised their weapons immediately, but The Hefei settled them down.

Both men went to the corner of the hotel where the injured man pointed at the interstate to an abandoned school bus. Bishop watched in horror as the injured man flipped his flattened hand in the motion of "on its side." Bishop's heart froze. *He is telling The Hefei about a school bus lying on its side. Oh Jesus - Terri. The firefight he heard last night. This guy must have been shot in the fight and is telling the boss where it had happened.*

Bishop expected The Hefei to sound the war drums and gather up the braves, but he didn't. The biker king had finished his business and was ready to talk some more. His buddies were still nowhere to be seen. Bishop could just imagine The Hefei's frustration as the half-drunk biker bragged about his manly accomplishments with the girl. Bishop was sure The Hefei wanted to go collect scalps, but the war party would have to wait as he couldn't insult his guest. It was almost dark when the biker crew finally departed for their side of the bridge.

There was still enough light for Bishop to make out The Hefei talking to two of his men. He looked to the west at the sun, and then made the motion of "to hell with it" and pointed to the east as if to say, *we will hit them at sunup*.

Night Signs

The next few hours were the worst Bishop could ever remember. He was so worried about Terri he couldn't think straight, and lying in a fixed position for almost the entire day was giving his body fits. He had been tempted to sneak down the ladder before it got completely dark. It had taken all of his willpower to stay put.

When the light finally faded, Bishop began rushing to get back. He wasn't paying attention while swinging over the rail to the ladder, and a piece of his gear caught on the edge. Two fingers, barely hanging on, saved him from falling to certain death. The rush he received from the close encounter with his demise served to sharpen his focus, and kept him from taking any more dangerous short cuts.

It took him almost an hour to get back to Nick's house, and the closer he got, the more he dreaded bad news. He took a rock, whistled, and threw it on the roof of the house. That was the signal for, "I'm coming in, and please don't blow my head off." The rock had no more bounced off of the roof than Terri was running around the corner toward him. She almost knocked him over, jumping into his arms, kissing him over and over. He couldn't stop smiling, so relieved to see her unharmed. She finally came up for air, and started talking so quickly he had trouble understanding.

"Oh my God, Bishop, I'm so glad to see you. It was awful. Are you okay? They were everywhere. Did you see anything?"

It took Terri a bit to settle down. As they walked around the corner, Bishop looked at Kevin and Nick and instantly knew something was very wrong. "We lost Grandpa," was all they said.

Bishop replied, "I'm so sorry. Look, I don't want to be an ass, but we have to get out of here right now."

Nick and Kevin both perked up and looked at him.

"They're coming. You shot one of them, but he made it back and reported to the boss. They will be here in force and hit us at sunrise. We have to get moving."

Everyone immediately started scrambling around and loading the trucks. Nick's truck did not have a lot of diesel fuel left, but it ran fine. The boat had been unhitched long ago. Boxes, supplies, and virtually anything they could find was retrieved and loaded into the truck beds.

Bishop estimated they had less than an hour left when they were finally ready to go. He could see Nick and Kevin talking, and went over to make sure everything was okay.

"We can't find the keys."

"What?"

"You heard me - we can't find the keys to the truck."

Another mad scramble ensued with everyone looking everywhere for the keys. Bishop was sitting in the truck, bending down with his head craned for a view under the seat when he sat up and thought, *No, it can't be that simple*. He pulled down the visor, and the errant keys fell into his hands.

"Found them!"

Bishop had two monocles and couldn't decide how to distribute them. He figured there was enough moonlight so that Nick could follow Terri and him without headlights and not rear-end them. Terri left the driveway and turned away from I-10, heading back the way they had come. Bishop was in his normal position in the sunroof, scanning. They removed the brake, reverse, and dome light fuses from Nick's truck, so they could move without any lights giving away their position.

Bishop exhaled when they were a mile away. When they were 10 miles from the house, the sun poked through the clouds to the east. They found a trail leading back to a wooded area and pulled in to regroup and rest.

Everyone was burning adrenaline, so they set camp quickly. Hammocks were hung, tripwires set, and truck beds reorganized. They built a fire after Nick and Bishop scouted in all directions. Bishop savored that first taste of coffee. They ate a little breakfast, but Bishop was the only one really hungry. Terri made some oatmeal and dried beef. It wasn't half-bad, given the conditions.

They agreed on a schedule for sleep and keeping watch. Bishop got to close his eyes first and was mad as hell when he woke up seven hours later, Terri having taken his shift.

After stretching and more coffee, Bishop told everyone about his day on the billboard, leaving out the part about the girls. He displayed his sketches and answered questions for over an hour.

Nick and Terri told Bishop about the firefight and how Grandpa had died. "He was a retired Marine and died with a weapon in his hands," was all Nick said. Kevin was very quiet, but responded quickly when Nick asked him to do something. Bishop was worried about the boy, and so was Terri. She hung around him constantly and was always asking his help when doing so might take his mind off of things. He seemed not to mind.

When Kevin and Terri were out of earshot, Nick leaned over to Bishop and explained, "Terri shot the last one off of the top of Kevin. Both the attacker and Kevin had empty guns, and the guy was getting ready to bury his knife in my son's chest. Terri shot him seven times."

Oh shit, Bishop thought, *that's her first time."*

"She puked for ten minutes, and then just sat watching the fire for hours. I tried to comfort her, but hell, I'm divorced and don't understand women at all. Her coping with it right now is all an act. Keep an eye on her."

"Damn this world."

"Look partner, old war horses like us have enough trouble dealing with that shit. I remember the first time I was 100% sure I had killed a guy, I wanted to eat my own barrel and be done with it. The only thing that stopped me was the belief that my buddies needed me as much as I needed them. The other men in my platoon, the ones I had sweated, bled and suffered with, were depending on me. You need to make sure she understands you need her. End of marriage counseling session – I'll send you my bill."

Bishop thought it over for a bit. "I don't know about women, but you don't do so bad with people, Counselor."

They sat quietly and poked sticks in the fire. Terri and Kevin were busily making something on one of the open truck gates, whispering the entire time. Bishop finally looked up and said, "Nick, we are going to start a war."

Nick's face didn't react at all. "Now *that* sounds like fun."

Starting a war

There is a ritual involved when preparing to go into harm's way and any man who has ever readied himself for battle has experienced it. In reality, all of the equipment plays a dual role – it is essential for the fighter, as much as for the fighting. Regardless of a handmade bow with a quiver full of arrows, or an M4 rifle with a chest rig full of magazines, men who were about to go into combat have always taken some measure of comfort from their kit. The countless hours of training extrude a confidence with the tools of the trade. Sometimes, that confidence can be the difference between life and death.

In an odd sort of way, preparing for a fight was not much different than preparing to ride out a hurricane or survive an earthquake. Lists are made, equipment is secured, and everything is checked for readiness two or three times. While an approaching storm would require having enough food, an approaching gunfight requires enough ammunition. Items like medical kits, a good knife, water, batteries, and food are essential in either situation.

Bishop was not as experienced as Nick, who after many years in a wartime army, had "loaded up" many times. Despite the gap in their experience, both men knew their lives would depend on each other. Their mood was professional, quiet, and focused on helping one another. Straps were pulled so tight they caused pain. Pouches and bags were pulled, thumped, yanked and slapped. Nothing could make noise or fall off. After they had strapped on over 30 pounds of equipment each, they donned goggles and masks. When they were finished suiting up, they would have made a great recruiting poster for any Special Forces unit in the world.

Bishop looked over at Kevin, who was watching their every move. He kept thinking that if he messed up, he might be responsible for the boy's father not making it back. *I wonder if Nick is looking at Terri and thinking the same thing.* Bishop knew he had done all right at the Brazos River, but this was going to be a much more complex operation. He had to work with another man, not alone. Another difference was that they would be moving quickly and executing a "hit and run" type of attack. At the river, he had remained stationary for most of the fight. Nick seemed to have sensed Bishop's self-doubt. He grabbed Bishop's shoulder and in a low voice said, "If you *don't* have doubts, you are dangerous. It's the guys who are cocky that fuck up. Let's go kick some ass."

Bishop and Nick were in full "Jedi Knight" mode as they approached I-10. Their route took them under the Endless Salad Bar sign, and Bishop made a note to tell Nick about his pissing contest when they made it back. They crossed I-10, making their way to the Biker's side, and then headed for what Bishop thought was the Biker's headquarters. It really wasn't that hard to find - they only had to follow the music. They approached a single story block building that had once been a small pub.

The biker bunch has posted sentries at the expected places, but Nick was suspicious. "They could not have held off The Hefei and his boys with this level of security. We have to be missing something." Bishop agreed, and they took their time scanning and scouting the area. At one point, Bishop stopped and listened to the voices coming from the building. He heard the normal laughter and background voice noise you would expect when eavesdropping on a party. He almost laughed out loud when he heard a voice yell, just above the others, "The soldier told the Major, you use the camel to ride into town, sir!" followed by a lot of laughter. Bishop knew that joke, and it was a pretty good one at that. After an hour of searching, they couldn't find a single tripwire, hidden guard or even a stray mousetrap anywhere. Besides the four men with rifles at each corner of biker headquarters, they couldn't locate any other security. Bishop whispered, "Peace Dividend?"

"I don't buy it. Remember that old saying - if it's going well you are walking into an ambush."

"I just can't see anything else."

"We are not in a big rush here. Let's look around one more time."

They made another full circle of the building and found nothing. "I don't get it, but we have to do this now. "

Their plan was to kill the guards, bust in the door, and shoot the place up. Simple, effective, and no doubt, the Biker Army would blame the Banger Army; and war would be on. The Biker hive had about 30 meters of open space they would have to cross. Each corner guard was within the line of sight of two others. The problem for the guards was they could only be looking one direction at a time. The problem for Nick and Bishop was they could not be sure which direction the guard was looking. It there had been any reasonable light, it wouldn't have been difficult, but there were only shadows from what looked to be a few candles inside of the building, and all of the curtains were closed.

Nick looked at Bishop and whispered, "Ready?"

Bishop looked around a few more seconds and started to reply when he heard, "The soldier told the Major, you use the camel to ride into town, sir!" with the same voice and the same laughter following it.

"Hold!"

Nick gave Bishop a questioning look, and Bishop waved him back. They retreated about 50 meters away from the building, and Bishop explained what he had heard.

Nick shook his head, "Well those clever bastards. Who would have thought they were that smart? A decoy building as a diversion, complete with repeating sound track - how cute."

"Don't go getting all high and mighty, we almost fell for it."

"Good point."

Knowing there was a decoy changed what they were looking for, and it did not take them long to find the *real* Biker headquarters. What gave it away was the smell of urine, as most of the boys just went out back and relieved themselves. They had originally bypassed the building because it looked unoccupied. Boards covered broken glass in the windows and a quick glance indicated black, hollow windows with collapsed timbers hanging inside. When they encountered the heavy odor of urine, they studied the building carefully and realized it was all a façade. The windows were covered with paintings of a collapsed interior. The broken glass was painted on as well. It was not five minutes before a light suddenly appeared out back when a door opened and closed quickly. One of the bikers was delivering a bag of sandwiches to the guards over at the decoy.

Bishop watched as the man walked toward the decoy structure, and noted the guy stopped some distance away from the guards. The sandwich delivery boy whistled, and then threw the bag over 20 feet to the nearest sentry. Bishop thought it odd the guy didn't just walk up and hand over the meal. *Why was he being so careful about approaching that building?*

Once they had confirmed they had the correct hideout, finding the real security should have been easy. They found the first two quick enough, and thought they had the entire layout in their minds, but Nick stopped them again. "This just is not right. They wouldn't leave one entire side of their main quarters exposed like that. We are missing something."

"I agree. Let's take another look."

The unguarded side of the biker nest faced a slight slope. There were two overflowing dumpsters about 50 meters away, a small strand of trees just beyond the dumpsters, and then a pile of wooden pallets at 110 meters. Bishop scanned all three of the possible hiding places and saw nothing. They split up and approached the dumpsters from the rear on opposite sides. Despite the stench, they peeked around the dumpsters and found nothing but rotting trash. The strand of trees was next, and it proved empty as well. They spread out again and approached the stack of pallets from the rear. They got as close as they could without any potential sentry hearing them and visually searched every bit of the random scraps of wood. They looked at each other with questioning eyes. They were about to move off again, when Nick snapped his fist up in a motion that meant "Hold."

Bishop froze, watching Nick, who handed Bishop his rifle and pulled out his knife. He started crawling on his belly toward a pallet that was lying slightly off from the pile. Bishop could tell where he was going and wanted to be ready to help, but there was nothing there except a pallet lying on the dirt. *Dirt? Why was there dirt? There was grass everywhere else.* Bishop watched as ever so slowly, Nick approached the pallet. When he was almost on top of it, he reached out to the dirt and pushed down with his fingers. They sank easily into the soft soil. Nick moved his hand six inches and gently probed again. His fingers sank into the dirt as easily as if he were dipping them in water. He turned and looked at Bishop and spun his finger in the air. *Is there anyone around?* Bishop did a complete 360-degree check with the NVD and saw no one. He looked back at Nick and gave him the thumbs up.

In almost one movement, Nick pulled back a piece of cardboard, lightly covered in dirt, and struck downwards with his knife, one, two, three stabs in a flash. He rolled off and caught his breath. Bishop kept watching the area with his NVD, waiting for any reaction. None came.

The sentry was in a shallow trench covered to look like the surrounding ground. Often referred to as a "spider hole," a man would lie in the trough keeping watch through a narrow opening. Using a spider hole had it advantages, as a well-constructed hide was almost impossible to detect. It also had is disadvantages in that the man in the hole had very limited peripheral vision. Nick had just demonstrated the results of what could happen if the hide were discovered.

While Nick caught his breath, Bishop grabbed the dead guy by the boots and dragged him behind the main stack of the pallets. Nick repaired the spider hole so it would appear as before, and then joined Bishop.

Bishop looked up and shook his head. He whispered, "No jacket on this one. No colors. Damn glad you saw him though. If he had any skill with that rifle, we would have been easy meat when we hit that building."

Nick held up the rifle he had pulled from the hole. It was a military style bolt-action sniper rifle with a pretty good scope. They searched the body, and Nick pocketed about 20 rounds of .308. Nick pulled up the guy's sleeve during the search and tapped Bishop on the shoulder. Bishop looked down and saw a tattoo on the dead man's arm that said, "1S1K." One Shot One Kill was the motto of military snipers. *We were very, very lucky.*

Bishop moved off toward the next sentry, who was lying on the roof of a small outbuilding. Bishop had detected him because the guard kept moving. In the three minutes Bishop had observed him, the guy had scratched his head at least four times. Most sentries, when taking cover on a roof, are concerned about someone coming up behind them. It's very common to set up a tripwire to avoid being surprised from behind. As Bishop went to the ladder leaning on the side of the building, he looked it over very carefully. When he saw the tripwire, he almost laughed. On the fourth rung from the top, there was a piece of string which was tied to a beer can, no doubt full of rocks. Bishop would've found that one even without the NVD.

He slowly climbed the ladder, shifting his weight on each step very carefully. When he got to the top, he stood on his toes and peeked over. He really couldn't see anything, so he raised the NVD and took another look. He saw a man, lying on his side, not moving at all. Scattered all over the roof were beer cans. The man made a noise and Bishop ducked down. He heard the same noise again. The guy was snoring.

Bishop now had both a moral problem and a technical problem. The technical problem was the beer cans all over the roof would make it very difficult to approach the man without making noise. The moral problem was in killing a drunken, sleeping man. *No wonder the guy had been scratching, he was lying in a pool of beer.*

Bishop knew that despite what people watched on TV, knocking a man unconscious was very difficult. There were only a few areas of the skull where a blow would do that, and most of those caused permanent damage. Bishop did not know where or how hard to hit a man to knock him out – just something he had ever learned.

Another myth was that you could cover someone's mouth, and he would not be able to make noise. In a training class at HBR, an instructor had asked the students to cover their mouths and then try to make noise. While the yelling was not as loud, it sure wasn't quiet by any means. Bishop decided to let Rip Van Winkle have his beauty rest, but would disable him from causing any problem.

Bishop climbed up onto the roof, and carefully plotted his path to the sleeping biker. He slowly reached down, picked up each beer can, and set them upright so they would not roll around and make noise. It took him three minutes to make the 12 feet to the guard. *At least the cans are stacked neatly now.* Beside the now loudly snoring man was an AR15 rifle. Bishop could take the magazine out, but the old drunk might have more ammunition on him. Instead, he picked up the rifle and pushed out the hinge pin. With the entire inner workings exposed, he pulled the charging handle back and then removed the bolt carrier group. He pulled the retaining pin, and the firing pin dropped into his hand. He put it in his pocket, and reassembled the rifle in less than 10 seconds. *That will drive him crazy trying to get that weapon to fire.*

Bishop carefully laid down the rifle and got off the roof.

At the same time Bishop was stacking beer cans, Nick went after the third sentry. They had detected the man from his body odor. He was in a tree on the north side of the building. Through the night vision, Nick could see someone had nailed three boards together to make a nice little tree house. *They probably put him up there because this dude stinks to high heaven.* One problem with being in a tree is that several angles are normally blocked from view. The other issue is that falling can hurt like hell. Nick worked his way quietly to the base of the tree where the man could not see him because of the trunk. He stopped, and said in a challenging voice, "Hey fuckstick, you awake?"

The guy looked in the direction of the voice coming from the ground. But Nick moved just a little and the trunk obscured his view. "Yeah, who is that?"

"The boss wants to see ya – right fucking now." Nick said in a gruff voice. "You been doing his old lady or something?"

"Fuck you and him. Who is that?" The guy leaned out just a little more to see who it was. Nick sprung around the tree, grabbed the sentry's leg, and pulled hard. The biker fell out of his tree house, hitting his head on the way down. He landed flat on his back with a thump and a loud "whoosh" as the air was knocked out of his lungs.

Nick was over him immediately and put the barrel of his rifle in the guy's mouth, "It's just little ole me," he whispered menacingly.

Nick made sure his new friend was absolutely certain making *any* sound would result in a painful death. The guard's hands were bound with a nylon tie. When Bishop appeared, Nick had the guy on his knees, facing the tree. Nick pointed to the back of the biker's jacket and then held up a scrap of the patch he had cut off. It was a critical part of their plan.

"Ready?"

"Ready." Nick took his knife and held it under the biker's throat, then let the knife slide straight down, cutting his shirt right down the middle. Nick took a long piece of the cloth and used it as a blindfold on their prisoner, then commanded him to stand up. They guided him toward the fake headquarters, pointed him in the right direction and instructed him to start walking. He was told that if he stopped, he would be shot in the back. The Biker started walking toward the fake HQ while Nick went prone and waited. Bishop trotted back to the real headquarters and took cover in a small strand of trees.

The blindfolded guy kept walking toward the decoy and got to within 35 feet before one of the guards challenged him. "Who is that?" The blindfolded man didn't know what to do. As far as he knew, the guy who had pulled him from the tree was right next to him. He decided to keep walking and not say anything.

The guard could see the outline of someone approaching. He didn't want to shoot one of his brothers, but the guy was walking dangerously close to the pits. When the blindfolded guy was at about 25 feet, the guard could clearly see it was Joe, but what the hell was he doing? "Joe, stop, man. Stop!" he yelled.

Three things happened in quick sequence. First of all, the guard turned to run. Almost simultaneously, Joe stepped in the pit, which was actually a trench about 30 inches wide and covered with sod so it would blend in. In the trench was a simple tripwire, which connected to a three-bottle set of propane in the house. The strategy was that if an intruder stepped in the pit, he would engage the wire and set off the trap. The third event was the destruction of the decoy building, which exploded in a loud, bright ball of flame. Nick promptly shot the other guards, who had been blown away from the building and were trying to get up.

Bishop felt the heat from the blast almost 150 meters away. He brought the ACR up to his cheek and noticed he now had a nice silhouette of the real headquarters in his rifle's sight, thanks to the burning decoy. It took almost 20 seconds before the back door flew open, and two men came running out with rifles. They didn't make it more than three steps. Bishop saw two of the window paintings come down, and moved his aim to about six inches above the top of the foundation.

Bishop knew that most people go prone when bullets start flying into a room. It is just a natural instinct to "get down." Even if someone remained standing or hiding behind cover, the rounds coming through just above the floor could break ankles and legs.

He started pouring fire into the building at that low level. He emptied a magazine of 29 rounds, hit the ejection button and slapped another in. The empty went into his dump pouch. He noticed Nick was now at his right and had started working rounds into the building as well.

The two men fired four magazines each and then took off. On their way past the still burning decoy, Nick threw the shells he had taken from the sniper into the fire. He could hear them start to cook off as they made their getaway. The cooking rounds would give pause to anyone who might decide to chase them.

Most guys would call it a night and head home, but their plan was only half-complete. They went straight along I-10 on the biker side for about one mile, running all the way, and then crossed over to the banger's side. They avoided the campers, who were also looking toward the now raging fires. Nick and Bishop started their approach to the Hefei's hotel.

Bishop had sketched the field of cars, next to the hotel parking lot, in as much detail as he could while under Endless Salad Bar. He and Nick approached the hotel from that direction, using the rusting hulks as cover. Through the NVD, they could see the closet guard was looking at the fire on the other side of the expressway and not in their direction. *After all, it wasn't every day you got to watch a big fire over at your enemy's camp.* Bishop and Nick moved in close, raised up in unison and opened up with their rifles.

They knocked the closest guard down and then charged into the hotel's parking lot, shooting anything that moved. They probably didn't hit much, but that was not the goal. Once inside of the perimeter, the over watch guards on the roofs couldn't tell friend from foe. The guards could only see swirling shadows and outlines of people running around and shooting. Bishop had identified the weakness in the Hefei's security almost immediately. Now the bangers were paying the price of relying too much on roof top sentries.

Bishop had guessed that most of the guards lived in the hotel, so he and Nick pounded relentless fire into the rooms. *I wouldn't want to be in that hotel.* While movies and television shows portray walls that stop bullets, in reality, they don't. Bishop knew their rounds were blowing through walls, doors, and air conditioners. Many of the bullets probably came out the back of the structure. The inside of those rooms had to be living hell. In addition to the hot lead coming through the walls, there would be glass, wood splinters, chunks of concrete and other projectiles looking to find human flesh. They ran from place to place just laying down fire and then moving again. People were running, screaming and shooting all over the area. It was utter chaos.

Using a full magazine, Bishop gave The Hefei's room special attention. *This will teach you not to invite us to the BBQ.*

After they had emptied eight magazines each, they retreated back into the field of cars. As suddenly as they had appeared, they were gone. Bishop knew they had done well because the shooting kept going for 15 minutes after they disappeared into the night. He hoped the bangers were chopping each other to bits. When they were well clear of the area, Bishop asked Nick if he had planted the biker's patch, removed from the sentry on the other side. Nick nodded. "They can't miss it."

Bishop and Nick made it back to the camp right at sunrise. Terri was up already, having relieved Kevin for the watch. The two men came into camp as giddy as two schoolboys that had just perused their first playboy in dad's dresser drawer. They were smiling, laughing and full of "you should have seen Bishop when that guy" and "you should have seen Nick when he" remarks. They each grabbed something to eat, and began cleaning weapons and refilling magazines. They had used almost 700 rounds between them, and Bishop thought it had been a good investment.

Terri knew both men were putting on an act. Their matter-of-fact behavior, after just having taken several human lives, was a mutual support system used to avoid thinking about the ramifications of their actions. They could look at each other and say, "He is not showing remorse or doubt, so it must be okay." She had watched Bishop after he had been forced to kill and knew it troubled him deeply. She had seen the change in her husband, and knew that all of this was going to come back and haunt him one day. *I just hope we can help each other get through it.*

Battery Management

They remained at their camp for two more days. Nick and Bishop were planning a scouting trip to I-10 and the intersection to see if their attempt to initiate a war had worked. There was a chance they would have to irritate the two parties again.

Bishop was going through his battery management routine. Each rifle used at least one battery, with a couple of them taking three different sizes. A weapon's mounted flashlight, holographic optic, and illuminated reticle scope all required different sized batteries. They NVD took batteries as well. The two that Bishop owned, purchased at different times, required different sizes. Even his pistols, which had laser pointers in the grip, required batteries. Fortunately for Bishop, the electronics industry had a limited number of options available so he only had to manage three different sizes of batteries.

He and Terri had been on one of their first trips together to "The Ranch" when he first realized there was a problem with batteries. He went on an early morning trip to see what kind of wildlife was still in the area and the density of their population. He brought his first NVD along to see how it performed in the field. He left their campsite early and was using the device to climb a narrow trail where a misstep could lead to a nasty fall. Of course, the NVD went blank at the worst possible moment, and he had to stop right where he was. He kept spares in his kit, and dug around until he found them. Over the course of the next few minutes, he managed to lose both his rifle and the battery cover for the NVD. The rifle tumbled down 30 feet, banging his very expensive optics on sharp rocks all the way to the bottom. He couldn't find the battery cover either.

He went back to the camp, stumbling around in the dark on the way, and managed to tear his pants in the process. At first light of day, he began the search for his weapon and battery cover. He spent almost all day to recover the weapon, and he never did find the NVD cover.

During the ordeal, he discovered that all of the new batteries stored in his kit were worthless. His sweat had soaked the packaging over the last few months, and they all had corroded.

That little adventure was not lost on Bishop. Thinking more about his teams at work than personal survival, he later had written a battery management and storage procedure for KBR that received a positive review from The Colonel.

On their way back from the ranch, they stopped at a very high-end camping store to take a break from the road. Bishop was wandering around when he found a "Universal Solar Battery Charger." The product was a solar panel that rolled up like a tiny sleeping bag. It was about the size of a pillowcase and contained two wires which connected to a small case where the dead batteries were to be placed. The product came with several adapters to handle different sized batteries.

After the typical married couple exchange over cost justification, he purchased the product along with two new shirts for Terri as a counter balance. After all, the shirts *were* on sale. That shopping trip almost spiraled out of control when he snuck into the ladies changing room and attempted to "molest" Terri in the little booth. The timing of his entry was perfect as she was pulling a top over her eyes. Of course Terri screamed, alerting a rather butch female store employee who charged in and proceeded to whoop Bishop's ass thinking he was a pervert. *That woman had zero sense of humor or romance.*

When they had returned home, Bishop started testing the little solar charger, and it worked well. He created a spreadsheet of each type of battery required and went through all of the manuals to find the expected battery life of each device. Some searching on the net provided a source of rechargeable batteries. He entered the number of "charging cycles" each size of could withstand and purchased enough battery inventory to last 50 years. He used small waterproof plastic bottles to store his rechargeable batteries.

Bishop spread the solar charging panel out on the hood of the truck and started charging the batteries he had been using the last few days. The night vision was the biggest battery hog, and he and Terri had been using it almost constantly since they had left Houston. Every other morning he had been exchanging their batteries and recharging the drained ones. His HBR procedure had recommended all security personnel learn to change the batteries in their devices at night. He could replace the NVD batteries with his eyes closed.

Kevin was sleeping, and Terri was taking count of their food and water while Nick was on watch. Nick had a radio with him, and Bishop set the other radio on the hood and turned up the volume so he could hear it as he moved around camp.

"Hey! I have activity on the road...anyone there?"

Bishop ran to the radio and keyed it, "Camp here."

"I hear engines...lots of engines coming down the road. I can't see anything yet, but something is happening."

"On my way..."

Bishop grabbed his armor, vest and rifle as Terri woke up Kevin. Bishop ran about 100 meters to the road, and as he approached where he thought Nick was hiding, he could hear the engine noise himself.

He couldn't find Nick, but then saw an arm waving about 20 feet away. *Damn Ghillie suit, I might have tripped over him and hurt myself.* Bishop ran over and went prone next to Nick.

"Rovers?"

"I don't know. I have never have seen Rovers use more than one vehicle at a time."

They were in a wooded area that overlooked the road slightly below them. In about a minute, they saw three motorcycles, followed by a pickup truck, then two more motorcycles and another pickup truck. *What the hell*, thought Bishop, *we are on the gangbanger's side of I-10. How did these guys get through?*

As Bishop and Nick watched, the convoy passed slowly in front of them. Two of the lead riders wore bloody bandages. The first pickup had boxes, black trash bags and gas cans in the back. The next two riders passed, and then they saw three men with more bloody bandages lying in the back of the second pickup truck. The little parade passed by and proceeded north.

They listened for a few more minutes as the sound of the convoy faded away. Nick and Bishop radioed Terri and Kevin and gave them a quick report so they could relax a bit. The two men followed the convoy on foot for almost a mile to make sure they were gone.

When they got back to camp, Bishop said, "I don't understand. The head biker guy was not with them and they were on the wrong side of I-10. How did they get through? Why would they leave if they had won the war? I need to know what is going on up there."

Nick agreed, and they started making plans for yet another trip to the I-10 exit they had both started calling Gettysburg.

Gettysburg

That night, as Bishop and Nick approached the interstate, they noticed the smell of something burning even before they could see any flames. They decided to go up on the interstate about a mile east of the exit and work their way down to where they could see the underpass. Bishop had remounted his scope on the big rifle, but was unsure if it were still zeroed in. They could see the glow of larger fires on both sides as they got close to the exit. Hundreds of people remained in the area with their makeshift camps. Bishop first noticed the hotel burning. It was down to its block walls with one of them collapsed. The Steak House was smoldering, nothing but a heap of blackened wood and coals. They worked their way down the line of cars stranded on the exit ramp and didn't see any soldiers from either side. Bishop wanted to get a good look under the bridge to see if the roadblock remained. As they continued down the ramp, he saw three men, all with rifles, standing by the underpass. He studied them, trying to determine which side they were from. He could not see any biker colors. They looked ragged and older than any of the gang's soldiers.

Bishop whispered to Nick what he was going to do. Nick reminded him that it was "his life, but he would take good care of Terri." Bishop cracked a smile, shook his head, and moved off.

Bishop swung his weapon around to his back, stood up, and started walking toward the three men. When they finally saw him approaching, they showed no concern. He walked up and said, "Hey."

One of the three nodded, and the other two replied, "Hey," back.

Bishop continued, "I've been off in the woods for a few days trying to scrounge up some meat. I got back a little bit ago, and the whole world has changed. What happened?"

"You missed the battle?"

"Battle?"

"Yeah, the Northerners attacked the Southerners two nights ago. It went back and forth until this morning. Both sides hurt each other so bad, they all just packed up and left. A couple of the boys and I were picking up rifles from the dead because we wanted some payback for all their shit. I think they knew we were sick and tired of being fed scraps like a bunch of animals, and they all lit out of here."

"So the road is open?"

"Hell yeah, you can walk to the ruins on this side or that side all ya want. I see you have a gun. If they come back, will you help us?"

"I'm not much good with it. I never did get any meat, but I will help if I'm still around. I have family a few miles south of here, and I've been waiting to get through."

Bishop left the three men with a big smile on his face and started walking back down the road directly toward his camp. No need to bypass any guard posts, worry about over watch shooters, or be concerned with running into roaming guards.

Nick appeared out of the darkness at his side and was smiling.

"Damn it's good to live in a free country again."

Crossing a free I-10

After they returned to camp, everyone started packing up and arranging their dwindling supplies. Bishop noticed Kevin and Nick were engaged in a very serious discussion and figured he would not interrupt them.

Terri had managed to wash a set of clothes for each of them in a nearby stream. Bishop stood in the shallow water and bathed, shaved and brushed his teeth. He felt like a new man, and Terri commented that she might be able to stand being in the truck with him again.

When he returned to camp, Nick walked over, "Kevin and I have talked it over. We are going to stay."

"What? Stay where?"

"We are going to stay at the exit. We only have a little diesel left in the truck, and we have decided that we want to stay and help these people reorganize and make things a little better. I don't have any place to go, and even if we found diesel, we would double your problems out west – we eat a lot."

"We would figure it out. We could make it work somehow."

"No sir, our minds are made up. I am sick of hiding and sneaking around. I want Kevin to meet some nice girl and live as close to a normal life as we can make out of this shithole. I think I can help those men at the bridge, and I'm worried that if they don't organize quickly, some other group will take charge, and that could even make the situation worse than it was before. We are staying right here and holding our ground."

Bishop and Terri both tried to persuade Nick to stay, but he remained stubborn. They were ready to go with about three hours of daylight left. After hugs, handshakes, goodbyes and tears, they pulled out of the camp and headed for the I-10 underpass that had changed all of their lives forever.

Central Texas - September 16, 2015

The landscape was changing as they headed south. It was becoming flatter and dryer with far fewer trees. Through the NVD, Bishop could not tell how far he could see, but the open country provided for far greater visibility than any they had traveled so far. He was trying to decide if that were a good thing or a bad thing when Terri's voice sounded with serious concern, "Bishop, I think there is a police car ahead of us."

Bishop snapped his head around and instantly saw two red flashing lights in the distance.

He told Terri to slow down, but she already let her foot off the gas, and the truck was losing momentum. Bishop tried to judge how far ahead the lights were, but couldn't.

Terri, to conserve gas, let the truck coast to a complete stop. Bishop never took his eyes off the lights trying to figure out what they were.

"I don't think that is a police car. They are flashing too slowly. Police lights are normally faster than that."

Terri thought out loud, "Fire truck? Ambulance?"

Bishop shook his head, "I don't know. Let me get the big rifle."

After Bishop retrieved his rifle, he propped it onto the side mirror and studied the lights with the scope's 24x magnification. He lowered the rifle and said, "They are blinking intersection lights. That doesn't make any sense. There is no road on the map or the GPS. We haven't seen electricity for days and there are no other lights on the horizon, so why would only those lights have juice?"

Terri offered, "Maybe it's a red light district? If you smelled a little better you might be able to get a date."

Bishop laughed out loud.

He set the big rifle in the seat beside him and popped his head out the top again with the night vision. Terri started moving the truck forward very slowly. It felt like it took forever for them to get closer to the red lights. When they could clearly see the poles and wires over the roadway, they coasted to a stop.

Bishop got out and began walking toward the lights when he noticed a road sign that said, "School Zone Ahead."

He continued until he was standing under the flashers and saw that they were suspended above a new driveway that branched off of the main road. The driveway led to a sign that said, "Future Home of the Mustangs. Your tax dollars at work - Scheduled Completion 2016."

He remained puzzled by the electrical power and soon discovered a solar charging system was on the other side of one of the poles.

As Bishop walked back to the truck, he could see Terri standing beside it, stretching and completely exposed. He thought, *we have to get to West Texas soon. We are getting tired, sloppy and careless.*

They both got in the truck, and Bishop teased, "You were right, it was a Bordello."

"Sure didn't take you very long," Terri remarked with a mildly sassy tone to her voice.

"Well babe – it has been a while."

He explained to Terri what he had found and added, "I don't think the Mustangs are going to have a good season this year."

They passed the future home of the Mustangs and Bishop started thinking about the solar panels and the lights. *Things must not be so desperate around here or those would have been looted days ago. It's not as if the locals can't see them.*

As they proceeded south, the population density continued to decrease with every mile. There were not many options for roads either. Bishop asked Terri how she was doing and she replied that she "could use a break."

They stopped, took a "rest area" break and grabbed a quick snack. The sun was peeking over the horizon, and it would be full light soon. As Bishop looked around, he could see only flat land all the way to the horizon. The vegetation ranged from none to patches of scrub oak and clusters of knee high cactus. There was not a phone line or power cable in sight. This was open grazing country, where the cattle's brand was a sign of ownership, not a fence.

Bishop opened the atlas on the hood of the truck and studied it while he ate dried fruit and beef jerky. He frowned, looked around, and turned to Terri, "No place to hide."

Terri gazed over the land and hooked her thumbs in her pockets. In her best cowboy twang she observed, "Sure would be hard to bushwhack us round these parts."

They were soon on their way having decided to chance driving during the day. As they approached their next turn, Bishop saw a sign that read "Road Closed Ahead" and grumbled an annoyed "Shit." When they reached their turn, sawhorses and orange cones blocked their route. A small sign read, "Bridge Out."

Bishop didn't want to believe it, so he moved two of the sawhorses, and they continued down the allegedly closed road. About two miles ahead, they ran into another large group of sawhorses and cones. Sure enough, the bridge over a small, impassable wash was no longer in existence. The road simply ended in what appeared to be a giant bicycle ramp.

"Bishop, if you want to try and jump that, I'll let you drive while I walk across."

"I always wanted a cool name like Evil. Maybe this is my big chance?"

They got out and Bishop checked to see if their 4x4 could make it across the dry wash, but it was too risky. Stones slightly larger than a basketball covered the bottom, and busting an axle on the truck would mean the end of their journey. Even if they did make it across the rocks, he was unsure about climbing the opposite bank.

They were comfortable spending the day there, until Bishop found fresh ATV tracks while checking the wash. Someone had recently been in the area, perhaps hunting feral hog. "Terri, that road we were on runs right into Brewster, Texas. According to the Texas Tour Guide, Brewster is a bustling metropolis of 348 nice people and one old sour head. It has a gas station, a post office, one café, and a combination hardware and feed store."

"I wonder if the restroom is clean at the gas station."

"I think we need to risk staying here. I'm too tired to think straight and need some sleep. Let's pull the truck over there."

"What about the hog hunter and the ATV tracks?"

"I have an idea."

They pulled the truck off of the road into a small strand of scrub. Bishop pulled his machete out and began to hack off short branches of the small oak trees that spotted the area. After about an hour, he had a small pile at the front of the truck.

He hunted in the back for a bit and came out with a large cargo net. He held it up to Terri and said, "Nothing up my sleeve," but received no reaction from her. *Clearly she is tired and doesn't appreciate my sophisticated humor.*

Bishop poured water on the coal black net and rolled it around in the dirt with his boot. He poured a little water on the truck and threw several carefully filtered handfuls of dirt on the truck. Terri observed, "I bet you liked to play in mud as a boy."

He began weaving the branches into the net, and Terri came over to help him finish the pile. They carefully draped it over the truck and then walked off a bit to view their handiwork.

Terri couldn't believe it. From more than 50 feet away, the truck was almost invisible.

They anchored a hammock between the back of the truck and a scrub oak that barely held the weight. Bishop made a sunshade, and they were set. They took turns sleeping and keeping watch the rest of the day.

When the sun started to set, they both took a quick sponge bath to remove the coating of sweat caused by sleeping in the heat of the day and proceeded to pack everything up.

Bishop checked the gas and was not surprised to see they were down to a quarter of a tank. He took the two five-gallon cans they had left and poured them into the tank. It moved the gauge to slightly more than half of a tank.

He and Terri went over the map again and reached a decision.

The Brewster Roadblock

They decided they didn't have any choice and proceeded toward Brewster. It was completely dark by the time they could see the outlines of the buildings in the distance. Bishop was studying the road ahead using a combination of his night vision and the scope. The moon was providing more light than he would have liked, but it did help his spying.

"Stop!" he said suddenly.

Terri stopped the truck immediately.

"There are two pickup trucks blocking the road. I can't be sure, but I think there are men all around them. Either it's a guard post, or Brewster is having a rush hour traffic problem."

Bishop studied the roadblock for a while and considered their options. "I think we are screwed on this one. We may have to backtrack."

Terri touched Bishop's arm, "I have an idea."

After listening for a few minutes, he responded, "No! Absolutely, positively not!"

Terri put her hands on her hips, "Bishop, this is 2015. Women have the vote; we make almost equal pay, and we serve in combat units. The days of you men having all the fun are over."

It took some persuasion on her part, but he eventually agreed. When he thought about it later, he realized that there had never been any doubt Terri was going to win. *Never marry a woman smarter than you no matter how nice her boobs are.*

They backed the truck up about 200 yards and pulled off the side of the road into some scrub. It wasn't well hidden, but would have to do.

Bishop checked their gear while Terri got ready behind the truck. She came walking out and even in the low light, Bishop let out a wolf whistle.

They kissed and both said, "Good Luck – love you" at the same time.

Bishop took off through the scrub and brush using his NVD to avoid falling into the cactus.

Terri marked the time with her watch, gave him a ten-minute head start, and then started walking up the road to the roadblock.

Of the three guys on guard duty, one was asleep, and the other two were swapping stories of past conquests while commiserating about how horny they were. The one young man had just finished a tale about his last trip to the River Walk in San Antonio and his chance encounter with a really hot babe. His friend was saying, "Dude, you are full of shit. Stuff like that never happens. Hot women don't just fall into your lap like that."

Just then they heard a female voice call out somewhat suggestively, "Hey, at the trucks! Anyone home?"

One of the guards reached inside a truck, pulled on the headlights and sucked in his breath.

Terri was standing in the road about 75 feet away. She was dressed in a micro-miniskirt and was barefoot. She wore Bishop's chest rig, and the straps barely covered her otherwise bare upper body. An M4 rifle slung across her shoulder, and her hair was pulled up in a ponytail. She looked like a calendar girl for the National Rifle Association.

She covered her eyes from the suddenly bright light and made sure she turned sideways just enough to flash them a little boob.

There was no reaction from the guards for several seconds, and she thought she made a mistake convincing Bishop to let her try this. Before long flashlights were combing the areas beside the road to see if she were alone. *Not completely stupid*, she thought.

She could hear hushed voices coming from the trucks and could just imagine the debate that was going on. Pretty soon, a voice yelled out, "Why don't you set that rifle down, and come on up here?"

"No thanks. I'm good right here. Why don't you get that fucking light out of my eyes so we can talk?"

"What do you want?"

"What I *want* is to shoot your dumb asses and pass on through your town. What I *need* is to pass through your town and perhaps get some gas."

She could hear them laughing quietly.

"This road is closed. No one other than the people who live here can pass. The last strangers we let through robbed us and shot two people."

"I can trade."

This brought more laughing and more hushed discussion.

"What do you have to trade?"

"I have ammunition and whiskey. You ain't Indians are ya?"

She could clearly hear them laughing now, and her response sparked even more debate.

"How about we just roll out there and grab that pretty ass; and after we are done with you, we go find your car parked up the road and just take the ammo and whiskey? How's that for a trade?"

"You wouldn't like that trade because right now, two of you are in the crosshairs of very powerful sniper rifles, and if you even scratch your balls funny, you will be cut in half."

"Bullshit. You probably have one person with you, and they are probably guarding your car. Set the rifle down, or we will sit you down."

She almost smiled when the flashlights started searching the surrounding brush again.

"Fine. You boys don't want to do a fair trade – you can kiss my ass." Terri spun around, flipped her skirt up enough to show her bare bottom and started walking back up the road, hoping they wouldn't shoot. She also hoped that Bishop had not seen her flash the boys because the removal of her panties had been a last minute addition to the plan.

"Hold on!" came a shout from the trucks. She stopped, but didn't turn around.

"Why should we believe you got us covered? Tell me that."

She spun, making sure the skirt flew up when she did and yelled back, "Look guys, I have been driving for two straight days. I'm tired, almost out of gas, and my boyfriend has had the shits and cramps. Do you want to do a trade or not?"

God, I hope he didn't see that skirt fly up, she thought to herself.

"Tell ya what. We will let you pass if we can have a little party with you and some of that whiskey. We won't hurt you - we just want to have a snip or two and a little fun. "

Terri acted as if she were seriously considering their proposal. She shifted her rifle around just a bit so that the front sight caught on her skirt. She shifted the rifle just a bit more, and it pulled up her skirt. *COME ON BISHOP*, she thought, *I A RUNNING OUT OF OPTIONS HERE.*

Bishop had actually been behind the guard trucks before Terri had ever shouted her first challenge. He had a 12-gauge pump shotgun and had been watching the show since the beginning. He had almost made his move twice when Terri's act had stopped him. He could see the three guys guarding the road were between 18 and 20 years old and really didn't know what they were doing. The fact that they were young and piss poor sentries allowed him to relax a bit and just watch the show.

When he saw Terri's skirt start to come up, he decided she was either enjoying the hell out of her little tease, or she was getting desperate. Either way, he had had enough, stepped around from behind the truck, and chambered a round into the shotgun.

A pump shotgun makes an unmistakable noise when a shell is chambered. The pump handle is moved forward and backward making a very distinct sound that many people have described as sounding like "Oh shit" in gun speak.

Bishop's shotgun clearly announced, "Oh shit" to the three men, and he immediately added, "Put'em down, boys. Show's over."

The man closest to Bishop started to turn and received the hard plastic stock of the shotgun into his ribs for his effort. He dropped his weapon and fell to the ground cursing. The other two just stood there, and Bishop could smell urine as one of them had wet his pants.

"I said put them down. Nice and slow, just like in the movies. Nobody is going to get hurt unless you move too quickly."

Both men slowly bent down and placed their guns on the ground. Bishop told them to take two steps forward and then kicked their weapons away.

He then took out a set of nylon "tie strips" and secured each man to the side mirrors of the pickup trucks. He reached in and turned off the lights that were still shining on Terri and then yelled out to her, "Hike that skirt up any higher and you will have to strike a deal with me."

One of the men snorted, and Bishop kicked him in the shin.

"Ok boys, I am unhappy. My wife just had to show off all her goodies because you idiots didn't have the good sense to strike a fair deal for some ammo."

One of the men started to say something, and Bishop slapped him across the mouth. "Shut the fuck up, hayseed."

Terri walked up about then and just stood quietly to the side.

"Now gentlemen, we are going to have a little discussion. How many ice packs you boys need after we are done depends on how honest you are with me."

He pointed the shotgun at the oldest and said, "How long before someone comes out to relieve you?"

"I don't know what time is…"

Bishop kicked the man in the other shin.

"YOU!" he yelled at the next man, "ANSWER THE QUESTION!"

"They come at 7 a.m."

"Next question, is there a roadblock like this on the other side of town?"

"Yes."

"Good. Now the next question, is there anyone on guard in the town?"

All three of the men just looked at each other and didn't say anything. Bishop stepped close to the second man, reached down and cupped his testicles. The man inhaled sharply and screamed when Bishop pulled them up.

"OK, OK, OK, oh god mister, OK."

Bishop let off a little pressure, "I'll rip them off if I don't get a straight answer. Is anyone on guard in town?"

"No, gawd damn it…NO!"

"Two more questions. What is the signal that you boys need help?"

"Three shots followed by one shot. Everyone comes running when that happens."

"Final question, do you think my wife is hot?" Bishop brought the shotgun up to his shoulder when he asked them the question. All three men looked at each other, then Bishop, and then the shotgun.

Bishop had never heard so many "umms" and "errrs" and "ahhhhs" before in his life.

Bishop laughed, but Terri had never heard him laugh like that.

He spun around and instructed in an ice-cold voice, "Terri, come here please."

Terri was hesitant, but walked over. Bishop looked down, and her blood went cold. In the moonlight, she had seen a look in his eyes like she had never seen before. She could feel her throat getting tight, and her heart rate doubled.

He leaned over and said in a whisper, "Never do that again."

Busting through Brewster

Bishop roughly checked the men for any knives or other weapons. As he approached, they tried to cross their legs to protect their testicles, which caused him to snicker. Bishop flung their weapons far out into the scrub, soon followed by their car keys. Terri left to bring their truck forward and arrived as he was asking the guards how much gas was in their tanks.

As Bishop started to drain their tanks, he told Terri to shoot the guards if they moved. He also noticed she had put on more clothes.

Once the gas was drained from both of the roadblock trucks, Terri and Bishop took off for downtown Brewster. Central Texas was dotted with similar towns. Most were originally settled on railroad lines or where there was water. In more recent years, they role changed to supporting nearby cattle ranches. Brewster consisted of a few businesses clustered around the main highway. The small downtown was surrounded by side streets of modest homes.

When they got to the town, Bishop pointed for Terri to park behind the feed store.

He got out of the truck, fired his rifle in the air three times and then once, and climbed back in.

It was about three minutes before two pickup trucks came from the south, zooming past and heading to help the other roadblock. "There they go. Let's get out of here."

Terri raised her night vision, hit the accelerator, and spun the tires taking off. As they headed south, they noticed movement around the sleepy town and knew other reinforcements were trying to wake up to answer the alarm.

She accelerated the truck to almost eighty and much to Bishop's relief, kept her focus on the road. After a few minutes, he said, "Terri, slow down – the gas mileage."

"I don't want them to catch up to us."

"They won't. Right now they're searching the town to make sure we aren't robbing the feed store."

"Bishop, how mad are you?"

"I'm not mad at you at all. Why do you think I'm upset?" he replied in a flat tone.

Terri's tone made it clear she wasn't buying his response. "Bishop?"

"I did get a little upset when you turned your back on three men with guns who had already threatened you. You didn't know if I were there yet or not. That put you in danger, and the thought of your being hurt naturally upsets me."

"Bishop, if you are mad at me, please just yell and get it over with. That whole thing did not go down like I thought it would, and I probably messed up several times."

"I, um, well – I'm jealous and proud at the same time. This whole thing is so crazy. We had to put you at risk so we could drive down a road? I don't know – I shouldn't be mad I guess, it's all a little confusing right now."

"I didn't enjoy that little charade if that is what you are thinking. I was scared shitless and didn't know if you had fallen in a hole or been eaten by a rattlesnake or what."

"Terri, you showed guts back there, and I know you had to dig deep to hold it together. What is making me so mad is the fact that you had to do that in the first place. No man wants to see his wife have to stoop to that level just to pass through a one-horse town. Now that I think about it, it's the world I'm mad at – not you."

Bishop was silent for a bit, and then leaned over and kissed her on the cheek. He whispered, "I love you with all my heart. All is well between us, I swear it."

She smiled and rubbed his cheek and hair, and then they went back to watching the road.

"By-the-way, your bikini trim is sexy as hell babe. All the guys thought so."

She started to slow down quickly, and Bishop questioned, "What are you doing?"

"There was a sign in the feed store's window that said 'PIG FEED 50% OFF.' I was going back to get you some."

They drove off into the Texas night, laughing.

Welcome to Meraton

A nice place to visit

Meraton, Texas was a small railroad town about 100 miles North of Big Bend National Park. The census listed the population at 894 residents in 2010. The entire business district was on a single two-lane road that was the only way in or out of town.

Meraton had experienced a small economic boom in the late '90s from what many of the locals called "The Art Revival." The century's end marked the beginning of large city artists settling in smaller western towns. Many told themselves the simpler lifestyle provided a creative work environment. The lower cost of living probably contributed to the migration as well.

As the artists moved in, they opened shops; which in turn encouraged folks to stop, shop, eat and even spend the night. Meraton was also famous for The Manor Hotel. Back in the days when the railroad was the only way to travel between Houston and El Paso, Meraton was a logical place to stop and let passengers, railroad executives and crew spend the night. The Manor was built to provide the finest in western hospitability to those weary of travel. The facility still provided refuge even though guests now arrived via mini-vans and SUVs, rather than the great iron horses of the past.

The Manor was considered by almost everyone that stayed there as one of the best places in the world to relax. The high, dry air combined with hand-manicured gardens made for a magical oasis in the barren west Texas desert. The rooms were traditional ranch house decor, but everything was real, not reproductions. Even in the year 2015, there were no TVs, phones, or internet at The Manor. There were, however, some of the most comfortable rocking chairs in the known universe sitting in front of each room overlooking the gardens, gazebo, and scenic paths through the grounds.

After the artists came the chefs. Probably for similar reasons, many small, western towns found themselves with new restaurants opening that served some of the finest cuisine anywhere. Meraton was especially attractive to the culinary crowd because of The Manor and its guests.

Main Street in Meraton had four nice, art galleries, three good restaurants, and The Manor Hotel. There were several side streets with smaller, humble homes.

Of course, all of this was unknown to The Force as they pulled into town. They had been navigating through the sparsely populated region avoiding civilization as best they could, but had no option of bypassing Meraton. There were simply no other roads.

The thugs were surprised when people casually waved or nodded in their direction as they slowly drove down Main Street. When they stopped and asked someone about a place to stay, The Manor was the natural response.

Spence needed more information, but didn't want to get too close to Mexico with his vulnerable treasure. He had told The Force, "Look, we are some bad asses, no doubt. But we are only five men, and these drug cartels have death squads of 50 or more. They have the best equipment, the best training, and the best intelligence network on the planet. We are stupid if we think we can roll into their turf and either take over, or pass through without being noticed. "

Spence decided to get close, but not too close, to the border and hole up. He would wait, learn, and then decide his next move. Meraton was looking like the perfect hideout as they were running low on fuel.

Central Texas – September 17, 2015

East of the Pecos

Bishop and Terri were making a wide swing south and west around San Antonio. Their progress was good because the area was so lightly populated. They were driving almost straight west now on a two lane state highway through very arid terrain. Small patches of cactus dotted the otherwise barren and rocky dirt. There were no homes, telephone poles, or fences at all. Every now and then he would see a water tank or windmill used for the few livestock this land would support. Bishop knew that some homes did exist, but they were usually far off of the road and out of sight.

This area of Texas had been originally divided into a small number of ranches having thousands of acres each. Because the land was so poor, it took several acres per head to support the animals. If the early ranchers wanted a herd of any size, they needed a lot of land because there was not enough nutrition per acre to keep the herd alive.

None of the ranches here had thrived. Raiders from Mexico, the occasional dry year, and the ultra-harsh lifestyle kept the early settlers from doing as well as they had in other parts of Texas. In the early 1920's, gasoline-powered cars and trucks allowed good, quality feed to be delivered to the cattle. Railroads would bring in grain from other parts of the country, and some small towns sprung up along the lines. The ranchers could take their Model A Ford trucks to the town and buy bags of feed. They used the rail lines to ship their four-legged products back east.

With the non-native food source being available, there was little need for so much land. Property taxes, driving distance to deliver the feed, and other circumstances caused the big tracts of land to be divided and sold off.

The cost of feed, fuel and the rugged environment meant that current day ranchers in the area barely kept their head above water. The typical ranch house became an old mobile home purchased second hand, hauled in, and used until it fell apart. The cycle repeated, with the new trailer parked adjacent to its predecessor.

Despite the poverty, Bishop knew these were proud, independent people. They knew the land and their families, in some cases, had been on it since before the ink on the Declaration of Independence dried. The loss of electric power would have little impact here and may have gone unnoticed completely. Because of this difference, he and Terri were driving more and scouting less. Bishop just didn't think a truck going down the road at night would attract any attention from the few people in the area. He remembered his first trip through this part of Texas.

Years ago, as a college student, Bishop wanted to see the big city of San Antonio. He had a young lady friend who owned a beat up old car, and they had decided to take a grand adventure together. The car broke down right in the middle of nowhere. It was over 100 degrees outside, and Bishop had enough sense to just stay put. The car would provide some shade, and the thought of walking along miles of baking highway did not seem like a good idea. Someone would be along soon.

They sat there for over three hours without a single car or truck coming along. They were thirsty, hot and hungry having started the trip with little money and even less experience. The first car that came along just kept going. Bishop had waved wildly at the elderly lady driving the old beat up truck, but she just ignored him and kept on going.

By late that afternoon it was over 105, and Bishop's lady friend continued to shed clothing all afternoon to stay cool. She was lying in the backseat, down to just her bra and panties when she said, "Bishop, you can take me right now if you have the strength."

He didn't have the strength, and that seriously concerned him. Within an hour, he saw the second truck of the day coming down the road. This time the driver stopped. Bishop and his lady friend were given some water from a dirty old igloo in the back of the truck and a ride to the next town. They used all of their money getting the car fixed, and just headed back home with two bad headaches and the same number of plastic milk jugs full of water.

Bishop's analysis of the locals was right on, but did not take into consideration other westward travelers who had become stranded in the rugged environment. He had not been sticking his head out the sunroof very much the last few hours because there was really nothing to see. He was in the backseat, still looking around when he saw sparks fly across the hood of the truck. Before he could say anything, a small hole appeared in the window to his left; and something hit his arm with a hammer-like blow.

"Go! GO! GOOOO!" he yelled at Terri, and she floored the gas pedal.

Bishop had dropped the NVD and couldn't see anything. He reached up to feel his arm and pulled away a sticky, wet hand. "Fuck!" he said, and Terri almost wrecked the truck trying to see what was wrong with him.

"I've been hit. Keep going, and watch the road. Don't stop."

"Are you OK? What's going on Bishop? What just happened?"

"Someone was shooting as us. Just keep going, and watch the road. I am hit in the arm. I'm fine."

A Deer Kills the Hunter

Alberto could not remember how long it had been since he had been at the high-rise apartment in Covington, Kentucky shooting at trucks on the bridge. He had avoided the American authorities while trying to reach El Paso, which is where he was supposed to have crossed the border days ago. When the American society had begun to fall apart, he realized he had to avoid everyone. He lived in Beirut as a child and had seen this type of behavior before. *Every man for himself was what they would call it here in the west*. He had used all of his military skills and training to reach Texas and had stolen a truck outside San Antonio two days before. While hiding in woods, he came across two men hunting. They shot a wild boar; and as they were cleaning it, he came up behind them, took their weapons, and shot them both. He found their truck and headed toward El Paso.

He believed the animal that jumped in front of his truck was called a white tail deer. For sure it was some sort of antelope, and he had hit the animal so hard it broke his windshield and caused him to swerve off of the road. The truck rolled twice, resulting in a broken collarbone and a fracture in his right leg. He had limped along that first day for hours without water. While he was accustomed to arid climates, these plants were strange to him, and he had not been able to find any that produced moisture. The throbbing in his leg was so bad he could no longer walk, and he settled in a small gully. As the sun began to set on the second day, he knew he was dying from dehydration. He still had his rifle and would use it to stop the first car that went by.

When he first heard the noise, he thought he was either hallucinating or there was ringing in his ears. He lips were blistered, and he was having trouble breathing, but his eyes were not failing yet. There was enough moonlight to see a truck going down the road without any lights. He had to stop it; this was his last chance. He brought the rifle to his shoulder and almost lost consciousness from the effort. He calculated the truck was driving very slowly since it was dark, and it used no lights. He led his aim with the hunting scope and pulled the trigger. He didn't know if his shot had been good, but realized the truck was moving much faster than he had originally thought. He centered quickly and pulled the trigger again.

He turned his head to see if the truck stopped, but it didn't. He heard its engine race and fade into the distance. He decided to sleep for a bit. Maybe he would dream of home and his favorite mosque. He said a prayer and closed his eyes.

They never opened again.

Wounded

Terri was driving over 80 mph, and Bishop asked her to slow down to 50 or so. He started digging around in his "blow out bag," a first aid kit strapped to his chest rig. He was not sure how bad he was hit or where the bullet was. He was breathing okay, but the entire left side of his body was numb and tingling except his arm and shoulder – they hurt like hell. He could not use his left arm at all, and was fumbling around with various dressing and bandages in the bag, not sure what to do in the dark.

Terri said, "Bishop, I think it's raining. There is water on the windshield."

"Rain, here? No way."

"I can see it, Bishop. I'm going to need the wipers."

Bishop looked up, but couldn't see anything but black. Without his night vision, it was like staring at a wall. He said, "Rain is not impossible here. I guess that will help cool it off a bit."

Terri responded with, "What is this light blinking on the dash mean?"

Bishop looked over her shoulder. "Oh shit. Pull over."

They got out of the truck, and Terri wanted to see his wound before doing anything else. She took the paramedic sheers from his blow out bag and cut away the blood-soaked sleeve of his shirt. Holding a flashlight in her mouth, she could tell the bullet had entered his upper arm right through the triceps, and exited into his ribs. With his body armor on, she couldn't see anything beyond that. While the arm wound looked clean and had missed bone, the rib entry point was still bleeding badly. She dressed the wounds as much as possible, but all of Bishop's equipment prohibited her from applying a proper bandage. Bishop felt exposed along the side of the open road and refused further treatment. He talked Terri through opening the hood of the truck.

The first shot had punctured a radiator hose and sliced it badly. The "rain" Terri had seen on the windshield was actually the truck's anti-freeze and water spraying out of the cooling system. It did not take long for the level of critical coolant to be depleted and the engine to begin overheating.

Bishop was feeling weak. His entire left side was now wet with blood, and his head felt like it was going to split open. He had Terri retrieve the sleeve she had cut from his shirt, and he wrapped the discarded rag around the radiator cap. When he twisted the cover, it blew off in his hand and showered him with steam and droplets of scalding water. He spun away from the spray, flaying his burning arm while spinning in small circles. His movements were accompanied by the angry recital of every known curse in his extensive vocabulary. He finally sat down in the middle of the road and continued to fill the air with vulgarities, some newly created on the spot. Eventually, his voice lowered, and then he sat silent for a few moments.

After he had recovered from the shock of the burn, he asked Terri to find the duct tape. He knew it would not hold forever, but hoped it would work until a better solution could be found. He used a flashlight to show her where to wrap the tape, and she began to refill the radiator with drinking water. Their supply of water was down to less than 20 bottles, and filling the radiator to the point where Bishop thought they could drive without damaging the engine. They only had four bottles left to drink.

He looked at a map while she tried to get more bandages on his wounds. It was such an awkward position to work on. She got an idea from a large compression bandage in the kit. While elevating his bad arm, Terri wrapped some duct tape as tightly around his chest as possible in order to get pressure on the wound and hold the bandage in place. When she moved his arm, she noticed his eyes roll up in his head and his knees bent just a little, but he never said a word.

Bishop felt vulnerable along the side of the road, but there was no place to go. He knew they needed time, water, and somewhere safe to hide until he could get his act together. As he studied the map, he saw a place that he had been years before. They had no other choice.

Terri helped him into the truck and laid him down across the backseat. When she got back in, he said, "Sanderton - follow the signs. I'm going to sleep for a bit, wake me when we get close."

Terri drove down the dark highway until she saw a sign giving the distance to Sanderton. She was torn between driving fast to take care of Bishop and driving slower to take care of the truck. She settled on a speed somewhere in between "Grandma Moses" and the "bat out of hell."

Sanderton, Texas – September 18, 2015

Sanderton had been founded as a watering station for the Georgia-Pacific railroad shortly after the civil war. The town had flourished for several years despite its isolation and proximity to the Mexican border.

Since the 1980s the story had been quite different. The town had experienced a continuing decline in population primarily due to the success of other towns in the area. By the year 2000, it was a completely uninhabited, semi-modern ghost town. There were still four boarded up buildings at the intersection, with weeds, fallen shingles and small bits of scrap iron scattered around the paved areas. Its primary role in the last 20 years was a destination for teenagers to sneak away and have beer bashes.

As far as the State of Texas was concerned, Sanderton still existed, but the U.S. Government had closed the Post Office years ago. It had been located in the General Store, and when that shut down, there was no place left to house it.

As Terri slowed and approached the intersection, she realized that this was the first town they had entered without sneaking, scouting or crashing through since they had left Houston. The few buildings still standing were within sight of each other, and she drove around each one making sure there were no other cars or sign of recent visitors. She had to be careful because broken glass and debris was scattered everywhere. She decided on a building that looked to be in the best condition and offered a little cover for the truck. There had been a small lean-to built behind the structure, and there was still enough of it standing to hide the truck. While anyone going down the main road would not be able to see it, the hiding spot would not hold up to a closer inspection. *This will just have to do for now.*

She checked on Bishop. He was still breathing well, and his pulse was strong. When she touched his wrist to check it, he moved and changed his breathing just a bit. She decided to let him rest while she nosed around a little. *Damn him*, she thought, *I am picking up his bad habits.* She started to grab her

9mm pistol, but had felt more secure with the rifle at the roadblock. She knew the basics of how it worked, and Bishop's favorite one was lying on the floor of the truck. She pulled it out, made sure it was loaded and a round chambered. She made sure the safety on.

This rifle didn't have a weapon light, and she really didn't want one. She walked around the truck for a bit, peering through the night vision and listening. She went back to the truck to check on him again and tried to see how much he was bleeding. She knew that was her first job – stop the bleeding. Because of Bishop's position in the truck, she really couldn't tell how much blood he had lost since it was running through the crack in the seat. The white light of the flashlight made it difficult to judge his color. *At least he is still breathing, and the blood has not started running out from under the seat.*

She locked the truck and proceeded to explore the building she had picked. There was a double front door surrounded by windows, all of which were boarded up. When she stepped on the front porch, she almost fell through the rotten wood. *Good,* she thought, *it will be hard for someone heavier than I am to sneak up on us.*

Terri checked the back door, and it was boarded up as well. *Whoever closed this place down really didn't want anyone inside.* Knowing she was going to have to break in somehow, she decided on the back door. That would leave the front undisturbed in case someone passed by. She checked the 2x4 boards that were nailed across the rear entrance. They were all solid and tight. She thought about trying to pry them off, but figured that would take forever, and she didn't have anything to pry with anyway.

She opened the back of the truck and rummaged around, but couldn't find anything that would help. She dug out a pair of her blue jeans and wrapped them around the middle two boards. She found a piece of rusty iron rebar lying nearby, put it between the legs of the jeans, and started twisting.

On about the sixth turn one of the boards cracked. She hoped it would break soon because she didn't think she had the strength to twist it many more times. She put all of her weight into it, and the bar went half a turn and the top board went "pop" and came loose. She managed to tear the board away, and repeated the process. In about five minutes, she had removed all but the bottom and top boards. The ruined jeans were thrown to the ground.

Behind the boards was a solid sheet of very thick plywood nailed to the doorframe. Her kick accomplished nothing but hurting her foot. *Is anything you see on television true?* She thought about trying to shoot the board off, but didn't want to make the noise and was not really sure this plan would work. She grabbed a nearby rock that was about the size of a softball and threw it as hard as she could. It bounced off, almost hitting her as it rolled back.

It was time to regroup and think for a little bit, so checked on Bishop again. His pulse had slowed. Rolling him a few inches to the side revealed the entire back of the truck seat was covered in blood. *This is not good. I have to get him inside where I can work on him or he is going to bleed to death right here in the truck.*

She returned to look at the door again, but just couldn't figure out a way to get it open. *I have got to get this done, and right now.* She went back to the truck, started the engine, and inched it slowly toward the door. She knew the front bumper was engineered with a big rubber component that stuck out and hoped it protruded enough to meet the door before the rest of the bumper hit the doorframe. At this point she didn't care if she hurt the bumper or not – she had to get Bishop where she could dig the bullet out. Moving the truck forward bit by bit, the bumper engaged the plywood door with more force than anticipated. The truck jolted enough that Bishop moaned, but the plywood gave way on one side. Terri backed up and re-aimed. This time she was able to better control and soften the impact. The second push left the plywood hanging loosely in the frame. She backed up the truck and got out to examine her dirty work. One good strike with her hand sent plywood crashing inwards, creating a small cloud of dust when it landed.

She retrieved a flashlight from the truck and used the night vision to scan the inside first. The NVD showed her a small back room, completely empty. The flashlight revealed falling plaster on the floor and a few cobwebs.

The main part of the building proved to be empty except for one old chair, a few boxes of yellowed paper, and some scrap wood lying around. Dust covered everything.

Terri pulled both hammocks out of the back of the truck and suspended one between two columns that ran through the middle of the main room. She pulled over the chair and tested it – It would hold her. She laid the other one out flat on the floor. She then ran back to the truck and retrieved the large medical kit and a small box of books Bishop had packed before they left. The last four bottles of their precious water came inside next.

It took a few attempts, but Bishop finally opened his eyes to look at her. His pulse sped up, and she thought that was a good thing. She told him where they were and that it was safe, but he had to get up and get inside. He nodded and with her help, managed to get out of the truck and into the building. She took off his chest-rig, body armor and cut his shirt away. Guiding him to the floor hammock, she had him lay on his stomach so she could see the damage. .

The bullet had entered through the upper arm and exited into his rib cage through the opening in his armor below the armpit. She remembered seeing something on TV once that talked about how bullets can take random paths through the body. She traced the path of the bullet by the swollen, purple flesh. This one had been deflected by his ribs and traveled upwards into the muscle covering his shoulder blade. There was no exit wound. The bullet was still in there. She ran back and retrieved two flashlights and using the duct tape, secured them to the columns shining down on Bishop. He turned his head a little and told her he was worried about the light. He wouldn't relax and tried to get up, so she walked around the building quickly to make sure there wasn't any light leaking out that would be detected by passersby. He relaxed a little bit and seemed to go back asleep.

The arm was still bleeding, but most of the blood was coming from the entry wound on the rib cage. She looked around in the box of books and found the US Army Survival Manual. Its third chapter was about treating bullet wounds in the field, and she read it as quickly as she could. She checked his pulse again. It was even faster than the last time. She flipped through the book and re-read the section on shock. An increasing pulse rate was a sign Bishop was going into shock.

She grabbed a clean shirt and spread it out on the dusty floor. She spread out the contents of the medical kit and took a quick mental inventory. As she was getting organized, Bishop turned his head and said, "Baby, I need water. I need it real bad." She grabbed a bottle, and he drained it without pausing. He said, "I'm so thirsty. I think it's because I'm losing blood. I could drink ten more of those. I've never been so thirsty." She handed him another, and it was gone in a few seconds. They had two bottles left. She started to use one to wash off the wound, and remembered the two bottles of bourbon that were in the truck. They were a door prize at a company party, and Bishop had brought them along for bartering.

She used the expensive bourbon to wash the dried and caked blood away from the torso wounds. She would deal with the arm later. Much to his displeasure, she pushed gently on his shoulder to see if she could find the bullet. There was a red streak that started at the entry and when she followed it around, she found the bullet about one half inch below the surface of his skin in the muscle below his shoulder blade.

"Bishop, baby, I found the bullet."

"It has to come out. How deep?"

"Less than an inch. I'm going to have to cut you. I don't know about this Bishop."

"Terri, I love you. That bullet has to come out, or I'm dead from infection. You are going to have to cut it out."

"Do you want some booze? They do that in the movies, you know."

"No, but a bullet to bite on might help," Bishop joked to lighten the mood a bit.

"Funny. This is all swollen and purple back here, and I think it's going to hurt. Are you ready?"

"I was born ready. Terri, I say crazy shit when I'm in pain. Do you promise not to hold it against me?"

"I promise. Okay, here goes."

She took the scalpel from the medical kit and opened the sterile wrapper. Her first attempt to cut his skin barely drew blood because she didn't press hard enough. She pushed harder and the skin sliced open. Bishop tensed, but didn't say anything. She pulled apart the skin with her fingers and stuck tweezers in the incision, causing Bishop to inhale sharply and arch upwards.

"I HATE YOUR MEATLOAF!" he growled.

She smirked and thought, *I don't make meatloaf*, then dug around very gently with the tweezers until she felt the bullet.

"THOSE NEW SANDALS LOOK LIKE OLD LADY SHOES!"

He's delirious because my sandals look great. She tried to put the tweezers over the bullet to pull it out, but the skin would not stretch enough, and she didn't want to tear the skin and hurt him.

"YOUR ASS LOOKS FAT IN THAT NEW BATHING SUIT!"

This time Terri pushed the tweezers deep and hard, grabbing the bullet and tearing tissue - but it came out.

Bishop was panting and sweat was beading up all over his back. Terri set the bullet down and poured more bourbon over the wound to clean the blood. She dried the surgical site, opened a packet of antibiotic powder, and sprinkled it on the wound. Then she pulled out a suture, threaded the enclosed needle, and poked him with it, waiting on his next outburst. When he didn't say anything, she proceeded to sew and bandage the incision. She decided to let the entry wound drain after reading the army manual. She put a sterile strip on top of the wound and then focused on his arm. He weakly drank another bottle of water, this time taking much longer to do so.

She started concentrating on his arm, when she thought she heard a car go down the road. She turned off the flashlights and went outside with the night vision to look around. She couldn't see or hear anything except a coyote far off in the distance.

After she returned, an examination of Bishop's arm made her second-guess working the shoulder first. While it did not seem to have bled as much as the other entry, the entire top of his arm was swollen and purple. When she moved his arm to get a better view, blood poured out of the exit wound. The injury was bleeding heavily inside of the "tunnel" created through his flesh as the bullet bored through.

She was at a complete loss as to how to stop the bleeding. Pressure and bandages were a simple fix, but how do you stop bleeding inside of a hole like that? She re-read the manual again, but it was not much help. Bishop moved his head a little bit and said, "It's so cold in here. Why is it so cold?"

Terri thought it was anything but cold. She was dripping in sweat, and Bishop's bare back and forehead were beading up as well. *He's going into shock.*

She tried to remember anything she had ever read or seen about how to stop bleeding. She had been watching a survival show once where they cauterized a wound with gun powder, but that had been on the outside of the body. She flipped through the Army manual again and didn't find anything about cauterization of wounds. *I have no choice here*, she thought, *he is losing blood and if I don't get it stopped, he will die.*

She got up and walked around for a bit, trying to think. She stepped on something that felt different from the floor, and realized there had been a coal stove here at one point. The floorboards stopped at a large iron plate, and she could see where the stovepipe had gone through the wall. She kept walking around for another ten minutes, and then checked Bishop's pulse. It was really fast now, and he was very pale. I'm going to have to cauterize that tube inside of him, but how? What did she have to use to sear the wound? And once she found a tool that would work, how would she manage to heat it to the right temperature for burning the flesh?

She thought about the car engine, but it was filthy under the hood. She thought about building a fire outside, but anyone nearby would see that for sure. She didn't think burning the booze would make it hot enough. It took a little bit, but she finally formed a plan.

She ran outside and found a pile of old bricks. She grabbed as many as she could carry and brought them into the building. On the old stove plate, she stacked them into a circle. She used her rifle barrel to punch out the plywood covering the hole where the old chimney had been vented through the wall. She went back outside, retrieved a piece of tin siding, and leaned it against the wall such that the top just barely covered the old smokestack exhaust. After gathering some of the scrap wood and yellow papers, a single click of a disposable lighter started the fire. Terri draped Bishop's body armor on one side of the tin to channel the smoke out.

She watched the wood start to burn while nervously fiddling with the lighter. Her tired mind drifted back to the day they were in the camping store looking at various fire-starting options. Flint and steel, waterproof matches and various other devices were available. She remembered how Bishop had said, "I am not spending $40 on some fancy thing I'll probably lose anyway. Let's buy a big package of lighters for four bucks and keep them handy." He had spread them all over the place, and she stumbled across at least three stashed in the truck cab alone.

Bishop kept a rifle cleaning kit on his chest rig. She had watched him take the metal tubes and screw them together to make a long rod. He would shove the rod in and out of gun barrels to clean them. She hunted around until she found one of the rods and thought it was the perfect size. She screwed three of the pieces together and then wrapped a "handle" using a piece of Bishop's shirt to keep it cool.

After checking him again and looking at the results of the surgery, she scrubbed the arm wound, deciding it was now or never. She carried the gun-cleaning rod to the fire and stuck it in the flames.

"Bishop, your arm won't stop bleeding. I'm going to have to hurt you again. I'm sorry baby."

His voice was distant and weak, "What are you going to do?"

"I have to stick a red hot rod inside of you."

"I thought that was my job."

"Breathe deep. I'm so sorry, Bishop," and a single tear slipped down her cheek as she shoved the hot metal all the way through the wound.

Bishop screamed and jerked, but she had been ready for that. She pushed and pulled in almost one motion, hoping to get it in and out before his fuzzy brain reacted from the pain. The smell of his burning flesh made her gag and turn away. He panted and rolled his eyes a few times and then settled down. She heard him whisper, "Remind me to be gentler next time," and passed out.

Terri checked outside again, but didn't hear or see anything. She took some of the fishing line and an old can and made a tripwire like she had watched Bishop do a dozen times in the last few days. She intended to stay awake, but fell asleep in the chair watching him breathe.

Water, Water Nowhere

Terri heard something that snapped her head up. She rubbed her eyes and looked around, letting it all come back into her mind. She heard the noise again, "Terri – water." It was Bishop, and she rose up out of the chair and went to his side. He weakly drank a bit of water, but she thought he looked a little better now than before. She glanced around the room, trying to determine the source of the light that streamed from above. Her eyes adjusted in a few seconds, allowing her to make out the skylight in the roof of the building. Yellow, crusted, and old, it still let in light, which meant the day had dawned. She looked at her watch and gave Bishop another dose of the broad-spectrum antibiotic they kept in the medical kit. He swallowed the pill and went back to sleep.

An inspection of her surgeries found that the wound to Bishop's ribs had stopped bleeding and looked fair - for a gunshot wound. There was still purple bruising and a lot of swelling, but no pus or red color.

The arm was a different story. It was not clear to her if it were worse or just the same. The bleeding had stopped completely, but from the elbow up, the arm was almost twice its normal size and was still very dark blue and puffy. She adjusted his arm to elevate it as the book said, causing him to half-protest in his sleep, but he did not move it back. There was no sign of infection.

Terri went outside to use the ladies room, carrying her rifle and proceeding cautiously. As she passed the truck, she heard dripping and looked under the front to see a small damp spot in the sand caused by a slow but steady drip. She had a throbbing headache that really intensified when she stood up. She went around to the back and squatted, but was surprised that very little urine came out. *Odd*, she thought, *I normally make quite the puddle in the morning*.

Her stomach then started doing its new trick, and she tried to vomit, but there was nothing to come up. She dry heaved a few times and then the feeling passed. *I can't get sick now*, she thought. As she went to take a drink to wash down two aspirin, she realized it was the first water she had swallowed in hours. She was dehydrated and embarrassed because of the countless speeches Bishop had given her about drinking enough water. She finished half of their last bottle of water and thought about the situation. She had no idea of how to fix the truck, but knew whatever the solution, it would require water. She had done everything she could for Bishop, but he was going to require water. She was dehydrated and needed water too. Water should be the first priority.

As she walked around the building, she studied the landscape in all directions. Barren hills that looked like a volcano had recently erupted bordered the little hamlet to the north and east. Sharp purple and dark brown rocks jutted out in every direction and steep-sided ravines could be seen in the distance. There was not a green plant in sight except for the weeds in the paved areas of the ghost town. To the far south, the land gradually sloped downwards into a dry, flat desert.

Through a valley of small multi-colored mountains, the two-lane highway that brought them here could be seen snaking its way back and forth. She could see for quite a distance, and thought in any other situation the sun rising over the mountains behind her would have been a picture worth taking.

Another two-lane highway intersected and went to the north right in front of the building they occupied, but it crested a rise about 400 yards away and disappeared. The north was the only direction that did not provide for a long distance view, and she made a note to explore that direction first.

Water. It seemed like every survival show, book and movie ever made focused on water. They had purchased a water purification system for camping some years ago. It looked like a small bicycle tire pump and pushed the source liquid through ceramic filters to get rid of the bad stuff. It was slow and difficult to pump for any period of time, but was worth having in case of an emergency. Bishop once made her sample a drink of some puddled, muddy water he had filtered, and she quickly spat it out. The water may have not been dangerous, but it sure tasted like sour muck to her. It was that experience that resulted in there always being several cases of bottled water in the pantry next to the hurricane boxes. They had packed those cases of water before leaving Houston, but now there was only half of a bottle left. If the truck had not required so much water last night to fill the leaking radiator, there would have been plenty to get to Meraton. The purification kits were in their backpacks, stacked in the truck bed. If she could find water, she could either boil it or run it through the purifier.

She went to check on Bishop and found he was very warm to the touch and sweating again. A fever meant infection, and she thought about giving him another pill early. *No, I need to give the anti-biotic time to work, and there are no signs of any red streaks or pus.* Her assessment caused him to stir, and he wanted another drink. She opened the last bottle, and he took a few mouthfuls before going back to sleep. She took two swallows herself and put the cap back on. She had to find water.

She went back outside and checked the road as far as she could see. It was empty. She put on her "ninja suit," as Bishop called it, and prepared to explore. Her ninja suit consisted of a body armor vest he had purchased for her years ago and a photographer's vest with lots of little pouches where she stored various items that she might need handy. She also grabbed a rifle.

She did not want to get out of sight of their building, so she started by looking around the other three abandoned structures neighboring it. One had been a gas station, but the entire rear wall had collapsed years ago leaving only the façade in front. The other two were a mystery as to their original purpose, but after poking around them, she decided they were not safe to enter. She then widened her search and found nothing that even hinted at helping them. At one point, she thought about walking a little distance into the surrounding mountains, but dismissed the idea quickly. If she fell and twisted an ankle, they were toast. A rattlesnake or other poisonous bite would have the same result, and she could not go far in any direction without losing sight of their building.

She decided to walk up the hill to where the intersecting road disappeared and see what was on the other side. She stayed off of the pavement and hoped a car would not suddenly appear over the hill because there was no place to hide. She tracked up the rise cursing the weight of her ninja suit the entire way. When she reached the crest, the view on the other side provided more of the same landscape she had been eyeing all morning. The road meandered north through ever larger mountains for as far as she could see. She looked around a little bit and could see nothing of value. At the top of the crest, she noticed a hard, packed path leading off of the road to a small fenced in area. It appeared that years of heavy truck tires driving to the fence wore the path before her. She walked over and looked, but there was nothing inside of the area, and she had no clue why trucks would drive there. She was tired from her hike. It was getting hot, and they had had a night from hell, so she decided to head back down the hill to check on Bishop again.

On the way down, she started to get angry. *Why did someone shoot at them? Why were they even here? Why did Bishop guide her to this stupid, bumfuck town?* As her anger started to boil over, she realized it was not going to help them get through this.

She entered the building and took off her gear. Bishop was still asleep and still felt hot. She made up her mind to take another small drink from the quickly disappearing bottle and limited herself to one mouthful. It took all of her discipline not to drain the whole thing. She checked her watch; time to give Bishop another pill. She woke him up and made him take it, which was not easy. She had to pull the water away from him and a little spilled, which made her really mad – "Damn it Bishop!" He looked at her with distant eyes and whispered, "What's wrong?"

"I can't find water, and we don't have much left. I feel like shit, and I hate this place and don't want to die here."

"Other than that Mrs. Lincoln, how was the play?"

Bishop's remark made her even more upset, and she took in a deep breath preparing to let him have it. Something inside stopped her, and she began laughing. He tried to laugh as well, but the motion hurt him, and then he started coughing. The effort exhausted what little strength he had left.

"That will teach you to be a smart ass."

He just nodded and closed his eyes again. Terri checked his wounds and found the entry wound on his ribs was bleeding again.

She paced around the building for a bit, but it was getting too hot inside to move, so she just sat and thought, staring at the last little bit of the water. Bishop moaned again and tried to roll over but gave up.

More to herself than Bishop, she said out loud, "These people who lived here had to have water. I can't find any wells, tanks or anything. How did they get their water?"

Bishop moved his head slightly, and without opening his eyes, whispered one word, "Gravity."

Terri thought about what he had said for a minute and figured he was dreaming. She went through everything she had seen on her tour this morning and couldn't recall anything that had to do with water. *What if I think about it the opposite way? What did I see that I can't explain? I always wanted to be an archeologist, so now is my chance. I will determine how the ancient tribe of Sandertonsoians lived, worshiped, ate, and most importantly, drank.*

It was too hot, and she was too tired to put her gear on. She didn't even want to carry the rifle, so she nonchalantly tucked the 9mm in her belt as she left the building. A quick check of the sky did not show any rain clouds on the horizon. In fact, there was not a single cloud anywhere. She chose to return to the gas station first and walked across the road. She poked around gently, and cautiously moved some boards and patches of rotten dry wall. Something caught her eye right before she was about to leave for the next building. *Was that a*

broken piece of toilet bowl lying under those crumbled bricks?
She ignored the risk of spiders and snakes and went further
into the rubble. She rearranged the debris on the floor,
eventually spotting the base of a toilet. *There it was!* Behind
the base, going into the concrete foundation was a pipe. *So
they did have running water!*

She ran back to the truck and found the shovel they used to
dig cat holes. She went back to her discovery and started
digging right outside the foundation where the pipe
disappeared. The shovel was not intended to dig large holes,
but the soil was mostly sand and soon her efforts were
rewarded with a metallic "ding" when the shovel struck
something hard. She cleared the dirt away and there was the
pipe. She looked in the direction of the pipe and could see
nothing but open desert. It pointed to the top of the rise where
she had just been. She began walking in a straight line
following the pipe to see if she had missed anything. The path
led up the rise through the desert.

She crested a small lump of rocks and saw a deep ravine that
eroded through the surrounding terrain. It was about ten feet
deep and almost as wide. She looked for a place to cross, and
saw a large steel pipe spanning the wash. It was headed
almost the same direction as the water pipe, and when she
followed its path with her eyes, it lead directly to where she had
found the fenced area at the top of the hill. Bishop's word came
back to her, "Gravity," and she now understood.

She verified her findings and now concluded her research to
determine how the inhabitants of Sanderton had quenched
their thirst. Her primary evidence was inside the fence at the
top of the hill. At first, she found nothing, but as she walked
around, a patch of ground felt different under her feet. A few
scrapes of lose dirt later, she saw a large steel door in the
ground that had the words, "Markel Water Storage Systems,
Dallas, Texas" on it.

It all made sense now. Trucks delivered a full load of water to
the top of the hill into this tank. Gravity, as Bishop had tried to
tell her, pulled the water down the rise to the buildings below
and provided pressure. It was a simple system, but she
thought it had probably worked well. Now the important
question was if there were any water left in the tank. She could
not get the rusted, heavy steel lid open, and guessed it would
lead to some sort of cap or valve that would be even more
difficult to access.

As she walked back down the hill to their building, she felt better. She knew that mental attitude was an important part of survival, but had always discounted that advice. She now understood what a difference hope could make, and she reminded herself to always remember that. She checked on Bishop, who was about the same as when she had left. *Now,* she thought, *how to see if there is any water in that tank.*

She found a long piece of steel rebar and hurried back to the gas station pipe she had uncovered. After a little probing and prying, she put all of her weight on the rebar pole, using it as a lever to snap the old pipe in two. Nothing, dry as a bone. Determination overrode her disappointment, so it was back up the rise, wanting to get another look where the pipe crossed the wash. She noticed a bulge in the pipe at the edge of the ravine. She brushed away years of caked-on dust and mud and found a valve. There was no handle, just a hole with a stem and the words open, close and drain stamped into it. She dug around some more and found an open side to the valve that would have drained the water into the gully. *So that's how this ditch got here*, she thought, *someone had opened this valve to drain the water. After so many years, the water had washed away all of the soft soil and left this trench.*

College Showers

Bishop was dreaming of heat and being thirsty. His dream wandered back to the time when he and his college girlfriend were stranded along the road. The truck that had picked them up had a huge tank on the back and was headed to Sanderton. After giving tho desperate kids a drink, the driver had provided a ride back to the town. On the way, Bishop learned that the truck was delivering water to Sanderton and the entire tank was filled with the potable liquid. Bishop had thought water an odd cargo until the driver explained to Bishop how the water system worked. Bishop was in his first year of college and was studying Fluid Dynamics, so anything to do with gravity and pressure held his interest. The man looked over at the still hot and sweaty kids and told them he had a special treat for them when they got to town.

He pulled his truck up to the top of the rise and motioned them to follow. He walked about 50 yards down the side and came to the trench. "I have to flush the tank every time to make sure there isn't any sediment. Watch."

He stuck a wheel valve key into the stem and turned the handle. Water began spraying out of the valve and down the wash. He looked at Bishop and his girl and said, "My grandkids love to play in there. Go cool off. I'll yell before I come down to close the valve."

Bishop and his girl looked at each other and scrambled down the hill into the big shower of wonderful cool water. It was not long before they were pulling off their clothes and Bishop hoped the guy really would yell before he came down the hill.

Terri took her shovel and banged it on the side of the valve closest to town. It sounded hollow and empty. Then she banged on the pipe closest to the tank, and it gave a completely different tone. It was full of water or mud or something. She studied the valve for a while and realized there was no way to tell which state it was in – open, closed or drain. There was also no way she could open it. *Why is everything in this place such a bitch to get in, open, or find?* Her mind drifted back to the door of the building, and that led to an idea.

She filled the back of the truck with everything she could find that would hold water. She combined the plastic bins that were partially empty of the food they had been eating, gathered up all of the empty water bottles and threw in a few trash bags for good measure. She found Bishop's big, camping backpack and removed the 100 feet of climbing rope he kept there. After driving the truck to the top of the hill and checking the roads, she unloaded all of her containers and put them at the bottom of the wash. The rope was easily looped around the pipe and secured to the trailer hitch on the truck.

At first, she didn't think the truck would to be able to break the pipe. When the truck lurched forward the first time, she thought she had done it, but the rope had just become untied. On the third attempt, the wheels spun just a bit, and the truck moved forward again. She shut off the engine, ran to look over the edge of the ravine, and saw water spraying through the air.

She rushed to the bottom of the wash and filled her cupped hands to smell the water. It smelled fine and was much cooler than the surrounding air. She started filling everything she had carried down the hill while letting the water soak her as much as possible, careful not to drink any. Before long, she had peeled off her clothes and became only the second, naked young woman to enjoy the Sanderton waterfall in the last 25 years.

Skinny Dipping

Terri didn't know how long she stood under the water, but it seemed like a long time before the flow weakened. She washed her clothes and hung them to dry in the sun. The water pouring over her had helped with her attitude more than anything she could remember. *Now we need something to drink.*

Her clothes dried quickly in the hot sun and dry air. After dressing, she began hauling the water up to the truck. She felt bad that she had just left the truck blocking the road. If someone had come over the hill it might have caused an accident, but this had been an emergency. It took several trips up and down to get all of the water loaded, and she refilled the radiator with one trash bag. There was enough water pouring out to refill it. Carrying all of the water up the hill made her break out in another sweat. After the last trip she couldn't resist standing underneath the dwindling flow to rinse off one last time.

It took her almost the rest of the day to boil all of the water she had collected. She wasn't sure how long to let it bubble, so decided on ten minutes per full pan. Her first thought had been to use the camping purifiers, but they were slow and required a lot of energy. She considered a fire outside, but was concerned about someone passing by, and she wanted to stay close to Bishop.

Using only the small mess kit pans that were in their packs, she would boil one and let it cool while she started another. She had filled all of their containers and used a plastic bag of water to wash off Bishop as best she could. She was careful to keep the underground water from his wounds, fearing any little critters that may be living there. Bishop seemed to respond well to the bath having spent the day inside the hot building. As soon as the boiled water had cooled, she and Bishop drank all they wanted.

Terri made one last trip to the waterfall that afternoon and placed an empty bin under the drip in order to salvage every last drop. It finally ended its flow later that day, and she used that water to clean the inside of the truck because Bishop's dried blood had started to smell really bad.

Bishop spent the next two days sleeping and drinking water, but on the third day was able to get up from the hammock and walk around. He wanted to know every single detail about what had happened during the three days he had been in "la-la land." He even ate some chicken noodle soup that afternoon.

Afterwards, he took her hand and they walked outside to look at the mountains. He gently touched her face and brushed her hair. "Terri, I am so impressed at what you did the last few days. I really don't have the words. I am proud, grateful and very, very happy you are my girl. No one could ask for more. No one could have done better. You saved our lives, and I love you very much. Thank you."

Terri's eyes started to water, and she pulled him closer. "I was so scared. I had to help you, Bishop. I couldn't let you die. I love you."

On their fourth day at Sanderton both of them woke to a very strange noise. Bishop had installed a "blackout curtain" in the front of their building so he could keep an eye on Terri as she moved around the ghost town. It was just after sunrise, and the sound was like someone playing a drum with a bad rhythm. Bishop stood and looked outside and was shocked to see three men on horseback riding down the road. Were it not for the blacktop, the men would have been perfect extras in any Hollywood western. Slickers, dusty hats, and rifles in saddle holsters gave them the look of being ready for trouble. They never even glanced at the ghost town and just kept riding at a slow gait. That night, Bishop and Terri could hear gunfire at a great distance, but couldn't tell where the shots were coming from.

The only other activity around the area occurred on the morning of the fifth day. Terri was looking through the rubble of the gas station, and Bishop was watching her from his perch in the building. Without warning, a pickup truck came over the rise from the north. Terri froze right where she was, but had no chance of finding a hiding place. The man driving the pickup stopped at the intersection and looked both directions, then kept on going. Terri swore later the man looked right at her, but Bishop was unsure. Terri wanted to leave before the man in the truck returned with some of his friends. Bishop thought that was a good idea.

But there was still the matter of the busted radiator hose. Bishop had Terri concentrated their efforts on finding a piece of rubber hose to fix the truck. Bishop knew the heat of the coolant would melt duct tape again, but hoped to insulate the broken hose with rubber and wrap the tape around the outside. Terri had found some hose, but it was crumbling and worthless, so he had her searching for any sort of pliable, soft metal that he could use in the same way.

While she couldn't find any suitable rubber or soft metal, Terri did find two rusted pipe clamps. Bishop used a little of the engine oil they'd packed for the truck to soak them for several hours and get the rust off. After their bath, the clamps worked. He took a tin can and pounded on it with a hammer for an hour to get the shape he wanted. Bishop was finally satisfied that they had the truck at a point where he felt that it would not drink more water than they would.

The Great Sanderton Bug Out

There was a single road between Sanderton and Meraton, and Bishop was uncomfortable at having no other option. Although there was practically zero population in the 100-mile stretch between the two towns, they had heard and seen at least two cars and three horses using it. The gasoline taken from the roadblock could get them to Meraton. Bishop's land was about three hours south and west of Meraton. Since he had grown up in the area, he wondered if contacting old friends to obtain gasoline might be an option. He knew the chances of scavenging between Sanderton and Meraton were very low.

They waited until dark and slowly pulled away from their home of the last week. Neither of them were sad to see it go, and they both enjoyed the truck's air conditioning. Bishop could raise his arm up to about shoulder high, but it was still very weak. While he had always practiced shooting one handed, his skills were never as good as using both, and he prayed there wouldn't be any trouble.

Meraton, Texas – September 24, 2015

Are those lights, or are you just glad to see me?

They were traveling at 30 mph and both were keeping a keen lookout for anything unusual. The land was open, mountainous desert for as far as the eye could see and had been that way for hours. Bishop asked Terri to stop, and she pulled to the side of the road. He could see lights in the distance and was sure it was Meraton. "They have electricity!" he told Terri.

To be accurate, Meraton had lights, but not electrical power. The county had decided that Meraton had a chance to become the next big growth area for the local tax base. This was primarily due to the artistic and culinary crowd that had previously relocated there. Since these people were a little more "liberal" than the traditional Texas resident, going "green" was thought to be a way to attract even more relocation and growth. When federal grant money became available in one of the seemingly endless programs to create jobs, the commissioners had jumped on it and received funding to install solar streetlights.

Not to be outdone, The Manor installed a solar system for its pool and garden lights and immediately marketed itself as a "green" destination. The good citizens of Meraton really didn't care much about green energy, they were happy to finally have streetlights in their growing little town.

To Bishop and Terri, the entire town appeared to have power, but what they were seeing was actually the twinkle of six new solar powered streetlights and glow of The Manor's gardens. Bishop scanned with the big rifle's scope for almost 15 minutes and didn't see any moving cars. He did notice several horses tied in front of one building. The Manor had numerous cars parked along its entrance, which fronted Main Street. If he had been returning from a two month hunting trip in the Glass Mountains, the town would show no sign that a major collapse in society had occurred while he was gone. Everything looked absolutely normal.

They talked it over for a bit and decided to boldly drive right into town. As they approached the outskirts, Bishop asked Terri to turn on the truck's headlights and they put away their

NVD equipment. The first business on the edge of town was a gas station. Bishop noted that it looked like a normal, closed gas station - no broken glass or evidence of looting at all. They went by a few dark, art galleries, and everything looked fine. The entire length of Main Street showed no clue that anything was wrong. Everything seemed as it should on a weekday night after all of the businesses had closed for the day.

The building with all of the horses out front didn't have a sign, but Bishop could see candles burning inside.

They pulled around to the back of The Manor's grounds and parked in the rear lot. Bishop was unsure of what to do. He didn't know if he should just walk up to the door and ask if there were any vacancies or scout around for a bit with his rifle. As they were talking it over, Terri saw a man looking out of the garden gate at them, and thought he had a rifle. She pointed, but by the time Bishop looked up, he was gone. "Let's drive around a bit more and see what is going on."

There really wasn't much of Meraton to drive around and see. The small city park, complete with fishing lake and the only trees in town, was closed, but that was normal at this hour. They passed the cemetery, and Bishop nervously made a bad joke about *people just dying to get into the place*. Terri started to punch him in his sore arm, but stopped at the last moment. They drove through two small sections of homes. A few had dim light glowing through the windows. None appeared to have been looted.

They wound up back on Main and were heading to The Manor, when Bishop saw two men getting on their horses. Terri stopped right in the middle of the street, and Bishop got out to investigate.

"Howdy," he said to them, carefully positioning his body between the men and Terri.

"Howdy. That you driving around town, mister?" one of them asked.

"Yes sir, we haven't been here for a while and wanted to see what had changed."

"Not often people waste gas like that these days. We saw you drive in from the east. Where from?"

"Houston," Bishop replied.

"Houston? How long ago did you leave Houston?"

"About a month ago - something like that. We wanted to take the scenic route."

"We ain't seen anyone come from the east in two weeks. I heard it was purdy bad. That true?"

"You heard right." Bishop pointed to the building they had just left and said, "Is everyone having a church social?"

Both of the cowboys laughed, and the older one said, "Naw, that's Pete's place. He just opened up before the electric went out. He is out of the hard stuff, but he has beer and maybe some wine for your lady over there. If you're thirsty and have something to trade, he will make it right."

The other cowboy added, "We ain't had a stiff drink for going on three weeks. There's a bright side though. Bill ain't fell off his horse since then neither."

Everyone, including Bill laughed and after a bit, Bishop questioned, "If I could provide something a little stronger than beer, could I swap it for information?"

"Depends on what ya got to trade and what you want to ask. But hell, I don't know any secrets, so let's give it a try." Both men dismounted and re-tied their horses. Bishop noticed they both wore side arms, so he decided to take his .45 and told Terri to do the same with her pistol. She gave him a look that said, *do you really think I would go in there without it?* While they parked the truck, Bishop noticed several faces watching them through the window.

Bill waited while the other man went back inside, and Bishop could hear laughter drifting out from the door. Bishop asked Bill if the truck would be "Okay" where it was. Bill just nodded and turned to go inside the bar. Bishop dug the full bottle of bourbon out of the back and locked the camper shell anyway.

He went in first and looked around. Were it not for all nine of the men inside wearing pistols, it would have looked just like any Country and Western watering hole in this part of the world. The shotgun lying on the bar was another dead giveaway that this was not your typical small town icehouse.

As Bishop paused to take it all in, he couldn't help but wonder if this were what it had been like in the old west. The distinct smell of the horses, candles, and saddle leather filled his head. It all seemed to belong to another time. There were no video games, and the television over the bar was dark and quiet. The only noise was the low, gentle hum of people with nothing else to do but talk to other people. He wondered how many times this scene had been played out? He and Terri were the strangers, arriving in town at the local saloon. The townsfolk, half-bored, half-nosey, and concerned about troublemakers, were trying to size them up without giving insult or acting like they cared. If the situation had not been so serious, Bishop would have been tempted to hook his thumbs in his pockets, belly up to the bar, and declare, "Barkeep – I got three days ride in mah throat and need to wash it down." *Terri would pull her pistol and shoot me on the spot.*

The neon signs above the bar were dark, but there were enough candles to see quite the assortment of animals mounted on the walls. A few signs, advertising different brands of beer and other refreshments were scattered among the trophies. It was a small town smoke-filled barroom, complete with peanut shells on the floor. He could see two women in the place, so clearly it wasn't stud. Everyone turned to see what was happening as they darkened the door. And when Terri walked in behind Bishop, all the men tipped their hats and said "Ma'am."

Bishop and Terri went to a corner table, and he pulled out her chair. Before he sat down, he slowly removed the .45 from his belt and then took the bottle out from under his arm. Everyone tried not to stare at them, but Bishop recognized they were the center of attention. A short, stocky man came out from behind the bar and said, "I'm Pete, and this is my place. I'm sorry, but we only have warm beer and wine. It's the best I can do right now." Bishop shook the barkeep's hand and then reached for the bottle and handed it to Pete, who held it up to the light, and then let out a whistle. He looked at Bishop and shyly commented, "I wouldn't have anything of this quality even if the trucks were still delivering."

Bishop reassured him, "Pete, I would like to share that with everyone. We are celebrating tonight and don't have any old friends here to join us. Would you do the honors for anyone who would like a drink?"

Bishop could see smiles breaking out all over the bar, and Pete went around showing everyone the bottle. While most had no idea of what it was, one thing was certain - it was not warm beer, and that was good enough for them. Pete poured the first two glasses and mixed water with the dark liquid. He brought them around and sat them on the table in front of Terri and Bishop. Soon, everyone had a drink in their hands and looked at Bishop. He held up his glass and toasted, "New Friends." Everyone took a sip.

After the second round, the locals started talking, and conversation flowed freely. Bishop and Terri split up for a little bit when Terri started talking to one of the other women. The men gathered at the end of the bar, and Bishop joined them, absorbing as much information as he could.

At one point, he looked up and saw two men walking around his truck. He stuck the .45 in his belt and started to head for the door, when Bill stopped him. "They won't bother your truck, mister. They're two of that group staying down at the Manor. They have been there for going on ten days now. After they first came into town, they shot one of the Lazy T's hands, but claimed it was a fair fight. They have a man with them, seems to be the leader. He keeps them in line, and there hasn't been any trouble since."

Bishop watched as the two guys circled the truck twice and then headed on down the road. He could see they were both carrying long guns under their jackets and their eyes were always looking around.

"Are there any rooms at The Manor?" he asked.

"I'm not sure, but I wouldn't stay there. I've heard those Ohio boys are awful mean, and most folks staying there have left. I don't think Harry is even manning the front desk anymore."

One of the cowboys asked a woman, "Is Betty still taking borders at her bed and breakfast?"

"She would if they were clean, quiet and had something to barter with."

Pete returned the bottle to their table with about one quarter left in the bottom. Bishop waved him off and said he could have it. Pete replied, "Thank you, but you should reconsider. Money is no good here anymore. We all trade for what we need, and this is a high value trade."

Bishop and Terri got directions to Betty's house and stood up to leave. Bishop nodded at Pete as if to say, "Thank you, and we will be back."

Pete nodded and smiled, as if to say, "You are welcome anytime."

Bishop and Terri said good-bye to all of their new friends and left to find Betty's B&B.

Bed and Breakfast and Guns

There were still candles burning in the windows when they found Betty's. It was a single story stucco home about a mile outside of town. It had a nice yard and looked welcoming. Bishop recommended Terri go up to the door. But before she could knock, a middle-aged lady with a round face appeared. Bishop's heart stopped when he saw an old double barrel shotgun in the woman's hands. It didn't take long before she set it down, and the two girls were talking like old friends. Terri waved at Bishop, and he got out of the truck as Terri introduced him to Betty.

Betty didn't have any guests, but she wanted to know what they could trade. She listed eggs, flour, laundry soap and toothpaste as the things she needed. Bishop offered some detergent, but that was the only item from her list they had to barter with. Betty looked over his shoulder and asked if his truck had air conditioning. When he told her it did, she then inquired if it had a CD player, which it did. Betty said she would take two loads of laundry soap and one hour sitting in the truck so she could listen to her music in the cool air.

Bishop smiled and said, "Deal." They shook hands.

Betty had a carriage house and suggested Bishop park the truck inside since there "hadn't been any law around for days and days." Bishop took her up on her offer, pulled the truck inside, and closed the door. The garage even had a lock.

Their senses heightened from their experiences of the last few weeks, Terri and Bishop were more aware of their surroundings. Normally the sound of pots and pans banging around a bit might have gone unnoticed. But in these still unfamiliar surroundings, the noise awakened them soon after daybreak. The sound startled Bishop, and he tensed up momentarily. His fears quickly subsided, wooed by the delightful aromas wafting through the air. They dressed and headed downstairs to greet their host. They enjoyed some coffee as Betty presented them with breakfast burritos, complete with rice, a little ham, and a touch of eggs. Mealtime conversation centered on everything they had learned the night before.

The power had gone out in Meraton about the same time as the electricity failed in metropolitan Houston, according to the refugees that had drifted through town from that direction. At the time of the blackout, the residents didn't pay much attention because that kind of thing happened now and then. A few years before, power had been out for two days, and there hadn't been any storms of any kind.

The man telling Bishop the story was not sure, but he thought it had been a week or so before folks noticed there had not been a Texas Ranger or a county sheriff drive through town in days. The delivery trucks also stopped coming to town about the same time. A Park Ranger had driven up from Big Bend National Park and spread the word that Martial law was declared in the big cities, and the roads were all closed. The Ranger purchased some batteries, loaded up as much food as her SUV would hold, and headed back toward the park. No one had heard from the park rangers since.

The townspeople also realized that travellers had stopped arriving from either direction. This was a major concern at first, because so many of the local businesses made their living from the tourist industry. Everyone had had a good laugh when one of the bar patrons related the story of the first town meeting when the owners of the two gas stations were in a panic about not being able to sell their gas. The preacher looked at them and inquired, "How would you pump it out of the ground without electric power anyway?"

So the town had resorted to the habits of the old days. Horses were common, as many of the surrounding ranches had dozens of the animals. Many of those who resided inside the city limits kept their own horses with friends or relatives who had "enough land." Weekend rides in the Glass Mountains were as common here as a round of golf in other places.

Another account from the night before involved an 18-wheel truck that had pulled into town. The driver had parked the big rig at the gas station seeking a mechanic. His tractor and trailer were riddled with bullet holes, and he relayed a tale of how he barely survived Midland, Texas with his life.

Over time other people drifted through town with little bits of news and rumor. One man passing through had said El Paso and Juarez were on fire and claimed that you could smell the dead from ten miles away. Rumor was that the U.S. Army and the El Paso police force had barely established order when the starving people from Juarez broke through the bridge to come north. Gunfire erupted, and a kind of cross border war started. Someone else had heard that the drug cartels and the Mexican Army had joined together and were fighting the people of El Paso.

Alpha, the next town 120 miles down the road, was said to be all but abandoned. The town's primary industry was a chemical plant, and an explosion released a poison cloud that killed hundreds. Several of the local ranchers found dozens of thirsty people wandering through their lands and gave many of them shelter, while others had received gunshots.

Fort Stockdale, the nearest city to the north was under control of the county sheriff. Always considered to be a bit overbearing, he organized the people and took over complete control. It was also rumored that if you wanted to live "under his protection," you had to follow his rules and work in the community doing what he wanted. Another patron at Pete's added that a lot of the deputies had moved their families to the town and stayed there.

Not all of the stories recounted at Pete's the night before were doom and gloom. Almost everyone at the bar had cheered up when the subject changed to the town's latest enterprise. A few weeks before, a local ranch foreman had brought in a freshly butchered cow and parked along Main Street with it strung over the side of his truck. His rifle had broken, and he put up a sign offering to trade beef to anyone who could fix the gun. The town's seamstress noticed the traffic generated from the man's offer and saw her own opportunity. She had a dozen eggs from her chicken coop that were going to spoil, so she set up a card table with a sign offering to trade the eggs.

By day's end, there was a makeshift farmer's market all along Main Street, and it had been growing ever since.

Commerce had not all been civil however. Two attempts had been made by "strangers passing through" to rob one of the gas stations. Both holdups had been answered with loads of buckshot and thus failed. The town organized its own "posse," and when shots were fired, an unofficial police force would come running. Almost everyone carried a firearm, but so far, no big gunfights had occurred except for the night the Lazy T's hand was shot.

"Those boys from Ohio are bad news," one man said at Pete's. "They're hard-looking men with mean eyes and won't step aside for anyone on the sidewalk." The story was that they came into town as a group, found The Manor, and moved in. At the time of their check in, there had been about 20 other guests at the inn. Only a few days later one of the families just got in their car and left. Peculiar behavior, given the current state of things, for folks to just take off like that... All kinds of rumors flew around town that the mother and teenage daughter looked like they had been beaten, and the man was in even worse shape, but that was just rumor. Someone else claimed they saw one of the men going into the hotel late one night with a local Mexican girl slung over his shoulder. The witness had run to Pete's and told the few customers what he had seen. The Lazy T ranch hand was a big guy, a little drunk, and he decided it was his time to be a hero. He was shot that night, and none of the locals knew what really happened.

A group of the town's men got together and went to confront the accused. The situation had almost gotten out of control. "Those five were going to shoot it out with all fourteen of us, and they almost seemed eager to do it." The leader, someone had called him "Spence," had defused the situation by claiming that the shooting was self-defense. He postured that his man had been confronted by a big drunken cowboy who pulled a gun. "What would any of you gentlemen do if that happened to you while you were guests in a strange town during these bad times?" No one could dispute his claim. No one really wanted to have the first shootout on Main Street in over 80 years, so they let it go.

"I don't let them in here anymore," said Pete, "and ever since, they have stayed to themselves and lay low. A few 'tourists' tried to get a room at The Manor when we still had stragglers coming through. I would see them go in, and then come out quickly and leave."

Speculation about the mysterious travelers ran the spectrum. "They're waiting on something," one man said decidedly.

Someone else added, "We see them walking to the market now and then, but that is about it. Over the past few weeks, any time a car or truck comes to town, they are among the first to check it out. It just seems to me like they're waiting on someone. Why else would they stay?"

The Art of the Deal

"That's laundry detergent?" Betty asked with a skeptical look on her face.

"Sure is." replied Terri, "Let me show you."

Terri was holding what looked like a thin stick of gum with a mint smell and color. She and Bishop had found the handy little packets a year ago at a camping store. They had purchased toothpaste, body wash and laundry soap, that other than the color, were all the same shape and size. The little packets contained 50 strips each, and were about the size of a pack of breath mints. After experimenting with them, Bishop purchased several, and they had gone into their camping packs and hurricane boxes.

Terri and Betty were standing next to a big tub in the back yard. Betty carried out two baskets of dirty laundry and filled the tub with water from her old, hand well pump. Terri immersed the strip in the tub of water and waited a minute for it to dissolve. She stirred the tub with her hand a few times and soap bubbles started forming on the surface.

"Well I'll be," was all that Betty had to say as she started washing clothes. Terri helped her, and in less than an hour, the clothesline running across the backyard was full of billowing colors drying in the sun and light breeze.

After the laundry was done, Terri heard strange noises coming from their bedroom and rushed to see what was wrong with Bishop. He was on the floor trying to do pushups, and clearly his bad arm was giving him trouble. After a heated debate about his not resting enough to let his body heal, she had given up, and let him do as he wished. Despite the spat, she returned later to check on him. She smiled when she saw he had his rifle and was moving it around in all kinds of directions like it was a dance partner. She had watched him do this at home for years. He had called it "gun ups" and "doing the rifle dance." She just thought it was silly. Bishop had tried to explain to her that exercising with the rifle made it become an extension of his body. He tried to draw analogies, like a baseball player repeatedly swinging a bat, but it was all lost on her.

Bishop was mad. He couldn't do any of his exercises without a lot of pain, and a couple of times he stopped just short of tearing open his wounds. He had attempted one-arm pushups, but his injury had taken its toll. He was just not strong enough yet. The swelling in his bad arm was almost down to normal size, and he had dodged the "infection bullet" due to Terri's good work and the pills. Despite his limitations, he had managed to work up a sweat and went to the backyard to wash off with the well water.

He dried and put on clean clothes. He moved the truck out of the garage, thinking Betty would want her hour in the cool air soon. He really didn't mind letting the truck idle for an hour as it would use little gas, and he needed to re-check the radiator after the truck had warmed up to make sure his repair was in good shape.

He backed it out of the garage and turned it off. He figured it was a good time to take a quick inventory. He unlocked and opened the cover for the truck bed to see what they had left. He just finished his mental list of the contents and shut the small hatch when he heard a voice from behind. "Nice truck."

He hadn't heard the three men approach. They were standing about 20 feet away, spread in a semi-circle eight to ten feet apart. They all had AR15 rifles, held them military style, and carried them properly.

"Thanks," was all Bishop said. He was so mad at himself his ears were ringing as he didn't even have a butter knife to defend himself. He was also scared as hell.

The man in the middle nodded toward the back passenger window where the sniper's bullet had left a hole. "Looks like you had a little trouble."

"Yeah, it was a hunting accident."

That brought a laugh from all of them, and one of them said, "I can just imagine what you were hunting." The leader continued, "We are not from around here, kind of stuck and waiting on some friends to show up, but they are late. We saw you pull into town last night and wondered if you had any news from back east?"

Bishop's voice was terse, "I can't really tell you much. We were camping for a few weeks at a hunting lease down by Brownsville. We started heading home and had all kinds of trouble finding gas and lodging. I have heard rumors, but really don't know many facts. We have been avoiding people as much as possible."

Spence digested Bishop's story for a bit, and said, "I saw some rifle cases in the back there. What were you hunting?"

"Mister, I don't know you, and we have just traveled several miles of bad road. Around here, asking questions like that after sneaking up on someone is not only rude, but dangerous."

Bishop watched as anger flashed through the man's eyes like wildfire. All three of them shifted their rifles and Bishop heard one safety click off. The noise caused the leader to look hard and the man re-engaged the safety on his weapon. Spence calmed down and said, "My name is Spence, and we didn't mean to be rude or scare you. These days, you can't be too careful."

Bishop saw movement out of the corner of his eye, and then Terri was behind one of them carrying her rifle.

"Everything okay, honey?" she asked in an innocent voice.

"Everything is fine, darling. I was just having a chat with my new friends."

One of the men started to turn toward her, and the unmistakable metallic sound made by the moving safety on Terri's rifle stopped him cold. "This big gun makes me nervous. Last time I had it out, I pulled the trigger by mistake, and it kept shooting all afternoon. It holds so many bullets, you know."

Spence sized up the situation. "Well sir, thank you for your information. I wish you good luck on your trip home. Something tells me you are going to need it. Let's go boys."

Bishop watched as the three men left. They moved like a well-trained rifle squad, and he was impressed. After they were out of sight, he gave Terri a hug and a kiss on the cheek. "You saved my ass again, baby."

"This is becoming a habit Bishop. I thought you were supposed to protect me?" Terri said with a wink.

Betty stepped around the other corner of the house carrying her shotgun and said, "I sure am glad they didn't shoot up that truck of yours before I got a chance to listen to my music." Bishop gave her a hug too.

The Meraton Mall

After everyone had settled down, Betty retrieved her knitting needles and two music CD's. Bishop inquired about her musical tastes and was a little surprised when she replied, "I have the Boston Pops doing Stravinsky recorded live in 1998.

It is soothing, and Brandon's violin solo in the 4th will make me happy all afternoon. I haven't listened to this Verdi in a long time. He tends to be a little melancholy."

Bishop started the truck and showed her how to adjust the stereo and air conditioning. He left her cranking up the volume and mumbling about "How these CD's just didn't have the fidelity of her tube and needle-based equipment, but would have to do."

After an hour and a half, he went back outside thinking something might be wrong. Betty was sitting with her head back and her eyes closed, tears running down her cheeks. He tapped on the window and was relieved when she smiled and opened the door. "Oh I'm so silly, that just moves me to tears," she said and went inside the house.

Bishop found Terri to discuss what supplies were left in the truck, which was not many. It had taken them so much longer to get here than they had planned. After hearing what had happened to the town where he had rented the storage bin, there was little hope that their supplies would still be there.

The entire conversation put them in a sour mood. After a bit, Bishop looked up and said, "Come on girl, let's get ready to go."

"Where?"

"I am going to make the ultimate sacrifice for you, Terri. I am accompanying you to the mall."

As they got ready, Betty appeared with three small melons from her garden and a piece of paper. She had overheard them say they were going shopping and asked if they would try to trade the fruit for anything on the list. She would stay put and reassured Bishop not to worry about his truck.

Betty then added, "Now watch that old man Turner and his counting. I don't know if he is old or crooked, so just watch him if he is there. That Wauneta woman is honest, but sometimes her apples have worms, so inspect them real careful if she has any." She continued to provide a "Meraton Consumer Report" regarding several other products and vendors.

Bishop borrowed a pillowcase and threw some items in along with Betty's melons. He slung a rifle over his shoulder like a hunter, not forward like a solider, and made sure Terri had her pistol in her belt. They began the walk to town.

Fifteen minutes later, it was so hot outside they could see mirage waves rising from the valley floor in the distance. When they got close to town, the first thing Bishop noticed was the smell of horse manure sizzling in under the Texas sun. The second thing was the noise. There was music playing from somewhere and a low buzz of people, animals, and even a wagon being pulled down the street. He counted at least 20 horses tied up to improvised hitches and a similar number of pickup trucks parked randomly around the area. At least 200 people were walking, pointing, bartering, or leaning against anything handy.

Many of the trucks were parked with their beds facing the street and tailgates open, storefront fashion, to display the goods that were available for trade. Someone had set several cafeteria-type tables up along the sidewalk where anyone could just sit down, spread their items out and put up a sign if they wanted. No business license required.

"I wonder if the fall fashions are in yet."

"Terri, am I going to have to take away your MasterCard?"

"Just try it big boy." Terri replied as she playfully reached for her pistol.

Bishop noticed that almost everyone carried a weapon of some sort. He saw everything from old bolt-action rifles to cowboy six shooters. His modern M4 was not unique. Many similar carbines could be seen in the gathering. He was glad to see that everyone was comfortable and non-threatening, even with all of the "iron" being displayed in the crowd. Terri could read him like a book. "In my eyes, your gun is the biggest in town cowboy, so relax a little bit."

They slowly walked up and down the street taking it all in. There were "stores" full of candles, homemade sausage, vegetables from local gardens, and even some bulk bags of rice and beans. A pickup truck at the end of the street had the biggest crowd, and the couple strolled over to see a Mexican man offering baby chicks. The eventual egg producers were going fast.

Pete had set up the equivalent of a "watering hole kiosk" where he was actively negotiating with the gentleman standing in front of him. The fellow repeatedly offered a small nugget of gold for trade. Pete didn't want the "useless metal," and the thirsty fellow pocketed his trinket before leaving disappointed. Pete waved at Terri and Bishop, and they returned the greeting before moving on.

A yummy aroma soon attracted their attention. Two older Mexican women were pounding dried plants into flour, and mixing a batter to bake in a small adobe oven. It smelled delicious, but Bishop wanted Terri to wait before they traded anything.

After they toured both sides of the street, they sat down on some steps and rested. Bishop noted that the mixture of people in the market matched his memories of the town from years ago. Many of the residents of Meraton were of Mexican descent, but probably more American than most of the whites. Bishop knew that many of their families had resided in what was now called Texas for hundreds of years. Since the whites had moved west and started ranching, an easy co-existence had developed. The original families had grouped together, normally where there was water, in order to keep the Indians at bay. Their healthy, strong sons had become ranch hands and foremen. Families indigenous to the area took jobs on the ranches in the lean years when pooling resources just made sense. A kind of symbiotic relationship was created giving security to the families and providing workers for the haciendas. There were also many skilled craftsmen in the community. Quality boots, saddles and other tack were always in demand as were the skills of blacksmiths and silversmiths. The family unit in their culture reigned supreme. The elderly were respected and taken care of, and even today it was rare to see grandma sent off to a nursing home. When Bishop had been growing up on the ranch, over half of the hands were of Mexican descent. He came to like their culture and respect them as hardworking, dedicated people.

Still, there was an economic divide between the two races, and Bishop never understood how it existed. As he pondered this thought, he realized that in the coming years, the evolution of this community might well reverse that situation. For generations these people had to make or grow the necessities they couldn't afford to buy. They were not *as* dependent on electricity or other modern conveniences as compared to the typical Anglo. If the modern society didn't recover, they would have the skills to survive, if not thrive.

There were also many Anglos. It was not unusual for a man to get enough of the tough ranch life, and opt for the social amenities of "city life" as he aged. Accustomed to hard work, these folks normally had little trouble finding jobs in more urbanized areas as construction workers, janitors and other laborers. Some, who had saved their money, worked at odd jobs now and then, and just enjoyed a simple, quiet retirement. All in all, the two cultures made it work in most of the American southwest.

Bishop couldn't figure out the exchange rate in the street-wide flea market. Since money had no value here, he didn't know how to assess the worth of his goods. He had seen a potpourri of items for sale. Everything from old rusty tools, to a table of expired medicines, and even homemade knit socks were offered at the outdoor bazaar. He decided to take the plunge and see if his wares had a market here.

He and Terri moved to an empty spot on a table and started spreading out his merchandise. He sat out a quarter bottle of whiskey, a hand full of shotgun shells, 15 rifle shells, two cans of Tomato soup and Betty's melons.

At first, he thought it was all for nothing. People walked by, nonchalantly browsed at his small storefront, but continued down the street. After a bit, several men walked past, briefly glancing at the ammunition. They moved on, barely breaking stride, only to make a quick turn and come back by again. *They are playing hard to get, completely disinterested,* Bishop realized.

Terri made some smart remark about Wal-Mart having no competition at their table and sauntered off to peruse the "drug store" table.

An older man stopped, pointed at the shotgun shells, and looked at Bishop as it to ask permission to pick one up. Bishop nodded, and the man examined a sample shell, scrutinizing it more thoroughly than most car buyers do before purchasing a new mini-van. He shook it, smelled it, and twisted it every way possible. Bishop was ready to say "enough" if the guy started to bite it. The old fellow set it down on the table, exactly where it had been and asked, "What size shot?"

"That'd be #1 steel," Bishop replied.

"What do you want for them?"

"Well, that depends. I have a lot of things here on my wish list. Do you have any of…" and he started reading first one item, then the next.

After Bishop read his list, the man said, "I have two rolls of toilet paper. I will swap you for all of those shells."

"No can do," said Bishop. "I'll trade one shell per roll."

The man whistled and rolled his eyes like Bishop had just asked for his first-born child. He then proceeded to inform Bishop that toilet paper was in short supply. Not to be out-negotiated, Bishop held up the shell, and retorted, "You can't use the Sears catalog to shoot vermin, but I can use it to wipe my backside."

They finally settled on two rolls for three shells, and the customer was satisfied with their established "exchange rate." The two shook hands and Bishop's first customer went on his way. Bishop was setting the rolls of TP on the table to make it look like he carried more inventory when a commotion on the street drew his attention. Two of the Ohio men were strutting down the sidewalk. Both men had been at Betty's house that morning. They pushed some kid out of the way and were bumping into people as they walked, glancing at the different tables. Bishop wondered if they were alone, but soon picked out a third man on the other side of the street. He looked around for Terri, but couldn't see her anywhere. He swung the rifle around to his front, keeping it pointed down. As he watched the men progress toward him, he saw one stop and pick up an apple and look at it. He made some comment, and then threw the fruit down on the ground. They were laughing and pointing and even paused to hassle a younger girl that walked by. *Typical bully bullshit*, thought Bishop, *how many times have I seen this before?*

It didn't take long for them to see Bishop and his table. They looked across at their friend and motioned for him to meet them in the street. Spence was not with them.

There was an old brick building right behind Bishop's table. He stood up and took two steps backward so that his back was close to the wall. The men made a straight line toward his shop.

"Well, well lookie here," one of them said. "Where is your lady friend at? It's awful brave of you to leave the house without her."

He looked down at Bishop's table. "She is going to be pissed with you selling off her ammo like that. Did she give you permission to sell that?"

They all thought this was very funny, but Bishop didn't laugh. He watched their hands on the rifles. Most men will take the safety off of the weapon and then raise it up. It was only the very well-trained who managed both actions in the same movement. If Bishop saw a safety being taken off, he was coming up shooting, period.

Right at that thought, a shadow fell across one of the men and everyone looked up to see Bill on his horse towering above them. He tipped his hat at Bishop and said, "Everything all right?"

Bishop kept his eyes on the three men, "Yeah, everything is just fine. These men are homosexuals and were offering to give me a blow job in trade for some ammo. I declined, and they're not happy about it."

This really pissed them off, but their thumbs stayed off the safeties. One of them said "Fuck you, you..." but the back end of Bill's horse suddenly swung around and almost knocked him down. Before any of them could react, the horse pivoted again and pushed them all back one more time.

Bill said, "I'm sorry boys. Old Nubbins here is a little fidgety given the big crowd and all, please forgive him." The men looked at each other and at the large crowd that had gathered to watch. They decided to move on, glancing over their shoulders and giving Bishop and Bill *that look*.

After they left, Bill turned to Bishop and teased, "I bet you got beat up a lot as a kid with that mouth of yours. Have you always thrown sticks at mountain lions?" He winked and ambled down the street.

Terri pushed her way through the crowd, inquiring what happened. After Bishop had explained his bargaining methods, she pretended concern. "Damn it Bishop, we just moved in, and already you are pissing off the neighbors. Now behave yourself before these people get out the tar and feathers."

Bishop responded with his characteristic reply. "Yes ma'am," he said.

The Shoot Out at the Market

Bishop continued to trade and swap as best he could, but the members of The Force had taken the fun out of it. He kept an eye out for the troublemakers in case they showed themselves again. He had successfully acquired a few items on his list, as well as a couple on Betty's, and decided he had a pretty good day. The crowd was beginning to thin, and vendors started leaving, so he and Terri called it quits.

He was putting all the stuff back in his pillowcase when three shots rang out, and someone screamed. He threw Terri down on the ground hard, and took a knee in front of her while bringing his rifle up. People were running away from the shots, and Bishop had no idea who was the shooter and who was not. At times like this, he was grateful that his rifle had a holographic red dot sight on it. This allowed him to keep both eyes open while scanning. Wherever he looked, the rifle was aimed at the same spot. When the street was almost clear, he grabbed Terri by the back of the shirt, literally lifting her off of the ground, and moved her into a doorway close by. He turned and looked at her extremely pissed expression and snapped, "Stay here. Stay down; and get that fucking pistol out right now."

He could care less how mad Terri was at that moment because down the street he could see a horse lying on its side with a man pinned underneath it. *Bill, oh God no, not Bill.*

Bishop moved through the market, keeping close to the walls and using anything he could for cover. He zigzagged across the street and changed speeds, always pivoting his head and rifle right and left, up and down. It took him less than a minute to reach where Bill was lying. Bishop could tell the shots had come from around the corner of the building next to him. He got as low to the ground as he could and popped his head around once and then back quickly. Nothing happened, and his mind replayed what his eyes had just taken in: *An empty street, nothing in the shadows, but a few places for someone to hide.*

He took five big steps backward and then ran as fast as he could toward the corner. When he was almost even with it, he leapt into the air and flew feet first like a runner stealing home in a baseball game. Landing in a perfect slide, he angled his feet down and they caught, making him pop straight upright. He ended up standing with his rifle scanning all around. Nothing happened.

He cleared the back of the building with a glance and then hurried to Bill's side. The old cowboy's leathery face was wrinkled with pain, and he had tears running down his cheeks.

He looked up at Bishop and struggled,
"Nubbins...Nubbins...they shot my Nubbins."

Bishop looked Bill over, and knew instantly he was not going to
make it. He had two wounds in his chest, and one was
bubbling air. Nubbins was dead as well, having taken a shot to
the temple.

"Bill, who shot you? Who did this

"I think..." cough...cough..."I think I got one of...." and he died
in Bishop's arms.

Bishop set the old cowboy's head down gently on the street
and pulled his hat over his face. Movement made him turn
immediately, but it was Pete heading to Terri's side in the
doorway. Pete carried his shotgun while Terri rubbed the slight
bruise on her leg, but Bishop could clearly make out her pistol
in her hand.

Bishop looked around and saw Bill's weapon lying on the
ground underneath Nubbins. He pulled it out and looked it
over. Bill had fired a single shot.

Bishop then went back to check the area where Bill had been
ambushed. He found three shell casings of 5.56, the type used
in AR15 rifles. He turned to leave when he noticed something
else a few feet away. There was a small drop of blood on the
ground. He walked a few steps further and found another . . .
and then a third. *You got one of them, old-timer. You sure as
shit got one of them.* Bishop noticed the blood trail led straight
to The Manor Hotel. He stood there, fully exposed in the
middle of the street, his eyes first fixed on the hotel and then
back on Bill's body.

His anger began to boil, driving him into a crazed fury. *I don't
give a shit. I just don't care. I bet I can get all of those fuckers
before they bring me down.* Adrenaline mixed with a lust for
blood and revenge spiked through his veins. He inhaled
deeply, about to roar a battle cry and charge the hotel, but then
something stopped him cold.

It was Terri's voice that brought him back from the brink.
Poised to wreak havoc on his enemy, he wanted so badly to
unleash absolute violence using his weapon until it was empty
and then pull his knife and slash until his arms could no longer
move. That all mighty, all powerful, all-encompassing urge for
combat was beaten down by a soft, almost weak voice.

Somehow, it reached through the blood raging in his ears, and three words registered in his brain.

"Bishop – please don't."

The Manor Hotel – September 25, 2015

Spence was as mad as he could ever remember being. He had been taking a dip in the pool to cool off when he heard the shots. He knew his men were out in the market and had warned them numerous times about causing trouble. *We are lucky. This is probably the only place in a thousand miles that has food and a good place to wait this out. The only way we can fuck this up is to cause trouble. Keep your noses clean, and let me finalize our trip to Mexico.*

Spence was nothing if not a good judge of men. His read on the local people was that many of them were as tough as nails, but really just wanted to get on with life. If The Force left everyone alone, they could spend their time in Meraton in relative anonymity.

The first rape and shooting had been bad enough. It was after that incident when he finally accepted the fact that his Force was really nothing more than a bunch of thug criminals. He had almost shot them a couple of times himself. He showed restraint due to his own realization that they all needed each other now. However stupid these men were, there was safety in numbers. He had lost track of how many times their numbers had gotten them though bad situations on the trip here from Ohio.

He jumped out of the pool and went for his rifle without even dressing. He went to the gate and saw his guys running toward him, one of them bleeding from his head. They stumbled inside the gate, and he could see that his man had been lucky. The wound was bleeding a lot, but the bullet had only grazed his head.

Spence kept vigil over the gate, thinking the entire town would come after them with pitchforks and torches. He was watching as Bishop flew around the corner doing the baseball slide, and he knew immediately who it was. *Damn*, he thought. He wished later that he had shot Bishop right then and there. But seeing the single man as no threat, he lowered his rifle. He noted Bishop glaring in his direction and guessed he could see the blood trail. When Spence saw the look in the man's eye, he half-expected him to charge the hotel by himself. He hated to admit it, but deep down inside he was glad when Bishop spun away and left.

It's on

Bishop and Terri hurried back to Betty's without a word between them. When Bishop had thrown Terri down, she had skinned her leg and ripped her pants. Bishop was feeling so many different emotions, he couldn't sort them out. He had taken a huge risk at the Brazos River Bridge and had gotten lucky. He had taken bold steps at the I-10 overpass and again, had gotten lucky. How long would the luck last?

He also understood that men like The Hefei, this Spence character, and whoever was running the show at the bridge were going to keep civilization from reigniting. He had just manhandled his wife because of this human slime. He knew she was mad at him, and he didn't blame her. Why did there have to be people that caused, no, forced that reaction? Bill's face kept popping into his mind, enraging him more and more. *He helped me, and now he is dead.* Bishop also felt guilty because he had provoked the showdown in the market. He should have backed off and let it go. *Now a good man is dead, and I am to blame.*

What they had found at Meraton had given them hope. No one person had organized what was essentially the re-start of a productive society. It gave Bishop something his soul needed so badly, faith in his mankind. People like Spence seemed to always destroy that faith.

Soon Betty was fussing over Terri like her own daughter. Following suite, Bishop made sure Terri was okay, before adjourning to the bedroom. He emerged in full "ninja" gear.

"What are you going to do, Bishop?"

"I'm going to stop a lot of people from being killed is what I hope to do. Don't worry babe, I am not going near those guys tonight. I'm worried the good citizens of Meraton will try to force them out of that hotel. A lot of people are going to die if they try that."

"Bishop, do you think Betty is in danger? I mean, they know we are here, and they don't like you very much."

"They are going to be worried about the townspeople for right now, so I think you guys are safe here tonight. Stay alert though – I could be wrong."

Bishop went back to town, traveling a different route just to be safe. If he had been Spence, he might have decided another ambush was worth the risk. On the way, he gathered his thoughts about his arch-nemesis and his little gang. It was completely dark as he approached the town.

As expected, everyone was at Pete's. Bishop crossed Main Street far away from the glow of the solar lights and was approaching from the darkest area he could find. He finally settled about 50 yards across Main from Pete's, lying in a small drainage ditch that gave him good cover and a clear view through the front window of the bar. The entire place was packed, and Bishop wondered how many beers had been raised already tonight. There was a cowboy standing by the bar giving a little speech and he could hear a few of the words. As he had expected, they were downing a little "liquid courage," gathering their mettle to confront The Force. The speaker, as best he could tell, was doing a good job of whipping up the townspeople. He went on and on about how they should just go burn those bastards out after what they had done to Bill. Someone opened the front window to let in some air, allowing Bishop to hear the conversation more clearly, "There are only four of them. We have almost 20 men here, and I know all of you want them out of our town. We can make torches, throw them at the hotel, and shoot the bastards when they come out!"

Many people in the crowd agreed, and several shouts of "Hell, yeah!" and "Let's go!" drifted over to Bishop's position.

Bishop was scanning up and down Main with the NVD, checking all of the alleys and dark patches where the light from the high poles above could not reach. He was about to get up and try settling everyone down when he became aware he was not alone in the night air.

The man was hiding, prone behind the wheel of a pickup truck parked a few blocks away from Pete's.

Damn, I can't believe Spence made this mistake. He divided his forces, and this changes everything.

Spence had anticipated the reaction of the townspeople. They would be in shock for a few hours, but after that wore off, they'd be out for blood. The horseman his men had killed had been popular and was by default the town's sheriff.

There were supposed to have been two men from the Mentone Cartel come to Meraton and visit him by now. He had sent two different messengers with his offer to obtain safe passage to the coast. The decline in the U.S. economy and years of continuous civil wars had weakened the cartels financially. Ten years ago, the offer to pay for protected passage through their territory would have been laughable, a mere pittance compared to their coffers.

Spence was hearing rumors that Mexico had fallen into complete anarchy, just like the U.S., only worse because of the cartels and their control before the fall. He had originally wanted to go to Mexico to escape U.S. law enforcement. That was no longer a concern to him, as every single bit of rumor and gossip indicated there would not be any law in the U.S. for years, if ever.

So why should they run to Mexico?

The trip from Cleveland to this remote West Texas town had also proven to him that it truly was a jungle out there. Even with their numbers, skills and his leadership, they had barely pulled through. This was the only place they had found that even remotely seemed to be livable. Before his men had caused this latest round of trouble, he had hoped to slowly make good with the locals and gain their trust. Then, he would execute these criminals he had brought with him and take over the town. If his knowledge and leadership had enabled success with this bunch of vicious animals, imagine what he could accomplish with an entire town full of sheep.

"They will be down at the bar." He had told his men. "They will be down there drinking to build up their courage. I want a pre-emptive strike. I want you to drain a bottle of gasoline out of the truck and go give them an old fashion barbeque, only they are going to be the meat."

Anybody got a light?

Bishop knew the man had skills just by watching him. He stayed very low and took his time, working gradually up the street to Pete's bar. When he was within a few feet of the entrance, he calmly stood up and walked to the center of Main holding a glass bottle with a rag stuffed in the top. He reached in his pocket for what Bishop knew would be a lighter.

Bishop pulled the trigger and the glass bottle shattered with the impact of his bullet. He pulled the trigger a second time, and the man went to the ground with shattered right knee. Before he could roll over and even reach for his weapon, Bishop was standing on his arm.

All of the people in the bar heard the shots. Everyone who could turn to look out of the front window did so. They could see a man lying in the street holding his leg. Before any of them could get out into the street, they saw another man standing over him.

They were a little unsure of who the second man was. He was wearing a baklava and heavy glasses that covered his eyes completely. His chest was covered with numerous pouches and gear. He looked up at everyone pouring out of the bar, and yelled for them to stay back.

The smell coming off of the large puddle of gasoline convinced them to listen to him. The firebomber was beginning to recover from his shock and pain. After kicking the weapons away, Bishop walked over to the crowd, turning to address the man lying on the ground. His voice was disconcertingly calm when he asked, "What were you doing with that bottle of gasoline, friend?"

"Fuck you."

Bishop fired a shot that missed the puddle of gas by inches. The bullet sparked off the pavement.

"What the hell are you doing?" the man yelled.

"What were you doing with the gasoline?"

"Spence told me to firebomb the bar," the man confessed.

Everyone in the crowd started talking at once, but no one moved.

Bishop shouted over the noise, "Who shot Bill?"

"I don't know I wasn't…"

Bishop fired another shot, and it sparked as well.

"Jesus Christ, I'm covered in gas. If you hit that gas…" stuttered the man.

Bishop said calmly, "Who shot Bill?"

"It wasn't me, Mister…I swear, it was one of the other guys."

Bishop turned around to the crowd and said, "This man had a bottle of gasoline with a rag stuffed in the top. It's called a Molotov cocktail. He was going to light the rag and throw it through the window into the bar. The bottle would have broken, and the gasoline would have ignited inside. Many of you would be dead or badly burned by now. Then he was going to stand right there and shoot anyone who managed to make it out the door."

Everyone in the crowd looked at each other and several cursed under their breath. Bishop waited a bit, and went a little closer to the man. "Why are you and your friends here?"

"We are waiting to go to Mexico. We are waiting on the cartel to come here and escort us in."

Bishop did not expect that answer. He said more to himself than the man, "You are drug runners?"

"Fuck no. We robbed a bank and have hundreds of pounds of gold and other stuff. We just want to go to Mexico. I told you what you wanted to know man. Can I move out of this gas?"

"No, not yet. I have a few more questions."

"Jesus, my leg is killing me. Come on mister. Let me out of this - please."

"How bad is the man hurt that Bill shot?"

"Not bad. It was just a scrape."

"How many people are still at the hotel?"

"I don't know, maybe ten or so. Spence forces them to stay in their rooms mostly. They saw us unloading the loot, and he didn't want any of them spreading it around."

Bishop walked close to the man and asked him a couple more questions that no one could hear. He then turned to the gathered crowd. "He was going to burn all of you alive. I'm going into the bar to have a drink. You can do with him what you want, but remember the bad guys down at the hotel are expecting to see a fire. My vote is you give them one."

He pushed through the crowd and headed into Pete's. He heard the firebomber start yelling, "No, please, no! Please don't . . . " and then a gunshot – followed by screams. There was a big fire on Main Street.

Bishop wanted to go into Pete's to sit for a moment and think through his next move. He sat with his back to the street and drank some water from his kit. *Spence made a mistake by dividing his force. I bet he won't do that again.*

What's the password?

Spence was standing by the garden gate waiting to see the blaze brighten the night sky before his man returned. He thought it was odd to hear shots before seeing the glow of the flames. He heard some yelling and another shot. *I wonder if he had to shoot someone outside before he threw the cocktail.*

When he finally saw the flickering light from a fire and heard the screams, he relaxed a bit and started thinking about next steps.

Spence signaled the other men to stay alert at their sentry posts, but warned about shooting their own man when he returned. His man was to work his way to the back gate, where they would challenge, "Ohio" and he would respond, "State." It was dark by the back gate, so the code word was necessary to avoid an accident.

One of the sentries indicated he saw movement, and Spence yelled "Ohio," and the man yelled back "State." Spence opened the back gate, waved him in, and turned, walking back to a table in the gardens where the debriefing would occur.

It was Bishop who entered the gate, not the bomber. Bishop passed through the gate not knowing what to expect. He felt bad that he had lied to Terri about not coming near the place, but what he had learned required he act now. He could see the outline of a man walking ahead of him toward a table in the garden. He closed the gate behind him, just like their man would have done, and tried to locate the others he knew would be in the hotel gardens. He couldn't see them. He broke off into the shadows and used the night vision to scan the area.

Spence turned around expecting to see the bomber behind him, eager to report. He was pissed he was not there and thought, *"Where did that dipshit go?"* He finally decided the guy must need to take a leak or something, so he stood and waited.

Bishop tried to move quickly without noise, but his progress was slowed because the garden's ground was covered with noisy pea gravel. He wanted to work his way around to get behind Spence. He was hiding under some stairs when he heard someone above him. The stairs were metal, without a kickboard, and Bishop could see the man above was carrying a weapon. *Not likely a guest.* He could barely make out a bandage wrapped around the guy's head. *Bill almost got him, and I will finish the job.* Bishop had several nylon ties stored on his chest rig. In his role at work, they were issued to serve as handcuffs, but over the years he had found many different uses for them. He pulled out three of the ties and connected them together into one long strip of plastic. He secured one end to each side of the stairs making a tripwire across the steps.

Bishop knew there were four men he had to engage. He could see Spence by the table and was aware of the guard at the top of the steps. He had to locate the other two before they realized their bomber was missing.

He caught movement out of the corner of his eye and located the third man 50 feet away. This guard was patrolling between two sections of the gardens and carried a rifle. Bishop scanned again using the night vision, but couldn't find the last guard. He jumped when Spence yelled. "Hey! Tim! Where the hell did you go?"

Spence was looking for his missing man, and Bishop knew he had to act fast. He assessed the situation and didn't like his options. *Maybe this wasn't such a bright idea after all.* Spence didn't have a weapon in his hands, but Bishop was sure one was close by. The two guards had rifles and were no doubt alert now. He had no idea where the fourth guy was. The Manor's gardens were almost two full acres and divided by low adobe walls and rows of hedge. The last guard could be anywhere.

Bishop didn't like his chances in a prolonged game of cat and mouse. There was too much cover and too many places to hide. He moved away from the stairs and took refuge behind a gazebo. His back was close to one of the main walls of the garden, and he had a reasonable angle on the three known targets. *I will make this area my Alamo.*

Time was running out. A quick glance at Spence showed he was looking at his watch and appeared annoyed. Bishop had a quick fantasy of killing Spence with his bare hands. His "mind movie" had them rolling around with blades slashing and blows being landed by fists and feet. He quickly dismissed the Hollywood hero's version of the ending. His shoulder and ribs were throbbing, he was tired, hot, sweating underneath all of his gear, and he had broken his promise to Terri. *I am sick of all of this,* he thought, *and I want it to end right now.*

He raised his rifle, centered the red dot on guard's chest, thumbed off the safety, and slowly squeezed the trigger. Two shots rang out, and the man crumpled to the ground instantly. Bishop swung the rifle in Spence's direction, but he was already diving to the ground. Bishop fired, but knew he missed.

The guard at the top of the steps came running down fast. His boot caught on the nylon tripwire, and he became airborne, landing with a thud on the bottom step. He was trying to get up when Bishop slipped up behind him. The guard heard a scrape of gravel and started to turn toward the noise, when Bishop's rifle butt smashed into the side of his head, right where Bill's original shot had just missed.

By now, Spence had recovered from the surprise and picked up his rifle. He instinctively knew where the shots had come from, but doubted the shooter was still in the same spot. He couldn't be sure how many foes he was up against, so he remained behind cover. He heard a loud "thud" by the stairs and saw movement. He aimed and sprayed several shots, trying to draw a response.

Bishop was moving away from the stairs when he felt Spence's bullets crack the air beside him. He went prone, fired back, and then rolled away.

The missing guard had been at the far end of the gardens when the firefight had erupted. He was cautiously working his way back, when he saw Bishop dive to the ground and start shooting. He could see enough of Bishop's silhouette from the muzzle flashes to know he wasn't a friend, and let go a long burst of automatic fire.

The ground around Bishop erupted with flying rocks, dirt and debris. He rolled left and snap-fired two rounds back at the new attacker. *Now I know where the fourth sentry is.* He got up and tried to scramble for cover when a round slammed into his rifle, barely missing his hand. The kinetic energy of the bullet snapped the rifle out of Bishop's grip, spraying small metal fragments into his skin. Still attached by its sling, the rifle fell between his legs. Bishop tripped, fell and skidded across the ground.

Bishop's right hand was completely numb from the shock of the bullet, and wouldn't respond. He tried to crawl away to find cover; but the bulk of his gear, tangled rifle, and worthless hand all impeded his progress. He rolled onto his back and managed to pull his pistol with his left hand. He flicked the safety off and waited on the fourth guard to come closer.

Bishop knew this was it. He had little chance in his current condition against one man, let alone two. As he lay panting for breath, he wished he had given Terri a better kiss goodbye. *Did I tell her I loved her before I left? Did I tell her I was sorry I hurt her in the market?* He saw the shadow of the fourth guard approaching cautiously and tried to be still. He knew any sign of life would cause the man to empty his magazine, and at this range there was no way the guy could miss. Slowly, he pointed the pistol in the man's direction, hoping the movement would be undetected. *It's now or never.* Bishop started firing the .45 caliber when the man was about 25 yards away. With aim and a good hand, it would be an easy shot. Using his left hand and not aiming, it would be a miracle. Bishop emptied the 8-round clip but couldn't tell if he had hit anything because the muzzle flash had blinded him. He started to eject the empty clip when a nearby voice made him freeze. It was Spence, and he was very close.

"That's four of my guys you have killed tonight. In a sick sort of way, I should thank you. I was going to eventually kill them myself."

"You're welcome…in a sick sort of way."

Bishop heard Spence moving, and his vision was beginning to clear. Spence circled around him and finally stood ten feet away pointing his rifle at Bishop's head.

Spence, anticipating the coming coup de grace, was curious. "What's your cause man? I mean, why get involved in all of this? I know you just came into town. Do you have a hero complex or something?"

For the first time in his life, Bishop couldn't come up with any words. He could only lay there thinking of Terri and wishing this guy would just get it over with.

"No matter," said Spence, and he slowly and deliberately raised his rifle to take careful aim.

Bishop closed his eyes and waited for the flash, or pain, or whatever someone felt at the end. He jumped when shots rang out. It took him a few seconds to realize he was still breathing. He opened his eyes and looked over to see Spence lying on the ground.

The fourth guard was standing over Spence's body. The man looked down and growled, "So, you were going to kill us anyway. You wanted all of the loot for yourself. How did that work out for ya, motherfucker?"

Bishop could see a large, dark stain of blood on the man's shoulder where one of his pistol rounds had found its target. The guard staggered toward Bishop and raised his rifle. He suddenly convulsed, jerked and spun as several gunshots rang out. His body corkscrewed down to the ground, as it was hit several times.

Bishop craned his head to see the source of the gunfire, and saw Terri, Pete and several of the town's men running toward him. Terri threw down her rifle and almost jumped on top of him.

"Are you okay? Where are you hurt?"

"I'm okay...really...I'm okay. Just help me up," Bishop answered.

Feeling gradually returned to Bishop's hand. After two bottles of water, he was walking around trying to shake it all off. Terri checked his wounds, and miraculously everything looked okay. Pete had explained to Terri what happened, and she waved off Bishop's apologies for having gone after The Force.

After he had regained his strength, Bishop banged on each of the hotel room doors. He yelled "police" as he knocked, and anyone who answered was told that they were now free to go. The townspeople, drawn by the noise of the firefight, began to console the terrified guests.

After the hotel guests had been released, Bishop walked through each room, hoping not to find any more bodies. The third room he checked was locked, and no one responded from inside. He went back to Spence's body and searched his pockets for the key. He opened the door carefully and detected the anticipated booby trap inside the room. It was a rather large pipe bomb. He disarmed the device and pointed his flashlight inside.

Bishop could make out boxes of stacked food and ammunition. He could also see several steel containers full of gold, jewelry and other stolen items. He closed and locked the door behind him, leaving the booby trap unarmed.

Pete walked up behind him and asked, "Did you find their loot?"

"Yes, it's behind that door. I think we should have a town meeting in the morning to discuss what to do with it."

"Why don't you take it? You saved a lot of lives here tonight. You deserve it."

"There are some things in there I would like to have, but it's not what you think. Let's talk about this in the morning. I'm beat."

The Ranch, West Texas – September 27, 2015

Bishop and Terri slowed down, pulled to the shoulder of the highway and stopped. They had left Meraton that morning and had not seen a soul on the road since. Bishop looked up at the familiar mountains of his childhood and smiled at Terri.

"This is it. I hope everything is still like we left it."

They turned off the road and engaged the four wheel drive as there was no lane or driveway, just flat, hard packed dirt and rocks. Normally the added traction would be unnecessary on this soil, but the truck was loaded down with supplies from the hotel and several hundred pounds of gold. It had been decided that the gold would be a magnet for trouble, and the town was better off without it. Bishop had promised to return it when the town was ready and had a plan to put it to good use. He had drawn a map to his place and Pete stored it in the small safe he kept in the back office, promising to send someone when and if Bishop were needed.

Bishop and Terri pledged to come back and see everyone in a month or so after they had settled in. There had been tears, hugs and tight throats all around as they had left. As they were pulling out of town, Bishop saw a large Hummer entering Meraton. He had looked at Terri and said "Oh shit," thinking the drug cartel finally arrived to meet The Force. He had turned around and followed the vehicle directly to The Manor. He pulled out his rife and began walking to meet the town's new visitors, thinking that this nightmare was never going to end. He was a little taken aback when an older man got out of the Hummer, followed by a middle-aged woman and two teenage kids. Bishop slung the rifle around to his back with the barrel pointed down and approached them.

"Howdy, welcome to Meraton," he said.

"Thanks, I am Dr. Richard Hopkins, and this is my wife and grandchildren."

The two men shook hands.

The Doctor continued, "We've heard that there is, well, some sort of order here. I hope it was not just a rumor. We're so tired and barely got out of Houston with our lives. Is this place sane?"

Bishop laughed and said, "It is as sane as anywhere I have seen in two months. Doctor, you say?"

"Yes, I'm a GP, and my wife is a teaching, well, *was* a teaching physician at the University of Texas at the Medical Center."

Bishop nodded, smiled, and said, "Walk about four blocks down that way. You will see a bar with a small sign over the door that says "Pete's Place." Go in, and tell him Bishop sent you. You and your family will be welcome here and probably as safe as any place in Texas."

"Pete's Place, okay. A bartender runs the town?"

"He is only a part-time bartender. His real job is Mayor."

After a small rise and another stretch of flat ground, Bishop and Terri approached the old ranch road that led to their canyon. If they had turned left, the old road wandered for over a dozen miles past watering tanks, holding pens and outbuildings no longer in use. They turned right and eventually dead-ended at a ravine that had been cut from the surrounding mesa by wind erosion thousands of years before.

As the canyon walls began to rise above them, the road suddenly ended. Years ago, Bishop had carefully cleared a path of any obstacles allowing them to continue deeper into the desert even though it appeared as if there weren't any path at all. They wound around boulders and slabs of rock the size of homes that had fallen from the steep cliff walls. As they made the final turn, the surrounding vegetation changed and became greener from a spring that dripped just enough water to make a difference. There were even a few trees.

In front of them was the camper, just as they had left it on their last visit. Two small pecan trees had survived as well as the high desert pines Bishop had planted years ago. One of the pecans was actually providing shade for the trailer.

They got out of the truck, and Terri came around to hug him. They stood by the truck for several minutes just holding each other.

Terri finally looked up and said, "Bishop, I have something I need to tell you."

"What's that?"

"I'm pregnant," she announced, searching his eyes for approval.

He was stunned . . . shocked . . . and finally, he smiled and softly replied, "I love you baby," and pulled her close.

After they talked about the new addition to the family for several minutes, Terri claimed to have an urge to nest and went to the camper to look inside and see how dirty it had gotten since they were here last. Bishop walked behind the 30-foot long aluminum bullet house and found their "hot tub" was just as he had left it. The ten-foot wide natural "cup" in the rocks was still full of water from the spring. It was just as clear and inviting as he remembered it. The tub overflowed into a small channel in the rocks and continued until disappearing in the sand. Bishop had made a small "dam" that allowed the cup to fill, but believed it had originally formed naturally over the years due to water dripping from the slight overhang above. When he poured the concrete, he made a small "gate" so water could be diverted to a flat area of ground where he envisioned having a garden one day.

He looked around the tub and saw numerous sets of deer and rabbit tracks, which told him his idea was popular with the local residents as well.

He could hear Terri opening the windows on the camper and fussing already. "This place is a dusty mess Bishop. How could it get so dirty in here without you living in it? I need a bucket of water and some soap right now, or I'm going to sleep in the truck."

He waved his hand dismissing her, but said out loud, "Yes dear."

He went around a large boulder and then up a short narrow path until he was facing the cliff wall. He dug his keys out of his pocket and unlocked a large stainless padlock. He pulled hard on a big steel door which was scavenged from the bin of a grain hauler. The door opened to reveal the "bat cave." The "cave" was really not a cave at all, but more of a deep indentation in the rock face. The five-foot high entrance opened into a room about the size of a one-car garage that had plastic storage bins stacked along one wall. He looked for the one labeled "cleaning" and found it toward the bottom of a stack. After digging out soap for Terri, he looked around the room thinking, "*I would like to build a workbench over there, and I could reload over there, but first I should build a playground slide off of that rock and hang a swing from the top."*

"Bishop, where's my soap?"

He smiled and rushed out for the camper to tell Terri about his idea for a playground. He was so excited thinking about his role as a new father that he completely forgot about her soap.

(The End)

Epilogue

Bishop was working on the meat, dipping salt from a large container. He had the venison spread out on a rock letting the sun do its work, drying out the lean strips of soon-to-be-jerky. When he first heard the noise, it sounded like a large flying insect buzzing around nearby. As he looked for the source, it dawned on him it was a sound he hadn't heard in months – an airplane was flying overhead.

It took him a few seconds to determine the direction of the small craft because the engine noise was echoing off of the canyon walls. When he finally spotted it, he could see it was making a wide, slow turn off in the distance.

He picked up his rifle and yelled a warning to Terri, who immediately left the camper and headed for the "bat cave." She was with child and didn't appreciate having to move quickly, but did so without protest - other than a dirty look. They agreed early on that the bat cave was a much safer place to be than the camper, and it had become their "storm shelter" at any sign of trouble.

Bishop watched the plane circling above his property. He lost sight of it when its route took it behind Mill's Peak off in the distance, and he wondered if it had left their area when it failed to emerge on the other side.

He jumped a little when it suddenly appeared right over his head from the back of the box canyon where they had been holed up for months. The plane made a quick loop and flew directly back at him, tipping its wings from side to side as it zoomed overhead on its second pass.

He watched the small aircraft circle off to the west, and then heard its engine change tone as its nose started angling lower toward the ground. The pilot was landing the plane, not far from Bishop and Terri's place.

He lost sight of the plane as it vanished behind the canyon wall, then heard the engine sputter momentarily before the sound disappeared as well. He couldn't tell if it had shut off, crashed, or simply landed. After waiting for several minutes to see if it reappeared, he decided the plane was on the ground somewhere close by and went to get Terri.

"I don't know what to do. We don't know anyone with a plane, and what the hell would they being doing way out here anyway?"

"Bishop, you have to go check it out. We won't get any sleep if we are worried about someone creeping around. The baby and I will be fine here – go make sure it's okay."

Look for the next book in the *Holding Their Own* series, *The Independents,* due Spring of 2012.

Made in the USA
Lexington, KY
11 October 2012